Jo Thomas worked for many years as a producer, first for BBC Radio 5, before moving on to Radio 2's *The Steve Wright Show*. In 2013 Jo won the RNA Katie Fforde Bursary. Her debut novel, *The Oyster Catcher*, was a runaway bestseller in ebook and was awarded the 2014 RNA Joan Hessayon Award and the 2014 Festival of Romance Best Ebook Award. Her follow-up novels, *The Olive Branch* and *Late Summer in the Vineyard*, are also highly acclaimed. Jo lives in the Vale of Glamorgan with her husband and three children.

You can keep in touch with Jo through her website at www.jothomasauthor.com, or via @Jo_Thomas01 on Twitter and JoThomasAuthor on Facebook.

Readers can't resist Jo Thomas's feel-good fiction:

'Romantic and funny' *Sun*

'A perfect pearl of a story. I loved it' Milly Johnson

'Well worth a read' Carole Matthews

'Jo's trademark warmth and wit sing from the page . . . I adored it!' Cathy Bramley

'Perfect escapism' *Marie Claire*

'Sunny and funny' Veronica Henry

'Perfect summer read' Liz Fenwick

'An utterl
adventure

'Perfect fo
My Weekly

'A heart-warming tale' Ali McNamara

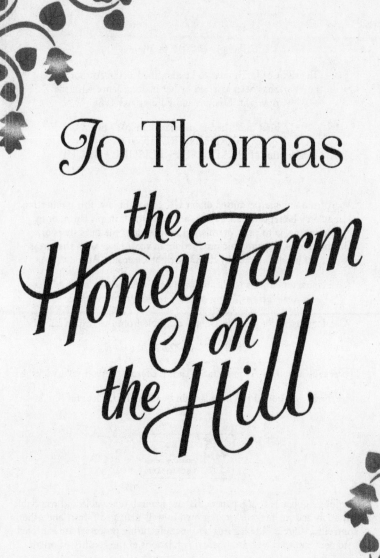

Jo Thomas

the Honey Farm on the Hill

REVIEW

First published in paperback in 2017 by
HEADLINE REVIEW
An imprint of HEADLINE PUBLISHING GROUP

5

Cataloguing in Publication Data is available from the British Library

ISBN 978 1 4722 2374 6

Typeset in Caslon by Avon DataSet Ltd, Bidford-on-Avon, Warwickshire

Printed and bound in Great Britain by Clays Ltd, Elcograf S.p.A.

HEADLINE PUBLISHING GROUP
An Hachette UK Company
Carmelite House
50 Victoria Embankment
London EC4Y 0DZ

www.headline.co.uk
www.hachette.co.uk

For my brilliant editor Emily.
Thank you for coming to find me and bringing me home to Headline.

Hello all!

Welcome back if you've read my other books and, if you're new to my world, welcome and come on in. I'm Jo Thomas and I write about food, families and love, with a good splash of sun and fun thrown in.

When I write I'm always dreaming about a new life overseas and this book is no exception. This time we're in Crete, the largest of the Greek islands.

For me, starting a new book always feels a bit like opening the pantry and seeing what ingredients you've got in. When I thought about Greece, I pictured the makings of a Greek salad: crumbly white feta, shiny black olives, crunchy cucumber and juicy red tomatoes. But when I arrived in Crete I realised there was so much more to discover about this mountainous country and its food. According to Greek mythology, the god Zeus was born in a mountain cave in Crete and was looked after by a nymph, Melissa, who fed him milk and honey. The honey in Crete is amazing. It's flavoured by the wild herbs that grow in the mountains, specifically dittany or *erontas*, which translates as 'love'. And it's here I found the heart of my story.

With teenagers of my own at home, I also wanted to write a book about a woman who is trying to work out who she is once her daughter leaves home and she starts trying to come to terms with her empty nest. Because sometimes in life you have to go back before you can go forwards.

I do hope you enjoy Nell's journey into the heart of the Cretan mountains.

Me agápi apó,

Jo

X

Acknowledgements

Firstly, thank you to James Villas for a wonderful week in Crete that gave me the backdrop and setting for this book and enabled me to explore the island and find the ingredients I needed for my story. Thank you to Vamos Traditional Village who promote ethical, sustainable eco-tourism and agro-tourism in Crete and who run cookery lessons and trips to meet the local food producers in Vamos.

It was there I met Koula Varydakis-Hanialakis who runs a wonderful Cretan cookery course in an old olive press in the town. It was there I learned about the health benefits of Cretan cookery and how to make simple food special by using the herbs that grow on the island and, in particular, in the mountains. And it was there I first saw dittany!

One of my really special memories of my time in Crete was a meal we had in a small mountain village at Dounias Traditional Cretan Food, where the owner and chef Stelios took time to show us his farm and kitchen, where everything is grown locally and cooked on wood-fires. If you ever visit Crete and find yourself near Drakona, do go!

To write this book I also needed help with understanding bees, and Barbara and Harold from the Cardiff, Vale and Valleys Beekeepers' Association were wonderful, introducing me to the bees at Dyffryn Gardens and showing me the basics of beekeeping. Any errors here are entirely of my own making!

And finally, a huge thank you to my brilliant editor Emily Griffin, for setting me on this publication path; for your faith, encouragement and support, helping me harness my ideas and giving me the wings to fly. I'll miss you.

Prologue

It all began the day the Christmas decoration factory burned down.

'Bloody hell, it's like New Year's Eve at Winter Wonderland,' says Angelica. Her festive red and green tinsel-edged earrings flash in the late-June sunshine as we huddle together outside, watching the orange and yellow sparks shoot up from the factory roof.

Bang! Crackle! Bang, bang! Fizz . . . bang!

We jump back as the factory's electrics explode and fire takes hold. There's an almighty crash as part of the roof collapses. We gasp in unison, huddling tighter together and shuffling backwards at the same time.

'Christ!' Angelica, one of my closest friends despite the ten-year age difference between us, is the first to speak. 'That was right over where you were sitting, Nell!'

I stare at the hole where the roof used to be, sparks and smoke spitting out of it like an angry volcano. I can't reply. My blood runs cold and I feel my hands begin to shake. She's right. I was sitting just under that roof beam only a tea break ago.

Gracie coughs like she's trying to dislodge a bone from her throat . . . a whole leg bone by the sounds of it.

'You all right, Gracie?' I reach down to put a hand on her back. Gracie is my other close friend at the factory. She was my nan's next-door neighbour for as long as I can remember, and she's mine now, ever since Nan died and I took over the house. Gracie is just five foot tall, and almost as wide, wearing one of her signature shapeless nylon dresses. Although in her late fifties, she looks much older. She nods, still coughing.

Another fire engine arrives, blue lights flashing and sirens wailing. The girls from packing let out a roar of approval as the firemen leap from the engine, as does Rhys from baubles, who's wearing two of them as earrings. Most of the girls are wearing tinsel round their necks and wave it like cheerleaders' pompoms as the firemen leap into action pulling out their hose.

'I will be,' says Gracie in her gravelly voice as she slowly straightens. Pulling out a packet of cigarettes from her front overall pocket, followed by a lighter, she sparks up, puffing smoke into the air, where it mixes with the thick black smoke chugging out from the factory roof. She drags deeply on the cigarette between her long, hooked painted nails, exhales, then growls, 'Better now.'

Sporadic bangs, sparks and flashes take us by surprise, making me leap out of my skin, but the girls from packing cheer again. 'Better than Bonfire Night, this,' says one in a dayglo vest top and a flashing gold Santa hat.

I shove my hands in the back pockets of my worn and comfortable calf-length jeans. I live in jeans – I wear them to work, to the pub, at weekends. Angelica thinks I have a vintage look going on, but it's really just about reusing things, like the chequered shirts and the fifties bomber jacket I found

2

in my nan's attic, and scarves made from bits of fabric to keep my unruly red hair in place. I roll the toe of my lace-up canvas pump around in the fallen white ash in front of me and push my hands deeper into my pockets, my collection of wristbands and bangles bunching together.

'All my Christmases come at once,' says Rhys from baubles, fanning away the heat and smoke with a 'Santa Stop Here' sign. Gena, who works in the luxury crackers team, lets out a laugh like a machine gun that makes us all wince and put our fingers in our ears. It grates up and down my already shredded nerves like fingernails on a blackboard. Gena usually gets this response when she laughs. It's the reason she's been moved off Christmas deely boppers – those headbands with baubles on springs that can smack you in the eye if you nod your head too much – at the front of the factory. Instead she's been put on crackers at the back to try and stop her high-pitched laugh from carrying across the factory floor.

'Stand back, please, stand back.' A fireman in a big black suit and a large white helmet waves his arms at us, and we shuffle back again with a few good-natured catcalls, mostly from tinsel, trimming and fairy lights. As we move, there's another huge bang and the remainder of the factory roof around the hole over my work station, blows off, showering pieces all over the car park.

'I guess we're not going back in today then?' says Angelica. She clicks away on her phone, taking photos of the explosion and posting them on Instagram. As one hand takes a selfie, the other does a thumbs-up.

I look over to our managing director, short, fat Alwyn

Evans, who is smoothing his comb-over nervously as he talks to the fire officer.

'Might as well go to the pub.' Angelica puts her phone into her big cream and gold handbag and hangs it over her shoulder.

I cough as the smoke catches in my throat. My chest is tight and I feel a little light-headed. I'd like nothing more than a sit-down and something to settle my nerves. I look at the hole in the roof again. My whole body is shaking. That could have been me gone if I hadn't got out. I shake my head in disbelief and reach for my own phone, running my thumb over the keypad. I just want to hear my daughter's voice and to tell her I miss her. I do miss her, badly.

'You coming, Nell?' Angelica asks.

I shake my head. 'No. I gave my last twenty to Demi last night at the bus station.' I check my phone for messages. There are none. I wonder if now would be a good time to ring, or if she'll be busy. Who'd have thought, my daughter, nearly eighteen, and living in London. I look up at the roof.

'She's gone then, your Demi?' Angelica asks. 'Didn't fancy the job in packing? Decided to go for this posh job in London?'

I nod, feeling the tears that keep filling my eyes, determined not to let them fall.

'Lucky beggar. Wish I was off somewhere exciting, instead of stuck here.' She folds her arms and her bag swings violently.

'I took her to Cardiff last night to get the bus. She promised to text when she arrived safe and sound.'

'Blimey, I'm amazed your car made it that far. And she's

4

really ditched her A levels and gone to get a nannying job in London?'

I nod again, because I'm not able to talk properly through my tight throat.

'Strong-minded, that one,' Grace pipes up. 'Just like someone else I know . . .' She smiles at me and coughs, and I try to smile back, wishing I could see the funny side of this. The truth is, I'm petrified for Demi. Not yet eighteen, and living in London with a family I've never met, working as an au pair. She thinks I'm worrying too much, that I've got to understand she's grown up now. But she's so young. I told her to wait, to do her A levels; she has plenty of time. But she insisted A levels weren't for her and she was ready to go. I'm just not sure I'm ready to let her.

'They have to fly the nest sometime. Just like you did. Your nan was beside herself when you went off travelling. But you came back safe and sound, a bit bruised maybe and with some surprise news. But you coped. The world kept spinning.'

My face falls. I wouldn't change having Demi for the world, but I wish I'd seen a bit more of life first. I just want something different for her. Maybe this is the best thing. I manage a smile

'At least you'll get the remote control to yourself now.' Gracie stubs out her cigarette on the low red-brick wall and then coughs some more.

Angelica's mouth turns down. 'It's a scary place, though, London. Who knows what lunatics are lurking around those street corners.'

For a moment none of us say anything, and a hole in the

middle of my heart, loosely held together, seems to rip right open. The colour, whatever is left of it after the shock of the fire, finally drains fully from my face. I could strangle Angelica . . . and I just want to bring Demi home.

'Oh God, I'm sorry, Nell! How stupid of me! Of course she'll be fine!' Angelica grips my wrist, her face screwed up in apology, and the tears I've kept in start to pour down my cheeks. Neither Angelica nor Gracie has children, but they've been like brilliant aunties to Demi over the years. Angelica buys her fabulous outfits for birthdays and sends over magazines with the latest fashions for her to look at. And Gracie has always been there, just next door, with a full biscuit tin, a listening ear and a couple of quid if Demi runs to the shop to get her milk and fags.

At the end of the road an ambulance whizzes past, sirens blaring, and I wonder again if Demi is safe. It's just her and me; she's all I have.

'Come on, I'll buy you a drink. You can owe me.' Angelica links her arm through mine, not taking no for an answer, and we join the other groups of workers heading for the pub, tottering on their high heels, snowman deely boppers bobbing up and down.

Just then, my phone pings. I have a text, from Demi. The first since I left her at the bus station last night.

Here safe and sound. House is amazing. I'm going to love it here. x

That's all it says, but I hold the phone close to my chest and breathe a sigh of relief.

'Oh hiya, Nell love.' I turn to see Gena, gripping on to one of her co-workers and grinning at me like a Cheshire cat. I have no idea what she's got to be so happy about. With the factory fire, we're all going to be out of work and out of pocket. I nod.

'Gena.'

'Sorry to hear about your Demi ditching her A levels. You must be gutted. Not the college type you thought she was going to be then.' She smiles that Cheshire cat smile and her friend sniggers.

I bristle and squeeze my phone as if it's her neck. Breathing as deeply as I can, which isn't very with my tight chest, I lift my chin and look her right in the eye. 'Actually, she's doing really well, Gena. Got a fab job in London. She's just arrived and is settling in.' I wave the phone and grit my teeth.

'Oooh, too good for us!' Gena is pulled away by her giggling friend. Her laugh grates on me all over again. 'You off to the pub?' she asks.

Angelica nods curtly. 'Seems as good a plan for the afternoon as any,' she says, clutching my arm tightly as if I'm going to do a runner.

'You coming, Gena?' her friend asks, orange in clinging vest and flashing fairy earrings.

'No, I've got other business to see to.' She gives the three of us a little wave as she teeters out of the car park on to the main road and heads in the opposite direction.

My hands are shaking even more and I don't know if it's the shock of the fire or Gena's catty comments. I'm sure Demi will be fine. She's a smart girl, I tell myself, trying to loosen the grip of the doubts wrapping themselves around my heart.

* * *

'It doesn't look as if the factory's going to reopen any time soon. Rhys heard the firemen talking . . . it could be a couple of months.' Angelica puts a bottle of white wine and three glasses on the ring-stained round table in front of us; a selection of crisps, nuts and pork scratchings tumble from under her arm.

'And we're on zero-hour contracts. I guess that means they won't be paying us then,' Gracie grumbles, ripping open a bag of pork scratchings.

Realisation suddenly hits me like I've been whacked with a sack of spuds. I'm skint! I have no idea how I'm going to survive if the factory is shut. No work, no money. I gave Demi the last of my savings from the jar on the dresser that I'd put aside for a weekend in Tenby. The only thing I've got of any value is my car, and that's only worth a few hundred quid.

'We're never going to find anywhere else to take us on at such short notice.' Gracie confirms exactly what I'm thinking.

'We should go on holiday.' Angelica beams, unscrewing the bottle and filling the glasses.

'Some hope. I haven't even got my share of a bottle of wine!' I accept a glass from her with thanks and take a slug of the sharp, warm wine.

Angelica sits down and leans forward excitedly. 'We could always go WWOOFing!'

'I beg your pardon!' Gracie chokes on a pork scratching and has another coughing fit.

'WWOOFing!' Angelica repeats with a wicked smile.

'I've heard about that. It happens on the common . . . in cars . . . exhibitionists!' Gracie takes a sip of her drink to recover.

'Not dogging, Gracie!' Angelica hoots, and even my low mood lifts. 'WWOOFing! Worldwide . . . um, working on organic farms, or something like that. You volunteer to work on a farm in return for bed and board. You can do it practically anywhere.'

'What, like in the Bahamas?' Gracie frowns and then looks like she's imagining herself there.

'So that's you sorted out, Gracie. Where would you go, Nell?' Angelica is enjoying the game, and why not? We can all dream. 'You can have a moment to think.'

But I don't need one. My hand instantly goes to my throat, remembering the weight of the necklace that used to sit there. There's one place that's still close to my heart. Somewhere I didn't think I'd ever get to see again.

'Crete. I'd go back to Crete.' I suddenly feel like I'm falling into one of the big fluffy clouds that used to drift across the skies there. 'Not that I haven't loved being here and being Demi's mum,' I say quickly, blushing. 'But in Crete . . . well, I think that's where I finally became me. Grew up. Knew what I wanted in life.' I remember the feeling of confidence I found there. I had everything to look forward to. The plans we made to run a small boutique hotel there on the mountainside, my future laid out like a map in front of me.

'Why don't you go then?' Angelica says.

'I couldn't do that!' I laugh off her ridiculous suggestion and try and shake the sadness that comes with remembering, taking another sip of the disgusting wine to bring me to my senses. This is real life, in the Frog and Bucket, drinking acidic white wine.

'Well, what are you going to do then?' She sits back, glass in one hand, a handful of peanuts in the other and she tosses one up and into her mouth.

'You could spend some time with that man of yours.' Gracie raises her eyebrows. 'Snap him up before someone else does. He's been waiting for Demi to finally be off your hands. Now's your chance.'

Maybe she's right. How else am I going to fill my time waiting for the factory to reopen? And Mike moving in, paying half the bills, would really help me out. Perhaps this is fate. It's time the two of us finally put our relationship on a firmer footing, rather than just darts night on a Thursday and a takeaway curry on a Saturday. It would certainly take my mind off Demi being away.

'You're right, Gracie.' I slap my glass back on the table and push all thoughts of Crete out of my head. 'That is what I should be doing.'

I reach into my handbag, feeling fired up, and grapple for my keys, trying to ignore the monkey key ring that Demi bought me on a school trip to Bristol Zoo. Seeing it makes my heart twist again. Demi is fine, I remind myself. Her text said so.

'I'll surprise him. Turn up early!' I attempt a surreptitious sniff at my clothes to see if I smell of smoke. Then, leaving Gracie and Angelica with the rest of the wine, I head out to the car park and my battered Ford Ka. The sun has gone and it's beginning to drizzle. I try to ignore the memory of the Cretan blue sky that's now started taunting me.

This is exactly what I should do right now: finally make an honest man of Mike and ask him to move in. Even Demi told me it was time I put him out of his misery and got on with my own life now that she doesn't need me around. I throw my car keys up in the air and catch them, walking purposefully towards my car. I can't wait to see the look on his face . . .

I pull up outside Mike's flat and get my spare key from my bag. I slide it into the lock, feeling surprisingly excited, push the door open quietly and step over the threshold. Then I freeze, hearing that familiar irritating laugh . . . coming from the bedroom. I thought I'd surprise him, but it looks like someone has beaten me to it. I step back out and pull the door to as gently as I can. Suddenly the laughter stops and I hold my breath.

'Mike? Did you hear something?' I hear.

'No, now get back to bed!' And then that laugh again, running through me like the sound of a dentist's drill.

I let out the breath I've been holding with a long, slow blow. Then, with shaking hands, I slip the key through the letter box and listen to it fall on to the mat before lifting my chin and walking away with as much dignity as I can muster, that laugh still ringing in my ears.

It's over . . . Just like that, it's over.

Chapter One

I take a deep breath as I step out of the plane door and on to
the steel platform at the top of the steps, lifting my face to
the hot Cretan sun. The wind catches the ends of my curly,
red hair, just as I remember it doing last time I was here,
eighteen years ago. I gather my hair up in one hand and hold
it at the nape of my neck as I make my way slowly down the
steps. That's when it hits me. That smell, filling my nostrils,
my head, my chest, catapulting me back to a time when I
was young, happy; when anything was possible. I sigh bliss-
fully, despite the nerves turning somersaults in my tummy.
The aroma of wild mountain thyme on the wind wraps itself
around me in a huge hug, and I hold the handrail tighter to
steady myself. It feels as if no time has passed at all. I touch
the necklace at my throat; I'm still getting used to its weight
again. My heart fills and the widest smile spreads across my
face. I'm here. I'm actually here.

'Excuse me, madam, is everything OK?'

I turn to see the flight attendant and a line of impatient
faces behind me. A group of young girls are giggling, fool-
ing around with excitement, and suddenly I'm reminded
of the sound of Gena's shrill laugh coming from Mike's
bedroom. The memory makes me shudder all over again,

leaving me suddenly cold despite the intense heat.

As I walked away from Mike's ground-floor flat that day, from a relationship in which I thought it was just me stalling and we were waiting for the right time to take the next step, I realised that everything had to change. For seven years I had known where I was, what I was doing every day of the week. I'd had someone there to share the odd takeaway and telly night with. Now it was just me, and I felt like a balloon with its string cut, not knowing which direction to fly in.

'Everything all right?' asks the flight attendant again. I look at her and at the queue behind me, the harassed expressions of the parents with the child who was sitting near me. I look down at the man in ear protectors, overalls and a high-vis jacket despite the heat rolling in a haze off the tarmac, holding his hands up against the bright sunlight as he squints at me. 'Do you need a hand?'

'No, no . . . I'm fine. Just perfect, in fact,' I say, pulling down my sunglasses from my head, making my hair fly about even more. Despite my thrill at being here, my nerves spin like acrobats in my tummy. I take one more deep breath, then grip the handrail again and continue on down the slightly swaying steps, snatching glances at that oh-so-familiar landscape.

'Goodbye, thank you,' says the flight attendant. 'Hope you have a good stay.'

'I hope so too,' I reply, gripping the pendant in the palm of my spare hand.

The brilliant blue sea is just beyond the airport. Large jagged rocks are dotted along the shoreline, white spray dashing against them. All the while that scent is still there, like a good friend that has come to greet me, and suddenly all my nerves start to seep away. I did the right thing coming here, I tell myself as I make my way across the hot tarmac towards the terminal building. The sun's reflection is bouncing off the glass like it's part of a welcoming committee. I have no idea why I was so nervous, or why I've put this off for so long. I haven't felt like this in . . . years! It was time to get away from the empty house. To get a life of my own, as Demi insisted during our rather stilted Skype call on the night of the fire. I'd wanted to tell her how much the fire, the roof caving in, had scared me, and how I wanted her to stay safe and that I'd always be there for her. In return she told me about the posh house she was living in, describing the decoration and the fluffiness of the towels in her en suite in detail. I could never have given her those things. I bought what I could in second-hand shops and post-Christmas sales. Gracie was always popping round with little finds, a marked-down shower curtain or a dented tin of who-knows-what. Surprise dinner, we used to call it. A far cry from the sorts of fancy meals Demi will be eating now, by the sounds of it.

At least here I can get away from the loneliness and the heartache. I can forget about the idea of Gena and Mike together and take time to be myself again . . . or remember who I was, at least, and the dreams I once had. I clutch my bag and shuffle forward on the worn blue linoleum floor.

'*Kalimera*.' I smile nervously when I reach the front of the queue, and the passport control officer nods slowly.

'*Kalimera*,' he replies, opening the pages of my passport. Then, '*Efharisto*.' He thanks me and hands it back, smiling. The nerves settle again and I walk towards the exit.

'Hello,' I hear the passport officer say behind me to the family with the boy who used my seat as band practice all the way here. They have a teenage girl with them too, on her phone, barely grunting at her parents when she's asked to take out her headphones for immigration. 'I can't get Wi-Fi,' she wails, and I have a sudden pang, wishing Demi was here.

I pull out my phone and switch it on to see if I've got any signal yet, desperate to hear from her and to let Angelica know that I've arrived; that I did it. Gracie doesn't have a mobile, but Angelica will tell her my news. I might even find a postcard to send her.

When I finally decided to book my plane ticket out to Crete, I rang Angelica, desperate to persuade her to come with me. If I was going to do this, I wanted her by my side. But despite my best efforts, she turned me down. Wendy Davies, Alwyn's personal assistant at the factory, was pregnant. They'd found out at hospital when she'd had a funny turn after the fire. Angelica had been asked to step in to oversee the repairs and to get the factory up and running again.

'It's my big chance, Nell! If I can run a Christmas decoration factory, well, the fashion industry is just a step away. I could be in charge of a fashion house in London in no time. Following your Demi to the smoke.'

She couldn't turn it down, I knew that. I don't think she believed I'd actually get on the plane on my own. But I suddenly had to know. I couldn't just sit in an empty house waiting for Demi to come home. I was going to return to where I'd left off, with or without Angelica's support. I had to. I needed to know that the decision I'd made all those years ago was the right one. Let's just call it unfinished business. I touch the pendant around my neck again.

And anyway, there were only so many times I could watch reruns of *Mamma Mia!* and *Shirley Valentine*. Sitting there on the settee a week after the fire, having finished a packet of Hobnobs and started on a box of Cheerios, I realised I was standing at the top of a slippery slope. So instead of watching *The Holiday* again, I heaved myself off the sofa and started spring-cleaning, wiping away tears as I cleared drawers and cupboards, trying to take my mind off how much I wanted Demi home, and how frustrated I felt by the wasted years I'd spent with Mike.

There were boxes that hadn't been touched in years under my bed and on top of my wardrobe. Stuff I'd put away and hadn't looked at. Baby clothes, paintings and cards Demi had made. Old clothes, a pair of cut-off shorts I'd customised with stick-on gems and patches. Nan obviously never threw away anything. And that was when I found it: the necklace. Under a pile of photographs. I'd taken it off when I'd gone into hospital to have Demi, bundled by Nan into a taxi, and never put it back on again. I picked it up. The little ruby in the corner was duller than I remembered, but still there. The black leather lace was worn. As I looked at the silver, now greying, outline of half of the island, it all came rushing back to me, the person I was before. This felt like fate, what with the fire, Gena and Mike, and Angelica talking about WWOOFing. As I fastened the pendant around my neck, it felt as if it belonged there.

With my phone in one hand I googled Crete, then, with Gracie's initial horror still ringing in my ears and making me smile, I looked up WWOOFing and working abroad. An advert on a volunteering website jumped out at me: *Help wanted in a honey factory in Crete*. I love honey, especially Cretan honey – I remember the taste so well – and I know all about factories. It was perfect. In just a couple of moments I'd gone from utter despair to booking a flight on my supermarket saver points, all from my phone on my bedroom floor. With the factory closed for the foreseeable future, what else was I going to do? I'd sold my old banger and had the money from that to tide me over. WWOOFing seemed like a perfectly sensible idea. I was getting a life and it wasn't costing me anything.

'Find yourself a gorgeous Cretan waiter!' Angelica shouted as I got into the taxi to the airport. Gracie was on the front step of her little terraced house next door, puffing on a cigarette, watching the world pass by as usual. Other neighbours appeared at their doors to see what all the fuss was about. I shook my head at Angelica.

'That's the last thing I want,' I told her. There was only one man I wanted to find. Then perhaps I'd remember who I was too . . . because if I wasn't Demi's mum, or Mike's girlfriend, who was I?

Now I step outside the terminal building, my nerves returning with the heat, not knowing how I'm supposed to be getting from here to where I'm staying.

A battered old truck with dents in every panel and a black and white wire-haired terrier barking for all it's worth in the open boot pulls up in a cloud of yellow dust. I step back, putting my hand over my mouth, but still coughing. The window is open and a man in a large crooked-brimmed hat with a scarf around his neck, looking like something out of an Indiana Jones movie, leans out.

'Woof!' barks the man gruffly. He's about my age but with a face that says he's lived many more lives than just this one. I can't see much of his expression, his hat casting a shadow over it, but it doesn't look like the brilliant sunshine is making his day any brighter. Hoping that he finds whoever he's looking for quickly, I turn away, looking for some sign of an official representative sent to meet me.

'Woof!' the man barks again, sounding as fierce as the dog. The family with the teenagers emerge through the sliding doors behind me and glance at him suspiciously. He rummages through a pile of rubbish on his dashboard, pulls out a crumpled piece of paper and waves it, seemingly at me. 'Woo . . . *fer*?' he repeats slowly, eyes narrowing.

I look from side to side and then step forward. He couldn't be waiting for me, could he? A sinking feeling creeps over me as I take hold of the paper and look at it.

'Oh God! Yes! I mean *nai*!' I try and breathe despite my tight chest, my nerves made worse by this man barking at me, leaving me hot, tongue-tied and blushing. 'WWOOFer . . . yes, I'm a WWOOFer,' I finally manage.

He nods, grunts, nods again and then leans over to open the passenger door with a shove, the hinges creaking loudly. '*Ela!* Come! I'll take you,' he says.

My mouth is dry and a knot tightens in my stomach. My fickle friend, the warm, welcoming scent of wild mountain thyme, has deserted me, no doubt gone to meet other returning guests, and in its place is the stink of engine fumes and some kind of other smell that could be animal-related.

I hold the back of my hand to my nose as I drag my case round the back of the truck and wrestle it into the cab. As soon as I get in after it and shut the door, the truck shoots off, a plume of yellow dust billowing in through the open window as we career out of the airport and slew round the first roundabout.

Clutching my case, a barrier between me and the driver, I glance across at him. His eyes are fixed on the road ahead. His hands grip the wheel, making the veins on his dark forearms stand out. He has a scar down the side of his cheek that I can just see under the brim of his hat and above the scarf.

Suddenly I realise that he is watching me in the mirror, emerald-green eyes with golden flecks whipping between me and the road ahead. When he looks at me, they narrow like a sniper's, as if he's suddenly spotted his prey and is keeping a watchful eye on it. The scenery whisks past as we head away from the airport towards the coast road, and all my resolve leaves me.

I'm in a truck with a man I don't know, travelling at speed. I have no idea where I'm going or who I'm staying with, and clearly this driver doesn't do small talk. Suddenly the excitement that filled me when I first arrived is turning to mild concern, possibly with a hint of panic in there too. What have I let myself in for?

Chapter Two

I grab the dusty handle and wind the window right down to let out the smell of . . . well, I'm not really sure what, and let the scent of the wild thyme in. I stick my head out and breathe in deeply, trying to relax the knot of nerves in my stomach and focus on the mountaintops in the distance.

Shifting uncomfortably in my seat, I catch another glimpse of the driver's piercing eyes snatching a glance at me, as if sizing me up. I have a strange sense of foreboding and familiarity as we leave the graffiti-sprayed concrete walls of Heraklion. The last time I was here . . . well, let's just say I didn't think I'd ever come back. I tried to keep this place locked away in a secret box in my head while I focused on bringing up Demi, working, paying the bills, but now it feels like the fire at the factory has blown the lid off that Pandora's box.

We head out along the coast road, dust spraying up from the wheels. It's stiflingly hot. I look back to check the dog is still safe in the back of the truck. He looks in his element, leaning his front paws on the side, holding his head up to the wind, letting the air fill his lungs. I look out of the window and do the same. The feeling of familiarity pushes aside the sadness I felt when I left here last time, with my broken heart and the secret I was carrying, and happy memories begin to surface.

Foamy white waves crash against the rocky coastline following the brilliant blue sea to my right. On my left, high cliff faces lead up to the mountains and their towering peaks beyond. Flanking the roadside is a series of bamboo-covered stalls, little huts made of odd bits of wood nailed randomly together, some smart, some barely standing, all selling football-sized oranges. This seems to be a job for the older generation; ancient men and women, mahogany brown, with lined faces, sitting in the shade waiting for passing trade to stop. I wonder how many of them were doing this when I was last here; how much has changed.

My driver still doesn't speak, and I'm struggling to work out how to strike up a dialogue with him. His face is completely shut down, not inviting any conversation at all. I don't even know who he is. Is he just an employee, taking me to where I'll be spending my placement, or – God forbid – is this the man I'm going to be working for and living with for the next two months? I really wish Angelica had come with me. She would have asked all the questions I'm dying to hear the answers to but am too shy to ask. She just shoots and thinks later.

I weigh up my options and finally come up with: 'It's hot.' I'm stating the absolute obvious and tut to myself. What I really want to ask is whether the Zeus's Vista holiday resort is still there, and has he heard of the Papadakis family. Does he know a man called Stelios, and if so, what's his life like? Is he married? Is he happy? Does he ever mention a girl he once met . . . ?

The driver grunts and nods, his eyes sliding towards me again, then back to the road. He's chewing the end of a small stick, rolling it around his mouth. What would Angelica have said? She'd have made him clean out the cab before we got in it, that's for sure, in case her clothes got dusty. Angelica has a way of getting what she wants, just throwing herself into things. That's why she's where she is right now, I suppose, running the factory renovation. I imagine her strutting round the site in an oversized fluorescent jacket, hard hat and four-inch stilettos, carrying a clipboard and telling the workmen she has her eye on them.

Gracie, on the other hand, wouldn't have cared about the dust. Gracie is very easy-going, but she would never have come with me. She hasn't left her house, other than to go to work, and bingo at the weekend, since her husband died when I was still in primary school. Since then my nan and I, and then Demi and Angelica, have been all she's had. We've worked together since I started at the factory on fairy-light testing.

I decide to take a picture on my phone and text it to Angelica and Demi, to break the painful tension in the cab. I snap a photo of the clear aquamarine water and send it to them both; I'm far too self-conscious to take a selfie in front of my travelling companion. I wonder what Demi would think if she could see me now. Sometimes I get the feeling she's starting to feel the same way about me that I used to feel about my mum, like we're worlds apart.

I love Demi with all my heart and I know I should feel happy for her. A new life, with a professional family in London: it's an amazing opportunity. So why do I feel like a huge black cloud is hanging over me?

I realise that I'm still in shock. A big part of my life is over. The same week that Demi left home, I lost both my job and my boyfriend. For as long as I can remember I've been 'Demi's mum' at the school gates; or 'Mike's girlfriend' down at the pub. That's who I was. Now . . . well, now I'm just Nell. I'm not even 'Nell who works in the Christmas decoration factory'. That first evening after the fire, I didn't have to get tea for anyone or put the washing on. I didn't have to go looking for my hairdryer in Demi's room or pick up wet towels from the bathroom floor. I had no idea what I was supposed to do.

As we whizz down the coast road, I am pulled firmly back into the here and now. I hardly recognise the place. If my driver wasn't making me feel so tongue-tied, I'd ask if we were going the right way. Instead I watch the road signs until I see one I recall and know that we are indeed heading in the right direction. But it's nothing like I remember. I actually feel my jaw drop as I look around at the changed landscape.

Brand-new holiday resorts have sprung up all the way along the coast road since I was here last. Clusters of hotels and restaurants, like newly birthed villages, built into the coves and onto the rocky ridges around them; holidaymakers swimming, inflatables bouncing on the white waves, terraces covered with young people in bikinis and knee-length swimming trunks, eating, drinking and soaking up the sunshine. Angelica would have been in her element. I can just picture her, new bikini on, full face of bright make-up; cocktail in one hand and a waiter hanging on her every word. I wonder how many holidaymakers ever actually leave these resorts and head up to the mountains.

Why does everything have to change? A little wave of

anger bubbles up in me. Demi and I were happy, just her and me and her two honorary aunts. Why did she need to go and look for more? Why did Mike want more than I could give him? I hold the door frame and crane my neck, looking at the overcrowded pockets of half-dressed neon-clad tourists. What if everything about the man I'm looking for has changed and is unrecognisable? Him, the town, his family. What if it's all gone?

My case starts to slide towards the driver as we swing round a big bend, but he doesn't flinch as I grab it. We're passing another bay and another resort, only this one I remember only too well, like the familiar smell of a long-lost lover, bringing back memories as clear as if it were yesterday.

In an attempt to cool down, I pull at the ends of my knotted shirt, undoing it and stripping it off, revealing my vest top underneath. I remove the scarf from around my hair, an old bandana of Demi's, and shake out my curls. My bangles and plastic charity bands jangle to match my nerves. The driver gives me another sideways look. The resort is bigger than it used to be, way bigger, like someone's gone mad with Lego and built on lots of different new blocks, but this is the place all right. The resort where I spent a summer working. The place I've wanted to come back to. This is where I left 'me' behind.

My driver starts to indicate away from the coast and up towards the mountains on the other side of the road. The indicator makes a loud, confident ticking noise. I strain my neck back as we turn off the road to catch a last glimpse of the Zeus's Vista resort, reluctant to lose sight of it. Because now that I've found it again, I want to hold tightly on to the memories it's bringing back and not let go.

Chapter Three

The higher up the mountain we travel, the tighter and more frequent the bends. I daren't look down. I hold my breath as we swing round them, nothing between us and the sheer drop down the craggy rock face beside me, where even the trees look to be clinging on for dear life. Along the roadside, every few feet or so, are little model houses, lit on the inside by candles, like doll's houses. Some are beautifully designed.

My driver takes his eyes off the road for a moment to look at me, and then at the little houses. 'For lives lost along the road,' he says flatly, 'and for those spared.'

We pass a small white chapel with a blue bench outside and a bell above the door. I remember that chapel. I remember the first time I saw it. And the smell of pine trees. Once again I'm bombarded with memories. I try to breathe slowly to steady my nerves. This is what I've come here for, I remind myself.

The further we travel, the more I recognise: the tree in the middle of the road with white paint halfway up its trunk; the view down through the mountains to the resort below. I remember the excitement I felt at the prospect of a whole day ahead of us to spend together. And of course the nerves about meeting his family for the first time. As nervous as I feel now, knowing I'm about to retrace the steps of my past.

Higher and higher we climb until I think we're going to go right to the top of the mountain and over the other side. Eventually we pass through a high gorge, coming out into the light and the town ahead. Vounoplagia. I recognise it straight away, like a painting coming to life before my eyes. I catch my breath. This is the town I have pulled out of my memory box every now and again and relived in my mind, usually in the depths of darkness at night. My stomach twists into a tight nervous knot as I recall a cocktail of precious memories: his face, his smile, his soft olive skin, the sound of his laugh. I'm actually here. As we drive into the town, perched high on the side of the mountain, passing square cream and terracotta houses on the road leading towards the main street, I remember it all as if it was yesterday.

This is Stelios's home town. And I could be about to see him again, at any moment.

We swing up through the narrow main street, lined with shops decorated with embroidered table runners, cream lace tablecloths and mats hanging above door frames and over big glass windows. I watch it all whizz by, wishing I had time to take everything in. Penknives and corkscrews are displayed on a big wooden board propped up outside a shop door. There is turquoise and deep orange glazed pottery on tabletops on long steps outside another shop. Nothing has changed.

The road widens to where a mountain stream runs down through the town, with a smart bridge, and a big plane tree shading a little waterfall. In front of us is the square, the whitewashed chapel with a big brass bell overhead. The road bends again: to the left is the old town, the Venetian part that was probably totally separate at one time; to the right, the newer town, with a supermarket built into the hillside, and below that a car park and a small school that looks eerily empty. But then it is the summer holidays, I remind myself.

I look towards the old town, trying to catch a glimpse of Stelios's family's restaurant – an old stone building with big wrought-iron gates into a courtyard, as I recall – but it's not in sight. Old men sitting in upright chairs on the roadside in flat hats, short-sleeved shirts, long trousers and braces, hands resting on sticks, watch us pass with unabashed fascination. Elderly women in scarves and black dresses gather with shopping baskets. It's almost as if the town is stuck in time. The only thing that strikes me as different is how quiet the streets are. There are no families, no children, no tourists. The shops are dark and soulless. The café chairs are empty.

As I look around, heart racing, mouth dry, trying to spot anyone I might recognise, I catch my driver staring at me again. It's as if he's measuring me up, and I don't know if it's the effect of being back here or his scrutiny that is making me more nervous.

'Is this your first time here?' It's the only time he's spoken since we left the airport.

I take a deep breath. I had wanted to come back, but I hadn't expected for so many of the old feelings to flood over me all at once like this.

'No,' I say carefully, still looking around and drinking in the scenery. 'But I've not been back for a very long time.'

At first he stays silent, just focuses on the road. Then he says quietly, 'A lot has changed around here.'

He appears to have reached the limits of his conversational capacity, and says nothing more. But I notice that the veins on the back of his hand stand out as his fingers tighten around the steering wheel and his foot pushes down on the accelerator.

To my relief, but also with a strange feeling of disappointment, we carry on out of the town. I want to be somewhere I can breathe the same air, yes, but not actually here. That would be too close for comfort.

The mountain that rises up behind the town of Vounoplagia, casting a shadow over the roofs of the houses, is covered in little trees and bushes that look like they've been embroidered on to its surface. I look up and see big, slow-moving birds circling the peaks amongst the fluffy white clouds. It's much cooler up here, to my relief.

More swings and turns and I'm beginning to feel like a child after too much ice cream at the fairground. Then, around another sharp bend in the road, the truck suddenly pulls off on to what looks like a rough track. The ground is rocky and we dip and sway. I bang my head on the window and my case bounces off the driver's shoulder and back at me as he spins around in a big circle.

We are right up in the heart of the mountain now, in a large turning area that looks like the sort of place holiday-makers use as a vantage point to park up and take photos. But there are no tourists here. Just a rough *No Parking* sign, hand-made, with a picture of a car with a big cross through it. Far down at the end of the track that runs away from the turning area and hugs the belly of the mountain, there is a rough stone smallholding.

The driver completes the circle and pulls back on to the road again, in the direction we've just come.

'Hey! We just came this way!' I say, suddenly feeling anxious. He says nothing, just carries on driving back down the road. 'Look, I don't know what's going on, but I want you to stop. Let me out!' I grip the door handle.

No sooner have the words left my mouth than we career off and hurtle up a wide path, towards a single-storey whitewashed building with deep-blue-painted metal shutters over the windows and doors. A pink bougainvillea tree is in flower, framing the peeling blue paint on the front door, with ceramic pots either side of it. There are newer single-storey buildings to either side of the house, also painted white and joined by a trellis holding up what looks to be a vine, bearing bunches of grapes. In front of the house a small group of people are standing, staring at us with intense interest.

'Just stop the truck!' I repeat sternly. The man is clearly deranged! Instantly we come to an abrupt halt, as does my racing heart for a second, and the handbrake is yanked on with a jerk and a crunch. I look around.

'Here,' he says with a raised eyebrow. 'The turning is too sharp to drive in from the direction of the town.' He gestures back towards the road. 'You have to make a turn.' This is as close to chatty as he's come. He starts getting out of the truck, and 'Your hosts,' he says with a nod towards the people standing in front of the low building. With a flood of relief I realise that this is it, my home for the next two months. I'm not staying with him!

I look through the dusty windscreen at the people

gathered in front of the low building. Standing with his hands clasped in front of him is a short, dark-haired man in his late forties with a thick moustache that curls over his top lip like a yard brush. He is wearing a bright yellow T-shirt, old and worn so it billows in the breeze, and dusty working trousers and boots. He lifts his battered baseball cap with a rough hand and scratches his head, then looks up at the sky briefly and nervously before replacing it and peering back at me. Next to him, a head taller, is a rotund woman about the same age, with dark hair scraped back from her face, wearing a sun-bleached and well-washed apron over her round tummy, which she runs her hands over to smooth. Next to her, much shorter than the other two, is an elderly woman. She is slight, with short grey hair held back with a clip. She is dressed in black and is fumbling in the large pocket of her dress for something.

I suddenly feel very strange: nervous, excited, with an overwhelming feeling of homesickness and a longing for everything that is familiar. Even Gena's laugh on the factory floor would reassure me of my rightful place in the world right now, rather than feeling that it's slipped on its axis.

I look from the straight-faced welcoming committee, still standing in a row, to the view down the valley we've just driven up. It's breathtaking. I have never seen anything like it. The sea is far off in the distance, sparkling like an intense dark-blue sapphire, and the mountains rise up on either side like the peaks on a baked Alaska.

I turn back to the three people staring at me. My driver is approaching them across the dusty driveway, pulling my case behind him. I push on the door of the cab, and it opens with a squeak and a creak again. I breathe in, waiting for the fragrance of wild thyme to slow down my racing heart. But it's not there. The aroma that greeted me as I stepped off the plane, that transported me back to when I was a young woman, starting out on life's adventure, has practically disappeared. How could that be? Is it that we're just too high up here? In its place is the smell of pine resin and warm baked earth. And . . . goats, I'd guess, looking at the line of long faces staring at me from in between the fence posts to the left of the flat-roofed farmhouse. Or are they sheep? I have no idea.

I step out into the warm sunshine, suddenly feeling stiff from the journey. Beside the truck, two cats are lazing in the cool of a covered seating area. Six tree trunks roofed with long dried leaves provide shade for chunky carved wooden benches and a table made from another thick trunk. My bright purple case is now at the feet of the three people staring at me like the wise monkeys. My driver greets them, shaking hands, then glances towards me with a curt nod.

'WWOOFer,' he announces gruffly by way of introduction, before turning back towards his truck.

I notice that he walks with a slight limp on the same side as the scar on his face, his right. It obviously doesn't slow him down, though, as he's back in the truck quicker than I can rustle up the Greek for 'goodbye'.

As the truck spins off in a cloud of orange dust, the little black and white dog yapping in the back, I turn to the three people standing behind my case, who look as unsure about me as I feel about them. They are staring at me as though

I've just arrived from Mars. And frankly, that's exactly how I feel.

'Hi,' I stammer, feeling like my mouth is full of the orange dust I'm covered in after my journey. 'I mean, *yassou!*' As I say the words, the reality of my situation sinks in. What seemed like a good idea on my bedroom floor with a head full of memories and a mobile phone in my hand is now looking like an absolutely mad one!

What good can possibly come of being here?

Chapter Four

'*Yassou!*' The younger of the two women takes me by surprise as her round olive-skinned face suddenly breaks into a wide smile and she opens her arms warmly towards me. Instantly my fear melts away, like ice cream slipping from its cone and hitting a hot pavement. Clearly my clumsy attempt at Greek worked, though I can see they're wondering what on earth I'm doing all the way up here on my own.

'I am Maria.' She grabs my hand and shakes it warmly, and then, as if unable to help herself, hugs me before she steps back and nudges the man in the ribs, chivvying him into action. 'My husband, Kostas!' She beams again.

He is slower to react, but now he too breaks into a smile. He has a large red mark on his nose and one on his cheek, and I wonder if it's contagious, or a bad case of acne.

'I am Kostas. Welcome to my farm and my home.' He holds out a hand towards the building behind him, and then gestures to the field and outbuildings beyond. The whole place looks like it could do with a bit of TLC. To the other side of the farmhouse is a huge vegetable garden, bulging with vegetables and fruit: bright red tomatoes, figs and oranges. Then he too puts out his hand to shake. 'This is my mother, Mi-te-ra,' he says slowly, as if teaching me a new word and introducing us at the same time.

'Mi-te-ra,' I repeat. He beams and nods but she doesn't smile. I offer my hand and she gives it the smallest of shakes, staring at me as if I have two heads. I run my hand over my mouth just in case I still have the remnants of my in-flight panini there. Maria instructs her husband to take my case, then leads the way into the house. I follow, taking a look around me: the goats or sheep to my left, the vine growing between two flat-roofed buildings on different levels. This is a farm on a hillside, literally. The silence, apart from the rhythmic baaing of the goats and sheep and the whispering of the wind in the bushes and trees dotted over the hillside, is noticeable. There is no one else around at all. No people, no buildings, other than the one I saw just higher up the mountain when we turned around.

I turn and take another look down the valley, through the mountains to the sea, feeling Zeus's Vista holiday resort drawing me in, like I have a connection with the place. And I do. I loved it there. I was so happy then. I wish I was back down there now.

'Let's get you settled, and then my husband will show you around the farm and explain what we want you to do.' Maria speaks really good English, I notice with surprise. 'We need help, you see,' she continues. 'The farm, well, there's lots to do, but no one is buying our fresh produce these days. The restaurants, there are no customers. The only money is with the tourists, and they're not here. They are at the resorts.' She nods down towards the coast. 'So, we are going to reopen our honey farm. We need you to help us get it up and running again. It had to close a few years ago . . .' She falters, and her smile drops. 'But now . . . well, we have to find other ways to keep our farm going.'

I feel for these people, even though I've only just met them. They're trying to make a living whatever way they can, by the looks of it.

'Well, one thing I know about is factories!' I say brightly. 'One is probably much the same as another.'

Maria's smile returns, slow and wide. 'So you will help us get the honey farm ready and the factory cleaned, and hopefully the bees will be happy to help us too!' Her worry turning to optimism, she gives a small clap. 'And you will help on the lower part of the mountain, collecting wild *horta* . . . How do you say?' She turns to her husband.

'Greens, wild mountain greens,' he explains, as if the more he moves his lips, the better will be my understanding of his English.

'. . . when they are called for by the restaurants. It's the two things we can grow here that none of the other farms can. Our honey used to be very special indeed. How do you say . . . magical?' she smiles.

'Medicinal?' I offer.

'That too,' she answers with another beaming smile.

'You speak very good English,' I tell them both, embarrassed by my attempts at Greek.

'We are taught it from very young.' Kostas holds out a hand to waist height. 'It helps, working with tourists,' he adds, then looks at his wife and shrugs. 'When there were tourists.'

'Not now, Kostas. Nell has just arrived,' she scolds. She smiles at me again, but still Kostas's mother, Mitera, doesn't say a word, just stares at me from the doorway to the kitchen.

Kostas ushers me inside. 'The wild bees, up the mountain . . . you must keep an eye out for them.' He scans the sky as if looking for World War Two bombers before pulling the door to firmly. 'They are not very happy at the moment.' He puts his finger to his lips. 'Not happy at all. I want to make them happy again. Happy bees will make plenty of honey!'

'Why are they unhappy?'

'They are having to work hard to find their food,' he begins, but before I have a chance to hear any more, Maria is leading me into the living room, with its tiled floor and big open fire. There's a dark-wood dresser against one wall and old black and white photographs above the door frames and in every available space. Behind that is a kitchen with a wide window looking out over the farm, which drops away steeply down a slope. On one wall there is an old black range. Kostas opens it up, reaches down to a woodpile beside it and feeds logs into the belly of the stove. I step back. The crackling flames and searing heat suddenly take me right back to the day of the fire at the factory. I shiver. Mitera lifts the lid of one of the three worn terracotta pots on the stovetop and beckons me forward to smell the stew bubbling away there. The aroma is amazing. Tomatoes, aromatic and herby; cloves, bay and cinnamon, making my mouth water.

'*Stifado*,' she says, and I nod, taking a couple more deep breaths.

'Here we cook simply but everything is made special by the herbs that grow,' Maria tells me, waving a hand towards the mountainside. 'We cannot have everything in life, but we can live,' she smiles.

In the corner of the kitchen is a bread oven, and Kostas picks up a long-handled paddle and pulls out a loaf, holding it up for me to smell. This time, not only does my mouth water, but my stomach lets out a loud rumble. Mitera breaks into a wide smile, revealing the gap where her teeth should be. Remembering too late, she reaches into her pocket, then puts her hand to her mouth for a second. When she drops it again, the full set is in place. 'Wonderful smell,' I tell her, understanding now why she doesn't smile that often.

'*Dakos*,' Kostas tells me. 'Twice baked.'

Maria gets out a teapot and four cups. She opens a tin and looks into it, her face falling slightly as if disappointed, but she shakes out the last remnants of the tin into the teapot and pushes a smile back on to her face. She pours hot water on to the leaves and carries the tray through to the living room, where she hands round cups of the steaming greenish-yellow brew.

'Come, we will drink it outside, in the shade. It is cool there. We will show you to your room after.'

She leads me to the seating area. The cats haven't moved. Kostas sits down at the long table with his back to the stone wall of an old low shed.

'Tea,' Maria tells me, 'from the mountain.' She waves a hand behind us. 'Herbs that grow there that make us fit and well.'

'Herbs that used to grow there,' Kostas mutters. Maria nudges him, and his tea slops over the rim of his cup.

'It's the herbs that used to make our honey so special,' she continues. 'Sage and marjoram, wild thyme. Of course back then we had dittany too, lots of it all over the mountain. Nowadays, not so much. Everyone wanted Vounoplagia honey!'

The tea tastes and smells of . . . well, of grass cuttings, but I drink it out of politeness, watching their delighted faces watching me. I wonder why they stopped making the honey, but sense I shouldn't ask.

'Delicious!' I lie, and smile, replacing the cup on the tray.

When everyone has finished, Maria leads me back inside, through the other side of the living room. It's cool and dark here as we step down into what appears to be the older part of the house.

'The bedrooms,' she tells me, pointing to a room each side, and I suddenly wonder whether I'm going to be sharing with Kostas's mother. But Maria beckons me on, beaming, back outside and across a path, the one covered in the huge bushy vine, then in through another door to a single-storey breeze-block building. Inside, it's been clad with tongue-and-groove pine to match the two sets of yellow bunk beds there, bright and new, in stark contrast to the rest of the house. Maria gestures around proudly. 'Your room!' she announces. 'Kostas, he made it especially.'

She shows me the small bathroom, and pulls up the handle on the shower in the corner to demonstrate how it works. But my eyes are drawn to the big window looking out over the valley, just like in the kitchen, and the mountain face beyond that, where the road stops and my driver turned the van around. I wonder who he is. A worker on the farm?

'The man who picked me up – does he work here?' I ask, wondering, if he does, where he sleeps.

Kostas has followed us in, and he shakes his head. 'Georgios? No. He lives further up the mountain, . . . amongst the bees up there.' He exaggerates the 'b', rolling his lips like they're made of rubber.

'He is a neighbour,' Maria tells me. 'The small stone house up there,' and I realise it's the house I saw when I first arrived, where he turned the truck around.

'A good neighbour,' she carries on, 'helps if we need anything, like picking you up whilst he was in town, and so on, but . . . he keeps himself to himself,' she says after consideration. 'Most of us townspeople do these days, sadly. The young people, they are all leaving. Nobody stays. They are—' But Kostas shakes his head again, and she stops.

How odd, I think. What on earth has changed round here? This used to be such a strong, close community. The farm is only a mile or so outside the town, and Stelios would talk about the place as if it was one big family. I'm about to ask Maria what has happened when she bustles me back towards the door and the farmyard, where the stretching cats are watching us with feigned interest.

'Don't mind Georgios, it's just his way,' she says, bringing my thoughts back to the rude man who drove me here. 'You won't see much of him; like I say, he keeps himself to himself.'

Good thing too, I think, feeling relieved and thinking that I might actually start enjoying myself here with these lovely people.

Mitera is sitting at the table in the shade of the covered

terrace with a big pot of potatoes in front of her. She's peeling them whilst looking out over the mountains and down the valley towards the sea, lost in thought. We're so high up here, it feels like I'm standing amongst the mountaintops. Below us I can see the terracotta roofs of Vounoplagia, smoke from wood fires spiralling up through the pine trees and over the shrub-strewn mountains. I wonder if Stelios is down there right now.

I can hardly believe I'm here. I've done it. I'm back! And with luck, very soon I'll finally find out the truth.

Chapter Five

Having deposited my case on my bed, I rub my hands together and turn to Maria. 'Right, tell me what I'm going to be doing.' I'm keen to get stuck in to stop myself worrying about Demi and turning over all the possible scenarios in which I might see Stelios again.

'So, you'll be on the farm in the mornings, and then the afternoons are your own. You are welcome to eat with us. Everything we cook is grown here on the farm. We haven't had any workers on the land for a long time, but now times are tougher than ever. We are so grateful to have you here.' Maria puts her hands to my cheeks. 'I hope you will be happy with us.'

I suddenly feel as though a fraud alert is going off in my head. Do they think I'm some agricultural specialist? The nearest I've come to horticulture is a hanging basket in the back garden. Maybe I should tell them. I stop in my tracks.

'I haven't got any experience with bees or anything. But I'm really hardworking, and quick to learn,' I finish, hoping that I've put the record straight. I want to make it work here. I want to help these people. To stay until I've at least got a job to return to. I want to escape the emptiness I felt at home. And all the time I'm here, there's a chance I'm going to see Stelios again. I *have* to make this work.

Kostas beams. 'Come . . . follow me.' As we walk away from the farmhouse, he looks left and right, searching the sky again. 'The bees,' he says. 'We must watch out for them and be ready. There has been some commotion on the mountain. They are guarding their hives up there.' I'm about to ask what sort of a commotion when he continues. 'We must be careful. I get a reaction, you see. If I get stung . . . phew!' He holds up his hands as if to show his head swelling, and puffs out his cheeks, then smiles.

I don't have time to ask any more as Kostas sets off down the worn, rocky path to the side of the farmhouse in a manner that reminds me of the mountain goats in the adjoining field. The smoke from the wood stove in the kitchen is filling the slightly cooling air. I follow him down the slope and the goats trot alongside us behind the fence, making an almighty racket, baaing and bleating as if calling to Kostas like he's a returning friend. He stretches out a hand to greet them, stroking the noses that are snuffling and curling towards his hand.

The fence is home-made, constructed from wooden pallets, the sort used in the factory back home for piling packed boxes of decorations on, ready for shipping out. Here they're on their sides and secured together with cable ties. Kostas shakes one, checking its sturdiness. Satisfied, he turns back to me. 'Every morning we milk the goats,' he points to an open-sided shed, 'and take the milk to the cheese factory in town. Here in Crete we use a mixture of sheep's and goat's milk to make cheese. The factory sells it to restaurants and to tourists,' he shrugs, 'when they come. But again, there's not much call for it these days.'

'Really? No tourists? I'd have thought visitors would be flocking here,' I say, looking out over the farm beyond the field of goats. This looks to be the real deal, a traditional Cretan mountain farm and the local town too. I remember tourists arriving in their droves in hire cars and on buses when I was here all those years ago. I even remember we got a lift on one of the organised trips taking tourists up the mountain for the day. Stelios was friendly with all the drivers. He seemed to know everyone. The coach dropped us in the town, on our day off from the resort and picked us up on its way back in the evening.

'It's different now. They want the free drinks in the resorts, the swimming pools, the fast food . . .' Kostas explains. 'That's why we need to open up the honey factory again. The tourists in the towns will still buy honey.'

'So why did it close down, Kostas, the honey farm?'

He turns away and carries on walking. 'The herbs began to disappear and we thought it would be good to leave the mountain alone for a while, concentrate on the fresh produce we grow here.' He plucks a green leaf from the grassy verge and hands it to me. 'Rocket! Taste!' he insists, and I tentatively put it on my tongue. 'Peppery!' he announces with a smile, and I nod and agree, eating the rest of the leaf.

'So, the herbs and the bees?' I push. 'You left the herbs alone to what? Grow back?'

He nods. 'But whilst we left them alone,' he looks around, 'others have moved in on the mountain. I was born here.

I don't want to have to leave. But if we can't find a way to make a living any more . . .'

He shrugs, and I notice that his eyes are watery. I turn away, giving him a moment, and look around me. I can see that this is more than just a farm; it's a little piece of paradise too. I can't help it. I want to know more. 'Why are the animals fenced in?' I ask. 'I thought the sheep and goats roamed free in the mountains.' Last time I was here, I remember, they were dotted all over the mountainside.

'Overgrazing.' He shrugs. 'It's part of the reason the herbs are dying out. It's safer to keep them fenced in these days.' He looks up at the mountain as if it can hear him. I follow his gaze. Safer from what, or who?

We turn to see a gaggle of geese walking towards us. I stand back and let them pass, and as I do, I notice that right in the middle of the gaggle is a duck, walking just like it's one of the geese. I point, and Kostas smiles.

'It's not about what or where you've come from but where you fit in,' he laughs. I have a funny feeling I could fit in here too.

We carry on walking down the hill.

'My workshop,' he says, and moves quickly towards a black corrugated-iron shed. 'We chop the wood every day for the oven and for fires in the autumn and winter. It gets cold here in the mountains, lots of snow.' He bangs his arms around himself by way of explanation, making me smile. 'And I am making new beehives!' He gestures proudly to the work going on there, beehives in different stages of completion.

A little cream-coloured dog jumps out of a wooden crate

lined with blankets and comes over slowly to greet me, wagging her tail but keeping her head and shoulders low to the ground, wary but keen to find out who I am. Following her out of the crate, one by one, tumbling and bouncing over each other, come three puppies. I'm bending with open arms to greet them when suddenly there is a loud bark that makes me jump back. I look up to see the black and white dog from the truck that brought me here from the airport. He bounces down the hill from the rough mountain road above the farm, and it's only as he gets closer that I notice his back leg is missing. He stands above me on the slope, barking rhythmically and incessantly as if on guard, until I put my hands up and step back from the cream dog and her puppies, understanding his message.

'OK, OK. I'm not going to hurt them,' I tell him. As I move away, one of the puppies, smaller and scruffier than the others, attempts to follow me, and the black and white dog darts forward, barking at me to stay back.

'Sorry, sorry.' I hold my hands up again, and Kostas throws his head back and laughs.

'He is very protective,' he says. 'He will be different when he trusts you.'

I keep backing down the slope until I'm on the worn path again. The black and white dog stops barking but looks to be keeping a close eye on me.

'Come.' Kostas beckons me on quickly to an old stone barn and opens up the big wooden doors. 'The honey factory,' he announces with a strange mixture of pride and disappointment.

I peer into the darkness at the rows of empty pots. Oh my

God, where on earth am I going to start? It's huge, and full of cobwebs. I hate spiders! I look at the ferns growing through the walls, and what appears to be a fig tree, and the daylight that is coming in through the roof. This is nothing like the factories I know.

'It will need to be thoroughly cleaned first. And then we will try and make friends with the bees again and see if they will let us have some honey.'

'Just one thing, Kostas.' I look around. 'Where exactly are the bees for your honey factory?'

His smile drops like a stone. 'Ah,' he says, as though I've popped his birthday balloon. He starts shuffling his feet, then shoves his hands in his pockets, looking at the dusty concrete floor.

'Kostas?' I ask again. I'm getting a really strong sense that there is more to this than a big old barn that's been left to rot. And if this trip is going to be everything I hoped, I really need to find out what's going on.

Chapter Six

'No bees? On a honey farm?' I ask incredulously.

Kostas screws up his face and waggles a hand. 'As I said, the bees are unhappy at the moment, the wild bees, up the mountain.' He shrugs. 'The herbs on the mountainside are disappearing; our precious dittany is practically nowhere to be seen. The bees are disappearing too. We need to bring them back to the farm. We need to tempt them here with new homes and plenty of herbs. No one wants to go high up the mountain these days. Not since *people* have moved in up there.'

'What people?' I ask, but he just shrugs, raises his palms and shakes his head.

'No one knows what they're doing, but it's best to stay away. We need to plant up the meadow here with some mountain herbs,' he points to the valley below the farmhouse, 'and try and tempt the bees into new hives where we can look after them and make sure they are well fed. If we can persuade a queen into our hives, we will have a chance.'

We continue walking along the path through the valley. When we reach the field on the other side, he introduces me to the Cretan cows that are grazing there.

'Always have some of these in your pocket and they will

be your friends forever,' he smiles, handing me a dark brown dried pod. I look at it, sniff it and then hold it out to a cow with a calf at her feet.

'Dried carob,' Kostas tells me. 'It grows everywhere. It is known as the lost treasure of Crete. When people were poor, especially in the war, everyone depended on this to eat. Especially up here in the mountains.'

I remember Stelios showing me carob pods on my first day here all those years ago, holding them out in the palm of his hand. He told me how they had kept many people from starvation during the Second World War, when towns and villages were cut off. 'Like chocolate,' he said. The cow munches on the dried carob and looks for more, and I smile. I dust off my hands, and then step back and look up to the mountain peak.

Back at the farmhouse, Maria is calling us from the kitchen.

'Ah, late lunch,' announces Kostas. On the way back into the house he shows me another room next to my bedroom where he makes his wine.

We sit in the shade outside and Maria brings out a large laden tray. She serves lentil soup with garlic, onion, carrots and a hint of orange and bay. My tired and flagging spirits are immediately lifted. Afterwards she brings out *dakos*, the twice-cooked bread covered in bright red chopped tomatoes, chunks of crumbling white mizithra cheese and black olives, sprinkled with freshly chopped oregano and drizzled with deep green olive oil the colour of a peridot gemstone. It is Crete on a plate, the tangy white cheese, juicy olives and tomatoes bursting with flavour all wrapped up in the glorious thick olive oil. Suddenly I feel as though I am right back to being eighteen again. My taste buds do a very happy dance indeed.

'It's a wonderful place,' I tell them, feeling revitalised after my early start to the airport that morning.

'After lunch, Maria will show you where we collect the greens. But you must be careful on the mountain,' Kostas warns. 'These are strange times. You will be safe if you stick to the lower slopes. No one will bother you.'

I nod, taking on board the warning and suddenly feeling like the shine has worn off the glorious painting in front of me.

'So who has moved on to the mountain? Who's keeping people away?' I ask as I run a forkful of *dakos* around my plate, letting the tomato juice and olive oil soak into the bread and soften it.

Both Maria and Kostas seem nervous, looking about them shiftily. What is going on? I wonder.

At last Kostas shrugs and then sighs. 'No one knows. No one speaks of it. The path that leads up over the mountain to the town the other side is closed.'

'Drugs!' Mitera pipes up, scanning the valley below. 'Like the other towns.'

'Ssh!' Maria silences her. 'There are many rumours,' she says.

'Drugs!' Mitera repeats.

Kostas sighs again. 'It may be poachers,' he says reluctantly, 'stripping the mountaintop of herbs to sell on to tourists.' He bites his bottom lip and his big moustache bobs up and down. 'Or . . . well, there has been a wave of this sort of activity across Crete, gangs moving into hard-to-reach mountain areas.' He looks around again. 'They plant drugs in amongst the olive trees and guard them ferociously.' Despite the heat of the sun, I feel myself shiver. 'Which is why we need to bring the bees back down to safety. If we can't reach them up there, we will bring them to us!'

After lunch I go to my room and unpack. I check my messages; there's one from Demi, telling me she's really busy, having a great time and going out with the family to a BBQ at their friends' house, which has got a swimming pool. I try to ring her, but it goes straight to answerphone. I want to tell her about Maria and Kostas and the bees and how Kostas's mother keeps losing her teeth. But I can't, and I'm left with an odd feeling of being snubbed and pushed out. I don't think I've ever spent this long without her.

There's a selfie from Angelica and Gracie, Angelica in her hard hat and fluorescent tabard over a low-necked blouse, short skirt and high heels, with Gracie pulled in at her side. They're on the way to the pub and missing me, they tell me, making their mouths downturned, although that might be Gracie's usual expression. But it makes me smile and a bit teary at the same time. The factory is going to be shut for at least two months, Angelica says. Gracie is just about managing to eke out her savings by the sound of it and I know I would have been in real trouble if I'd stayed. There's also a message from Mike, which I leave till last. He says he's sorry. He made a mistake. It was a one-off. He wants to talk. I hear Gena's laugh in my head and purse my lips. I have a past to find before I can think about my future. I press delete firmly.

* * *

Later, after a little afternoon nap on my new bed, as the heat goes out of the day, Maria leads the way up the mountain to show me where to collect the wild *horta*.

Kostas is pushing a rotavator, a cart-like thing with spiral blades, along the side of the valley, turning over the stony ground there, and I'm glad that's not my job. He calls and waves cheerily to us. Then he bends to plant out the herbs before watering them all.

Maria and I wave back and continue past him towards the field of cows in the valley that dips away behind the farmhouse and runs back up the rough track to their neighbour's small stone house.

'These are the greens we eat with our meals.' She nods towards the mountain. 'Wild mountain greens. Actually, I think *horta* means weeds in English. We are weed eaters!' She laughs and walks sure-footedly up through the field. I find myself dodging behind her as the cows start to gather around her, and she pats their heads and pulls carob pods from her pocket to feed them. When we reach the fence on the other side of the field under the pine trees, she unties a rope and pulls back one of the panels to let us out, tying it back up again securely whilst still talking. 'They must be picked, washed and served quickly, otherwise they lose flavour and nutrients. Of course, there are no pesticides up here. Here in Crete we love wild foods. It's part of the reason our diet is so healthy; that and, of course, the dittany.'

'The herb that the bees love, that made the honey special?' I say, taking it all in. She nods.

'It grows high up. It is a very special herb. It is known as *erontas*. Love,' she explains. 'Everybody wants the wild dittany.' She smiles with just a tinge of sadness at the corner of her mouth, then changes the subject. 'And so this is where I go for the greens.' She points up towards a small set of steps leading on to the gentle lower slopes of the mountain. 'We eat them boiled, with extra-virgin olive oil' – she indicates the twisted olive trees at the side of the track, their leaves lifting in the wind, showing their silver undersides – 'and freshly squeezed lemon juice.' She nods to the trees down in the vegetable patch, with lemons the size of rugby balls. 'They are packed with all the nutrients. People have foraged for *horta* since Minoan times. This mountain has always provided for our community. It looks after us.' She smiles again, her eyes twinkling.

We cross the hot, dusty track. To one side is the place where Georgios turned the truck when I arrived earlier. To the other, down the lane, is the small stone building, with the truck parked outside. In front of us, the worn steps lead up towards the mountain between strong-smelling pine trees. I follow Maria up, her big round bottom making her skirt sway ahead of me.

'We collect from here . . . and here,' she points to two patches of land, 'and then one place just a little way ahead, but no further,' she warns, her face dark and serious. I watch as she begins to pick the greens. 'No one will bother you here. Be careful not to take the root. We want them to grow again,' she tells me, putting the greens into the crate she's placed on the ground. I watch and copy, picking the greens and putting them in my basket.

As we work, we chat. I tell her about life back home.

How the factory burned down and that it will be shut for two months for refurbishment. I don't tell her about the roof, though; I've locked that memory away in one of the little boxes at the back of my brain, only visiting it at night, when I wake up sweating from a nightmare that I'm still in the building and the fire is taking hold and Demi is on the other side of it and I can't get to her. I tell Maria about Angelica and Gracie and that I recently split from my partner. I tell her how I hoped Demi would change her mind about going to London and would come home and resit her exams at a further education college; even stay on and do something like hospitality. I don't tell her that I've felt like a boat cut loose from its mooring since Demi's been gone, or the real reason I wanted to come to Crete.

She tells me that she and Kostas have been together since they were seventeen, and I have a little pang of envy. They are clearly devoted to each other. I don't ask about children. Something tells me that too may be tucked away in a box, at the back of Maria's mind. But she tells me how important it is that they get the honey farm up and running, and how she would have to go and live with her mother and sister in the city if they can't make a living on the farm. Her sister has just had another baby, her fourth. The apartment is full to bursting and there are too many mouths to feed there already. Her brother-in-law has struggled to find work. Jobs are hard to come by. Besides, city life would kill Kostas, she tells me; he hates not being outside. She tries to make light of it, but I hear how important this is to them. They have to make their life at the farm work.

* * *

That evening, after returning from the mountain, we eat *stifado*, the beef stew that Mitera showed me earlier in the kitchen. It is juicy and tender and melts in my mouth in a slightly sweet rich tomato sauce. There are the wild greens that we picked; the potatoes, soft and fluffy, that Mitera peeled earlier; followed by a large dish of fresh fruit – huge round oranges, figs and quince.

'And . . .' Maria says with the excitement of a child on Christmas morning, 'honey!' She puts the jar ceremoniously in the centre of the table. 'It is the very last jar from when we used to make it here. I have been saving it for a special occasion,' she beams, 'and now we have one! You are here!' she tells me, and I blush. 'The honey farm will reopen and we will have more.' Her face is positively glowing with happiness.

'Oh, you should save it!' I say, but she's having none of it.

They all look at the jar with smiles on their faces. The honey is deep and dark and looks like liquid gold. Then Maria places semolina halva on the table, a wobbling moulded desert, not too sweet, covered in almonds and cinnamon with a hint of cloves. Such a simple dessert, she tells me, but delicious. Kostas pours home-made wine from an orange metal jug as the sun starts to dip in the sky, big and orange behind the peak of the mountain to the side of the farm.

Maria serves the halva and hands round the fruit. I take some figs and sit them next to the halva. Then Maria twists the lid off the jar, which is shaped like a small Grecian urn, and hands it to me, eyes wide with expectation. I put my spoon in and drizzle the molten gold liquid over the figs on my dish; then, watched by three expectant faces, I bring the spoon to my nose and breathe in. It smells exquisite. At last I put it in my mouth and suck. It tastes fresh, as fresh as the mountain air, and aromatic. A delicate balance of sweet smooth nectar and the wild herbs.

'I can taste the thyme in there,' I tell them. 'A hint of sage, possibly oregano, maybe basil?' They nod, smiling broadly, eyes shining. 'But there's something else. Something different.' It's dancing lightly on my tongue. What is the other flavour? A woody taste, bittersweet, puzzling me. It's cooling and clean, slightly minty. It smells and tastes of Crete, of the trees, the mountain. There's a fragrant aftertaste, sitting on my taste buds, leaving a lingering flavour. 'That's the dittany, isn't it, the herb you were telling me about?'

They all nod together.

'It's . . .' I hesitate. It's different. Distinctive. It seems to elevate all the other flavours, balance them perfectly. 'It's . . .'

'Magical!' they finish for me, and I laugh and nod, and suck the spoon clean.

After dinner, I sit watching the sun set. This is such an amazing place, and Maria and Kostas are lovely people. I hope I can help them. I hope I can help get the honey factory set up and the bees into new beehives.

From high up on the mountain a round of what sounds like gunshots rings out. I look at Maria and Kostas for an explanation; they look at each other.

'It happens, there's nothing to worry about,' Maria says. 'It's way up on the mountaintop. Please, don't be scared off like the tourists have been. No one has been hurt. You are safe, I promise.' She looks at me earnestly, worried that I'm going to pack up and leave, no doubt. I smile.

'Where I live, on a Saturday night at pub closing, it's like the Wild West!' I joke.

Kostas tops up my wine glass and Maria offers me the platter of fruit, looking relieved. I gaze back up at the mountain, appalled that some sort of gang is keeping people – honest people who have lived here all their lives – from making a living. Well, I intend to do the best I can whilst I'm here.

When the sun sets, it gets dark, really dark, like someone's thrown a blanket over the world, and the stars look like bright crystals decorating a deep velvet sky. As I make my way to my bedroom, though, I can still make out the shape of the mountain, standing over us. I don't know if it's protecting us or intimidating us, but it's always there.

I pull my case out from under my bed and take out the photographs I've brought with me. Then, feeling ridiculous but unable to stop myself, I find Hamish, Demi's little teddy bear, and hold him to me, like I'm holding her close. It feels so strange to be back here, and to be without Demi. Now that I've seen the town again, though, confronted by all those memories, I need answers. Yet I can't just go straight down there and find Stelios and ask how he's doing. I need to make sure I don't give myself away too soon, keep my head down.

In the distance I hear the gunshots again and a dog barking. What on earth is going on? We really are in the middle of nowhere here. I shiver again and make a mental note to leave the bathroom light on, just to keep out the dark and whatever might be lurking out there.

Chapter Seven

There's a thick mist rolling round the farm the following morning like a cloak. I wake to the sound of bleating goats in the field outside my window. After a bowl of creamy, tart yoghurt with a drizzle of the honey Maria insists I have from the last of their limited supplies, I want to get stuck in to my chores straight away. Filling a bucket with soapy water, I drop a scrubbing brush into the bubbles with a splosh. Sleeves rolled up on my checked shirt, hair tied on top of my head with a red spotted bandana, looking like a fifties housewife, I'm ready to head towards the sad, empty honey factory.

Just before I head down the path, past where Maria is milking the goats and Kostas is rotavating and planting herbs, I take a moment to look up to the peak of the mountain, then back the other way to the distant sea, where the sun is starting to sparkle on the water like someone's dropped a pot of glitter there. The only sounds are the bleating of the goats, the hush of the breeze in the pine trees, and the gentle mooing of the beautiful brown-eyed Cretan cows, who watch us from their field on the slope above the farm.

This is so far from my life back home. On a normal day I'd be getting up, shooing Demi off to school, cutting it fine as usual, then rushing out the door to the factory, promising myself I'd tidy up as soon as I got in and be more organised tomorrow. In the evening, if I wasn't seeing Mike, I'd sit down with one of my favourite DVDs, knowing the next day would be just the same. My only pleasure came from the world I escaped to on the screen. And now here I am, as if I'm *in* one of those films!

Pulling back the doors of the honey factory is like opening up the decaying mansion and finding Miss Havisham in her wedding dress. Nothing has been touched for over ten years, Maria told me, perhaps more. I look around at the enormity of the task. There are piles of dusty jars covered in cobwebs. A huge vat with a turning handle on top that looks rusted up. Another tank that needs cleaning inside and out. There are shelves covered in dust, cupboards and boxes full of jars, lids and labels. I take a deep breath and decide to start by pulling out the ferns from the stone walls, cutting back the fig tree growing there too and then dropping to all fours to start scrubbing off the moss. If we are going to make and store honey here, it needs to be spick and span.

By the end of my first morning, I ache so much I can barely straighten myself up, let alone walk anywhere. Kostas comes across from the workshop to help me close up for lunch. We are walking together back up the track, discussing the design of his beehives, when suddenly he stops and stands stock still. His eyes widen in a mixture of excitement and fear and his cheeks start to quiver.

'Kostas? What's the matter?' I ask, looking round to see what's caught his attention.

He doesn't reply; just looks this way and that and then

turns and starts to stumble across the field, tripping over rocks in his haste and pointing up at the sky.

'B . . . b . . . b . . . !' I hear it first – a buzzing noise, getting louder and closer – and then I see it. A moving black cloud, shifting shape in the sky, heading towards us. I'm no expert but I'm guessing this is a swarm of bees; an angry swarm of bees. I freeze, backing into the corner of the open-sided shed, and stand flattened against the corrugated wall. I feel my heart start to race and my palms sweat, because those bees don't look like they are popping in for a friendly chat. I hold my breath, and to my relief they fly straight over the shed.

I turn to look at Kostas, halfway up the side of the valley, to see him beaming from ear to ear.

'Now all we have to do is get them to come and live here!' he says with crazed excitement. He holds his arms out wide. 'If we build it, they will come!'

Back at the farmhouse, after our close encounter with the flying squad, Maria ladles a soup of fat white beans, chunky carrots and celery, tomato and paprika into large round bowls.

'*Fasolada*,' she tells me.

We carry the bowls and basket of fresh warm bread out to the shaded table. 'Delicious,' I tell Maria, finishing my bowl and accepting seconds from the big pot. As we finish, I stand to help clear away.

'Leave those, I can do them. It's the afternoon; your time off. Why not go and explore? You can take my moped; it's easy,' she says, smiling mischievously.

I nod confidently, though never having ridden a moped before, I have no idea if I can do it, particularly when my muscles are so sore after a long morning scrubbing the walls in the honey factory. But if I'm going to find out if Stelios is still here, it seems to be the only way of getting around.

'Are there any jobs I can do for you while I'm out?'

'Well, you could deliver the goat's milk to the cheese factory just on the other side of town.' Maria smiles.

'Of course, no problem!' I tell her, wiping my hands down my shorts, wondering how I'm going to ride a moped carrying a bucket of milk.

This is it! I'm actually going to do it. I'm going to drive into town, retrace those steps from my past that I've dreamed about so often. Maria hands me her open-faced helmet from a hook on the back of the kitchen door.

'Wear this,' she says, looking at my shaking hands. 'You'll be fine as long as you take care. The moped may be easy to ride but the roads are . . . well, less easy. And the tourists don't always take the care they should,' she adds with solemnity.

I take the helmet and put it on, doing up the strap under my chin. Then I pick up the milk and head outside.

And as I straddle the moped, my back and legs ache and I realise I might actually be about to see Stelios again, face to face, And I have absolutely no idea what I'm going to say or do.

Chapter Eight

The little moped roars into life, louder than I was expecting; like Georgios's terrier, small but with a loud bark and plenty of attitude. Maria steps away, having shown me how to start it, and I give myself a pat on the back. I've managed to get the key in and pressed the ignition button. It's a start. Now all I have to do is work out how to actually steer and ride it. Can't be that different from a bicycle. Suddenly the engine erupts, belches and farts, scaring the life out of me.

'It does that!' Maria waves a tea towel and grins madly from where she's standing with Mitera by the front door. 'Don't worry!' Kostas is watching too, looking very worried. They are like proud parents witnessing their child take a first bike ride without stabilisers, full of trepidation and faith.

I focus really hard on the handles I'm gripping. I just have to open the throttle and . . . whooaaa! The bike shoots forward like a racer snake. I stick my legs out either side and lift them as it wobbles violently from side to side. It's not like a bike! And it doesn't slow down when I try and put my feet on the floor to get some control over the damn thing. Instead it snakes around this way and that, chucking up a cloud of orange dust. Lots of it, making me cough. I take my hand off the throttle to wave away the dust and stop suddenly.

I try it a few more times: stop, start, stop, start. Maria comes forward with the stainless-steel milk churn and slides it on to the footplate in front of me.

'Go!' She waves and smiles. 'Go and explore! Go and see the island!'

I don't wave back for fear of what will happen if I take my hands off the handlebars. But I do slowly open up the throttle, focusing on going in a straight line. I lift my feet and balance them either side of the cold milk churn, wedging it into place, and I'm off! Heading down the little dirt track to the road, hand on the brake, squeezing it and squeezing it, and then quickly trying to remember which side of the road to drive on. It's not the actual driving of the moped that's the hard part, I discover as I quickly get my balance; it's the steep incline that's the problem. I keep my hand on the brake, discovering that if I do lots of little squeezes it slows me down more than one long one, despite the jerky stop-starting of the bike.

But I'm out on the road, on my way. The wind in my face, the milk churn balancing between my feet, and in the background I can just about hear Mitera, Maria and Kostas laughing over the high-pitched whine of my brakes. This will give me something to talk to Demi about if she Skypes tonight.

At a sharp bend in the road, I stop the bike and stand with my feet either side of the footplate next to one of the ornate little houses with a lit candle in it. I remember this place from my drive up here with Georgios. On one side of the road is a sheer rock face; on the other, the ground drops away sharply to a deep gorge filled with twisted, wind-blown olive trees and tall green firs. I can smell the pines like someone has waved smelling salts under my nose, reviving me. There are needles all over the road, and the odd cone too. I bend down to pick one up and hold it to my lips. Then I stretch my neck to try and see the bottom of the gorge, but my head spins just looking at the drop, so I pull back. From a safe distance, it's one of the most beautiful views I have ever seen.

I set off again, feeling like Thelma and Louise on a road trip. Following the twists and turns in the road, I stop and start all the way down, getting the occasional rush of confidence before panicking that the bike is out of control and practically braking to a stop. It would have been quicker to walk at this rate! I finally manage a comfortable speed, relaxing enough to start leaning slightly with the movement of the bike; not easy with a milk churn balanced on the footplate. I swing round a corner confidently and smoothly, feeling pleased with myself, and am about to straighten up when almost immediately I have to swerve round a pile of rocks that have slid on to the road from the mountain on my right. Once again I catch a glimpse of the drop below. I glance down to adjust the milk churn, which has slipped, and look back up just as I hit a pothole, which nearly unseats both me and the churn. I wobble violently this way and that before catching the churn between my feet and righting myself.

Oh God, I hope Demi isn't out doing something as stupid as riding one of these. But I know one thing. If I can ride this bike on these roads, whilst balancing a milk churn, then I'm pretty sure I can get that honey factory up and running again.

As I arrive in the outskirts of Vounoplagia, rows of square two-storey houses start to pop up, nestled into the gentle slopes. The road widens enough for two cars to pass comfortably. I drive slowly towards town, the hot sun beating down on the road, throwing up the smell of melting tarmac. But at least it is a tarmac road and not the stony dirt-covered track up to the farm. I start to enjoy the feeling of the little tyres trundling me along as I approach the square white church with the big brass bell over the door.

All the shops are open, displaying their wares, and the restaurants have blackboards outside and orange charcoal glowing in the barbecues awaiting grill orders. But still no one is browsing, eating or shopping. As I pass, my red hair poking out from the back of my helmet giving away my foreign roots, my moped farting and belching, the locals stop and stare. So much for keeping a low profile.

I follow Maria's directions to the farm on the other side of town, where the local cheesemaker has his factory, and deliver the milk, unspilled, to the elderly man there with a nod and a few basic words of Greek that I manage to draw up from the depths of my memory. Then I take the empty churn and head back towards town, the road's familiar twists and turns drawing me in.

I stop at the supermarket, a little smarter and bigger since the last time I was here, but emptier too by the looks of it. I park the bike, my thighs still vibrating, and look around. Stelios could be anywhere. I glance back towards the shop, and my heart quickens as I turn and head for the doors. When I push them open, I'm hit by that familiar smell of strong cheese and the sound of whirring fridges and freezers working their hardest. It's cool on the tiled floor, and I pull off my helmet and shake out my hair.

'*Kalispera*,' says the man sitting behind the counter watching the world go by. But it's not him. It's not Stelios. In fact, there's no one else in the little supermarket, and my heart drops back down to its usual rhythm.

'*Kalispera*,' I attempt, and he nods and smiles. I grab a cold bottle of water from the full fridge and a postcard to send to Gracie, and pay for them both.

'On holiday?' he asks hopefully in stilted English.

I shake my head and take a much-needed swig from the water bottle. 'Working, with Maria and Kostas, on their farm.' I point up the mountain.

His face drops momentarily, but then he smiles again. 'Well, welcome to Vounoplagia.' He holds his arms out proudly, and I can't help but smile back and thank him. 'I am Samir. Here to help.'

I take another sip of water and wonder whether to ask about Stelios and his family. Are they still at the restaurant? Does he know Stelios? But I don't want to go jumping in there with both feet. I don't want to scare Stelios off, so I hang back.

'Thank you. *Efharisto*,' I say, and return to the moped.

As I finish my water, I stand and gaze out over the trees below. It's not quite such a good view as the one from the farm, but it's still amazing, and it hasn't changed since I was here last. I look around. Two men standing on the pavement opposite are openly discussing my arrival in the town, and the woman outside the tablecloth shop leans on her stick and stares at me. Well, I'm here, I tell myself. I might as well go and look. See if the place is still there. I climb back on to the moped, my thighs feeling the vibrations all over again, and roll off, more smoothly this time.

Approaching a fork in the road, I slow down and instinctively stick my feet out before heading down a narrow cobbled street. Immediately I see a difference in the houses. These are older, bigger and have Venetian-style arches with wrought-iron fences and gates. There are orange trees in the front gardens and beautiful purple bougainvillea growing over terraces facing out on to the road and in the direction of the sea. Behind them the mountain sits looking dark and sulky, as if the houses have turned their backs on it, ignoring its glowering mood. On the left-hand side of the road, lower down the slope, the houses are smaller, whitewashed and built around the incline of the mountain. The streets that lead off this lane are not wide enough even for one car to pass. The cobbles are worn and rounded and the rusting metal handrails shiny from hundreds of years of use.

I slow to a stop to let a man with a billy goat and two female goats pass. He is wearing a thick woollen jacket and hat despite the heat of the day and carrying a long stick, though he doesn't seem to need it. He looks at me as if I have two heads, his mouth falling open slightly, then misses his footing before righting himself and carrying on, still staring back at me. Honestly, you'd think I was some kind of celebrity, the way people keep gawping.

I take a deep breath and look down the narrow street. There in front of me are the wrought-iron gates of the restaurant, looking just as they did when I was here eighteen years ago.

I have to think about this. Am I really going to just walk in and say, 'Hi, I'm back, remember me?' I stand and stare for what seems a very long time. Then, from the restaurant, I hear voices – well, one voice. A man's voice, raised as if in disagreement. I have no idea what I'm going to say or how I'm going to play this, and instinctively I turn the moped around and start it up again, suddenly panicking that I'm going to be seen. I just don't feel ready. Not yet. I need to find out more about his life before I go strolling in and reintroduce myself. I have to work out how to do it, and today was just the start.

Chapter Nine

My days at Maria and Kostas's very quickly fall into a pattern. I wake early and work in the field whilst it's still cool, helping Kostas, watering and tending the herbs he's planted there and helping to plant more. Then Kostas works on his beehives, bringing them out one by one as they're finished and proudly putting them into position. Each day he checks the hives and I watch from a distance at the entrance to the honey factory, waiting for the thumbs-up. But every morning I get a shake of the head. No bees have come. He checks the skies, and as each day passes he gets more and more impatient. 'Why do they not come?' he wails. All I can do is sympathise and go back to scrubbing down the work surfaces in the factory.

On my sixth morning at the farm, I'm clearing out under the sink, armed with an upturned jam jar to catch any spiders that might be hiding there, when I hear screams coming from the mountain path just above where I've been picking the wild mountain greens. It sounds like Kostas. My heart leaps and races like a whippet down the racetrack. I drop my scrubbing brush into the bucket, letting soapy water splash everywhere, and run outside, through the cows' field and up the hill the other side, my walking boots that I bought from

Lidl when Mike and I took Demi to the Green Man festival last year slipping under me as the tiny rocks create a little landslide. I actually manage to jump the fence by lying along the top of it and sort of rolling off the other side, then catapult towards the worn stone steps. Coming towards me I see Georgios, running down the lane from his little stone hut. He must have heard the screams too.

'Sorry, sorry,' I say, slightly out of breath, only just managing to stop myself careering into him. He doesn't speak. I haven't seen him since he dropped me off last week, and frankly, I'd've preferred it to stay that way. He's still scowling at me now, and I'd like to ask if he's like this with everyone, or whether it's just me. Something about him seems familiar . . . But I don't have time to think about it now; there are more important things to worry about. I need to find out where those screams were coming from. I need to find Kostas. I glance briefly at Georgios, dodge round him and run up the path. Georgios follows just behind me, making me run faster, my breathing deeper, batting away flies from my face. It's hot now, and getting hotter.

'Kostas?' I shout as he suddenly comes into view, stumbling and sliding down the path. 'What's happened?'

'The bees!' he cries, clutching his head, and carries on running past me and Georgios towards the farmhouse. Georgios and I swap concerned looks. It's the only common ground we've found since I arrived.

I try to remember the number for the emergency services. Should I call? Would an ambulance be able to get up the road? Instead, I follow Georgios back down the path. His limp is only just evident and isn't slowing him up any.

At the farmhouse, Maria has her arm around Kostas and is leading him inside. She waves a tea towel at us. 'I have him . . .' she calls, and Georgios slows up, showering little stones over my feet as he puts the brakes on down the rough road.

'What happened?' I call, walking towards them.

'The bees,' Maria says, rolling her eyes. 'He went after the bees. A whole swarm came down through here. He followed them to try and catch them.'

Kostas is whimpering, holding his nose.

Maria tuts and shakes her head. 'He just wanted the bees to come to the hives. He has been working so hard on them. He just wants them to come before the summer is over,' she says, looking suddenly close to tears.

'Oh you poor things.' I turn to Georgios, but he's gone, just the tumble of tiny stones where he stood only a minute before.

I follow Maria and Kostas into the kitchen, where Mitera fills a glass of water from a big, battered metal jug. Maria sits Kostas down on a chair and puts cold water on a tea towel, then hands it to him to hold over his face. Going to the dark wooden dresser, she takes down a small glass jar with what look like a few dried herbs in it. She looks up at Mitera, who nods. Maria takes the kettle off the stove and pours hot water into a mug, then adds the herbs and hands the mug to Kostas. He takes his hand away from his face, revealing an angry red sting on the end of his nose, close to another and another. His cheeks are beginning to swell like a red balloon.

We suck in a collective breath, wince and take a step back.

It's only seeing our reaction, looking in turn at each of our faces, that Kostas realises how bad it actually is.

'Do we have any more dittany?' he asks, looking at the pathetic offering in his cup.

Maria shakes her head. 'Let's hope we get a visit from the messenger soon!' She looks out of the window.

'Who is the messenger, Maria?' I ask.

'He is sent by the gods. Ever since the mountaintop has become . . . well, out of bounds, someone comes. They bring a bunch of dried dittany and leave it on the doorstep for whoever needs it. The messenger always knows and always comes.' She nods firmly.

'This dittany . . . can *I* get it?' I ask, keen to do something to help. 'Do we have some on the farm? Has Kostas planted any?'

'Dittany is a special herb. It grows only here, in Crete.' She waves a hand at the mountain behind us. 'It has been used as an antiseptic . . .'

'Anti everything,' Kostas butts in.

'. . . since the beginning of time. The gods would seek it out. Zeus was born here. It is said he gave dittany to the island in gratitude for keeping his mother safe when she fled her husband to give birth to him. It is woven into our history here in Vounoplagia. This town is built on dittany. It is why we are . . . well, were,' she corrects herself, 'so healthy and lived so long. It's what drew people here.'

'I could go and find some if you want,' I say, turning and getting ready to go.

She shakes her head firmly.

'It grows only high up, in hard-to-reach places. In the

crevices on shady rock faces. Soft fuzzy leaves, arching stems, pale pinkish-purple flowers. No one goes that high up the mountain these days.'

She pours more cold water on to the cloth and puts it back on Kostas's face. She lets out a long, exasperated sigh, making her lips pout like Demi does when she's taking a selfie.

'So maybe . . .' I start to think out loud, but Maria is busy tending to Kostas, who is whimpering and looking very unwell. 'Maybe we need to plant dittany. And maybe if I can find it and bring it here, the bees will come back.' I suddenly break into a smile, feeling like a tiny seed has been sown. Why hasn't Kostas done this before? It's exactly what we need!

Kostas takes the cloth from his face and shakes his head. 'The mountain . . .' He tries to speak, but his lips have started to swell and Maria scolds him. Neither of them is really listening to me whilst they gently bicker in Greek to each other. Kostas looks like he's complaining loudly about the pain and Maria is waving her arms, presumably insisting he keeps the cloth in place.

'The bees won't be happy until love returns to the mountain,' Mitera says firmly in English for us all to hear.

Maria and Kostas both roll their eyes but smile as if indulging a young child. 'The Greek name for dittany is *erontas* – love. Mitera thinks the bees won't be happy until the dittany starts to grow again,' Kostas explains with difficulty.

'And some people think they won't be happy until long-lost loves are reunited once more,' Maria adds.

Mitera shrugs and lifts her chin, turning back to the sink with a look that says she knows she's right. She gazes out of the window as if expecting someone.

'You must stay inside,' Maria tells Kostas. 'Nell, could you help Mitera in the kitchen?'

'Of course,' I reply, glad to be of use. 'Shall I collect the greens, Mitera?' and she nods, her teeth rattling up and down in her mouth. I grab a basket and head out of the kitchen door.

I'm climbing up towards the mountain when I hear a rustle in the trees just above the cows' field, making me jump. I catch my breath and see a dark figure in the shadows. 'Hey!' I shout without thinking. The figure stops and looks at me. It's Georgios, and I let out a little sigh of relief. At least it isn't some gang member from the mountains. He stands as I march up the hill towards him. 'What are you doing here?' I ask.

'I was . . .' he hesitates just for a moment and then says, 'making sure Kostas was OK.' I'm confused. He looks as if he's leaving the farm, not arriving.

'Well, he's in the house.' I point. 'Maria says he has to lie down, but I'm sure he'd welcome a visitor.' I look up at the mountain and jut my chin out towards it, as if prodding the belly of a giant bully. 'Perhaps you could help find out what's going on up there. You're the last house up the mountain.' I look around. 'You must see what's going on.'

He steps out of the shadows of the pine trees. He's wearing his hat and his scarf is pulled up around his chin. The little black and white dog is at his feet. It barks at me and then at something in the distance. I look up and see the smallest of the puppies venturing down the hill towards us. He's warning it to go back. I know that if I make a move, the dog will warn me too.

Georgios looks at me sharply, his eyes narrowing like a sniper once again. 'I keep myself to myself. You would be wise to do the same.' There is something about him – something vaguely familiar – still there, scratching at the back of my mind.

The puppy does as it's told and turns back to the shed where its mother is waiting. I feel a little surge of defiance on its behalf. I lift my chin.

'I need to get up the mountain,' I say, more boldly than I'm feeling. But if anyone can help me, it's going to be this guy.

'No one goes up the mountain these days,' he growls, looking around.

I look at him squarely. 'Kostas needs some . . .' My mind goes blank. 'Some plant thingy. Soft fuzzy leaves, pinkish-purple flowers, the one in the honey.'

'Dictamus,' Georgios supplies. 'Otherwise known as dittany.'

'That's it!' I turn to him and attempt a smile. 'Can you show me where to get it?' I try and hold the smile. I want to find some and plant it up in the field.

'No,' he says flatly and with finality and turns to walk away.

I'm smarting, but I'm not going to let him see that. 'Look, just tell me where it grows and I'll find it myself.'

'You have to know where to look,' Georgios replies.

'Well tell me then!' God! This man's infuriating! 'I just want to help Kostas and Maria.' It's the least I can do after all their kindness, welcoming me.

'It's not safe.' Georgios snaps his head round to me, his

eyes flashing, unnerving me again. 'It's best if you just stay away.'

'But Maria said the town relies on dittany.'

He looks down and doesn't catch my eye. 'I know,' he says slowly.

'Kostas needs it. The bees need it. The whole town needs it. If I can just find some to bring down to cultivate in the herb meadow—' He cuts me off before I have a chance to go on.

'Nobody has been able to find the dittany since . . . well, since things started happening.' He looks up at the limestone tip of the mountain, as white as if it were covered in snow. 'Trust me, if there is any left up there, someone is keeping it very safe.'

He draws away slowly, his gold-flecked eyes resting on me, and I feel every nerve ending tingle. Something tells me not to go any further. Like deep water, there is a darkness behind those eyes that is unsafe and definitely not for swimming in, no matter how strong the pull.

Chapter Ten

I return to the farmhouse with the basket of greens under my arm to see Maria at the front door, bending down and picking something up off the step.

'It's here!' She straightens up, holding out a little sprig of something dried like it's the Olympic torch. 'A gift from the gods,' she beams. 'I told you. We just have to have faith and he delivers.' She holds the herbs to her chest; they're wrapped with a crocheted ribbon, I notice, like a corsage for a wedding.

'Is that the herb? The dittany?'

'Yes! The healing herb.' She beams again and holds the sprig to her nose, breathing it in. 'We have it, Kostas! It came! I knew it would!' She turns and makes her way back through the big blue door into the cool of the whitewashed house.

In the kitchen, she pulls the big black kettle on to the stove with a stained tea towel. Kostas joins us and tries to smile as Maria begins preparing the dittany. He doesn't look good. His face is an angry red, and swollen where the bees have stung him.

'I'll finish up outside,' I say. 'Are you sure Kostas doesn't need to go to hospital? I could try and drive the truck,' I offer, with more confidence than I feel.

'No, no. We will be fine now we have the dittany. We'll use it to soothe the stings rather than as a drink this time. But thank you. If you can do the herbs and check on the hives, that would be such a help.' Maria hugs me. 'You are brilliant! Thank goodness you are here. The gods are really smiling on us today!' she beams, her cheeks like rosy apples. She looks almost teary as she strikes a match and lights a candle in the window. 'To give thanks to the mountain, for the dittany,' she explains. 'And the honey factory is starting to take shape. A lot of people would have turned and run when they saw how much work it needed. And here you are helping us when we need you.'

I suddenly feel really . . . well, just that: needed. They need me here and that feels good. Really good. Like I'm somebody again. Nell, cleaner of honey factories, guardian of herb gardens! I may not be a Nobel Peace Prize winner, but it's a start. My shoulders relax and I find I'm holding my head higher than I have in a long time, and I can't help but smile back, feeling my throat tighten and my eyes prickle.

Maria starts grating half the dried leaves into a jug. Then she takes the kettle off the stove and pours boiling water on to the herb dust, stirring it with a big wooden spoon.

'I let it cool for a minute, then it will be ready to dab on,' she says, touching her own face. Taking the other half of the bunch, she pours hot water straight on to the leaves to make tea. 'We will leave it for ten minutes, then strain it,' she says, as if giving me a Cretan cookery class, but I'm a keen student, it's fascinating. 'We will add a little honey.' She picks up the jar we opened on my first day here and scrapes out the last of it. 'And now it is gone,' she says. Their last jar. She shrugs, smiles and tips her head from side to side. 'At least we have some dittany!' She kisses Kostas on the top of the head and then on his cheek, and he winces and cries out in pain, making her hug him to her tightly.

I wish I hadn't eaten the honey. I've been having it every day, with yoghurt for breakfast and on fruit in the evenings. If I hadn't, there would be more for Kostas. I feel bad. I have to try and help get the bees here and the honey factory up and running.

That herb seems to make all the difference. The bees obviously love it too. I wonder, what if I *could* find some and bring it to the herb meadow? It can't be that hard, can it? I go collecting greens on the mountain anyway. Georgios's words come back to me. *It's best if you just stay away.* I never did like being told what to do. Certainly not when my mum wanted me to go to Australia. She was moving there with her new husband, Bob, who she'd met on holiday in Benidorm. Bob worked in a boatyard. Everything changed when she met him. I refused to go with them. I didn't want to take orders from a woman who'd barely been there for my growing up and who had introduced me to more new dads than I could remember. I especially wasn't going to be told what to do after I rang her from my nan's and told her I was pregnant and she told me to think about things. That having a child had ruined her life. Ouch! That had hurt, and it made me build my barriers higher. She told me I should consider my options. There was only one option in my mind. I was having a baby and I was going to be a way better mum than she'd been. I was going to throw everything I had into it.

Kostas winces as Maria applies the blanched dried dittany

to his stings, waving his arms around complaining about the pain, his nose and cheeks glowing. She argues back and tells him to sit still.

I watch them, so at ease with each other, bickering yet clearly deeply devoted, and I feel a pang of . . . not jealousy exactly, but a sadness, deep down. Mike and I were never like that. We never bickered or rowed but we didn't care about each other like Maria and Kostas do either. We were just two lonely souls trying to convince ourselves we were a couple. But we weren't a couple, not really. Not like these two. I try and think of the things I miss about Mike, and with a heavy heart, I realise I can't actually think of anything. I realise that there has only ever been one love in my life, and that was Stelios, and I regret with all my heart letting him go. That's why I'm here. I have to find him and discover if he felt the same, and why he didn't come after me when I left.

I move away from the sink, where I've been cleaning the greens, and Mitera slips her teeth out and starts washing up. As she works, she gazes up at the mountain, as if looking for someone again. Is it the 'messenger' she is hoping to see, or somebody else? This dittany plant, if the bees love it so much, could be what Kostas needs to bring them to the farm. If I can just speak to Stelios, I'm sure he'd know what to do and where to find it. He knows this mountain inside out. I just need to pluck up the courage to go and see him. I know one thing for sure: I'm not going to go through life with any more regrets.

Chapter Eleven

Before bed, I Skype Demi. It's a frustratingly stilted call as I wonder whether now is the time to tell her that her biological father wasn't just a holiday romance but the love of my life, and that that's why I've come out here – to find him.

But she's busy telling me about her family that she's working for in London, and although she doesn't mean to hurt me, I can't help wishing I'd been enough of a family for her. I decide that now isn't the time to tell her about Stelios. I'll wait until I've found him. But every time I look at her, at the dimple in her cheek that appears when she smiles, I see him. I will find him.

I swap a couple of text messages with Angelica about the bees, the honey factory and the messenger from the gods. Then I get a surprise text from Mike, telling me again that he's sorry and asking if we can give it another go. I lie on my bed and think. Do I want him back? I know I don't love him like Maria and Kostas love one another. Do I want to settle for anything less? There is only one word that is going round my head. *No*, I type, and then slowly and firmly press send.

That night, I barely sleep a wink.

As dawn comes, I push back the sheets and get out of bed. There were strange sounds on the mountain last night, screams like a wild cat, and I'm sure I heard gunfire again. I go to the bathroom and stare in the mirror. Why is it anyone I ever care about leaves me? I splash cold water on my face and try and push the thought out of my mind. I hope Demi never sees me as I saw my mother: someone who abandoned me when I needed her most. It was why I could never have committed to a full-time relationship and let Mike move in while Demi was growing up. What if it hadn't worked out? I couldn't do that to her. I couldn't risk him leaving both of us.

I never knew my dad. When my mum moved to Australia, I went to live with my nan. And that was it. I saw very little of Mum, and by the time Demi came along, we were more or less estranged. She did send a card congratulating me, though I knew she was secretly horrified at the idea of being a grandmother. She returned for Nan's funeral, but didn't stay for the sandwiches and tea back at the house. She and Bob had to fly out early the next morning. She left with her make-up intact, not having shed a tear.

After the funeral, I returned home to Nan's house with Demi. It felt so empty without the woman who'd brought me up, who'd always been there for me and who had been the proudest great-nan in the world when Demi was born. Over the next few weeks I boxed up her belongings and tucked them away under beds, on top of wardrobes, unable to take them to the charity shop, vowing to deal with them in time. That first night I slept in Nan's bed and I never moved out, finding comfort in being close to where she had lain for all those years. It felt like she was still there with me as I brought up Demi, supporting me and cheering me on from the sidelines.

And she'd be cheering me on now, I think, telling me that of course I can find this dittany plant; that I'll manage just like I did when I had Demi, when I was scared to death of being a single mum at just eighteen. She told me I could do it then, and I did.

I hope with all my heart that Demi knows I'll always be there for her. I just wish I knew how to show her.

I throw more cold water on my face to chase away the doom. I need to walk off this black cloud. I dress quickly in cut-off denim shorts – the ones I customised with stick-on gems and patches. Demi would be horrified seeing me in them. I smile to myself. Maybe I'm just trying to remember who I used to be.

I slip quietly out of my room. Outside, the early-morning smell hits me as it always does, the damp earth warmed already by the sun, rich and full of minerals. Steam rises as the heavy dew evaporates, mist clinging to the mountainside as though a sheet of wonder-web has been thrown over it for Halloween. Cobwebs glisten, and there are snails with spiral shells everywhere, going about their early-morning business. Kostas loves to collect them, picking them off his wild rocket and turning them into his favourite lunchtime snack, heavy with garlic and served with *dakos*. The white clouds down the valley meet the rising mist over the mountaintops, and the orange sun is rising behind the dark, rugged peaks, where the skyline is washed pink, orange and light blue. I have goose bumps over my bare legs.

I head straight for the beehives, but there is no sound coming from them. They are empty still. I look up at the mountain, just as Kostas did, searching for signs. I need to get the bees to come. With Kostas laid up in bed, it's all down to me.

Maria is up early as always, and I hear pots and pans in the kitchen and smell the woodsmoke from the bread oven.

'Just off to pick the greens before it gets hot,' I tell her.

'But you must eat!' she scolds, stirring a pot of soup for lunch later.

I grab a basket and pinch a piece of white feta from under the domed fly cover in the cool cupboard whilst I'm at it, along with a large tomato freshly picked from the veg plot and a small bunch of grapes from a bowl on the side. I hold them up to Maria. 'Breakfast!' I announce, and she smiles.

'Kostas is like a caged lion, not able to go out. But I think he should stay away from the bees for just a while. They may remember him,' she tells me.

'Don't worry, Maria, we'll soon have the honey factory up and running.' I say it with a smile, but although I can clean up the factory, it's not going to be up and running without the bees.

I make my way down the farm track and up towards the cows' field, stopping to fill my bottle from the little waterfall. I take a bite of the fat, fresh tomato. The juice squirts out at all angles, and I try and stop it from running down my T-shirt. It's sweet and fragrant, nothing like the tomatoes I buy in the supermarket back home. I nibble the feta; it's rich, creamy and tangy, and I take alternate bites of cheese and tomato as I start to walk up through the field, feeling in my pocket for carob pods for the cows. I finish my breakfast just before I reach the path that leads up the mountain, and lick my fingers. Then I climb the fence and walk over to the vantage point, looking out as the rising sun throws handfuls of glitter across the brightening sea, the unmissable scent of thyme on the wind. My spirits lift as the fragrance takes me back to where I was happiest and safest, pushing me onwards and upwards.

Having climbed the stone steps, I start picking greens. After a while, I stop and look up the mountain, wondering what would happen if I were to go a little higher. Who knows, I might just happen on some dittany that I could take back to plant at the farm. I look down towards the house, checking that Maria and Kostas can't see me, then up at the rock face that rises behind the farm. With a deep breath, I seize the moment and start to climb. I'm just going to pick greens, I repeat to myself. And if I happen to stray a little further, well, where's the harm? If anyone stops me, I'll just feign innocence.

Leaving behind the wild *horta* spot, I spot a sign, bent, twisted and rusted: *No Entry!* Despite the heat of the August sun, I feel myself go cold. What the hell am I doing? Just go home, I tell myself. But no one has stopped me so far; I'll go a little higher. 'I'm just picking greens,' I repeat out loud. I take a defiant swig of water and wipe away any traces from my lips with the back of my hand, then resume my climb, holding out my arms to steady myself and grabbing rocks either side of the track as the uneven snaking track gets steeper.

I look around and wonder if I can find the spot where Stelios took me all those years ago; where we sat and ate a picnic and he told me about his dreams and plans to build a small hotel there one day. A boutique B&B where tourists could come to experience the real Crete and eat the food that grows here. I'd remember the view, that's for sure, by a small natural pool where butterflies flitted to and fro. That's another mental picture I've pulled from my memory box. We drank a bottle of local wine and made love amongst the sweet-smelling wild thyme. I could smell it for days afterwards; it made me light-headed with excitement.

The higher I climb, the more it feels like I'm seeing him everywhere I look, my heart lifting and dipping like a roller coaster. He could be just around the corner. I scramble higher and higher, faster and faster, feeling as if I couldn't stop if I wanted to. All the time I'm scanning the rocks, looking for the plants, thinking I've caught a glimpse of dittany, only to realise it's something else.

The day is starting to really heat up now. The mist is being blown away by the wind and the sun is reaching out behind it. The higher I go, the windier it gets. It keeps me cool, and I pull my baseball cap on, one of Demi's that she left behind, from a Beyoncé concert she went to in Cardiff. I move through the olive trees and the tall pine trees bunched together here. Their smell is so refreshing and their shade is dark and cool. My mind wanders back to Stelios, and I wonder if he ever built his B&B.

Suddenly I'm stopped in my tracks, literally. There's no clear way forward. The trunk of an old olive tree is lying across the path. It's not easy, but I manage to grab hold of the branches and pull myself over it, dropping on to the big rocks on the other side, out of breath and with scratches on my legs. If that's what Georgios reckoned was unsafe, I think I can say I handled it. I brush my hands, take a swig of water and allow myself a little smile of victory. Feeling pleased with myself, I keep moving on. I must be close now.

Eventually I reach a plateau and turn to walk out on to it. This is it! My heart leaps and swings like a gibbon in the treetops. This is the spot that Stelios brought me to. I hold my breath. What are the chances he's here? I'm above the farm, the cows below me. I look around. There's no hotel. But I can see it, the way he described it, as if it were yesterday. This is where we sat, where I felt so sure of life and my place in the world, next to the man I loved. He was right: this would make a perfect setting for a hotel. I wonder why it never happened. The natural pool is still there, all but dried up, though there are no butterflies like I remember. And there is no Stelios here either.

I gaze out over the wonderful view. I can see Georgios's little stone house, and an old open-sided barn next to it, right on the edge before the mountain drops away. I spot a field of sheep, penned in; it is like Kostas's farm but on a much smaller scale. It feels as if I'm up with the gods, it really does. I pull out my phone to take some pictures, but I can't send them to anyone because there's no signal. There's also no sign of human life. I'm alone, totally alone.

I go back to the path and climb a little further, only to find a big pile of rocks in front of me, a landslide, blocking my way. I look up to the ledge above from where they've come, and put my hand against the rock face. It's just a pile of stones, I tell myself. But it feels as though someone has put them here intentionally. The mist is below me now, rolling and tumbling away down the mountain in between the shrubs and trees as the sun reaches out its rays. And then it strikes me that nobody knows I'm here. Who would miss me if something happened? I feel small and insignificant all over again, and realise the stupidity of what I've attempted. If the dittany was that easy to find, the locals would be up here themselves, not depending on some messenger from the gods. I need to go back down before I get lost, or something happens to me.

I turn, suddenly feeling nervous. People have been using these paths for years, I remind myself, trying not to panic; centuries probably, before the roads were built. I hear a bird call and, holding my hand over my eyes against the glare of the sun, look up to see what looks like a golden eagle circling around the mountain peak. I look away, back down, hoping to see the path again. But I can't. I have no idea which way to go. It's like sand blindness; all I can see is rocks, all looking the same, and I've lost my sense of direction.

Actually, this really wasn't a good idea at all. Stelios, where are you when I need you? I think to myself, praying that this will be the moment he finally appears.

'Stupid! Stupid idea!' I say out loud. 'All alone up a mountain! Stupid!' I repeat to absolutely no one, or so I think.

'What the hell do you think you're doing?'

'Argh!' My heart rockets into my mouth.

Chapter Twelve

'I told you not to come up here. It's not safe.' It's Georgios. My heart sinks. Of all the people . . . Why couldn't it have been a group of tourists? Why him?

'I was picking greens, wild *horta*. Got a bit lost.' I try and brazen it out, sticking to my story.

'If you have your *horta*, please go back to Kostas's farm, and next time stick to the lower slopes.'

'What's going on? Who's doing this?' I ask, gesturing to the rock pile. 'Someone really doesn't want people up here.'

'We don't know what's going on. There is a lot of talk, but you can see for yourself, it's not safe.' He points further up the slope to another metal *No Entry* sign.

'But this mountain belongs to the town. It always has . . .' I stop myself, realising that I may have given too much away. I don't want anyone asking about my last trip to Crete. I want to keep myself to myself until I've found Stelios.

He looks at me, his green and gold eyes narrowing, and I suddenly feel all my brazen bravado seep out through the soles of my feet. 'Like I say, a lot has changed around here.' He glances away towards the coast, and just for a moment I wonder again . . . do I recognise him? Does he recognise me? But I doubt it. He's right. It was a completely foolhardy thing for me to do. Looking for greens, indeed!

Before dinner that evening, I drive into town and scour the streets for signs of Stelios and his family. I even park up and go to the taverna just down the lane from the restaurant, where I sit under the boughs of a big plane tree and order a glass of wine. The waitress nods and smiles at me. She doesn't say anything, but I know she's wondering why I'm here drinking wine on my own. As are the two old men outside the coffee house next door. Despite the laid-up tables and the menu boards, no one is sitting and eating. It's just me. I make my glass of wine last and write my postcard for Gracie, wondering if Stelios might pass by. The longer I wait, the more I know the locals are staring at me

The waitress puts a small plate of sweet treats in front of me: a square of *kataifi*, with chopped walnuts and what looks like golden spun thread on the top, the whole thing soaked in sweet lemon syrup; *galatopita*, golden and flaky, filled with mizithra cheese; and a small triangle of lemon cake. I start to say that I haven't ordered anything, but she puts her hand up, showing me that they're a gift, and I thank her.

On my return to the farm, I have a quick call with Demi, who tells me that yes, she's eating fine, and yes, she's managing her money. That she's left home now and is a grown-up. She sounds tired. She's told me that the children she looks after have no idea of bedtime. They sound like a handful. I wonder if she's getting the chance to meet new friends, other nannies, maybe a boyfriend. Or maybe I don't want that for her yet.

The Honey Farm on the Hill

That night as I lie in bed, my thoughts turn to Georgios and that look he gave me earlier. I'm trying to work out what he meant when he told me that a lot had changed around here. As I start to drift off to sleep, I hear gunshots coming from the mountain in the distance again, making me jump and get up to leave the bathroom light on for the night. I don't understand it. Why isn't Stelios doing something to protect the mountain from whoever is up there? Where is he?

Chapter Thirteen

The next morning, I'm on the lower slopes when Kostas, who is still supposed to be inside recovering, comes running down the mountainside towards me so quickly that I almost drop the basket of greens I'm collecting. He is wearing a white beekeeper's suit, the netted hat unzipped and flapping around, bouncing off the back of his head. In one hand he has a kettle, pouring out steam like a train as he runs, the other is holding an empty cardboard box.

'Kostas? Kostas?'

'Argh!' he wails as he passes me at speed, a gaggle of agitated bees behind him, buzzing like a high-pitched orchestra of untuned violins. I let them pass before following Kostas back to the farmhouse.

'I thought I might, well, encourage one of the queens away.' He is shrugging, sitting on a stool in the kitchen. 'Whilst it was still dark, while they were shut down, resting.'

Maria has put the kettle on and is reaching for the practically empty jar of dust and scrapings from the sprig of dittany left last time by the messenger. 'I told you to stay inside!' She bangs a cup of tea angrily down in front of Kostas. This time there is no honey to sweeten it.

'Then one got into my suit. It was like he was determined,

92

like a screwdriver trying to find a way in.' He sips the tea. 'The guard bees, they are protecting the hives like the Minotaur in the labyrinth eating humans!'

'They are just looking after their families.' Maria tries to be the voice of reason against Kostas's raging. 'What were you doing up there anyway? We agreed not to go up to the hives, but to encourage the bees down the mountain.'

'I couldn't wait any longer for them to come. I thought that if I took a queen bee and rehomed her, the others would follow,' he says sheepishly.

'Kostas!' she scolds.

'And then . . . well, they got all agitated and that one got into my suit and . . . ouch!' He winces.

'You have to stay inside until these stings all heal. And until the bees are less agitated. What if they remember you now? You have made them your enemy! We have Nell here, for now.' She swallows, as if wondering what will happen when I'm gone, and I wonder too. 'She's a natural. Like she was born here.' She smiles at me. 'The honey factory is nearly ready. It looks like new.'

'Well, I'm not sure about new.' I blush, but I'm actually very pleased with how it's looking. Kostas has mended the hole in the roof, and where there was once moss and ferns, the walls are scrubbed clean and the surfaces sparkle in the summer sunshine.

'Kostas and I have been talking. You have worked so hard in the honey factory. We want to repay you.'

'You give me my board and lodgings,' I cut in.

She holds up her hand. 'Once the honey starts to come in, we will sell it at the market. We would like to share the profits with you, by way of thanks. No arguments.'

I know that to turn this down would cause offence, and I can't deny the money would be very welcome. 'Thank you, that is very kind of you.' It *is* kind of them, and even more reason to get the honey farm up and running again. Who knows, maybe I could even earn enough to tide me over while I look for a new job back home, a new beginning so I don't ever have to go back to the factory.

Maria shakes out the very last of the dusty herb remnants from the jar, peering inside to make sure it really is all gone.

'You need more,' I point out, and she does her usual shrug.

'With luck the messenger will come soon and leave us some. We just have to send up a plea,' and she looks briefly to the ceiling, where pots and pans hang from hooks, much like the wooden dryer my nan had at home where we would dry Demi's babygros overnight above the boiler.

Maria taps out the last of the dittany into a bowl and pours boiling water on it from the big black kettle, then dips a cloth in and puts it to Kostas's new bee stings, holding it over his eye. I watch him grimace in pain. I wish there was more I could do to help. We all need the bees to come.

'What can I do, Maria? There must be something.'

'No, it's fine. You have already done enough. You have worked so hard for us. I'm fine. I just have to get those greens into town.' She nods to my basket. 'A restaurant called earlier. They have a booking. A table for lunch. They need the greens . . .' she looks up at the clock and pulls a face, 'now!'

'Which restaurant?' I ask cautiously.

She is dabbing Kostas's angry red swellings.

'The To Agrio Thymari. How do you say? Um, the . . .'

'Wild Thyme Restaurant,' I finish flatly for her, staring at her in disbelief.

'Exactly! Bravo!' she exclaims, and then laughs. 'Your Greek is really coming on . . . but you look like you've seen a ghost.'

And that's how it feels. My mouth is dry, and I shiver despite the heat of the kitchen. This is my chance. This is how I can get to see him. I have to do this.

'I can take them,' I offer.

'No, you have enough to do with watering the herbs and cleaning the honey factory. I can go.'

'No, Maria. You stay here with Kostas. I will go to town,' I tell her.

'Are you sure? You must hurry. They need them now.' She grabs the key to the moped from beside the door and hands it to me. My heart is in my mouth and banging so loudly I wonder if she can hear it. 'Just after the main square, where the church is, take the right turn.'

'All the way to the bottom, on the right,' I finish for her.

'With the courtyard and the big wrought-iron gates. One of the oldest buildings in the town. Venetian,' she says proudly. 'One of the few that wasn't destroyed in the war.'

I nod. 'Yes, I know it.' I look down at the key and notice that my hands are shaking. 'I . . . erm . . .' I swallow, trying to get my heart to sit back in my chest. 'I visited . . . years ago.' I look up at her and try to smile.

'You look nervous. Is it the moped? It's easy, no? And the

family are good people. Very kind. They could do with some luck too.'

My hands are still shaking, my heart thumping. I am about to come face to face with Stelios. This really is fate. At this rate I may just start believing in the gods' messenger myself. Part of me wants to rip the helmet off, go back to the honey factory and pick up my scrubbing brush. Run away and hide. But that's what I've been doing for the last eighteen years. Hiding away. I need to see him. I've been here for two weeks, waiting to catch sight of him. Now this is my chance. I'm about to finally come face to face with the one man I've ever loved. The father of my child. The question is, will he remember me?

Chapter Fourteen

I grip the greens in their box firmly between my feet on the running board as I ride down the mountain road, twisting this way and that, the wind making my eyes water and flicking up the ends of my hair beneath my helmet. I pass the supermarket, where Samir is sitting on the counter, looking out with a hopeful smile. I drive past the closed-up school, the church, the little museum telling the town's history through the war. On the uneven cobbled lane towards the restaurant, I nearly lose the box of greens. Those greens are my ticket back to Stelios. I slow down.

Finally I arrive. I swing off the bike, put down the footrest and slowly remove my helmet, shaking out my unruly hair. I look down at my arms, much browner than when I first arrived. My legs, too. I can feel the muscles burning after climbing the mountain yesterday. I pick up the box of greens and tuck it under my arm. Then I take a deep breath and walk towards the gates, stopping by the menu on the board. Next to it is a small, ornately carved wooden house with a single candle burning in it.

I put my hand on the rusting handle of the black gate and look inside at the courtyard. There are pots of red, white and purple begonias. The courtyard itself is on different levels; up a couple of steps there are tables with white cloths on them, brightly coloured water glasses and pressed napkins. Colourful cushions line the benches against the stone wall. The sun is streaming in on the intricately tiled circle and the small Grecian urn fountain right in the middle. Nothing has changed, I think, my heart leaping with joy. As beautiful now as it was back then.

Beyond the courtyard and a big single potted olive tree, I can see through a series of stone archways in the walls to the inside of the restaurant, where the walls are painted a soft sage green. Excitement is fizzing inside me. All my senses are being seduced. The smell of the bougainvillea and the herbs, the sight of the sunlight pouring in on to the tiled floor and bouncing off the coloured glass, the sound of food preparation in the kitchen. If there is anything more beautiful than this, I wouldn't believe it.

I find myself wanting to pull up a chair, sit down and let the moment last forever. Just like when I was here with Stelios. He was wearing a white shirt that day. There were tea lights along the long table. It was late in the season, much cooler than it is now. I remember the way his dark face was lit up by the candlelight . . . those green eyes. I remember sitting here with his family, drinking coffee and eating *loukoumades* – deep-fried, crispy, golden doughnuts drizzled in hot honey syrup with cinnamon – then walking up the mountain for lunch. That day was nothing less than perfection.

My second visit, less so. That was the day I was returning to the UK, when I came to find Stelios before flying home. I needed to speak to him and find out how he felt about me being pregnant, about our baby. I had to tell him. But he was run off his feet. We barely had time to talk things through. We ended up rowing, but I knew he'd come and find me when he was ready. He knew where I'd be. I was stubborn, just like Demi is now.

I should never have left. I should have stayed and fought for him, instead of letting his family persuade him otherwise.

'*Yassou!*'

My thoughts are interrupted by a shout, and a figure at the back of the courtyard waves to me. I've been seen. There's no backing out now.

'*Yassou!*' comes the voice again as if the past was just yesterday. The punishing midday sun is beating down on my head. My top lip is damp and my T-shirt is sticking unpleasantly to the small of my back. The figure emerges from the shadows and starts to walk towards me, a dark silhouette with the sun behind him. That figure, that walk, that voice. As familiar now as it was back then.

'*Yassou!*' I say through my tight, strangled throat. And I don't know whether to laugh, cry or be sick.

Chapter Fifteen

Oh God! I can't do this! I can't face him yet! I'm not ready. I step back, wishing I'd never come, and find myself dipping into the shadow of a large potted lemon tree there by the gates, sliding in between its branches. He's speaking Greek, quickly and furiously, holding a phone to his ear, the other hand up now, palm out, and shoulders shrugging. He's clearly not happy with whoever is on the other end. Stelios always did tell it how it was. I swallow. How on earth is he going to react when he sees me? Will he recognise me straight away?

He's still speaking animatedly and loudly into the phone, waving one hand in the air, two thin leather bracelets jiggling on his wrist. He turns away just before getting to me, holding the phone between his ear and his shoulder, to push two tables together. Finally he finishes his call, snaps the cover on the phone shut and pushes it in his pocket. Then, as my thundering heart is about to explode, he turns to look at me.

'*Kalispera.*' He nods, frowning slightly, a look of confusion on his face. But then it's not every day you see a red-headed girl hiding in your lemon tree clutching a box of wild *horta*.

'Stel—' The word rushes from my mouth, then catches in my throat. I can see his face clearly now, not a silhouette any more. His frown deepens, and my heart lurches, then plummets like a stone falling from the mountainside. He has all the family features: the same long nose, the dark green eyes, the swept-back hair showing the start of a widow's peak. But it's not him. I'm thirty-six now, and Stelios must be thirty-nine. This young man in front of me is closer in age to my daughter. A wave of nausea washes over me.

I take in his wavy dark hair, cut neatly at the sides, and the dimple in his cheek as he gives me a cautious smile, just like Demi's. The resemblance to Stelios is uncanny. The realisation slowly dawns on me, like the sun rising over the mountain in the mornings . . . If Stelios is married . . . My heart does that quickening thing again, pounding. If he has a family . . . I bite my bottom lip. My eyeballs burn. What if this is Stelios's son?

I try to digest this painful piece of the jigsaw. Is this why he never came? Did he meet someone else? A good Cretan girl, like his family wanted him to? I grip the box of greens so tightly I can barely breathe. I feel hot with anger. Staring at the young man in front of me, head cocked to one side, I feel fury at Stelios, fury at myself for not realising it before, and fury on my daughter's behalf for having being abandoned for a new family. I need to know what really happened, and I'll do whatever it takes to find out.

Chapter Sixteen

'Can I help you?' The young man frowns again as I step out from the branches of the lemon tree and stand firmly in front of him. I open my mouth to try and form a question, but the words jumble up and my mouth waggles up and down like I'm trying to free it from lockjaw. Where do I start? I try to think how to ask who his father is, when what I really want to know about is his mother. What is her name? What does she look like? Why did he pick her over me?

Then I spot it. The pendant around his neck. It's exactly the same as the one I'm wearing . . . the one Stelios gave me. My hand instinctively flies to my throat. An outline of half the island in silver, with a tiny ruby heart, on a black leather lace. He told me he'd had them made by a jeweller in the town. On the back was an engraved message: *In my heart, forever*. He gave one to me and kept the other half for himself.

Jesus! There was me thinking all this time that the necklace was some kind of special love token! Obviously they're two a penny. I want to leave, but something keeps me here. I quickly flip my necklace inside the neck of my T-shirt, feeling foolish and furious at the same time. I clear my throat and hold out the box of wild – now slightly wilted – greens.

'I've brought the greens,' I finally manage to say, and I can't help but feel like Baby from *Dirty Dancing*: the outsider, the interloper, a frump holding out a watermelon. 'From Maria and Kostas.' I try and generate some saliva in my mouth to help the words out, hoping I've said enough. I've certainly seen enough. 'Up the mountain,' I explain, but I still can't look him in the eye. It's too confusing. He looks so much like Stelios, the man I loved. I was just another girl, from another summer, to him. I was foolish to imagine there was a good reason he didn't follow me. Me with my stupid romantic ideas, believing in all those romantic DVDs I watch, thinking we had something special. That love would conquer all.

'You're late,' says the young man in front of me. It suddenly strikes me that if he *is* about Demi's age – maybe even a little older – then he was already around when I was pregnant with his half-sister. Stelios was already spoken for! I'm beginning to feel like a boxer in the ring, taking all the hits and finding myself clinging to the ropes for support. 'I rang Maria and Kostas hours ago.'

'I'm sorry. Um, Kostas . . . he's unwell. I came as quickly as I could . . . Sorry.' I want to slap my forehead. Why am I apologising?

'Oh. Is he OK?' the young man asks with what looks like genuine concern, though if he's as good a faker as his dad clearly was, that doesn't mean much. He holds out his hands to take the greens from me. For a moment I hang on to the box. He gives a little tug, but I don't let go. He gives me another curious smile and then tugs the box again, and this time, realising how ridiculous I must look, I let go. He puts the box on the stone wall behind him, then pulls out his wallet and hands me a couple of notes. Blushing at my own awkward behaviour, I take them, fold them in half and stash them safely at the bottom of my bag.

'Bee stings. The dittany helps,' I manage to untie my tongue enough to say. I catch another glimpse of the necklace and my fury returns.

The young man shakes his head in shared concern for Kostas. Then we both glance around. Our business transaction is over. I should just go. But I can't help but look in case Stelios is about to appear, maybe with his wife . . . or other children.

'Are you OK?' the young man asks. 'Do you need some water?'

'Great!' I say, grabbing on to this delaying tactic.

I watch him as he goes to the bar in the corner, then look around again for any other signs of life. When he returns, I take the glass and drink the water slowly before thanking him and handing back the glass.

'Just admiring your beautiful restaurant,' I say, smiling with huge effort. I need to dig a bit deeper, get a clearer idea of the situation here. 'It must be hard work running it on your own.'

'It's my family's place.' He returns the glass to the bar. 'Me and other members of my family. When they turn up!' He rolls his eyes as he washes the glass. I can't help pressing him for more.

'You and your family?' I nod and start to move around looking at the place. He's watching me, I can feel it.

'Been in the family since my grandparents started it. But I

run it now. Well, I would, if we had more customers.' He looks around and then pulls out his phone. 'And a waiter! That was who I was talking to.' He waves the phone. 'My father.' He rolls his eyes again, and my cheeks flare up and burn. 'His arthritis is playing up,' he tuts. 'For a town that has always prided itself on longevity and good health, suddenly everyone is getting very sick! My mother is visiting her sister, who is unwell . . .' He shrugs, as if he's already said too much.

Stelios has arthritis? I can hardly believe what I'm hearing. He was only a little older than me and was really, very fit. Always on the go. Despite how I feel about what he did to me, and to Demi, that's still very sad.

'So, you're working for Maria and Kostas? You're the WWOOFer?' He laughs, reminding me of Gracie and her misunderstanding, and I can't help laughing too. 'I heard about you coming.'

'Yes, I'm a WWOOFer.' I hold out my hands as if admitting to being an addict of some kind.

'And you're from the UK?' He starts working around the tables he's pulled together, straightening the tablecloth and laying out knives and forks.

I nod again, relaxing enough to ask the questions I need answers to, starting by getting to know more about this young man. I join him at the table and begin laying up the other side. 'What's your name?' I ask.

'I'm Yannis.' He straightens up, smiles and holds out a hand for me to shake. Oh that smile! Just like Stelios's. 'And this is the Wild Thyme Restaurant. And you are?'

That stops me in my tracks. I know how weird I must

look again. First I'm hiding in a lemon tree, then I'm helping to set a table, and now I can't remember my own name. But I don't want Stelios to know I've been round, snooping and spying on him.

'Nell,' I say. When I came to Crete last time, everyone knew me as Elinor. No one ever calls me by my full name these days. No one here would recognise me as Nell.

'Well, Nell, if you're looking for a job, I can't take anyone on full time, but I could use a hand today if you need to earn a bit of cash. Do you know how to cook these greens?' He turns round and picks up the box and looks at them. 'I'm suddenly short-handed,' he waggles the phone again, 'and for once I have a table booked in for lunch.'

I shake my head. 'No idea, sorry.'

And not being able to find any other excuse to stay, I turn to leave. But as I do, a thousand questions are still going round in my head. Was I just an affair? A silly girl taken in by a married man? Is this young man my daughter's family? And that stubborn streak tells me I can't leave until I've found out the whole truth.

I turn back. 'I have no idea how to cook wild *horta*, but I have done some waitressing before . . .'

I think back to when Stelios and I were working together at Zeus's Vista holiday resort. He was a barman and I started out as a chambermaid but got promoted whilst I was there to the resort restaurant, if you could call it that. Chips, chips and more chips. It was Stelios who got me the job. The waitressing jobs usually went to the local girls. It was better pay and better working hours than chambermaiding. No more early mornings whilst he was on late nights. Now, looking back, I wonder why he went to all that effort if he didn't love me.

'Great!' Yannis smiles. 'Do you want to . . . clean up a bit?' He looks down at my dusty legs and points towards the ladies' loo. 'We'll be the talk of the town. Two young people in the same place! Unheard of!' He laughs and heads off with the box of greens to the kitchen at the back of the building.

Being the talk of the town is the last thing I want. I try to balance one plate in my hand and the other on the heel of my palm, like I remember doing at the resort restaurant. As I hold my arm out in front of me, the plate on top wobbles and they both fall with a clatter to the floor. Yannis pokes his head out from the kitchen and raises an eyebrow, and I wonder what on earth I've gone and got myself into now.

Chapter Seventeen

Having cleaned myself up and practised the plate stacking a few more times without much success, I hear the crunch of tyres on the stony road outside and the grinding of a handbrake being yanked on. A minibus has pulled up outside the restaurant. It's silver with a yellow sun and *Henderson's Holidays* down the side. This is it. They're here. I breathe out through my mouth, feeling like a Greek opera singer in an amphitheatre preparing to perform. All I have to do is not drop the plates. Hopefully by the end of this lunch I'll know exactly where Stelios is and how to find him. I smooth down the apron Yannis has given me, lift my head and wait by the gates.

'*Yassou!*' I say with gusto as they arrive, practically scaring the group half to death. 'Sorry, that's all my Greek; we'll have to revert to English now,' I say, gesturing to the restaurant by way of a welcome.

A woman with a blonde bun on top of her head, wearing a tight yellow dress and high heels and clearly struggling with her suck-it-all-in magic pants in the heat, looks me up and down guardedly and does the same to the restaurant as she steps into the courtyard. I find myself bristling slightly. This place is beautiful. She must be able to see that. She's followed by a man in a smart cool suit who says 'Yassou,' back to me in perfect Greek and hands me his jacket, revealing a tight-fitting shirt, open at the neck. Another woman and a man follow them, nodding to me and looking around, their eyes drawn upwards as they step into the courtyard, obviously appreciating its beauty but talking in low tones. Lastly a tall man, blond, pushing his wraparound shades up on top of his head.

'Hi.' He gives me a friendly smile. 'This place is great.' He looks around appreciatively, and I find myself smiling back, my nerves dissolving.

I begin to hand round menus and take drink orders, not necessarily in an organised way. I'm all fingers and thumbs, like I'm at a job interview, juggling my notepad and pen and the menus and dropping the pen into the lap of the lady with the yellow dress. As I apologise and clumsily retrieve it, I wonder what on earth I'm doing here. I was eighteen when I last did this! A lifetime ago!

'Full of rustic charm,' the tall blond man says cheerily, giving me another warm smile, and once again I feel my confidence returning. You are thirty-six, for God's sake, Nell, I think. You have brought up a child and delivered more meals to the kitchen table than you can count. I hand round the rest of the menus and then fetch a large jug of iced water and the rest of the drinks from the bar. I'm feeling a lot more in control when Yannis appears from the kitchen, wiping his hands with a clean tea towel.

'Welcome to the Wild Thyme, my family's restaurant,' he says, and I'm suddenly reminded why I'm here. I'm not really trying to get a job. He explains the daily specials. 'Everything is grown here, local and in season. Simple ingredients made special by our wonderful mountain herbs. We have lamb *tsigariasto*, cooked long and slow. This dish used to be made from the wild mountain goats, the kri-kri, but these are now a protected species. This is served with wild *horta* steamed with olive oil, from our own groves here in Vounoplagia and picked fresh this morning by your waitress here, Nell, on the slopes of the mountain.' I find myself blushing.

'Brilliant,' says the blond man. 'So . . . rustic!' He uses the word again. 'Real old-world charm about this place.' And I'm hoping it's still a compliment.

The woman in the yellow dress doesn't look convinced and takes a sip of water, eyeing her glass suspiciously.

'We also have *soutzoukakia*, spicy pork meatballs in garlic, local red wine and tomatoes from my mother's garden. There is home-made moussaka made to my grandmother's recipe with aubergine, lamb and local cheese; stuffed peppers; and *choclioi*.'

'What's that?' the woman in the yellow dress asks.

'Snails, picked by my father!' Yannis beams, and the woman grimaces and takes another sip of water.

The blond man orders for everybody, suggesting they'd like to try all the specials. Yannis prepares them a large bowl of Greek salad, with home-made bread, dolmades – vine-wrapped parcels of rice – olives, a cheese dip, *tyrokafteri*, and *tzatziki*, a yogurt one. The garlic-and-rosemary sautéed snails are followed by steaming bowls of spicy pork meatballs and slow-cooked lamb, the wild greens glistening with olive oil and lemon. The guests talk between themselves as they eat, encouraged by the tall blond man to try each dish.

The smells are amazing and my stomach rumbles. The blond man laughs heartily.

'Hope you get yours soon,' he smiles, dipping bread into his bowl of sauce. 'It's very good. And all local and seasonal?'

'Of course,' I say, remembering how Yannis introduced the food.

When they have all finished eating, I start to clear the plates, my tongue poking out of the side of my mouth in concentration as I work.

'Can I help?' the blond man asks, watching me balance the plates on my hand like I practised earlier. They wobble precariously. I stick my tongue out further. The woman in yellow tuts. I grab the top plate before it falls and put everything back down on the table.

'No, no, I'm fine,' I tell him, and decide to stack them just as I would have done had it been Demi and her mates eating supper at home. As I pick up the pile, I go to grab a sliding knife, but he gets to it first and puts it back on top.

'Thank you,' I say, blowing the hair from my hot face with my bottom lip.

'Tell me . . . what's it like around here?' he asks. 'What's to love about this town?'

'What's to love?' I turn and put the pile of dirty plates down on an empty table behind me, then wipe my hands on the apron tied around my middle, covering my cut-off shorts. 'Well, just look at it.' I hold up a hand in the direction of the mountain. 'It's beautiful,' I say, meaning it. 'The views, the clean air, the sunshine.' I gather up glasses as I talk.

'You obviously love it,' he says, giving me a very white, shiny smile. His light baby-blue eyes smile too.

'I do.' I nod thoughtfully. 'I have loved it here for a very long time.'

'It's very quiet,' he comments, and smiles at me again, right at me. 'Not too quiet for you?' His eyes twinkle and my stomach does a little jump. Is he flirting with me? I blush.

'You wouldn't say that if you heard the racket on the mountain at night,' I say without thinking, and immediately regret it. Some help I am! Maria and Kostas want tourists to come, not be scared away. Duh!

'Oh?' He tilts his head with interest.

'Oh, y'know, kids,' I say. 'Just messing about, I expect . . . It's a very quiet town. Almost nothing happens here,' which is sort of true, I tell myself. 'Very soon we'll have our own honey factory up and running again on the mountain,' I tell him. 'The honey has magical health benefits. People will come for miles for it.' I find myself gabbling and wish I could stop.

'Really?' he says with interest. 'Well, you've certainly sold Vounoplagia to me. This is definitely the sort of place I'd like to bring more tourists from my holiday company.' He looks at me. 'Henderson's Holidays. I'm Harry Henderson. Let me know about the honey factory when it opens,' he says as he slips a business card into the front pocket of my apron.

'I will,' I say.

'Or maybe we could meet for a drink and you could tell me more about this magical healthy honey, or anything else that might be of interest to tourists here.' He smiles again as I nod and turn away, and I can't help the grin that spreads across my face as I make my way back to the kitchen with a pile of dirty plates and a little spring in my step.

'You look pleased with yourself,' Yannis says as he finishes arranging a huge plate of fresh fruit for dessert.

'I think I am,' I say. I've managed to waitress again for the first time in years, and to flag up the honey factory to a big holiday company who want to bring their tourists to see it. And I've been asked out on what I think is a date! Maybe I'm not so washed up after all.'

The tip Harry Henderson leaves puts an even bigger smile on my face. I try to share it with Yannis, but he refuses, telling me I've earned it. I add it to my wages. It feels good to have some money in my pocket. I look around the restaurant, sad to see it so empty again. It would be great for the town if more people like the table today came out here.

Yannis hands me a glass of cold water and I lean against the bar. This is my opportunity. 'So . . . it's just you and your dad here usually?' I ask.

He nods. 'And my mother sometimes, but not often these days. My sister lives in the city with her husband and her kids. Then of course there's my grandmother, Demetria, and believe me, you don't want to run into *her* when she's in a bad mood.' He laughs, but I suddenly freeze.

'Your grandmother is Demetria?'

'Yes,' he nods. 'A formidable woman.'

Stelios's grandmother was called Demetria. Could it be? Is she really still alive? And if Demetria is Yannis's grandmother . . . my brain slowly processes the information . . . that makes Yannis Stelios's brother! His much younger brother! So he isn't Stelios's son after all.

My brain goes into overdrive. Where is Stelios? Could it be that he isn't married with a family after all? And if not, why did he not come after me? A tiny, treacherous glimmer of hope rises up in me. I need to stay and find out more.

'I could work some more shifts if you like,' I say to Yannis. The palpitations start again. I could get found out at any moment. I feel like I'm spying, but I do need to know where Stelios is, and to speak to him. And when I do, what then? Will he be delighted I've gone to all this effort, or will I be a cuckoo in the nest?

'I'm afraid I couldn't pay you . . .' Yannis shrugs and shakes his head.

'It's fine. I enjoyed it. I can work for tips if you like. Something is always better than nothing.'

'You'd work for tips?' He doesn't seem able to believe his luck, and I can understand why. 'Don't you have your hands full working for Maria and Kostas?' he asks.

'Well, I have chores to do in the morning – watering the herbs on the farm and collecting the *horta* – but mostly I've been scrubbing out the honey factory, and that's nearly ready. Kostas has worked really hard making new hives and planting out the herbs to bring the bees in. But until they come,' it's my turn to shrug, 'we can't make any honey. I'm free at lunchtimes and afternoons until the bees return.' I smile.

'Please,' he says, gesturing towards the long bench filled with cushions. 'Please, come and sit down.' He looks serious, and I wonder if I've been found out already. I clutch my bag to me and follow him. He turns over a glass and fills it with white wine from a carafe in a small glass-fronted fridge by the kitchen entrance. 'Please.' He gestures again to the seat. 'Sit. I'll be back.'

He disappears to the kitchen and I take the time to look around the beautiful courtyard once again. Shaded from the glare of the hot afternoon sun, I lean into the cushions plumped behind my back, which, if I'm honest, is aching a bit. I'm not sure if it's from picking the wild *horta*, scrubbing the honey factory, walking up the mountain or riding the moped down it. Should I really be doing this? But I can't just come out with 'Where's your brother?' without raising suspicion. I rub the back of my neck to smooth out the tension there.

At that moment my phone chirps into life with a text. It's from Demi.

Will be working tonight, can't talk. All fine. D x

She's sent it with a picture of herself pulling a daft face and a thumbs-up. I sigh and smile wearily. This why I'm still here. I have to let her do her own thing and just be there if she needs me, I tell myself. I send her a couple of kisses back and then, knowing that no one is looking, put the phone to my lips, hoping that she realises how much I love her.

To distract myself I photograph the courtyard, pointing my phone upwards to get in the second level of seating with its white tablecloths and candles and the sun pouring in through the open roof, and text it to Angelica with a kiss for Gracie too. Angelica sends me back a photo of the factory, stripped bare and full of workmen.

I scroll through other images whilst I wait for Yannis, photos of Demi smiling, pouting, running along the beach on a day trip to Porthcawl, sandy bunches and a gap where her tooth had fallen out. I've never found the right time to tell her about Stelios. We were fine. Even after Nan died we were a tight little unit, Demi, me, Gracie and Angelica. She believed her father was just a holiday romance, and it seemed easier that way.

Just being here now, I feel close to him. Even though I still don't know why he never came for me. I touch the pendant tucked inside my T-shirt. Was it because I wasn't the only one? Did he give these necklaces to every girl he met? I sigh. Even if I wasn't the love of his life, I have to tell him about our beautiful, independent, strong-willed daughter . . .

'Everything OK?' Yannis is standing in front of me, staring down at the phone.

'Yes, fine.' I blink a lot, hoping he won't notice my watery eyes. He is standing with lots of little plates balanced on his hands and up his wrists, just like I attempted to do earlier and nowhere near as competently. He places them in front of me and then turns over another glass and sits down.

He holds out a hand to the food. 'Staff perks! Leftovers!' he beams. The smells are delicious, making my stomach rumble again, even louder than before. I hold it, embarrassed, and he laughs. There are small dishes of spicy meatballs, smelling of cumin, cloves and cinnamon; olive-oil-soaked baked peppers, brimming with fluffy rice; artichokes and broad beans in chunky red sauce; glistening dark-green vine-wrapped parcels, and bubbling cheese-topped moussaka. 'It's the least I can do. Besides, you need to be able to tell the customers how each dish tastes if you're going to help me here. And with my father out of action, you've saved the day.'

'So you want me to help out?'

'Absolutely.' He smiles and holds up his glass. 'I need help here, sure, but I also need to get customers into the restaurant. I need someone to be on the street, pointing them down here. I'll pay you a percentage of all the bills from the customers you get in. How's that?'

'Deal!' I confirm, and we clink glasses. I suddenly feel like I'm standing at the top of a black ski run, knowing it's going to be a bumpy ride but that there's no other way down. The more regularly I'm here, the sooner I'm going to come across Stelios. I have to do it. I have to know if Stelios ever thought of me . . . or of Demi.

Chapter Eighteen

'Hurry up! Time to finish in here for the day!' Maria is standing in the doorway of the honey factory, where I've been cleaning and scrubbing all morning. The surfaces, the honey spinner, the big settling tank and the jars, washed and rewashed to keep the dust at bay, are all ready for when the bees arrive.

She gasps. 'You've done brilliantly!' She looks around the scrubbed work surfaces and rows of clean jars. The honey spinner – or extractor, to use its proper name – takes centre stage in the middle of the room. 'This is where we will bring the honeycomb from the hives,' she explains. 'We scrape off the wax that covers each hexagonal cell, and then we put the wooden frame from the hive in here and we spin.' She turns the big handle on top of the circular metal bin that I've scrubbed to within an inch of its life. 'After that, we strain it over there,' she points, 'and put it into the jars. And that's it. Pure, natural wild herb honey.' She claps her hands together. 'We are ready!'

I pull my hands from the soap-sud-filled sink and peel off my rubber gloves. I have been here for just over four weeks and I have quite a routine going now. I get up early and water the herbs, then check the hives for signs of life – still none yet – before a breakfast of yoghurt with figs from the trees outside my bedroom. The sharpness of the yoghurt awakes my senses. I eat out on the front terrace watching the sun start to fill the sky over the sea.

After breakfast, I go to the lower slopes to collect the wild *horta*, taking time to watch the golden eagles circling round the peak as I look out for signs of bees. As the day heats up, I head for the cool of the honey factory to continue cleaning. It's been like the Forth Bridge. No sooner have I cleaned one area than another seems to need doing all over again, everything covered with the dry yellow dust that the wind blows in.

At lunchtime, I grab the makings of *dakos*: double-baked bread, tomatoes, crumbly white cheese and a few olives; or a bowl of Maria's wonderful soup that seems to be ever constant on the stove, then head out to Vounoplagia on the moped, always keeping my eyes peeled for Stelios.

I feel for Yannis; he's trying so hard to drum up regular trade. Each day we stand by the front gates, hoping to encourage people in with a small pile of flyers. But no one is passing. There hasn't been another big group at the restaurant since the table from Henderson's Holidays.

Earlier this week a group of four American tourists stopped to make a booking. They wanted to drive up to the mountain first, take in the views, maybe walk up. 'My mother told me about the herbs on this mountain. The best in the whole region,' said one of the women in the group.

'Well . . .' I started to tell them it might not be quite as they'd been told. Should I warn them not to go too high up, to stick to the lower slopes like the rest of us do?

'We'll go and have a look, and then we'll be back.'

But no sooner had they reached the vantage point than I heard gunshots coming from the mountain, and minutes later, they were slewing their way back down through the town, leaving it twice as fast as they'd arrived, looks of horror and disgust on their pale faces.

This town is never going to recover until someone puts a stop to what is going on up there. Someone is terrorising the mountain and I have no idea why. I tap the flyers in my hand. I've tried to ask Yannis about what he thinks is going on, but like Kostas and Maria, he tells me that no one knows and everyone seems too nervous to find out.

Every afternoon when I arrive at the restaurant I tell myself that this is the day I'm going to ask Yannis where Stelios is. But every day, try as I might to work the conversation around to brothers, extra helping hands, family get-togethers, he always finds a job to do, a reason to move the conversation on, and with it goes my resolve to face this head on. As soon as I tell him who I am, everything I've built between us could fall apart. And right now, I'm quite enjoying my little routine here. I have an extra place where I belong. For the first time in my life, I have to be patient, listen and wait. I'm not being hot-headed and stubborn; I'm waiting for my moment and actually enjoying it.

After lunch, Yannis and I usually share the leftovers, the dish of the day that has been prepared but not sold. Wonderful home-cooked dishes he learned from his mother and grandmother, and he tells me about his hopes and dreams. How he wants to leave the island, see the world, but has to run the family restaurant instead. If I try and ask why it's down to him, he shrugs and replies that that's how it is. It's life. He tells me how he hopes for change to come to the town, something that will bring it back to life again, but really he dreams of travelling and meeting as many young ladies who look like Britney Spears as he can along the way!

And usually after we have eaten, I drive around the town, scanning the streets, hoping to catch a glimpse of Stelios before I return to the farm and help out with feeding the animals and harvesting from the vegetable patch with Maria as the evening cools. But today, Maria has other plans.

'A day off!' she tells me. 'You are working too hard. The factory is ready,' she waves her hand around, 'and I'm sure Yannis will let you off. All the tourists will be at the market today. No one will be coming up here.' I start to protest that I'm happy working. It keeps my mind occupied. And I don't want to be away from the restaurant if there's a chance Stelios is going to visit. But she won't take no for an answer.

'Where are we going?' I ask. It feels surreal to think that in just a few weeks I'll be back home. I'm halfway through my time here. Will the house feel as cold and empty as when I left? I wipe my hands quickly.

'Mitera thinks you're not getting out enough.'

'I'm fine. I'm happy just doing my work, helping out in the restaurant and coming back here.' The more I have to do, the less time I have to think about Demi and the calls that seem to get less and less frequent these days. But if she's busy and happy, I know that's a good thing.

'She thinks you are working too hard and need to make some friends. She worries you might feel lonely. Come, I will help you to finish up, and then we will go.'

She comes to stand next to me at the sink on the side wall, picking up a tea towel and starting to dry the jars I've been washing.

'When I first married Kostas, I thought we had it all with this place. Business was good. People came to the mountain. Mitera and Kostas's father would make the honey here. Kostas would sell it at the front gate when the coaches came. The honey was something special. It . . . well, it came from the heart of the mountain.' There is a tear in the corner of her eye. 'I just hope it will come again.'

I can see how much the thought of losing the farm upsets her. I take the dried jar from her and put it on a tray, ready to take to the house for sterilising in the oven.

'When I finally stopped hoping that Kostas and I would be blessed with children, we poured all the love we had into the farm. I grew to love it as he does. Despite the winters!' She laughs and stops to wipe away the tears with her tea towel. 'You are lucky to have a daughter,' she tells me.

'I know,' I say, my throat prickling as I try to swallow. Demi hasn't disappeared out of my life, I realise. She isn't gone for good. It's just different now. I put a soapy arm around Maria and squeeze, leaving bubbles on her shoulder. Maria always puts on such a cheerful, brave face.

'Sometimes I wonder what we have done to upset the gods,' she says as she carries on with the jars, drying them thoroughly and placing them on the tray.

'Oh Maria, you haven't done anything. How can you say that? You are the most big-hearted, welcoming, kind people I have ever met! I wish I was half the person you are!'

She puts her warm hand on mine, squeezing and patting

it. 'Thank you,' she says, and I know there and then that a friendship has been made for life. 'But I worry what will happen if we can't get the bees to come.' She drops her head and sniffs, then rubs her nose and with a deep breath lifts her head again. 'Now come,' she says, brushing off any sadness in her usual bright way, 'it's a day off! It's time to go out.'

Out of the shade of the shed, the sun is burning hot, cracking the dry earth on the pathway back to the farmhouse. The goats stick their heads through the fence, clearly fascinated to see where we're going.

'Here, we'll take the scooter,' says Maria, grabbing the key and two helmets from the dresser just inside the door.

'Where are we going?' I ask as we climb aboard, Maria up front, her big bottom spilling over the seat like a soft pillow.

'Just into Vounoplagia.' She shuffles forward, starts the engine and calls for me to get on behind her as the little bike roars into life with its customary farting and belching.

'But what about Mitera?' I shout as I climb on to the hot plastic seat, wincing as I do. 'How will she get there?'

She turns to me and smiles from her open-faced helmet, like a big beaming moon. 'She walked, of course.'

'Of course,' I nod, silly me! Back home, no one walks. Gracie can barely make it to the shop at the end of the road and always sent Demi to get her fags and lottery ticket. We have a lot to learn from these people, I think, as Maria pulls out down the drive. I turn to wave at Kostas, who is standing sadly behind the fly sheet, like a dog left behind on a family day out, still looking out for signs of bees.

* * *

Once I've released my grip on her, Maria steps off the bike and pulls off her helmet. I follow, my knees shaking after the hair-raising ride, and she beams at me. 'Mitera wants to introduce you to her friends,' she says, nodding to the taverna at the end of the street leading to the Wild Thyme Restaurant, where I first sat watching for signs of Stelios all those weeks ago. She waves me forward to the main road, past the *kafenia*, where the same two men I have seen every time I've passed are sitting outside. I nod my head in greeting but they just stare at me, as before.

Maria ushers me up a couple of steps to the taverna's terrace area, which has an uneven flagstone floor and a few pots here and there, some cracked, others weatherworn and a bit green. Right in the middle of the terrace is a large plane tree under which empty tables and chairs are gathered. There is an open grill at the back, but the coals are unlit. She leads me past a waitress, who nods and smiles, and then up a couple of steps into a cool whitewashed room, where a group of women, all around Mitera's age, are sitting in a circle, crocheting by the looks of it.

'Ah!' Mitera puts up a hand. 'Our guest!' She smiles widely, having obviously stuck her teeth in securely this morning. 'Come, sit down.' She indicates a chair. The other women all look up from the stitching on their laps and stare at me. 'This is Nell, the WWOOFer!' Mitera says with a flourish, making me smile. She places something on my lap.

'Oh, I . . . I really couldn't,' I attempt to explain. 'I've never crocheted.' The closest I've come is sticking patches and shiny gems on the cut-off shorts I'm wearing.

'You can learn. I taught Kostas when he was a boy,'

Mitera tells me. Her English is far more stilted than Kostas and Maria's, but still very good. 'Everyone here has a little English,' Mitera explains. 'Since the British soldiers came in the war and then later as the holidaymakers began to arrive. This is Agatha, from the shop.' She points a finger to the main road, and I smile by way of hello. I've seen Agatha sitting outside before. Mitera goes around the circle introducing each of the women to me. They are all wearing black, all crocheting busily, and not one of them, I notice, is wearing glasses as they work.

Maria sits down next to me and starts to show me how to crochet. But I'm hopeless. I can't see what I'm supposed to be doing. How do these ladies manage it? They are talking amongst themselves and I get the feeling some of them are discussing me, leaning into each other and speaking in hushed tones, giving me quick glances.

'You all have very good eyesight and nimble fingers,' I say. 'No arthritis?' I add lightly, stretching out my already aching fingers.

'No, no.' The woman to my immediate left shakes her head. But some of the others tip their heads from side to side.

'We didn't used to. But . . . well, it's different now that we don't have so much . . .' Agatha stretches out her stiffening fingers, and they all nod in agreement.

'Some of us are starting to get more aches and pains now there is less dittany to be had,' says Gabriela, the café owner's mother. 'My husband suffers from gout. It is very good for that.'

'So how do you get the dittany when you need it?' I try

and focus on what I'm being shown, the old lady next to me trying to guide my hands by holding her soft dark brown ones, knobbly but not gnarled, over them.

They look at each other like I've entered a magic circle and asked to be shown how the trick is done.

'Same as for us,' Mitera replies eventually.

'The messenger of the gods?' I ask. I hear a sucking-in of breath around me, and a couple of the women look nervously in the direction of the mountain, as if something bad will happen if they let out the town's secret.

Mitera looks around the circle. 'Nell is one of us. She has worked hard to help Kostas and Maria,' she scolds them, first in Greek and then in English for my benefit. 'Yes,' she nods to me. 'Most of us here have had help from the messenger. Christina gets a delivery for her husband when his gout is bad; Gabriela for her hip; Agatha for her arthritis and her husband's gas!' and they all laugh and wave their hands around, agreeing, warming to me and the conversation, it seems.

'And it helps?' I ask.

'It is miraculous!' they all say.

'It makes you feel strong!' Christina looks at me with beady bright eyes.

'And sometimes frisky!' says Agatha.

'With your husband? Really?' Gabriela jokes.

'Maybe with yours!' Agatha retorts, and they all laugh again.

My neighbour reaches over as she attempts to help me and move my work on. They are all talking now, louder, mostly in Greek, laughing and joking.

'So, this messenger, who is it? What do they look like?' Suddenly the laughter stops and they all look at me.

'No one knows,' says Mitera. 'The dittany just appears, and . . . well, we're grateful.'

For the next couple of hours the women sit and crochet, telling each other of their families' aches and pains and joys and troubles. I wonder if I will hear news about Stelios. But once again, despite me telling them that I'm helping out at the Wild Thyme, there is nothing. No one mentions Stelios, the son who was going to build a boutique hotel and bring the tourists to the mountain.

'We should go,' Maria says finally, her cheeks full and rosy from time spent chatting and drinking coffee. And I feel my spirits lifted too. Stelios is tantalisingly close, I can sense it.

'Where shall I put this?' I stand with the crochet needles and yarn in my hand.

'I can do that,' Mitera starts to get up.

'No, let me,' I say. 'Is it over here?' and she nods. I open a cupboard door and then step back. There are piles and piles of crocheted circles in here, like the Leaning Tower of Pisa. I turn to look back at Mitera, at all of them working hard to crochet more circles that may never see the light of day.

Mitera shrugs sadly. 'Nobody comes to buy them any more,' she says, and I look at the towers of coasters and mats and then close the door quickly before they tumble out.

Poor Kostas and Maria; poor Mitera and the ladies at the crocheting circle. It isn't right. There must be a way of getting the tourists back.

I think of Harry Henderson. Attractive as he was, I'm not looking for a date or anything like that. But he was interested in bringing more tourists here. The whole town would benefit, I think, as we drive much more slowly back up the mountain, the moped bottoming out and scraping along the ground every now and again. The honey farm would draw tourists too. Maybe I should try one more time to find the dittany that will bring the bees to the farm.

I tell Maria I'm going for a lie-down, but instead I change into my walking boots and grab my bag and a water bottle. I'm going up the mountain, and this time, there's no way I'm going to let Georgios put me off!

Chapter Nineteen

The late-afternoon sun has disappeared and dark clouds fill the sky, replacing the strange stillness that was in the air when we returned to the farm. I'm feeling so enraged on behalf of my new friends. I know that wherever Stelios is, he wouldn't stand for this. These people just want to get on with their lives. They have a right to be on that mountain. It can't be so difficult to find some dittany and bring it down to the meadow to plant.

The heat is clammy and oppressive and there's a smell of herbs in the air. My well-worn black T-shirt with the Christmas decoration factory logo on the back clings to me, and I keep pulling at it in the patches where it's stuck. The wind is starting to pick up. An old feed sack escapes from the barn and whisks up the hill, making the goats scatter with fright. I chase it, capture it and return it before filling my water bottle from the stream in the valley by the sheds, trickling down from the peak of the mountain to the town below. Then, pulling my T-shirt over my mouth and nose, I make my way out on to the dusty road and up towards the mountain track.

My phone trills into life. It's Yannis, asking if I can help out in the restaurant this evening. It's his grandmother's birthday, he tells me; the whole family are coming. This is it. This is what I've been waiting for. Finally my patience has paid off. In just a few hours' time, I'll see Stelios in person. I type my reply, then shove my phone away, knowing I'm going to lose signal soon.

Reaching the area where I collect the greens, I pause and look down the valley. The neighbouring mountaintops are shrouded in grey clouds like fur collars, and I can't see the rooftops of the town below, let alone down to the sea. I look back towards the path I usually take to pick the wild greens, then turn and head straight on up, over the fallen trunk across the path. This time when I get to the landslide of fallen rocks I scramble over without hesitating. Dusting myself down, I keep moving forward, higher and higher. I have to find some dittany.

I'm heading for what looks to be a plateau. When I reach it, I pull myself up, panting, and look around in surprise. There are half a dozen different-coloured boxes, blue, yellow and white, standing on some old tyres on a flat piece of ground under the shade of some old olive trees, shimmering silver, their trunks bent, twisted and gnarled but still thriving; much like the elderly people of this town, I think with a smile.

I have no idea what's in the boxes. They're wooden and square with a catch at the front, securing the lid, and two slits either side of the catch. They could be holding anything. Then it dawns on me how high up I am. Is whatever is being grown or stashed away in these solid boxes why people are being kept off the mountain?

The sky is still darkening and it looks like someone's

thrown a blanket over the lower peaks, making them dark and moody. I feel myself shiver. I'm puzzled. If these boxes are the reason people are being kept away, why is there no one here guarding them? I look back at the boxes. Should I open one? I glance around again to double-check that there's no one else around. What would you keep in boxes like this? Stolen stuff? Phones and wallets from unsuspecting tourists? Perhaps it's a gang working the coastal resorts. Or maybe drugs, like Maria was saying; illegal groups working in the mountains, hiding their stash up here where no one will find it.

I step closer to one of the boxes, the wind whipping my hair round my face as it escapes from the hairband I tied it back with. One of Demi's I found in my hoodie pocket. Even that smells of her and makes me miss her. The wind fills my head with noise and my breathing gets shallower as I reach out a shaking hand. I look around again nervously, imagining myself coming face to face with the barrel of a drug baron's pistol. Maybe they're not expecting to be raided in the middle of the afternoon. Who would be stupid enough to do that?

I take a big breath and let it out slowly, then reach for the catch . . . just a little further . . . and flip the lid up as quickly as I can. I jump back, then peer in. Not drugs. Not stolen goods. Not guns . . . BEES! Buzzing very loudly! Stupid, stupid me. They're beehives, full of bees, and very unhappy ones by the sounds of it. So this is where the bees that Kostas has been chasing must come from. Not from the wild, but actual hives. But these aren't like Kostas's hives. I wonder who put them here. I need to get out of here, fast.

Suddenly there is an almighty bang and the shriek I was trying to hold in escapes. I bite my lip and whip back round to look at the beehives, six of them. The sky is dark grey and angry, just like the bees, who possibly think I'm after their honey.

'There, there, it's OK,' I say. I'm trying to sound soothing, but my voice is shaking. 'I don't want anything from you. Just go back to sleep . . . or whatever it is you do in there. Just go back to having fun. Nothing to see here . . .' Oh God! This is ridiculous. I'm talking to a box of bees.

Just as I reach out to try and close the lid, there's another bang and a huge crack of lightning rips across the sky. 'Argh!' This time I can't keep my mouth shut. I'm standing on top of a mountain and I could be electrocuted any minute. I'm not sure if that'll send the bees into hiding or make them angrier, but I'm not waiting to find out. I glance back down the way I came up. It looks a lot steeper and rockier than I remember. There's another rumble in the sky – or could it be buzzing? I've got no option. I have to get away from here. I put my head down and run forward, grabbing a rock on either side and starting to climb, higher and higher.

There's another crack of lightning, followed quickly by thunder, and the air is thick with anticipation of the rain that's going to follow. I need to find shelter, fast. I can feel my chest tightening and I tell myself to stay calm. I shouldn't have come. It's not my responsibility to solve everyone else's problems. I look up and spot another plateau. It's a steep climb, but I'm pretty sure I can see the opening of a cave. I have to push on. I screw up my face against the wind. Any minute I could be struck by lightning. Who would tell Demi?

How could I have put myself in danger like this? I can't believe I've been so stupid. I can't die on a mountaintop; I have to get into that cave. I reach out to pull myself up. The muscles in the backs of my legs and shoulders are screaming, but I have to keep going.

I take another quick look behind me. There is a dense black cloud heading straight for me. It's moving fast for a cloud . . . a noisy cloud . . . It's not a cloud! It's the bees! Forgetting my aching limbs, I catapult myself forward, grabbing at any bit of rock, heedless of sharp edges, stones falling away from under my flailing feet as I scramble frantically upwards, waving my arms around my head.

The buzzing is loud now, and really angry. My heart is hammering just as loudly and angrily. I swish my arms at them and they retreat momentarily before whooshing back towards me as one, this time even closer. 'Go away!' I shout, but it's no good, they're not going. They're right over me. I can't move forwards or backwards. Instinctively I throw myself to the floor, screwing myself up into a ball, my hands protectively over my head, bracing myself for what's to come.

Suddenly I'm lifted off my feet and dragged by my waist over the final lip of rock. I land with a thump on the plateau, just as there's another massive flash of white light overhead, accompanied by a colossal bang. Then suddenly the heavens open and big fat drops of rain start to splatter on my face. Huge drops, like water bombs. I'm soaked in an instant. I turn to see the bees retreating, no match for the downpour beating down on them. They're clearly very intelligent creatures. Relief floods over me, but it's short-lived. As I watch the bees disappear, I hear a familiar voice.

'Follow me! Quick!'

And I'm not sure which I'm more terrified of: the bees, the violent storm playing out above me or, with an expression even more thunderous than the sky, Georgios.

Chapter Twenty

'In here, quickly!' he barks, the rain lashing against his dark, angry face and bouncing off the rim of his hat. His eyes are screwed up against the stair rods coming down like spears, stinging my arms and legs. I wish I'd worn something other than these stupid denim shorts.

There's another almighty bang in the sky right above us, and this time I pick myself up off the ground, where the dust is quickly turning to mud, and throw myself towards the mouth of the cave, where Georgios is standing, his khaki shirt sticking to his arms and chest. Water is pouring off the rim of his hat like a rivulet rushing down the mountain towards the sea.

I fling myself against the cold, rough wall of the cave, gasping for breath, my heart thundering from exertion and terror. Noisily I drag in huge gulps of air. The muscles in my legs and the tops of my arms are cramping from pulling myself up the rocks. My hair is stuck to my wet face and I'm soaked through, my clothes sticking to me like a second skin. As I straighten up with my back to the cave wall, my eyes start to adjust to the darkness and I can make out Georgios's outline standing in front of me.

'What the hell do you think you were doing? You scared

me half to death!' I fire the first shot, lashing out before I get stung.

'What was *I* doing?' he splutters. 'I told you to stay off the mountain. It's not safe. You nearly got yourself stung to death, and if that wasn't bad enough, you could have been struck by lightning.'

As if confirming what he's saying, there's a huge crash of thunder and flash of lightning at the same time, making me leap out of my skin and my breath catch in my throat. I push the small of my back harder against the cold wall, shoving my hands behind my backside in an attempt to stop them shaking.

'Looks like trouble has a habit of following you around,' he practically growls.

'Sorry?' I glare at him. Did I just hear him right? How dare he? 'You don't know anything about me!' I snap. He's right, of course. I could have died out there. I turn my head to stare out of the mouth of the cave, knowing I can't get away from him until this storm passes. Even then, will the bees have forgiven me?

Neither of us speaks. The crackling atmosphere between us is as highly charged as the lightning ripping across the sky. It's like the gods have gone to war, lobbing spears between the mountaintops at each other. There's a thick white fog curling around the mouth of the cave, and I can't see further than the ledge I was unceremoniously dragged up, let alone the farm or the town below, or the mountain and sea beyond. I feel like I've been cut off from the outside world. Like I'm in limbo, waiting for the pearly gates to open. I'd be furious if Demi put herself in such danger. How did I think I would get away with it?

Eventually Georgios turns and moves into the shadows at the back of the cave. I can see that his limp is a little more pronounced now. I turn to face the storm again. I've gone from hot and shaking to cold and shivering. The dark clouds are tumbling and swirling around out there as though they're rolling round a glass bowl looking for a way out. I feel safe in this cave.

After a while, I smell something. It smells a lot like . . . burning! I sniff again and snap my head round to see that Georgios has lit a fire behind me. The smoke is tumbling and twisting its way up to the cave rooftop, and spilling out to mingle with the thick mist and fog outside.

'Here.' He holds out a metal mug towards me. 'Take this.'

'What is it?' I ask. I feel like he'd poison me at the first opportunity he got.

He sighs with irritation. 'Raki. Take it. It's good for shock.'

I'm about to argue that I'm not in shock, but instead I bite my lip, take the mug and hold it to my chest, reminding myself that I'm on top of a mountain in rural Crete, in a massive electrical storm, having almost been stung to death by a swarm of angry bees. I think shock is pretty much where I am at actually.

'*Efharisto*,' I manage to croak, before dropping my eyes and looking into the mug. The smoke plumes up around me, reminding me of the factory fire, and of the dreams that have rolled into my head every night since; where Demi is on one side of the blaze and I'm on the other, unable to get to her. My throat tightens and my eyes sting, and I blink a lot. Then, to stop both the stinging eyes and the tight throat and to push out the nightmare that keeps turning up like an uninvited visitor, I tip the clear liquid up to meet my lips. It makes my eyes smart again before it's even reached them, and I wonder what harm this drink might do me, but considering the risks I've already taken this afternoon, I part my lips and let it slide into my mouth. It has a clean, clear taste and it burns its way down my throat and wraps itself around my heart and belly, leaving me feeling like I've had my first lesson in fire-eating.

I look at Georgios, who is crouching by the fire, his head on one side. His dark brown forearms are covered in droplets of water, which catch the light like crystals as he leans in to blow on the flames. He looks up at me, the flecks of gold in his green eyes sparkling.

'You're wearing black,' he says. 'Bees hate black.'

He continues to tend the fire, breaking up more twigs and sticks and adding them to the blaze. Meanwhile I look around the cave, my eyes adjusting to the gloom. I think about the bees in those boxes, and wonder who put them there. Is there someone out there now, watching me? Waiting with a gun? I strain to listen, but can't tell if it's gunfire or thunder banging around the mountainside. Looks like I'm stuck here for the time being.

I glance down at my watch and feel Georgios looking up at me.

'I have to be somewhere,' I inform him. But he doesn't respond, just adds what look like herbs to a pot that is boiling merrily on the little fire. 'I'm helping out at the restaurant this evening. The Wild Thyme? You know it?' I have no idea why I'm asking him this, trying to make conversation when he clearly doesn't want to.

'Yes, I know it.' He blows on the fire, and I'm sure he's done it on purpose, as the smoke billows up and I have to put my arm across my face and cough.

'They're having a big party, a family party . . .' My mouth goes dry and I brace myself and take another sip of the fire water in my metal cup. 'It's Yannis's grandmother's birthday.'

Georgios sits back on his haunches. 'I know,' he says, giving away nothing more.

My stomach twists in a knot. Today is the day! I'm going to finally see him. I still have no idea where he's living, and I can't believe our paths haven't crossed yet. My mind has tossed around the various reasons why – perhaps there's been some kind of family falling-out. Has Yannis taken his place in the restaurant and he feels put out? Or has he just been working away, supporting his family? I'm sure he'll be there today for his grandmother's birthday, though – I remember how much he adored her.

The storm outside seems to be quietening down. The thunder is rumbling off into the distance like a bad loser after a fight, complaining and threatening that they'll be back for more. The lightning is doing celebratory flashes off over towards the sea, and the thick white clouds seem to be rounding themselves up to follow on behind. But the rain hasn't finished yet. It's still making its presence known, which I suppose at least keeps the bees away.

Georgios stands up and walks towards me, handing me another battered tin cup with a wide rim but no handle.

'Here, drink!' he says gruffly, and turns away, back to the fire.

'Oh no, really, I haven't finished this one.'

'It's mountain tea,' he says with a flick of his chin.

I lift the cup to my face, inhaling the steam, breathing in the herbs. I inhale again, this time deeper. The whole cave seems to smell of it. I take a sip that turns into a noisy slurp, and then choke. I put the back of my hand over my mouth. Great! That's all I need. Choking in front of Georgios. Then he'd have to save my life all over again, I never want to be that indebted to him. That would be just too much to bear. The coughing fit passes and I realise what a state I must look.

'Sorry,' I apologise, but he doesn't say anything; just stands up and walks away from me, across the cave. Rude! I think.

'Here.' He's coming back towards me carrying a log, which he puts down on the ground behind me. It's covered in moss and is crumbling at one end, but I don't care. Not so rude, then. My cheeks burn.

'It's fine. I'm fine really.' I step away from the wall and find that my knees are trembling, presumably from the shock.

'Sit!' he commands, and I want to tell him I'm not a dog and that no, I won't sit, but actually I'm really very grateful and know I need to just shut up for once.

With a cup in each hand, I hold them out in front of me and lower my backside down on to the log. Then I put the cups down and clear my throat. I realise I need to pay my debt of gratitude. I need to thank him and then, as soon as I can, leave and draw a line under this. I put the words in place in my head before I speak. 'Thank you,' I say. 'For what you did.' I know he probably saved my life. If he hadn't come along, things could have been very different for me indeed. I wonder what he was doing there to begin with.

He grunts and nods, but I can't see his face under the rim of his hat as he sits on another log next to the fire, his hands wrapped around a tin mug too. He's less confrontational now, almost softer. Was he there to look out for me or to warn me away? He obviously wants the storm to pass and to get out of here as quickly as I do.

I pick up and sip at the tea, but don't touch the raki again. I glance outside. The rain is still pounding down, but the warring gods have finally returned to their respective caves. I look back at the tea and take another sip, and suddenly my mind is whirring. This is what the villagers depend on. This is why everyone is getting sick – because there is no mountain tea, no dittany. But if Georgios has it, why hasn't everyone else?

'How did you get these herbs? The dittany?' I ask, more directly than I intended.

He looks up, staring at me from under the brim of his hat. His green eyes are darker in this half-light, but I still feel like they're boring into my soul every time he looks at me; like I'm in his sights. 'You have to know where to look,' he says, 'and where not to go.'

A shiver runs up and down my spine, disarming me. I can smell the woodsmoke weaving its way through my hair.

'You could take your T-shirt off,' he says abruptly, and all of a sudden I feel a rush of panic.

'Excuse me?' I say indignantly, guarded once more.

'To dry it.' He points to the fire, and there is a tiny trace of a smile in the corner of his mouth.

'It's fine.' I pull the wet shirt further round me, and feel like I'm sitting in a bath of cold baked beans. I try my hardest not to let the discomfort I'm feeling appear on my face. What is it about this man that I misread and overreact to everything he says? Why do I get the feeling he dislikes me so much? I reach for the raki and take a tiny sip to try and combat the baked beans effect.

He stands up. He's tall for a Cretan man. Kostas is very short, as are most of the other men I've seen in the town. He unwinds the wet scarf from his neck and lays it by the fire. I can see the scar now that runs like a burn up the side of his neck and across his cheek. He lifts his hat to reveal dark curly hair. He seems a lot less intimidating without them, almost like they're hiding him from the outside world. And the more I look at him now, the more I think—

'I told you not to come up here.' He cuts across my thoughts, looking up at me as he brushes the water from the rim of his hat into the fire, making it hiss and spit like a terrified wild cat. He's back to scolding me and I'm back to feeling uneasy all over again. It doesn't stop me arguing, though.

'The whole town needs the dittany,' I say. 'If they have it, they won't have so many aches and pains and the place will start to thrive again. The tourists will want to buy it.'

'The messenger will deliver the dittany to those who need it. He . . .' he pauses, 'or she . . . always does.'

I almost laugh, but don't. The messenger indeed! 'Who is this messenger? Where do they come from? I need to get in touch with them, because Kostas really needs that dittany, now!'

'Unless people stay away from the mountain, there will be no dittany left at all. No bees, no butterflies. No mountain.'

'What? But why?'

For a few moments he says nothing; there is just the gentle pitter-patter of the rain outside the cave. Then, slowly, he starts to speak.

'For years tourists have been coming up the mountain, helping themselves to the dittany to take home, ripping it out by the roots. Then there are the poachers. Dried dittany is big business in the shops on the coast. They strip one mountaintop and then move on to the next. If the dittany goes, the wildlife – the bees and all the other plants that rely on them for pollination – will stop thriving. Understand? If tourists keep taking the plants, we won't be able to feed our bees.'

I nod slowly. 'But I don't want to rip it out by its roots—' I start to say. He doesn't let me finish.

'In future, just stay away,' he repeats. 'No good will come of you being here.'

I blow out an exasperated sigh. So much for thinking I've seen a softer side of him, helping me out, saving me from the bees. Looks like I'm back to square one, and I don't think there's any chance he's going to help me look for a dittany plant.

From outside I hear a bark, and Georgios lets out a whistle by rolling his bottom lip inwards, a short, sharp, piercing note that makes my ears reverberate. His little black and white dog suddenly appears in the cave, and he smiles, bending down to rub its head. Not something I've seen Georgios do before, smile. I narrow my eyes. A memory is scratching furiously again at the back of my mind. There is something so familiar about that smile, and yet I can't believe I would have forgotten meeting this bad-tempered, irritable and guarded man.

'Have we met before?' I blurt out before I can stop myself. So much for learning to be patient and think things through!

He says nothing; just rubs the dog's ears once more, then reaches out for his scarf, tying it around his neck again, covering the scar as if putting his armour back on.

'Georgios?' I'm on a roll and can't stop, my mouth running away without my brain. 'What do you mean, no good will come of me being here?' I get the impression he knows a lot more than he's letting on. 'Tell me!' I push. Then I swallow hard. 'Do you know Stelios?'

He snaps his head round. 'Everyone knows Stelios around here,' he answers coldly, fixing me with those eyes.

I cross my arms and stand my ground. 'So is he married? Does he . . . does he have a family? I really need to know.'

'There is nothing you need to know, other than that Stelios's brother Yannis is working hard to keep the family business going. And it won't help, you being here.'

'I know Yannis! I'm working for him!'

'Yes. I know.' He replaces his hat carefully.

I have no idea what he's talking about. Of course I'm helping Yannis. I'm working for tips! Why all the secrecy? I really am getting fed up with it. It feels like they're all protecting Stelios and his whereabouts. I'm frustrated. I'm furious for Demi . . . and I'm furious with myself for never having told her the truth.

I walk towards the mouth of the cave. After all the rain, I

can smell the wild thyme and the conifers. It reminds me of the honey, and the smell when I came here with Stelios, when he swore he loved me as much as I loved him. I curl my fingers, squeezing them until my nails dig into my palms. Then I lift my chin to the sky, and as I do, the last of the dark clouds seem to roll away into the distance, letting the light back in, like a curtain swishing back on a clear, brilliant blue sky, with just a few white fluffy clouds to remind us of the turmoil that's been. The sun pushes through as quickly as the storm clouds rolled in, as if showing that her strength can match theirs.

I can see clearly now, very clearly indeed. There's something in here, hanging from the ceiling in bunches. Lots and lots of dried bunches. Someone is stashing something away. Could it be the hidden drugs Mitera was talking about? Is this where they're storing them once they've been picked from the mountainside? I snap my head back to Georgios. If he knows this cave as well as he seems to, he knows what's going on here. The gunshots at night. He must know everything.

His face darkens. 'I told you not to interfere with things you know nothing about. It would be best for everyone, for the family, if you left. If you like, I will help you, give you a lift to the airport.'

At that moment, something in me snaps. 'Ever since I arrived, you've had it in for me! Is it because I haven't kept off the mountain? Is that it? Are you worried the locals will discover that you know exactly what's going on up here? You know who's drying out whatever it is back there?'

My hackles are rising, like his little dog protecting its

pack. I reach out and grab my bag, then, with a quick look outside the mouth of the cave, left and right, for any sign of the bees, I leave as quickly as I can, sitting down on the ledge and shuffling off the side. I have to get back. I have to get to the restaurant.

'No, wait!' I hear Georgios shouting after me. I turn and catch a glimpse of him standing in the mouth of the cave. He holds out a hand, but I'm not stopping for anyone. I start to make my way down the rocks, fuelled by the fury I'm feeling, making quick progress back to the path. 'Wait!' I hear him shout again, but I keep going, picking up speed, nimbly negotiating my way across the rocks as if I'm an old hand at it.

'Wait! Nell!'

I stop abruptly. I didn't even realise he knew my name, but the way he said it, I know for sure now. We've met before. I just don't know where, or what I've done to him to make him hate me so much. I turn. He's right behind me, breathing hard, his chest rising and falling to match mine.

'If you tell anyone,' he looks back at the cave, 'about this – what you've seen in here . . .'

I match his stare. I'm not scared any more. I turn away and resume my progress over the rocks. 'You'll do what?' I toss over my shoulder.

'I will tell them exactly who you are, Elinor.'

I freeze. No one has called me that since I left here, when I left Elinor behind and became Nell.

'I will tell everyone exactly who you are and why you're here,' he says evenly.

Chapter Twenty-one

He takes two huge steps so that he's standing right beside me. We glare at each other, both still breathing heavily.

'Tell them what?' I narrow my eyes. 'If I tell everyone that you're in cahoots with whoever is keeping people off the mountain, you'll tell them *what* about me?' I cross my arms firmly in front of me.

'I know who you are,' he says slowly. The wind that has pushed the dark clouds away is swirling round the craggy rocks we're standing on, lifting my hair, wrapping strands of it around my face, and I try to swish my head this way and that to get it out of my eyes. 'I knew from the moment you stepped off that plane who you were. That you were back.'

'So you said. And who exactly am I, Georgios?' I lift my chin.

'You are Stelios's English girlfriend,' he says like he's swallowed vinegar. 'You're Elinor.'

All my nerve endings are standing to attention. It's like the electricity from the storm is still bouncing around between us, buzzing, lighting us up, sizzling as if one of us is about to get burned. 'I am,' I agree cautiously.

'And as I say, you being here will only bring upset. You ran away once before and left him; why not stay away?'

'I never ran away! I gave him time to sort things out . . .' The words catch in my throat. I know exactly who he is now. I can't believe it's taken me so long to work it out. I grit my teeth and try and take control. 'And you were his best friend . . . George.' Carefree, fun-loving, flirtatious George. Ever the party animal, never without a new girl on his arm. Always a smile and a laugh, always the charmer. You'd never know it now. I think back to when he took his hat off, when he smiled at his dog. It was enough to spark a memory. I stare at him again. Unrecognisable as the George I knew eighteen years ago. The George I thought was going to be best man at my wedding.

He and Stelios had worked the resorts together for years: George and his wing man, like Maverick and Goose. When I came along, at first George was unhappy with me for spoiling his fun, but he eventually accepted that Stelios and I were dating and soon we were like the Three Musketeers, going everywhere together: to the beach on days off; late-night bars after our shifts; beach parties where George would work his charm on the newly arrived holidaymakers, just after he'd waved the last girl off. We tutted, rolled our eyes, but that was George, so different from the man beside me now. I can't believe he's known who I am since the day I arrived, and he never said a word.

'Well if you know who I am, and remember how much Stelios meant to me, you'll understand why I want to see . . . see for myself whether leaving here that day was the right thing. You'll understand why I'm back.' I try to breathe more deeply. 'I picked this farm knowing it was near Zeus's Vista. Near Vounoplagia. But I had no idea how close. When

I realised I was just up the road from the Wild Thyme, well. I didn't want to cause any trouble, but I wanted to see him. To know he's happy. To find out why he never came after me. Is that so bad?' Hot, angry tears are blurring my vision and threatening to spill. I carry on with difficulty. 'No one needs to know I'm here, George. Just tell me, was there someone else when I was with him? Is that why he didn't follow me? Was I just a bit on the side, a summer fling?'

Georgios says nothing; just looks down at the ground as if searching for words.

'Ooof!' I puff in exasperation and start off towards the path again, swinging my arms as if they'll propel me faster down the slope.

'Wait!' he calls again, like before, but this time he catches up with me and takes hold of my wrist, stopping me in my tracks. 'You must promise not to say a word.' He raises his eyebrows and looks back towards the cave, and I follow his gaze. 'Not a word,' he repeats.

I can't stop myself; the words are out of my mouth on a tidal wave of injustice. 'What? So that no one finds out what you're really up to?' I think back to the bunches of drying herbs hanging from the ceiling, lit up by the sudden burst of sunlight. Drugs!

'What?' He frowns deeply, his dark thick eyebrows meeting in the middle. 'No! It's complicated. It's not your concern. It's better if you just go home now and stop interfering in things you know nothing about!' He is glaring at me as hard as I'm glaring at him.

'You know exactly who's keeping everyone off the mountain, otherwise how would you know about that cave?

You seemed very at home there. Are they giving you a cut for being the lookout? Keeping an eye out and scaring off anyone who comes this way?' I'm feeling like a ship whose sail has just been filled with wind, catapulting me forwards, unstoppable. 'You know who's scaring everyone off, but now the game's up! Just wait until I tell them all what you're up to. Stelios will put a stop to this, just as soon as I get to see him.'

I march off down the mountainside, no longer putting out a tentative hand to feel my way. I know exactly where I'm going. It's time we all found out the truth.

Chapter Twenty-two

At the gates to the restaurant I straighten up, pull my shoulders back and take a deep breath. I have to get in there. I'm late already. Georgios is beside me. He followed me all the way down the mountain and back to the farm, even driving behind me in his truck as I rode Maria's moped into town. I'm hot, bothered and grubby but determined to finally see Stelios for myself. There is no way Georgios is going to stop me. I flick my pendant inside the neck of my T-shirt and pat it for luck. I can't give myself away yet.

I reach out for the gate handle.

'Nell!' He grabs my elbow and my racing heart thunders even faster, like a young horse pushing towards the finish line in the most important race of its life.

'Let go!' I try and shake him off.

'This isn't a good idea,' he tells me firmly.

'What bit isn't a good idea? Me finding out why Stelios never came after me, never got in touch? Why I meant so little to him, me and his daughter?'

I was sure at the time that leaving was the right thing to do. We'd argued. He'd been surprised, confused by my news. He needed time to think things through. What were his family going to say? But I was stubborn as ever, hot-headed, and told him it was now or never. He was either in this with me or we were over. As he stomped off up the mountain to clear his head, to work out how to tell his family I was pregnant, it was his grandmother who encouraged me to leave. I thought it would give him space to work things out. And if he loved me like he said he did, and like I loved him, he would follow me, wouldn't he?

'He found out about his grandmother telling you to go.' Georgios breaks into my thoughts.

'He knew?' My blood suddenly boils up. '"If you love him, let him go," she told me. "Let him get on with the life he has here in Crete!" and that's what I believed I was doing, giving him the choice, not trapping him. That's why I never tried to contact him. I wanted him to be happy. But he never stood up to his family and told them it was me and the baby he wanted.' I'm raging now. 'My gorgeous daughter is not some kind of dirty secret. I have to speak to Stelios and ask him why he never came to find us.' I reach out and firmly grab the wrought-iron handle with one hand. As I storm through into the courtyard, Georgios turns away, putting his hands over his face in exasperation.

'Hey! You're late!' Yannis is carrying two large jugs of water from behind the bar by the entrance and looking really fed up. He stops in his tracks and looks me up and down. 'Couldn't you clean yourself up a bit?' he says crossly and nods his head in the direction of the ladies'. I glance down at my dusty clothes, still damp in patches, and push a stray lock of hair behind my ear, as if that's going to make me look any smarter.

I take a big gulp of air and look at the table of guests that

Yannis is heading for with the jugs. I haven't seen any of the family since I've been working at the restaurant, what with his mother spending time with her sick sister and his father suffering from arthritis. But here they all are. Stelios's mother, a big-busted woman in black, wearing lots of gold jewellery. Next to her, her grey-haired husband, a full head of curly hair, with a matching long moustache drooping from either side of his mouth, just as he always had. The round woman about the same age as me, sitting next to him, one arm resting on the back of the chair, is Stelios's sister, and perhaps that's her husband juggling a small child on his lap. There are two other children, aged about six and four, and I wonder if either of them are Stelios's; whether they are my daughter's half-siblings. Lastly, the elderly lady at the end of the table, her thin grey hair pulled back into a smart bun: Stelios's grandmother Demetria.

Everyone is there; everyone, that is, except Stelios.

I take another deep breath. '*Kaló apógevma*,' I say, rubbing my sweating palms down my shorts.

'Nell, there are plates to come out,' Yannis snaps, looking at me like I've gone mad, and maybe I have. Stelios isn't here. Maybe he does have a new life, on one of the other islands, or even abroad. Or maybe he'll be here later. My raging temper calms a little.

'Is something wrong, Nell?' Yannis frowns. 'Are you unwell? You look pale.'

I shake my head, the last of the raindrops flying from the ends of my hair. 'I'll just clean up,' I say hoarsely, but as I turn towards the ladies', the gate flies open and in storms Georgios, his face dark and furious.

'So,' he looks around at the table, 'has she told you?'

Yannis frowns again. 'Told us what?' He looks confused and understandably frustrated.

I glare at Georgios. Is he trying to cover his tracks here? Is he frightened what people are going to say about him? Maybe he's going to tell them himself, confess to what he's been up to. I cross my arms again, a habit I seem to have formed around him, defensive and protective, and cock my head to the left.

'Well?' I say.

'Well?' says Yannis, looking from me back to Georgios. 'Will somebody please tell me what's going on? I have my family waiting. Has she told us what?'

Georgios looks at me, rolling his top lip on his bottom one. I nod, waiting for his confession. He turns to the family, looking around at their still, set faces. 'Has she told you who she is?' he says slowly.

My jaw drops open. No confession! He's trying to cause a distraction by throwing me to the lions! 'Never mind who I am!' I say.

Stelios's mother lowers her white napkin and turns to look at me through narrowed eyes. Yannis is shaking his head as if he's walked into a parallel universe. He puts his hands on his slim hips.

I look at each of them in turn as they wait expectantly. They probably have no idea. I was just a young British girl who passed this way eighteen years ago and lost her heart, and who should never have come back to find out where she left it. They won't be in the least bit interested in me. It's Georgios we should be concentrating on!

'My name is Elinor, but everyone calls me Nell. I came to the island when I was eighteen . . .' I gabble.

'So . . .' Stelios's mother is the first to speak as she pats down the napkin in her lap. 'The rumours are true.' They all turn to look at her. 'I had heard there was a British woman with bright red hair in the town. It's you. You're back.'

'I . . . I . . .' I am completely thrown off my stride.

Demetria looks me up and down before turning to her daughter. 'It's her?' she asks in Greek. Stelios's mother nods and puts her hand over her husband's; he seems to have slumped into the cushioned bench and the greenery of plants along the ledge behind him.

My mouth is as dry as sandpaper. I turn back to Georgios, hoping he'll help me out, but he's looking at the ground and I wish it would open up and swallow me whole. It's Yannis who breaks the tension.

Chapter Twenty-three

'Who is she?' Yannis throws his hands in the air in frustration.

'Elinor! The one who broke Stelios's heart,' his sister says loudly, and I feel like a knife has been plunged into my own. 'And you have given her a job?' They all turn and look angrily at Yannis, whose jaw actually drops as he stares at me.

A burning hot flush travels up and round my neck, filling my cheeks and moving down to my earlobes, making them throb. There is something odd going on round here. It's not the same place I left eighteen years ago.

'It's true? You're Elinor? Stelios's Elinor?' Demetria asks slowly, reaching out a hand in my direction as if to touch me, to check that I'm real. I stand still, rooted to the spot. Much as I want to run, my body's having none of it.

'Nell?' Yannis take a huge gulp, realisation washing over him, and steps backwards, waving a hand across his face in something like horror. 'You're not Nell, you're . . . Elinor?' His mouth turns down in a grimace. 'I've heard about you, of course . . . I can't believe I didn't realise!'

'You were very young, Yannis. You were only four or five,' his sister says without taking her eyes off me.

Just wait until I explain myself and tell them what Georgios is actually up to. This is just him trying to throw them off the scent. I have nothing to be ashamed of, I remind myself. I just need to get this over with. I need to tell them about Georgios.

'Look, I didn't mean to cause any fuss,' I say. 'I just wanted to come back. To remember . . . that's all.'

No one says a word. You could hear a pin drop. Why is no one saying anything? Most people just look their exes up on Facebook. Why oh why did I decide to come and see mine in the flesh?

'So,' I swing my arms back and clap my hands in front of me, 'how *is* Stelios?' I try and push out a wide smile, as if I'm an old friend just popping in to say hi, but the lump rising in my throat says otherwise. 'Where's he living?' I look around at them; no one moves. None of the food has been touched. 'Is he married? Childr—' The last word catches in my throat and I try to jolly it out with a laugh that comes out more as a squeak.

Still no one says a word. Finally his mother speaks.

'No, Stelios never married,' she says softly, playing with the napkin in her lap.

My heart suddenly soars upwards, whooping with delight, roaring to life as if it's been resuscitated with paddles by a crash team of doctors. He never married! Maybe, just maybe there's a happy ending waiting out there for me. I've come back to see the only man I ever loved, and I find he's not married. My face breaks into a smile that reaches from ear to ear. I reach for the pendant and pull it out from inside my T-shirt. Yannis stares at it, his hand touching his own. I grip hold of it tightly, feeling it connecting me to Stelios in some way. If there is the slightest possibility of a second chance, I intend to grab hold of that and never let it go either. I shut my eyes and wonder why I didn't do this years ago. All this time I've been sitting at home, playing darts on a Thursday and having a takeaway on a Saturday with Mike, not letting myself think about this place, or about Stelios. Well, not any more. From now on I'm going to make every day count.

I take a deep breath and open my eyes, still holding the pendant. 'So,' I smile, 'where is he? Is he coming today?' I look around, bouncing on the balls of my feet.

Yannis looks from my face to the pendant around my neck again, not letting go of the one around his. I'm going to have a word with Stelios when he gets here, I think, for buying me a two-a-penny love token. I feel myself laughing. It's like I'm eighteen all over again. Who cares if they're two a penny? It's the necklace that's brought me back here . . . back to where I left my heart . . . back to where I belong. Me, Stelios and Demi, together at last. I feel like I could burst with happiness.

'Stelios isn't coming.' It's Georgios who finally speaks. 'I think it would be better if you left,' he adds quietly.

'Oh come on, Georgios, I know you're not happy about me being back, for whatever reason, but I'm not here to steal away your best friend.' I look at Demetria, who is sipping a glass of white wine that Stelios's father has poured for her. Despite the warm Cretan sunshine, the air has turned icy. No one is smiling like I am.

'Look, I just want to say hi, and see how he is, and then I'll go, I promise. I'm not here to cause trouble.' I bite the corner of my lip. Now is not the time to tell them about Demi. I have to speak to Stelios first. We've wasted too many years. I want to meet with him alone. I wonder if the same spark will be there. Will I recognise him straight away? Will it feel like I've come home when I see him?

'Stelios isn't coming,' Georgios repeats hoarsely.

'Well, look, just tell me where he is and perhaps I can swing by,' I suggest, rolling my eyes. I'm starting to get a bit fed up with Georgios's dourness. It's like he's performing some Greek tragedy.

He looks around the table, and then back at me, and when he speaks again, his voice is so quiet that I can hardly hear him.

'Stelios is dead.'

A nervous laugh escapes from my mouth.

Chapter Twenty-four

'Sorry?' I say dumbly, realising I must have misheard him. 'What did you say?'

'Stelios is dead,' Georgios's voice is more gravelly and husky than ever, barely a whisper, but this time I hear him clearly.

'He died in a car accident,' Yannis adds. 'When I was very young.' He holds the pendant around his neck as I am holding mine. 'This is the only thing I have of him. The thing that was dearest to him.'

I swallow and let my brain turn this information over, feeling like the world I know has fallen around me and I'm standing in the ruins, amidst the rising dust, wondering what on earth just happened. I look at Yannis's pendant and try and focus. He puts his hands to the back of his neck and undoes it, holding it up to mine like Cinderella trying on the glass slipper. It's a perfect match, but there's no Prince Charming about to swoop in to carry me off in a carriage. There is no happy ending here at all.

My jaw moves up and down but no sound comes out. There is a whooshing in my ears. My head is light and the brightness from the sun swirls in front of me. I stumble backwards.

'I'm so sorry, I . . . I have to go. Sorry for your loss. Sorry! *Kali . . . kali . . .*' I can't think of the word for goodbye. 'Sorry,' I say again, and I turn and stumble across the courtyard and out through the gates.

As if on autopilot, I climb aboard the moped and drive back to the farm, oblivious of the potholes I'm swerving round and the tree in the road that has caused me so many problems before. Nothing seems real. It's like I've stepped into one of my dreams that's turned into a nightmare and I'm hoping to wake up at any minute.

All this time, whilst I've boxed away my anger, my hurt, my heartbreak, my feeling of betrayal, he wasn't happily living another life; he wasn't living at all! As I pull up in the drive and head straight for my room, the tears that I've kept dammed up for all these years pour down my cheeks, like a tap that's been stuck and now can't be shut off.

Chapter Twenty-five

When I finally make it out of the bathroom, I know exactly what I need to do. I drag my case out from under my bed, unzip it and flip back the lid with more force than is necessary. The case bounces up and down on the bed.

You shouldn't have come! You shouldn't have come! a voice keeps repeating in my head. *I know!* I want to shout back, pressing the heel of my hand to my forehead to try and get it to shut up. I have to leave here, now.

Outside my bedroom door, the cats that usually laze in the shade around the sheltered tables and chairs have gathered to watch with interest, like an episode of *Gogglebox*, as I pick up clothes and throw them into the case, not caring about folding them. I just want to get packed up and get home as fast as I can. No matter how often I brush them away, the tears keep coming. I'm hot and getting hotter, my eyes blurry, like the heat haze rippling through the valley below where the goats are grazing. I can hear the team leader, bell gently clanking as she moves and the others follow. My cheeks are burning and red, maybe from the heat of the day or maybe from my humiliation. I can't believe I could have embarrassed myself and Stelios's family quite so badly. Talk about wading in there with my big feet! My mum was right:

I always was too gobby for my own good. Always sticking my nose in where it wasn't wanted.

Is that what Demi thinks: that I'm interfering in her life? If I hadn't tried to get involved in her business so much, maybe she wouldn't have wanted to leave home so young!

I am under the bed, trying to reach for my left shoe, when I hear the ringing. At first I think it's the goat bell again. Perhaps she's making a bid for freedom up the mountain. But as I squiggle my way from under the bed, I realise it's not the goat at all; it's my laptop, balanced on a wooden crate I found in the barn to use as a bedside table. I've got a Skype call. It's Demi! My heart lifts. I brush at the tears with the sleeves of my shirt, running a finger under each eye and then rubbing my face madly. I'm hoping she'll think my glowing cheeks and nose are just sunburn, and not because I've been crying buckets. I grab a pair of sunglasses to hide my puffy eyes and slide them on. Then, with one big gulp, I press answer.

'Finally! I was just about to hang up.' Demi's fuzzy face starts to come into focus, and at her chippy tone, I can't help but smile.

'Hey! How lovely to hear from you.' I try and speak brightly, but even I can hear there's a slight crack in my voice.

'Mum? You sound funny.'

'Must be a bad line,' I lie.

'Are you wearing sunglasses indoors?'

'It's so hot here, and bright,' I nod, 'I wear them all the time.'

'Are they my old One Direction ones?'

163

'Yes, work a treat.' I clear my throat. 'Now, how's it going? Tell me all the news. How's the job?' I try and drink her in through the tinted plastic in my glasses.

'It's great, really great . . .' Her voice trails off. Why is she ringing? And at this time? My gut instinct is to ask her what's wrong, but I know she'll just say 'nothing' and get cross with me.

'How's work?' I try and keep bright.

'The job's going really well.'

'Well that's good.'

'And the parents . . . really busy . . . They've got really, like, demanding careers, so they depend on me. They've said they couldn't do any of it without me. I'm their saviour.' She seems to be warming up. Maybe I'm worrying about nothing. Maybe it's only my life that's disintegrating, like crumbling feta cheese.

'That's brilliant, darling,' I say, and my heart does a weird rising and dipping. On the one hand I'm pleased and proud to hear it's going well in London, but it means I'll be going home to an empty house.

'What about you? How's the WWOOFing?'

'Well, I've finished cleaning out the honey factory, and I got chased by some angry bees and had to hide in a cave.' I don't tell her that Georgios had to rescue me from the bees. I don't tell her that I've just discovered her birth father is dead.

'Mum? Are you sure you're OK? You seem a bit—'

'Summer cold, that's all! Not used to the climate. Boiling hot in the day, but the temperature drops like a stone at night,' I say, sniffing and rubbing my nose. 'Course, when I was here before, I was down on the coast, not up in the mountains. But that was a long time ago. Everything's changed . . . everything . . .' I feel a catch in my voice and excuse myself to the bathroom. 'Just need to blow my nose,' I say, and stand up stiffly, my legs beginning to ache from the mountain climb.

In the bathroom, I blow my nose loudly, throw cold water on my face and take a deep breath before slapping on another smile and going back into the bedroom.

'Did I tell you about Mitera, Kostas's mother, who keeps losing her . . .' I pause. There's a shadow in the doorway.

'Sorry. I did knock.' Georgios gives a nod. 'You were . . .' He waves a hand at the bathroom. 'May I?' He pushes open the door and steps into the room, whilst his little three-legged dog sees off the nosy cats with a couple of warning woofs and lunges.

Once again, there's that feeling of an impending storm between us, filling the space, the air heavy with expectation and pent-up fury. We stand and stare at each other, neither of us able to break our gaze.

'Mum?' Demi says from the computer. 'You OK? Who's that?'

Georgios snaps his head round, and I make a lunge for the computer and slam it shut, scooping it up and clutching it to my chest.

There is a deafening silence between us. My heart is thundering like I've OD'd on Maria's fabulous coffee. It's getting to be a habit around this man. But I'm pretty sure I got to the computer in time. I don't need to make this any more complicated or upsetting than it already is.

'Who was that?' he says in his usual blunt way, tipping his head towards the computer I'm using like a shield.

I take a deep breath and force myself to look him in the eye. 'My daughter.'

He holds my gaze for a moment and says nothing, then his eyes dart around my bedroom, taking in the case on the bed.

'You were right,' I say. 'I should go. I shouldn't have come.' I don't know what I was thinking coming here. It was a ridiculous idea. I was eighteen when I came before. I'm not that person any more. Stelios is dead. Demi will never meet her birth father. 'I'll be gone as soon as I can. I won't be causing any more trouble for you and Stelios's family,' I reassure him.

'Running away, more like,' he says. His dislike for me is clear, and to be honest, I'd expect nothing less. But then indignation starts rising in me, as it seems to have a habit of doing when I'm around him. Hang on!

'You've been the one telling me I should go all this time! We're finally agreed on something at last. It's for the best.' I grab my nightie from my pillow and sling it into my open case. I can't stay. There are too many memories. I shouldn't have come and opened up wounds that have healed.

'Like last time.' He looks at me. 'You left because it was for the best. You and Stelios rowed, and then you left.'

How dare he? I open my mouth to tell him that I was doing what I thought was best for *everyone*, but no sound comes out. I'm tongue-tied and furious . . . again!

'I'll give you a lift to the airport,' he says, and turns to leave just as Maria appears at the door in her pink slippers and her usual wraparound apron. She is carrying a plate of glistening golden half-moon pastries that I know will be filled with fluffy soft cheese, and a slice of courgette pie made from the glut from the garden. Although I know how good they'll taste, my mouth is like sandpaper and my stomach a knot.

'You missed dinner. I was baking,' she says. 'I brought you some . . . What is this?' She looks at my case, and back at Georgios by the door.

'Nell is leaving,' he says bluntly.

'Oh no, please say it isn't true!' Maria looks at me beseechingly and puts the plate of pastries down on the windowsill. 'You can't leave. How will we cope? You are so good helping us here. Soon the bees will come, I know it. Georgios, tell her she must stay!' She turns to him, hands clasped. Below my window, two of the goats are having an argument, butting heads, each hoping the other will just back off.

'I . . . I really should go. It probably wasn't a good idea for me to come in the first place,' I say, my cheeks burning.

'But what has made you decide this? Don't you like it here, are you unhappy?' Maria is close to tears.

I look out of the window again, to the mountain behind.

'Are you frightened about what's going on up there? Is that it? Have you been scared off too? Will this never end?' Maria picks up her apron and holds it to her face. Georgios shifts uncomfortably.

'I love it here,' I hear myself blurt, as if my heart has just spoken for itself without thinking, and I quickly roll my lips together before it can do it again.

'Then please stay.'

'I can't,' I say, and Georgios narrows his eyes.

'Just until . . . well, until the honey farm is up and running, or until we can find someone else to help, though I'm sure they won't be as good as you. Unless, of course, you need to go home?' she adds quickly. 'Do your family need you?'

I look at the computer, and then at Georgios. What is there for me at home? Demi clearly doesn't need me. She's doing just fine. And with no news on the Christmas decoration factory reopening, I'd be going back to an empty house and no job.

'Please, we need you. Kostas needs you. Just until the bees come back to the mountain, until they are happy once more. And of course, once we take the honey to market, we can start to pay you back for all your work. Say you'll stay.' Maria's cheerful disposition has disappeared, her eyes filling with unshed tears.

Staying on with Maria and Kostas and Mitera has got to be better than going home to nothing, hasn't it? I have loved being here with them. Even if I have to put up with Georgios as a neighbour. I'll just have to make sure I avoid the town . . . especially the restaurant. I can't run away again. Right now, Maria and Kostas need me, and that makes me feel like I have to stay. I need to be needed right now. But can I really stay knowing that Stelios's family think I broke his heart?

Maria looks from Georgios to me. 'Look, I'm not sure what the problem is, but . . . please take tonight, sleep on it.'

'Perhaps Nell,' Georgios emphasises my name, 'should explain who she really is.'

'Who she is?' Maria frowns. 'What do you mean? She's Nell . . . from Wales.'

'She's Elinor . . . Stelios's British girlfriend.'

Her mouth drops open. 'Huh! So it's true. You *are*—'

Before she can say any more, there is a shout from outside, and we all rush out to see Kostas pointing and flapping his arms.

'The bees! See them? A swarm! The hives on the mountain must be overcrowded. They have thrown out the queen and half of her children. They are looking for a new home.'

I watch Maria and Kostas running down towards the hives. They have built this life together. Would Stelios and I have been like them? I wonder. Working together, sticking by each other? If only we had the dittany growing in the field. Then the bees would come to the farm and stay. The honey farm would be up and running. Am I really going to run out on all of this, or am I going to stay and finish what I've started?

Georgios gives me one last stare and turns to leave, past the goats and the herb patch, up through the cows' field to the lane above and his own house. I watch him go. Then I look up at the white peak above. At least while I'm here I still feel close to Stelios. He may not be here in body, but he is here in spirit, and I'm not sure I'm ready to leave him just yet. I gaze at the mountain, and the tears for what might have been sting my eyes.

Chapter Twenty-six

The following morning I am cleaning out the cupboards in the honey factory all over again, getting them ready to be filled with empty jars. The harder I work, the more it seems to distract me from the pain I'm feeling right in the middle of my heart.

'Take a break!' Maria instructs. 'You are working too hard. It is spotless in here. Everything is perfect.' She is holding a tray with a jug of water, a glass and a plate of pastries on it. She is such a caring woman. It is so sad she doesn't have children of her own. She would make a wonderful mum.

I wring out my cloth in the bucket of soapy water and renew my assault on the shelves. 'It's no bother,' I say, scrubbing with all the force my grief and hurt can summon up. I've been up cleaning in here since four a.m., going over the floor and all the surfaces again. My mind just keeps churning over and over what might have been if I hadn't left. What I still don't understand is why he never came after me. I wipe my face with the back of my rubber-gloved hand, hoping that Maria will take my tears for sweat.

As the sun began to rise earlier this morning, I went for a walk along the lower slopes of the mountain. I ended up ringing Angelica, waking her to tell her the truth about

Stelios. That he'd been more than a holiday romance; that he was my one real love and the reason I'd wanted to come back to Crete. Then I texted Demi, telling a white lie, to my shame, and saying my computer had been playing up the night before, which was why we'd been cut off. After that, I came back to the farm and set to work.

'Please, have some water,' Maria implores. My hair is tied back with a bandana, one of Demi's cast-offs from the big bin liner of stuff she gave me to take to the charity shop before she left. It's hot, even in the barn, and I feel myself dip and sway. A hand shoots out and catches me by the elbow, supporting me and guiding me away from the shelves. Usually I'd shake it off, unused to help, but today I'm grateful. My body sags. I've cried and cried, and there's nothing left in me.

'Come up to the terrace,' Maria says. 'Have something to eat and drink.' She guides me outside and back up to the shade of the table and chairs where the cats are in their usual place, lying in the cool. I rub my dirty hands over my face and peel my vest top from my sweaty back. Everything aches, but the physical pain feels good; it distracts me from the anguish I'm feeling. Is it the shock of learning that Stelios is dead that's made me so upset? Or sadness for what might have been? Or the memories I've raked up for his family? My mind is spinning.

'It was quite a day for you yesterday, from what Georgios said. You ran off so quickly from the restaurant.' Maria tops up my glass.

I sip the water and stare down the valley, in between the mountains to the coast, as if watching my past drift out to sea. Maria sits beside me in the shade of the covered terrace.

'Oof,' she says as her bottom lands on the bench. She hardly ever sits down. She's always working.

'I didn't mean to upset anyone,' I find myself stammering.

'So, you and Stelios . . . you were close?' Maria asks, filling her own glass with water. 'I don't get to the crocheting circle much, as you can see. I didn't know there was any talk in the town about you being here until Agatha, from the tablecloth shop . . . well, she thought she remembered, but her memory is a little hazy these days without her mountain tea. "The red-headed girl from the UK," she said. "Stelios's last love."'

I feel my heart swell at that. 'Yes.' I swallow. 'I spent the summer working in the resort down there.' I nod.

'So how does it feel coming back?' She smiles gently.

I look at her, and then back to the sea again. 'In some ways it hasn't changed at all,' I say. 'But then again, in lots of ways it has, if that makes any sense.'

She nods. 'The town . . . it's dying. A bit like its population.' She laughs, and I do too, in surprise at her black humour. 'No one wants to make the effort to go into the mountains any more. The tourists stay in their resorts down by the coast where they have everything they need. All their food, their drinks. When Stelios died, it was like the town died with him. We couldn't even go back up the mountain if we wanted to now, not until whatever is going on up there stops and the people keeping us away leave.'

I think about Georgios, knowing what's going on up there, and feel my shoulders stiffen. The injustice of it all weighs on me.

'Since Stelios died, Yannis has tried to make the restaurant

172

work, but there are no visitors. I think before long he will have to close. I don't think his heart is in it. All the other young people, his friends, moved away a long time ago. And if we can't get the bees to come, and the honey to flow again, then I guess we'll have to move to the city too.' She looks around. 'This is the only thing we have ever known. But without the tourists, without the businesses . . . Vounoplagia, the town, the mountain, it will die.'

We both sip at our water at the same time, lost in our own thoughts. I think of Stelios and how ashamed he would be if he knew what Georgios was doing, ruining his family's livelihood by helping out the gang in the mountains, whoever they might be, creating fear and worry for poor people like Maria and Kostas who don't deserve it.

Maria gets to her feet. 'Would you walk with me down the hill?' She pauses, then says, 'I would like to show you Stelios's shrine, on the roadside, if you'd care to see it.'

I look up at her kind round face as she stands next to me. I feel I have made a real friend here.

'I'd . . . like that very much.' My voice cracks.

As we walk down the hill, I think of how I wobbled and swerved my way down here that first day riding the moped. We stop on the sharp bend. There is a tree clinging to the mountain edge as if for dear life, and I step forward, putting my hand on its trunk, and look over the edge. A few loose stones fall over the edge and tumble, accelerating into the bushy green depths below. Maria grabs hold of my elbow. 'Be careful,' she warns.

Above us I can just see Maria and Kostas's farm and the field of Cretan cows, Georgios's above that, and then the mountaintop where the cave is. I look back at Maria. She is holding her hand out towards the beautiful little wooden house right on the bend. So this is Stelios's shrine. I have passed it so many times driving into town, trying to search him out.

'It is made from the wood of the olive trees,' she tells me, 'by hand.' She opens the front of the beautifully carved shrine and holds out a candle to me, and a wick to light it. I take them from her. Tears fill my eyes again, but this time they stay there; they don't gush like earlier.

The lit wick flicks and flacks in the wind, and Maria holds her hands around it, smiling as I try and light the candle. Finally the little blue flame takes and I place the candle in the box, next to the small picture of Stelios, just as I remember him. I smile at it.

'Thank you,' I whisper to Maria. She nods and smiles.

'So, you will stay on?' she asks quietly.

I feel so connected to Stelios here. I want to talk about my daughter, tell Maria how much she looks like him. But right now I can barely speak.

'Yes, I'll stay,' I manage. There's no question in my mind. I have to finish what I've started. My eyes sting with unshed tears. Maria wipes them with a hanky she's pulled from the front of her apron. I look down and see she is still wearing her slippers, and it makes me smile.

'I want to help,' I say, but what I really mean is that I want to make sure Georgios is stopped.

'We just need the honey to come back to the mountains. Then the town will find happiness again.'

I nod with her, and we gaze down at Vounoplagia below us. I can see the supermarket, the twisting high street, the old school and, if I'm not mistaken, Georgios's truck in the car park. As I watch, he climbs out, his slight limp just evident, and walks towards another car, from which a man gets out to greet him. They shake hands, and then, looking around him warily, Georgios reaches into his pocket and pulls something out. He hands it to the man, who sniffs it and nods. He shakes Georgios's hand, and then both men get back in their cars and drive off in different directions. As if I needed any more convincing that he was up to no good! A sense of injustice stirs within me crossly. Something has to be done.

Later that evening there are gunshots from the mountain again. Rounds and rounds fired off. We all look at each other as we sit around the table, but no one speaks.

Just before we say our goodnights, there's a gentle knock at the farmhouse door. I go to stand to open it, but Mitera is up like Usain Bolt from her chair, sprinting across the room, slipping her teeth in as she goes. It's as if she's expecting someone. She throws back the door and sticks her head out, craning to look left and right. But there's no one there, just a small bundle of dittany tied with a crocheted ribbon. Her shoulders dip with disappointment. Who is this person who leaves the dittany? Why do we never see them? I wonder how long this has been going on. Spitting her teeth back out and putting them in her overall pocket, Mitera hands the bundle to Maria and shuffles off to bed.

I have no idea how, but I mean to put a stop to the goings-on up on the mountain, and I can't leave until it's done, I think, as another round of shots goes off in the distance. I need to find out exactly what Georgios is up to.

Chapter Twenty-seven

The next morning I get up early again and pull on a warm hoodie. It's been another dreadful night where I dreamed of Demi and this time Stelios as well. We were at the burning factory, and no matter how hard I tried, I couldn't reach them to save them. Their outstretched hands were just out of my reach before slipping away. I try and shake off the memory and push myself out into the early-morning mist, low and thick, the greenery covered in heavy dew. I pull back my hair and stuff it into my baseball cap, and slap on sun cream. It may feel cold out here now, but by mid-morning the mist will have burned off and the sun will beat down, despite the north-westerly wind.

After watering the herbs and checking the still-empty hives, I start to make my way back up the hill to the other side of the valley that runs right through the heart of the farm, past the stream, where I fill up my water bottle, and then into the cows' enclosure, where I can cut through to the road above. Georgios's small farm is to the right and the mountain path straight ahead. The cows watch me and start to make their way towards me in a line through the pine trees, nudging and nuzzling me with their soft noses for the dried carob pods that they know I carry.

I smile, and pay special attention to a cow with a boisterous calf at her heels, making sure they both get some of the carob, rubbing them between the ears. The mother looks at me with her big brown eyes as the youngster barges around her back legs.

'None of these little ones come with a handbook!' I tell her, and find myself smiling.

Once my pockets are empty, I push on up to the wire fencing at the top of the field, the wind picking up the orange grit from the dusty road, making it swirl and my eyes sting. I hold my arm over my face. I know now why Georgios wears that scarf. The very thought of him makes my mood darken and my hackles rise.

I undo the string holding the wire panels together and let myself out of the field, retying it tightly. As I look to the right, I notice that Georgios's truck is missing. A sudden thought strikes me. If I want to find out what he's up to, this could be my chance. I could just look around his farm while he's away and – I can't believe I'm thinking it – maybe even his house! My heart jumps into my mouth and a big bass drum starts beating loudly in the space where it used to be. There's no one here but me. If he is one of the men up there with guns, warning people away, there's bound to be some proof of it in his house.

Instead of heading up the worn steps of the mountain path straight ahead, I do one more quick look around, then, with a sudden rush of impetuousness and no further thought, change direction, towards Georgios's house. The big bass drum accompanies me with every step I take.

I pass his goats and sheep in their enclosure – a temporary-looking fence, presumably so they can be moved from spot to spot on the mountainside to take in new grazing. Who'd've thought I'd be getting hands-on with goats and cows instead of reindeer with light-up noses? The place is completely deserted and quiet, and I feel like I'm the only person alive. Which is good, seeing as I don't want anyone to know I'm here. The only sound comes from the eagles circling the mountain peaks and the rustle of the wind in the trees. I take a picture and send it to Gracie and Angelica, and then to Demi. As I do, one of the goats comes inquisitively up to the fence, bleating at me, breaking the silence, probably wondering if I'm going to feed her. Then the sheep on either side of her join in.

'Oh God! No! Ssh!' I say, my heart thundering. I wave my hands at them. 'Please, shush!' I don't want anyone to know I'm here. I thrust my hand into my hoodie pocket and fish out the carob crumbs, throwing them into the pen. Then, as the animals turn away from me and start snaffling the dried scraps, I turn and run, heart still thundering, into the shadows of the small stone house.

In front of the low wooden door, I stop and listen. The house is small but looks to be on two levels. I give a gentle knock and listen again. Hearing nothing, I call, 'Hello?' then put my sweating hand on the wrought-iron handle and give the door a gentle push. It swings open. This is so unlike me, snooping – *breaking in*, a voice in my head says sternly – around someone else's house. But I need to know more. There must be some kind of proof in here that it is Georgios stopping us getting on to the mountain, stopping me from finding and cultivating the dittany plant that could save the honey factory. I know this is madness; I shouldn't be doing it. But the town is suffering. They need help. I can't just stand by and do nothing.

I step down into the dark room and my eyes adjust almost immediately. Inside it's just one room, with a fireplace built into the corner and a small black wood burner. The walls are whitewashed and uneven; it looks like it was once a barn or an animal shelter. There are varnished wooden beams across the ceiling. At the far end is a huge picture window with double doors facing out over the valley and the mountains beyond, which are covered in patches of firs, olive trees and shrubs. A small hand-crafted wooden balcony stretches out over the edge of the mountainside. There's a wrought-iron table and two chairs, and a stone fire pit with a well-used griddle lying over it and burnt-out embers in its belly. It's like a postcard, and for a moment I forget that I'm snooping around somebody else's house – or *breaking in*, as the stern voice reminds me again.

Off and over the kitchen in the corner is a rustic wooden staircase with hand-crafted rails like the ones outside. On the whitewashed walls of the kitchen area there are shelves made from tree branches, whittled and polished. There's a small cooker, and a red coffee pot on top of the stove. I walk around the table, made from wood to match the shelves, olive wood like the walls of Stelios's shrine . . . Stelios's shrine. I still can't believe he's dead. All this time I thought he had a new life, a wife maybe, children, a business. Whilst I have been plodding on, getting on with everyday life, he never even made it out of the starting blocks. The cloak of sadness wraps itself tightly around me again.

By the fire is a little stool, with curls of wood shavings and sawdust around its feet, and an abandoned branch and sandpaper. But that's it. There is nothing else here. I'm going to have to go higher.

I walk over to the staircase and put a foot on the bottom rung. With the fear and trepidation of a trainee tightrope walker, I tentatively climb the next step, and the next, until I can peer up into the big loft room above. There's a bed, a skylight overhead, and, at the end of the room, another picture window and an even more amazing view.

But there's nothing here to tell me what's going on; no clue as to what the gang are up to. I turn back down the steps, and that's when I spot it, on the kitchen worktop. A bird scarer. I've seen one once before, when I spent a summer strawberry picking on a farm in Kent with my nan. It looks like K9 from *Doctor Who*. A box, on legs, with a long tube that fires cartridges intermittently on a timer, making a big bang. On the floor is the gas bottle attached to it. 'Yesss!' leaks out of my lips, and my elbow and clenched fist pull back into my ribs with triumph. This is what I needed to find.

There are no guns frightening people off the mountain. And if I'm right, there is no gang up there either. It's just a bird scarer, backed up by rumours, making it sound like there are armed gunmen on the mountain. It's all a lot of noise, but no teeth! It's Georgios!

Chapter Twenty-eight

Closing the front door quietly behind me, I pull my hat down and, without looking back, march along the wide track behind Georgios's house that leads up the mountain. I've got to find out exactly what he is hiding in that cave where we sheltered from the storm. What was it hanging up in there? What drugs? Cannabis? Or something stronger? As I start to climb, I hear the rumbling of a vehicle out on the road, and I quicken my pace to match the quickening of my heart, hoping it's brave tourists and not Georgios returning.

The path gets steeper, and my boots scatter small stones as I march on purposefully. The early-morning mist is starting to blow off the mountaintop, taking the overnight chill with it, and despite the ever-present wind, the heat of the day is beginning to push through, making my skin tingle. I take off my hoodie, tie it around my waist and take a sip of water. One foot resting on a rock, I pull on Demi's sunglasses and dare myself to look around. I am hundreds of feet up, gazing down at the dark green vegetation at the foot of the mountain. My vision blurs and I turn away quickly, trying to shut out the fear that is telling me to go back down. That it's too high, I could fall. But despite the terror gripping me, I keep moving on. I have to make my way back to that cave.

I'm pretty sure it will provide the key to exactly what's going on here. Because if it's not a drugs gang, or poachers, or badass bandits, if it is just Georgios, what on earth is he up to? It's what Stelios would have wanted, I tell myself, and my heart twists at the thought of him.

There's a barrier at the end of the wide path, secured with a padlock. I duck under it and start clambering up and over the rocks. The sun is fiercely hot now and the wind has picked up on this side of the mountain. In the distance I can hear the faint sound of the bells calling people to church. But the higher I climb, the fainter they get, and the wind seems to be whistling its own tune up here.

I grab at the little shrubs in between the rocks to pull myself up, sometimes wobbling and reaching out for the trunk of the occasional small olive tree. I pray that I'm going in the right direction. I'm beginning to pant, and stop to sip some more water. Mid-swig, I hear it . . . buzzing. I'm on the other side of the plateau to when I was last here, but I'm absolutely going in the right direction. If I remember rightly, the cave is just above me, on the far side of the hives.

I carefully circumnavigate the bees this time, taking silent sideways steps, keeping my eyes on the hives and my back to the rock face until I'm safely round them. If only some of them would come and move into Kostas's new hives on the farm. I push on quickly until I spot the ledge above me, to the side of the worn path. This time, with a huge effort, I get myself up and over it. And then I'm in.

The cave smells damp. I run my hand along the cold, rough wall, heart thundering, then I pull out my phone with shaking hands, switch the torch on and shine it around.

I don't believe it. There's nothing there. Absolutely nothing. Whatever was drying out here, it's gone. He's hidden it. Or sold it. I'm exhausted, and every joint aches. I crouch down on my haunches, feeling like I could weep. He's moved it. Of course he has. He knew I'd come looking. I glance up and see a chink of light coming from the other end of the cave, as if it goes around a bend. Maybe, just maybe I need to keep going. I feel a little blip of hope in my flatlined heart. I still might find what I'm looking for. I stand up, take a deep breath and step forward.

That's when I smell it. It hits me like the hind legs of a goat. Wild thyme. I breathe it in again. The fragrance I remember so well, wrapping itself around me, reminding me of the place I love, the people I love, and exactly why I'm doing this.

'Looking for something?' says a familiar gravelly voice, and I'm stopped in my tracks. I've been caught.

Chapter Twenty-nine

I swing round and glare at Georgios, silhouetted in the mouth of the cave. He's leaning on a thumb stick, his little black and white dog at his feet. 'Where is it?'

His face is set and etched with anger, throwing me for just a moment. How can this be the George that I knew back then? How could Stelios's fun and flirtatious friend have changed so much?

'Where's it all gone?' I repeat. 'Whatever it was you were hiding here?' I take a deep breath, finding my feet again, putting myself back on course. 'I know what you're up to. It's you, isn't it! I know all about it,' I bluff, hoping he'll crack.

'Really?' He walks towards me, a faint smile in his voice. 'Is that why you went to my house and let yourself in? Did you find what you were looking for, seeing as you know what I'm up to?'

I feel like a mouse that's being teased by a cat. For a moment he says nothing and I feel myself squirm. He must have seen me from the road. 'You're the one keeping people off the mountain, aren't you?' I decide to push. I've come too far to back down now. I haven't seen anyone else on this mountain since I've been here. Despite all the rumours and the mysterious night-time gunshots, the *Keep Out* signs and

184

the blocked paths. 'There's no one else, is there?' I challenge him. 'It's just you!'

He lifts his head, hooks his thumbs over his belt and looks at me.

'Is it drugs? Is that what you're up to?'

'Drugs?' He smiles, infuriatingly. 'Look around you, what do you see? I'm not a drug dealer! There are no drugs here.'

'No. But you don't want people on this mountain. Why? What was drying when we were in here sheltering from the thunderstorm? If it wasn't drugs . . .'

And then it hits me like a smack in the face. 'Oh my God! It's dittany. You're dealing dittany! That's why I can't find any for the bees. You've taken it all!'

Georgios's green eyes flash angrily, his mouth set. His chest puffs out as he lifts his head, the scar just showing under his scarf. A muscle twitches furiously in his cheek under the dark stubble.

'So that's it. You're stockpiling it all for yourself. Cleaning up in a disappearing market. Selling to the tourist trade on the coast. Or perhaps you've got other contacts, paying you a high price for a steady supply.' I think of the man in the car park.

He narrows his eyes. 'You know nothing about what's going on up here.'

'I know that you're trying to scare people off the mountain. Well, you don't scare me!' I put my hands on my hips to try and stop them shaking.

'Don't breathe a word of this.' Georgios steps forward. 'You know nothing about what is going on,' he repeats.

'I know enough! Quite some business you must have

going. Well, you can't keep people off the mountain forever. They have every right to be here. Tourists should be allowed to come up here if they want to. Businesses are dying because of you. Family businesses that depend on the income from tourists.' I'm warming to my theme.

'I'm warning you.' He's rattled. 'Don't interfere in things you know nothing about! The sooner you leave, the better.'

I've hit the nail on the head. Georgios really is stockpiling the dittany for himself and selling it to the highest bidder, for a healthy profit. He's the reason this town is on its knees. He's the reason the bees are losing their habitat and we can't save the honey farm. He can't get away with it. People need to know there's nothing to be scared of.

I slide my hand into my pocket and touch the business card that Harry Henderson gave me while I was waitressing for Yannis. I turn it over. We need people to come back to the mountain, and I think I might know how to make it happen.

Chapter Thirty

When I arrive back at the farm, out of breath and hot from stumbling back down the mountain path, putting as much distance as possible between me and Georgios, Mitera asks me to join her at the crochet circle. I'm a little apprehensive about going back to town so soon, but at least Georgios won't follow me there, so I say yes.

Church is over and the women have gathered in the cool of the back room before returning home for lunch. As they crochet, they're discussing the townsfolk's latest ailments. Yannis's father is still suffering with arthritis, and Christina's husband's gout is still bad. All these problems, it seems, were practically unheard of in the community before the dittany disappeared. I bite my tongue. I have an idea how to put a stop to Georgios's little business, but I have to test out my plan first.

The talk quickly turns to Stelios. My presence has obviously caused quite a stir. Agatha from the shop recognised my red hair straight away, she says. It seems that news of my return has spread like wildfire through the town. I was nervous about coming here today, but Mitera insisted I needed to get out and about, and that no good would come of hiding away. At least with her by my side I feel well supported. Mitera, though, looks lost in her own thoughts, as if all this talk of the past has left her weary and melancholy. She is hunched over, barely working at all, just sighing and smoothing the piece of crocheting in her lap.

'Are you OK, Mitera?' I ask. 'Would you like some water? It's a very hot day.' She shakes her head. 'I'm sure everything will get better soon,' I try to reassure her.

'It will only get better when love returns to the mountain,' she says. 'When the dittany – the *erontas* – comes back. We need love to blossom here again.'

'And what about you, Mitera, did anyone ever bring you *erontas*?' I ask with a smile.

At first she is silent, and I wonder if I've offended her. Then she says, wistfully, 'They did . . . once. A long time ago.' She nods and looks back down at her crocheting, a big, intricate cream circle. 'I had hoped they would again one day, but I'm beginning to think it will never happen now.' It's like she's letting go of a dearly held dream.

She tells me how she used to get Kostas crocheting with her in the long dark winter nights, so that by springtime the shops would be full of tablecloths and mats for the tourists to buy. But I don't think her reminiscences are helping to take her mind off things. The honey farm is looking less and less likely to happen. The bees will soon be shutting down for the winter. If they don't come, then Kostas and Maria will have no choice but to leave the farm and move to the city. And what will happen to Mitera then?

Seeing her like this confirms in my own mind that what I am about to do is the right thing. I excuse myself from the group and step out of the cool back room, down the steps and onto the café's outdoor terrace area, where I take out my phone.

Half an hour later, I come outside again to find Harry Henderson sitting on the terrace, looking relaxed under the plane tree wearing expensive sunglasses. His blond hair seems almost white in the bright sunlight. He's wearing neat chinos and a cool linen shirt, and is studying the menu. I suddenly feel very scruffy, having not changed since my scramble down the mountainside. It's becoming a habit. I dust myself down and take a restorative deep breath. I am doing the right thing, I repeat to myself, thinking of Mitera and her big, sad brown eyes.

'Hello, Harry.' I step forward, sticking out a hand. He stands, pushing up his sunglasses to reveal eyes the sapphire blue of the sea. He takes my hand, then leans in and kisses me on the cheek, making me blush like a giddy teenager on a date. When he goes to kiss me on the other cheek, it takes me by surprise, and I feel ridiculously awkward, stumbling forward, stepping on the end of his toe. If he notices, he's too polite to say. I'd forgotten quite how attractive he is.

'I'm really pleased you called,' he says, knocking me off guard. 'I was hoping you would.' Not expecting such a warm welcome, I try to smile and think of something grown-up to say.

'Well, here I am.' I hold up a hand in a little wave. He really is incredibly good-looking. I tuck a stray strand of hair behind my ear in what feels like a vaguely flirtatious way. This would certainly be something to tell Angelica about. A date with a gorgeous man. That would let them all know I really was over Mike. Maybe it would be a way of moving on from Stelios, too.

There is a sadness that keeps filling my heart at the thought that we left each other on such bad terms. Me stomping off to the airport, him up the mountain, both waiting for our heads and the air to clear. But it never did. I keep replaying the final words he said to me, instead of all the things we should have been saying to each other. Both of us too pig-headed to put it right. Well, I'm going to start putting things right now. Hopefully by doing this, the regret will ease. I'm here for Kostas and Maria and Mitera, and for Stelios's family. I'm here to put right the damage Georgios is doing to them all. And if it comes with a date or two with a lovely man, well, why not?

'Please sit down.' Harry pulls out the chair next to him and, still blushing, I sit down quickly before my nerves get the better of me. As I do, I hear a crunch and feel a sharp prod in the backside. My heart sinks. I'd forgotten I'd put my sunglasses in my back pocket. Thankfully, he doesn't seem to notice.

'What can I get you? Would you like a drink? Wine?' He smiles, a wide, friendly smile, making me relax a little. He looks so different from all the other people here in the town. We must stand out a mile, me with my wilful red hair, and him, tall, blond and crisp.

'No, really, just a *kafé*,' I say.

'Oh go on, live a little,' urges Harry. 'Some of the local stuff can be quite good.' He gives me another one of those wide white smiles, and I nod.

'Thank you then, a white wine would be lovely,' and I

glance up at the bored waitress, who puts down her nail file and removes the menu, looking out at the main street as she goes, in the hope that busloads of tourists will start appearing.

The two old men sitting out on the road outside the *kafenio* next door are peeking in at the terrace as though Harry and I are a much-anticipated episode of *EastEnders*. I cast around for some small talk to break the awkward silence.

'It must be hot down there today.' I gesture in the direction of the coastal resort as the waitress puts my glass of wine in front of me, then sits down at a table to study hair extension samples from a box.

'You said you thought it would be good if we met, to talk.' Harry smiles again. 'You said you had some important information for me.' I take a sip of the wine. It has a fortifying effect, and I remember exactly why I'm here and what I need to do.

'You said to ring if I thought I could help you,' I say, feeling myself settle into my stride. It's not a date. It's business. 'You wanted to know more about the area, the mountain . . .' I swallow hard, imagining Georgios's angry, flashing eyes if he could hear me now.

'That's right.'

'Well . . .' I lean forward. 'Look around you. This town really needs an injection. Someone to bring tourists to the area again.'

'It's a totally authentic mountain village.' Harry nods in agreement, his voice a little louder than I would like. The two old men outside the coffee house are still watching us.

'It just needs tourists,' I point out.

'That's what we do. Bring in the punters . . . by the

planeload! Henderson's Holidays is my family's business. We want to move away from overcrowded beach holidays, offer something a bit different; spread our wings into rural and traditional Crete.' He smiles again, and I can't help but think of the plans Stelios had to build his small boutique hotel on the mountainside.

'Well, Vounoplagia could certainly do with some holiday-makers.' I look around at the empty café. The waitress lifts a light pink hair extension from the box on the table in front of her and holds it up to her peroxided head. Out on the main road, an elderly man, wearing a jacket that swamps him and a woolly hat, despite the heat of the day, is herding three goats through the town, two females and a male by the looks of it. The male is wearing a brass bell around its neck on a thick leather collar. The waitress waves a hand half-heartedly, and then checks her nails again.

'But it's a problem getting the locals onside,' Harry says. 'Look what happened the other week. We sold a tour, as a trial, sent some American tourists up here, a trip to an authentic Cretan village. We wanted to show the customers a place where the villagers thrive into old age . . .' At that moment, one of the old men starts coughing and finds he can't stop. His companion pats his back in useless camaraderie. 'Where food is gathered on the mountainside, where wild herbs and honey thrive. But it was a nightmare. They were halfway up the mountain when they were scared off by gunshots. It cost me a fortune in restorative raki and complimentary candlelit dinners. I need to know who's behind it and if it can be stopped.'

I nod, remembering the Americans who had stopped at

the Wild Thyme. Georgios's bird scarer cost Yannis a booking as well.

'The tourists have stayed away for a while. There have been rumours about gangs growing drugs on the mountaintops amongst the olive groves and guarding them with guns.'

He nods. 'I've heard about that. Is this what's going on here?'

I shake my head. It's time I told him. But if Georgios finds out I've revealed what he's up to, he could just move his operation to somewhere else on the mountain. I don't want him to get wind of what I'm doing. I need him to be stopped once and for all.

I take a deep breath. 'It's what people think is going on. It's what someone *wants* people to think is going on.' I take another sip of wine. At that moment, Mitera appears from the stairs to the back room.

'Are you OK, Mitera?'

She nods and tells me she's fine but is going home. She's just tired. I offer her a lift on the moped, but she waves a hand and says she's fine to walk, and I watch her go, more slowly than usual, as if something is weighing on her mind.

'Look.' Harry leans into me, interrupting my thoughts. I can smell his expensive cologne. 'Is there any information you can give me? We don't want to go wading in here without knowing what we're dealing with, but this place could be a gold mine for the tourist trade. Unspoilt Crete and all that. People would pay a fortune to come and stay here.' The man with the goats has stopped to talk to the two old men outside the café. The goats have wandered off and one is now attempting to nose into Harry's man bag. He gives it a gentle nudge with his foot, but it doesn't move. He focuses back on me. 'Look, these rumours about what's going on up there. Are you . . . one of them?'

I'm a bit taken aback and can't help but let a laugh escape. 'No. I work in a Christmas decoration factory!'

'Christmas decoration factory . . .' He nods as if I'm giving him a message in code.

'No, really I do.'

He nods again, slowly, then leans even further forward, his glasses tipping off his head. 'Whatever you can tell me . . .' He reaches for his bag, ignoring the disgruntled goat. 'I can pay,' he says, so quietly that I barely think I've heard him right.

'Oh no. I don't want any money . . .' I shake my head violently, making the round silver table wobble on its single leg. 'I just want to help. Make things better.'

'I see.' But I'm sure he still thinks I'm some kind of gang leader, and given the way I'm dressed – shorts, boots covered in dust, my hands and nails ravaged from constant cleaning – I can see his point.

I take a big breath. 'Look,' I say, 'there are no drug rings or guns up there. It's someone who wants us to think that. He's faking it to keep people away.'

'No drugs?' he repeats slowly. I shake my head, and move very close to him, so we're practically touching. 'It's dittany!' I say, almost in a hiss.

'Dittany?' he frowns.

'Yes. It's a herb, very sought after. But not an illegal one.'

'Dittany . . . I've heard of it. The souvenir shops sell it at the resorts.'

'It's a cure-all. It's what keeps everyone so fit and healthy in these parts, but it's becoming rarer. The local honey used to be made from it, and it has amazing healing powers and a wonderful aromatic flavour. But it's disappearing off the mountains. There's someone picking it, drying it and stockpiling it, then selling it, probably to the shops in the resorts. There are no drug barons with guns up there . . .' I'm about to tell him that it's not a gang at all, just one person, when I hear a voice.

'Hey! *Yassou!*' I jump and turn. It's Maria, her eyes lit up and dancing between the two of us, as if she's discovered love's young dream. 'Can I join you?'

'Of course!' I say, almost too quickly. 'This is,' I clear my throat, 'Harry.'

He stands and shakes her hand.

'Harry was in the restaurant the other day. He works for—'

'Owns,' he corrects with a wide smile.

'Owns a travel company. Henderson's Holidays.'

'Cretan culinary travels and tours.' He finally finishes shaking Maria's hand. Maria, though, is reluctant to let go, like she's found the winning lottery ticket and is determined not to relinquish it, her shiny cheeks beaming.

'Harry wants to branch out, take the tourists away from the coast and up to the mountains,' I explain, still feeling like I've been caught kissing behind the bike shed.

'Welcome, welcome.' Maria is still holding his hand and beaming.

'Well, I'd better get on,' he says, smiling at me. 'You've been really, really helpful. I'm sure we can look into this, get something done about it. Perhaps we could meet again?' He tugs discreetly at his right hand, which Maria is still holding.

'Yes, no problem,' I say, feeling flustered and blushing, much to my annoyance.

'It's been great meeting you.' He smiles at Maria and then gives his hand one final big tug, freeing it.

'Come again. Bring your holidaymakers,' Maria calls after him as he leaves some notes on the table, far more than the cost of our drinks. Brand-new notes, fluttering in the breeze under the white ashtray.

'What a lovely man!' Maria is still beaming from ear to ear and looking at me as if hoping I'm going to fill her in on all sorts of exciting details.

'Erm, yes . . .' I mutter. I watch as Harry gets into his new, shiny hire car. Just as he shuts the door, the goat takes a run-up and butts it, leaving a slight dent. Harry looks on in horror as the goat steps back and does it again. Before it can have a third go, he spins the wheels and drives off at speed, the dents in the door making it look far more like a local's vehicle.

'So . . . you managed to find one of the few available men in the area for yourself.' Maria smiles and orders mountain tea, but the waitress shakes her head and shrugs. 'Run out.'

'When did things become like this?' Maria tuts. 'No mountain tea! No wonder the community is getting ill. Still,' she smiles, 'they'll start to feel better if they know that nice young man of yours is going to bring tourists back to the town. We have all been waiting for this.' Her big bosoms rise like fluffy pillows under her sleeveless top and thin cardigan, and she nudges me playfully.

'He's not my young man,' I nudge her playfully back, 'yet,' and we both laugh. I'm going to make sure I do everything I can to help Harry bring his holidaymakers to the town. Feeling that a small celebration is in order, I turn to the waitress and order us two white wines. As the ladies finish their crocheting for the day and trail out from the back room of the café behind us, Maria and I chink glasses and smile at each other. Everything is about to change for the better.

Chapter Thirty-one

Kostas is standing in the doorway as we swing into the drive, me clinging on to Maria at the back of the moped for fear of slipping off, my legs sticking out either side of the bike. He's holding back the insect screen from in front of the door, waving his arms like a windmill as we pull up.

'It's Mitera! She went to bed as soon as she got back from town. Says she's unwell.'

'In bed! Unwell?' Maria flicks down the stand and is pulling off her helmet. 'Mitera never goes to bed in the day!'

'I know. She must be very sick.' Kostas drops his head and shakes it from side to side in big swinging movements. I'm worried he's about to burst into tears.

'Oh Kostas.' I put an arm around his shoulders. 'I'm sure she'll be fine. Probably just tired. It has been very hot.' I fan my face and hold it to the breeze, always happier to be back here further up the mountain with the cooling wind.

He lifts his head and looks straight at me with his big sad eyes. 'Maria's right. Mitera never goes to bed in the day. She hasn't even had lunch!' From the look on his face, I can tell that he's really worried. How much more can these poor people take? Once they had a thriving business, a small farm where they could feed themselves from what grew on the mountainside. They were a happy little family. Now there is no honey factory any more, Kostas is still recovering from his bee stings, Maria is exhausted, and now this! Mitera falling ill.

Suddenly I know what I can do. I know exactly what ... and where! 'Wait there! I'll be back.' I grab my hat from my bag, which I then sling across me, and stomp off towards the mountain path. I'm determined to get this family back on its feet, and nothing and nobody is going to stop me.

Chapter Thirty-two

The wind has picked up considerably and the sky has darkened, but I know exactly where I'm going this time. Somewhere around that cave the dittany must still be growing, and I intend to find it and bring it back. I march up through the cows' enclosure, then scramble up the rock incline to the fence and out on to the dusty lane. As I take the worn steps up the mountain, I can make out the smell of wild thyme riding on the wind, drawing me onwards.

Once I'm past the landslide, I begin to look for small plants with pinky-purple flowers. As I search, I can't help but turn around and look out towards the sea. Being able to see back to my past seems to give me strength, as if Stelios is willing me on. I take another scan around my feet and the rock ledges either side of me. There's nothing here. I am about to push on when I see him. Just below, with his sheep. His little black and white dog spots me first and I try to move off quickly before it sends up the alarm. But too late, it sees me and starts to bark. I just hope Georgios hasn't noticed me.

I keep moving up the mountain, more quickly now, my heart thumping, my mouth dry, feet and legs tingling with trepidation. But I'm not going to be put off. I reach out and up, using the rocks to help me. But now I feel like I'm being followed. I don't stop. I don't turn around, but I know he's coming up behind me. I reach the plateau with the hives, where the bees are murmuring to themselves, and clamber up the final ledge towards the cave. I have to get there before Georgios stops me.

Chapter Thirty-three

I reach the cave unhindered and switch on the torch on my phone, hoping to find a small sprig of plant left behind to take to Mitera. I'm scanning the floor when a dog's bark makes me jump.

'You again!' Georgios is standing in the mouth of the cave, just like last time. He is breathing heavily, whilst I am taking great gulps, exhausted from my dash up here and now drained and disappointed. I bend over and clutch my knees.

'Where is it?' I suddenly flare, straightening myself up. This can't all have been for nothing. 'I know it was here. There must be just a tiny bit left. I need it! Just one sprig for Mitera. You've sold it all, haven't you?' I'm struggling to catch my breath and it comes out sounding like a sob.

'Sold it?' he frowns, pulling down the scarf covering his face.

'You know what I'm talking about! The dittany!' I glare at him. 'I saw you! With a man! Exchanging the goods! I was at Stelios's shrine.'

He steps into the cave, his broad shoulders practically filling the mouth of it. Instinctively, I move back, tripping and nearly falling over the round pit where he lit the fire when we sheltered here from the storm . . . when this cave was full of drying dittany. If only I'd realised then what it was, but I don't know one drying drug or herb from another. I look back at him. This man has a strange effect on me. I'm not scared of him, but he makes me feel . . . unsettled, and I don't know why. I can't read him.

Suddenly he throws his head back and laughs. 'You think I'm selling it . . . First you think I'm a drugs dealer, and now I'm a one-man trader in dittany!'

'Well you won't be much longer. Very soon this place will be heaving with tourists again. It'll be full of people enjoying the mountain and holidaying here. I know exactly what your game is: you're a one-man band with a bird scarer! It's over. I've made sure of that.'

'What? What are you talking about?'

We stare at each other, like two gods coming out of their caves to claim ownership of what they both believe is rightfully theirs. But do gods' hearts thunder like mine is doing? I wonder.

'Maybe if you'd just asked me, I could have told you.'

'What?' I'm thrown for a moment, and I know that's what his intention is. 'Well, I'm asking you now! Where's the dittany? Have you sold it all?'

He turns away and sighs.

'Have you got any more? I just want a plant or two. For the honey farm. And for Mitera. She needs it . . .' I look around the floor, kicking at it with my boot toe. Still he says nothing, infuriating me. 'The townspeople have as much right to this mountain, and the dittany, as you do. Businesses have a right to be here! The young people are all moving away. Once the old people are gone, there will be nothing left at all.' I glare at him. 'Is this what Stelios would have wanted?'

'What did you mean when you said that there are tourists on their way?' He looks rattled, and I feel a small leap of satisfaction in my tummy.

'You'll find out. I'm not saying anything . . . not until I have a dittany plant to take back.'

'The bees won't come,' he says, losing patience. 'Please, you must go back down now.' He holds out a large hand.

'If I can plant it in amongst Kostas's other herbs, they will come, and the honey farm will start up again. There'll be dittany honey for everyone.'

'You don't understand . . .'

The clouds move overhead and a shaft of light peeps through from the other end of the cave, where I saw it last time. The smell of herbs is suddenly strong, as a blast of wind sweeps through. It must mean something. I turn and glance at Georgios, and then back at the light. There's definitely something there he doesn't want me to see. Well, I'm not going to be put off that easily. I may be a lot of things – a bit slow when it comes to realising that my partner's having an affair, a bit naive for thinking I could come here and find the love of my life, a bit lost without my daughter – but I am a loyal friend and will defend those I care about.

'If you don't tell me what's going on, I'll find out for myself!' I say.

His face darkens. I start stepping backwards, further into the cave. 'No! It's not safe!' He reaches out his hand to me. 'Come back!'

But I don't. Instead I turn my head to the far end of the

cave, towards the shaft of light and the smell of wild herbs.

'Oof! What is it with you? Why must you do the opposite to what is right!' He throws his hands up in the air.

I find myself smiling. This must be it, the place he's been trying to keep from me. I've done it. I knew he was hiding something. I turn and make a dash for the back of the cave.

'No!' he shouts. But it's too late.

There's an opening, an arch, leading towards the light. I go through it, throwing myself around the corner, reaching out to clutch the wall of the cave. Then all at once my heart leaps into my mouth and I skid to a halt, and only just in time.

Chapter Thirty-four

I'm teetering on the edge of a massive, head-spinning drop, my big toes hanging over the rocky lip. My hands fly backwards, looking for something to hang on to, and Georgios grasps hold of one of them, whilst I catch my breath. My head swims. It's like I'm standing at the opening of an aeroplane, thousands of feet up, ready to leap out into the green gorge below, the big blue sky above me.

'What is this place?' I say slowly. Below me is a deep, wide verdant valley, bushes and trees divided by the trickle of liquid mercury that is the river running through it. There are butterflies and, if I'm not mistaken, the odd bee moving from plant to plant. It's like I've stepped through the back of the wardrobe and into Narnia. Only I actually ran through the back of a cave.

I look around at the plants clinging to the craggy rock face to my right, just above a jutting plateau; soft fuzzy leaves, arching stems, pale pinkish-purple flowers . . . I turn to Georgios. 'I'm no expert, but I'd say that's dittany!'

We both look at the purple-tipped leaves on the little plants.

'It thrives well here in this gorge, where it's shady and where the moisture is trapped,' he says wearily, as if gutted his secret has finally been discovered.

'Who else knows about this place?'

'It's been a well-kept secret . . . until now.' He scowls at me.

It's like nowhere else I've seen on the mountain. Nowhere else I've seen ever, come to think about it. A pair of butterflies flutter past in front of my face, making me smile. The smell of the dittany is so strong, warm, fragrant, lemony, I almost forget my fear of heights, as if I've stepped into another world, leaving everyday life behind.

'It reminds me of how the mountain *used* to smell,' I say, not really realising I'm saying it out loud. 'This is the smell that I remember from my first time in Crete, when I visited this mountain. It reminds me of Stelios.' *And everything that happened then*. I close my eyes and let the scent wash over me.

'Well, now you've seen it, it's best you go.' Georgios's voice breaks into my thoughts, and I open my eyes to find myself staring straight at a dittany plant, almost within touching distance on the rock wall to my right. I tentatively reach out towards it.

'No!' Georgios puts a hand on my shoulder. I stiffen, thinking about him gathering the dittany, drying it, doing his deals, whilst other people can't get any. I think of Mitera and Kostas and Maria and the honey farm and am overwhelmed by a sense of injustice and urgency.

'I told you, just a plant or two at the farm will entice the bees.' I turn to look at him, and then back at the dittany, reaching out a little further this time. The gap is wider than I first thought, but I'm not going to lose face in front of him. He doesn't think I can do this. There's a ledge and I'm sure I can reach it. I stretch, testing the water, and when I realise I can make it, I grab hold of a rock and tentatively reach out a foot. If I can just climb on to the ledge and shimmy along, I should be able to reach that clump. With three or four little bounces I get ready to throw myself across.

'No!' Georgios shouts.

'You just don't want anyone else to have it!' I reply angrily.

'Come back,' Georgios shouts again, just as I take a deep breath and throw my weight forward on to the rocky ledge. *Made it!* I think, biting my lower lip and finding myself smiling at the same time. Kostas and Maria and Mitera need me to do this, and I'm blooming well going to.

Chapter Thirty-five

Holding my palms flat against the rock face, I hold my breath and step sideways over a small gap to another stony ledge. This one is more of a narrow shelf of rock hugging the side of the mountain, with a sheer drop to the valley below. I turn to the mountain face and press my tummy against it so as not to have to look down, and start to make my way along the ledge. I have to reach the dittany plant. I just need to shuffle along a little bit further. I grab hold of a rock and use it to hang on as I sidestep along. Clearly it's a well-trodden route. By Georgios, no doubt. I move along again, belly to the rock face, shuffle shuffle, slowly. Just then my foot slips on a loose bit of rock. My heart thunders and I stupidly glance down at the valley behind me. I catch my breath and cling on for grim death.

'Oh Jesus Christ!' I hear Georgios behind me at the cave entrance, huffing and puffing, making me even more determined to carry on. 'This is madness. Just come back and I'll get the dittany for you,' he calls over the wind whistling through the gorge, but I'm nearly there and the last thing I want is to let him see I can't do it. I hold on tightly with one hand and smile as I reach up for the purple-tipped plant.

'Don't take it from the root! It'll never grow back,' he

shouts behind me, and I roll my eyes but make sure I do what he says. Breaking off some of the stems, I pull my hand back and put them safely in the bag on my hip, and find I'm beaming from ear to ear. Yes! Get in! I think to myself. If I wasn't on a rocky ledge above a deep gorge, I'd do a fist pump. I look up and see another plant, just a bit higher up the slope. I could get that too, I'm sure. I really need to do this for Maria and Kostas. It's my way of looking after them like they've looked after me.

With renewed confidence, I start to climb, slowly and steadily, until finally I can reach out and gather the second plant – picking only the stems and leaving the root, of course. I don't turn round. I'm doing fine. I don't want to see Georgios's glowering face, putting me off. Plus, although it's a bit late in the day to be reminding myself of this, I'm not great with heights. I don't even really like the big wheel at Winter Wonderland. If I just keep facing the rocks, I'll be fine.

I can see another big bunch to my left. If I can get to that plant too, I should have a good bunch to take back. The bees are sure to start moving down the mountain, and in no time we'll have honey to share. I reach and look up, and suddenly I'm blinded by bright sunlight, pouring into the gorge as the sun slowly starts to set. My foot slips, and I desperately scrabble for a foothold.

'Oh God! Hel—' But I can't finish the word. Fear grips me tightly. My fingers ache as they clutch the rocks. My foot is working in tiny movements to find support, whilst my other leg aches too. My hand slips and my face screws up in fear. I can't do it. I can't find a foothold. I can't look round or down. I'm going to fall.

Suddenly he's behind me. His arms over mine, his body pushing mine against the hard wall. His hot breath on my neck melting the fear from around my throat, making me feel suddenly safe. But as the terror subsides, my racing heart and body feel like I've stuck my fingers into an electrical socket in the rain.

'Put your foot on mine, I will guide you,' he says evenly, and I do as he says, without question. 'You are undoubtedly one of the most infuriating women I have ever met. Why would you put yourself in such danger?'

I can't reply.

'Who else is going to give me the runaround, drive me insane with her mad ideas about bringing the dittany down to the farm, if you slip and fall?' he chides, and he lifts my foot with his and I don't resist, letting him guide it to a rock just a little further to the left. As it comes to rest, I move my hands back on to the rocks they were slipping from. I'm waiting for my racing heart to subside, but it doesn't. He's still there, his body covering mine and his breath on my neck.

'Thank you,' I manage, and it comes out as a sort of croak. 'I think I'll be OK from here.'

'Up there,' he nods to a ledge, 'keep going up. You'll be safe.'

'No, I think I should just go back.' I shake my head, all my confidence ebbing away. I feel like a child stuck halfway up the ladder of the big slide, too scared to go up or down.

'Keep moving up, it will be safer. Just reach there and catch your breath. Get your strength back.'

'No, I don't think I can. I'd be better going back.'

'It is never a good idea to go back,' he says clearly in my ear, despite the wind whipping round us.

I turn slowly to look at him, his face close to mine. I can see the old George under his hat, under his unshaven cheeks, and that scar is so much clearer now. I want to ask him how he got it. What happened to him? What changed him from the friendly, outgoing George I used to know? I feel as if all my strength has gone, like someone let the air out of the balloon. I turn back from him to look at the ledge, but as I do, I catch sight of the deep valley below me and I feel sick. Tears begin to sting and spill from my eyes, sliding down my cheeks.

'Go up, keep going forward,' he says, his forest-green eyes staring into mine, so close I can see the gold flecks and black circles around them. How can I tell him? I can't go forward, just as I haven't been able to move forward since I left this place where Stelios and I parted. I'm completely stuck.

Chapter Thirty-six

'Let me guide you,' Georgios says in my ear as we both lean against the rock face. I try not to think about how high up we are, or that Georgios is covering my body with his, because I'll freeze with fear. 'Just a bit further and you'll be there.' He nods to a ledge above, but still I'm stuck to the spot. 'Here, this hand here.' He puts his hand over mine. It's big and rough. Not like Mike's, I find myself thinking. He had small, smooth hands, as if he hadn't done a day's manual work ever.

Georgios grips my hand and tugs at it, but I'm not letting go of the rock. He tugs again, firmer this time

'No, gerroff,' I hear myself muttering petulantly, until he finally prises my hand from the rock it's clinging to. Despite my protestations, he reaches for my other hand and does the same. I am useless. Like a newborn baby. He lifts my foot with his, his body pressing against mine, protecting me from the prospect of falling, but still I can't move, despite my gung-ho confidence earlier. I'm tongue-tied, but all over my body. I can't move or string a sentence together, fear gripping me like a python. Only it's not a python coiled around me, it's Georgios, his breath on my neck, his lips next to my ear.

He starts to move my useless body up the rock wall. He leads, I follow.

'Now here . . . we're nearly there, just reach out . . .' We move towards the ledge. 'I can't help you on this bit. You need to pull yourself up on your own,' he says, firmly but the harshness all but gone from his voice.

I shake my head.

'You can do it. You got yourself out here. Remember how it felt before you felt the fear. Remember it and use it. Think of something that means everything to you and use it.'

'Only an idiot would put their life on the line like this . . .' I mutter.

'You must have been told. Dittany only grows in the most inaccessible places. Men have died trying to bring it to their loved ones. That's why it's the biggest show of love a man can make for his woman. To risk everything for this . . . it is true love.'

'That's why I wanted to take some back to the farm. To cultivate and grow it so the bees will come where they're needed.'

'Sadly,' Georgios takes a deep breath, 'the dittany will not be tamed. Many people have tried to cultivate it, but it does not have the same medicinal properties when grown in towns or farms; only in the wild, up high.'

'What?' I can't believe what I'm hearing. 'You mean it's all been for nothing? It won't grow if I take it down to the farm?'

'It will grow, but not the in same way. It will not have the same health benefits if we cultivate it.'

'Why didn't someone . . . why didn't you tell me?' Angry, frustrated tears prickle my eyes.

'Would you have listened if I had? I tried to stop you.'

'Oh for God's sake!' I could kick myself, if it were physically possible.

'The bees will come in their own time, when they start to thrive here. I put the hives up on the plateau when I discovered wild hives in the trees. I moved the bees into them to help them breed. When they get crowded, they will look for new homes close by, hopefully at Maria and Kostas's honey farm. They will find the dittany for themselves, seek it out. And if the bees do their job well, the dittany will flower and thrive too and hopefully start to work its way down the mountain. So . . . listen to me. Think and focus. Think of something or someone that means everything to you.'

He's right. I got myself into this mess. And him! I have to try and get us out of it. Shaking, but this time remembering not to look down, pushing away the images that keep trying to muscle in and make my head swim – the drop below me, the river at the bottom of the gorge like a snail's trail – I take a huge breath and think of Demi. My daughter, who I love. And in seeing her face, I see Stelios, as I do every day when I look at her. What would she think if she saw me like this? What if I wasn't there to protect her? My nightmares swirl in amongst my thoughts. She only has me! What if she needed me and I wasn't there for her . . . dead on a mountainside because of my own stubbornness? Suddenly I feel a surge of . . . something, I don't know what: maternal protectiveness maybe? I need to get to safety to be there for her. I can feel the urge building inside me as I look up and focus on the ledge above me. Throwing myself forward with more force than I thought possible, grabbing at rocks and tufts, scrambling, running, I launch myself up and over the ledge.

'Yes!' But as I stand and roar in triumph, I hear rocks falling in my wake and suddenly a shout and a tumble. And my euphoria evaporates like mist from a windscreen, and my blood runs cold.

I throw myself to the dusty ground and peer over the edge to see Georgios lying on the narrow stony ledge below, blood seeping from a cut above his eye, under the rim of his hat. Rocks are still falling all around him from the little landslide I created.

'Georgios!' I shout, but he doesn't respond, slumped against the rock face.

Chapter Thirty-seven

'Georgios!' I shout again. 'Wake up! You have to wake up!' The sun beats down on my neck, burning, punishing me. I wriggle forward on my tummy until my chest is resting on the ledge. Just don't look down! I tell myself. But how can I not?

'Georgios!' I shout again, but he doesn't reply. It's no good; there is only one thing for it. I'm going to have to go back down. I swing my legs round and sit on the ledge, my vision dipping and diving as I look down at the valley below and the rocks still tumbling down the mountainside, picking up more and more companions on the way.

I take a deep breath and begin to slide down on my bottom, but this just makes more loose rocks fall. I stop, turn around and start to descend slowly backwards. Finally I reach out a hand and can grab hold of Georgios's.

'Come on, Georgios, come on.' I tug at him but he doesn't move. How the hell am I going to get him off this mountainside, and even then what am I going to do with him? An air ambulance will never be able to land in this place. I look back up the slope. I have to think how to get him up there. I put my arm round his middle and try to pull him, but I'm terrified that if I pull too hard we'll both fall backwards and follow the stones I sent tumbling.

'Georgios, wake up. You're in the gorge. The secret one with the dittany. I . . . you helped me. But now I have to get you up to that ledge,' I say urgently, hoping he'll snap into life, but although he murmurs something in response, he's still drowsy. Blood is trickling over his eye and down his cheek. I dab at it with my sleeve. I wonder if I could leave to get help. But anything could happen while I'm away. This is Stelios's best friend lying here injured. I have to try and put right the mess I've caused, and there is only one way I'm going to be able to do that. I have to remember the things he said to me.

I step around him, and this time it's me that guides him up the rock wall. He may not be making much sense, but he is responding to my instructions as I guide him to his feet, gently and slowly, talking to him all the time, trying to keep him from falling back into unconsciousness. I look again at his familiar face, and at the scar that travels up from his neck to his cheek under the stubble. 'Left foot up,' I tell him. I take a deep breath and lift his foot, and he lets me guide him, but from the expression on his face, his leg is paining him. All the anger of earlier has gone. Now we're fighting for survival, and my heart is beating in terror. But I've been scared so many times before, as a parent, on my own, not knowing what to do for the best, sometimes getting it right, sometimes getting it really wrong. And I just had to keep trying. I was all Demi had, and right now, I'm all Georgios has got, whether either of us likes it or not.

'Come on, Georgios, stay awake,' I say, watching his head starting to nod again. 'Just a few more moves.' I'm puffing as we reach the ledge, my muscles aching. I get him to the lip, then I reach round him and pull myself up, gently this time so as not to disturb any more rocks. Lying on my tummy, I grab hold of the old olive tree, which creaks and groans and cracks, and reach down to drag him up, heaving and calling to him.

In fairness he makes every effort to help me, and finally we do it. Out of breath and exhausted, dusty and hot, but we do it. He's lying on the rocky outreach. I look around. Now what? I wonder.

'There's shelter,' he says weakly, as if reading my thoughts. 'A cave. There . . .' He vaguely rolls his head upwards. A second cave here inside the secret valley, I realise.

'OK, let's get you to your feet.' I scramble up and, using the groaning olive tree for support again, help him to stand, slinging his arm round my neck and putting mine around his waist for support. I can smell him as he leans on me, dusty yet pine fresh, like the conifers further down the mountain, around the cows. I think that will be one of my all-time favourite smells when I leave here. I look around. We are so high up now, I think I might actually be knocking on heaven's door. I realise how far away I am from Kostas and Maria's farm, the town, the coast road and home. A very long way indeed.

The wind blows the rocky dust around, lifting the ends of my hair, filling my head with the lemony smell of the dittany and the fragrance of other herbs – thyme, oregano, marjoram, like a heady cocktail.

'Over there.' He manages to point, and I narrow my eyes to see the opening of another cave a little way above us. I push off from the olive tree, which gives one last groan and actually keels over behind me, hitting the ground with a swish of dried leaves, and turn towards the cave, shivering with fear and exhaustion. Georgios is limping, practically dragging his leg, but together, arm in arm, we make it to the dark opening. I wish there was a light switch. I will never take electricity for granted again, I vow to whoever might be listening, if I can just get out of this alive. And I will never go up another mountain again either. We step inside the cave and I lean Georgios against the wall, where he slumps and slides down. I'm not quite sure what to do now. But if this was Demi or one of her friends, and not someone I was running away from only an hour or so ago, I'd do this . . .

I reach out tentatively and untie the scarf from around his neck, then gently pull it off, revealing his scar. I lift off his hat and put it beside him, then dab at the cut over his eye with the scarf. I wonder if there's any water around here. I stand up and look out from the cave mouth. There's a stream, clear water tumbling over the rocks, through the greenery, fast and furious. Not like the trickle back down at the farm. I run the scarf under it and wring it out. Then I get my water bottle from my bag and fill that up too. Putting my cupped hands back into the flow, I take a drink and then splash icy water over my face. Maybe I'm hoping it'll wake me up from this nightmare, where I'm stuck up a mountain, a really high one, with a man who can't stand the sight of me.

I take a deep, restorative breath of the heady air around me and go back into the cave. Georgios is leaning against the wall, his hat by his side. I hold the damp scarf to the cut above his eye, which is now swollen as well as bleeding, and hope it will stem the blood. Because if it doesn't, I have no idea what to do. I unscrew the lid of my water bottle and hold it to his dry and dusty lips. Some goes into his mouth, but most of it trickles down his chin, through the dark stubble and around the scar. If I could just find a cup to help him drink from . . . I wonder if there's anything useful in here, like in the other cave. Maybe a fire I could light. Some raki wouldn't go amiss right now either.

I pull out my phone and turn on the torch, shining the light up and around and then to the back of the cave. A scream catches in my throat at the image staring back at me from the shadows. The sound brings Georgios round, his eyes suddenly wide, looking from side to side, bewildered.

'What the hell is this place?' I say.

He slowly takes the scarf away from his head and seems to come round more fully, sitting up straight as if he's been woken from a deep sleep to discover he's in a completely foreign land. Then he sees what I'm staring at and, realising there's no immediate danger, slumps back against the rough stone wall, returning the scarf to his bleeding head.

'Georgios . . . what the hell is this?' I repeat, looking back up at the pictures staring down at me. One of Stelios smiling, and next to it, one of Georgios. Lying in front of them, a little bunch of dittany, tied with the crocheted ribbon that I've come to recognise. There's a cluster of candles, too. At the back of the cave there is an even bigger pile of dried dittany.

'I think you'd better tell me what is actually going on!'

But as I turn back to Georgios, I see that he has slumped down again and seems to have slipped back into uncon-sciousness.

Chapter Thirty-eight

Telling myself not to panic, I check the screen of my phone.

'What are the chances of me getting help?' I say out loud, not really knowing who to call. Maria maybe? She'd know what to do. Maria is one of life's copers. I hold the phone up as high as I can and wait for the appearance of just one little triangular bar.

As I thought: up here . . . no signal. I slap the cover shut and for a moment wonder what I'll do if Demi is trying to ring, but as her phone calls, texts and Skype calls have become as rare as hen's teeth, I probably don't have to worry on that front. She's doing her thing, she's happy. Whereas I . . . I need help and I don't know how to get it. I'm not a trained nurse. I'm not even the first aider on the factory floor . . . that's Angelica. I'm just a mum who works in a factory and has developed a knack for picking greens and cleaning. I rely on my phone for everything these days. And now I have no idea what to do.

I take the scarf and go back to the stream, rinsing it and wringing it out again. I look up to see two eagles circling, so close it feels like I could reach out and touch them. Huge birds, with massive wingspans, managing something that looks like it should be impossible, flying around the rocky peak, casting shadows over the rocks below. Gritting my teeth, determined not to give up, I go back to the cave. The water from the stream is ice cold. With shaking fingers, I crouch down and hold the scarf over Georgios's eye again. Just then, a gust of wind whips into the mouth of the cave, bringing with it the strong smell of wild thyme and dittany, wrapping itself around me in one of its reassuring hugs, and I breathe in deeply, taking strength from it. I can do this, I tell myself.

I have to get us warm, make a fire and boil up some of the dittany from that big pile. I'll put some on the wound above his eye and make some tea too. Everyone's always telling me how restorative it is, a cure-all. Let's hope they're right.

I look around. There are matches on the stone shelf by the pictures. I pick them up and strike one, putting the flame to the candles there. The orange light illuminates the faces in the pictures, and I catch my breath again. It all feels very surreal, like I'm standing in front of a shrine. I look up at Stelios's smiling face, just as I remember it, and next to it, Georgios. But if this is a shrine, why is there a picture of Georgios? Georgios isn't dead. I glance round at him slumped against the cave wall, holding his scarf to his head, then back at the pictures, and wonder whether to just snuff the candles out, but I need the light, I tell myself sensibly, and quickly turn away from the pictures and start searching.

I find a cup and a billy can – well, I'm guessing that's what it is: a tin pot with a handle. It's on a stone shelf next to the drying dittany. Someone obviously comes up here a lot. It's smaller and more homely than the other cave, I find myself thinking, and then realise how doolally I'm sounding, comparing caves like I'm browsing through Rightmove on my computer. I go out to the stream to fill the billy can with water. This cave has an outside waterfall, I hear myself saying, as if I'm an estate agent. The mountain air is sending me round the bend! Or maybe it's just my way of dealing with the situation: up a very high mountain, on the edge of a gorge, with a wounded man and no idea how long we'll have to stay here.

Having filled the billy can, I take a moment to look around. I wonder if I can see down to the farm. I wonder if there's a way of getting Maria's attention. But the valley is well hidden, which is why it's stayed a secret for so long. I look up to the cave roof. If I could get up there . . . I put down the can and scramble up, and then a little higher. From there I can see down to the road, the farm, and Vounoplagia like a toy town below it. I try and see if I can spot Maria, but there's no one there. I wonder if this is where Georgios comes to set off the bird scarer.

I sit for a moment taking in the wonderful smells, letting the warm sun and the breeze brush my face. I am in another world. I am amongst the clouds, so high up it's like I'm in a parallel universe. But I have to get on. Get Georgios upright and find our way back down the mountain. Clinging on to the branch of a tree, I scrabble down and back into the cave, determinedly not looking at the pictures, not catching the eye of either of them.

'Here, drink this.' I hold the cup of mountain tea to Georgios's face. I've made a fire, boiled the water and added the dittany, just like I've watched Maria do. Let it sit and then poured some into the cup, leaving the leaves behind.

At first he doesn't respond. 'Georgios! George?' I try, which feels more familiar now I know who he is. His eyelids begin to flicker and he opens his eyes, looking a little bewildered. I lift his face by hooking my finger under his chin, and put the battered metal cup to his mouth, tipping it gently. The first few drops just sit on his dry lips, but then, very slowly, his lips move, drawing in the tea.

Smoke from the fire curls up and out of the mouth of the cave. Maybe someone will see it and send help, I think, though I know in my heart of hearts that they won't. There's only Maria down there. Mitera is in bed and Kostas doesn't go out at all now. No one knows this place is here. It's cold in the cave and I'm glad of the fire.

I take Georgios's scarf and dip it in the mountain tea, the dittany aromatic and pungent. I hold the scarf to the wound and then bring the cup to his mouth again. Neither of us says anything. There is a huge elephant sitting in the cave, but right now, it's dozing, and I'll leave it that way until Georgios comes round a bit more. Some of the tea trickles out of the side of his mouth, but he lifts his chin, wanting more, raising his hand to hold the cup. When he's finished it, I stand. He seems more awake now, and I'm beginning to feel relieved.

His eyes dart around the cave, then back to me. 'I have to go,' he says suddenly, and makes an attempt to stand.

'What? No!' I put out a hand to stop him, but I needn't have.

'Argh!' He slumps back immediately, clearly in pain as he puts weight on his left leg. I watch as his head dips and sways too, and he puts his hand to it as he slides back down the wall.

'Here, let me see.' I move forward.

'No!' he snaps, and I step back. 'Sorry, I mean I'm fine,' he says, although he's clearly not. 'Try and help me to stand.' He looks at me. 'Please. There's something I have to do. Somewhere I have to be.' He holds out a hand.

'You can't stand. You need to just . . .' I have no idea what he needs to do. If it was Demi, I'd make her sit on the sofa and bring her hot milk, like I used to before bed, or if she had a nightmare. But he's attempting to get up again. Instinctively I step forward and hold out both my hands to support him. With a huge effort, he's pulling himself up the cave wall, dragging at his left leg, pain and exertion etched across his face. I step in beside him and let him put his arm around me as he heaves himself upright and tries to move forward, the other hand clutching his leg, which is clearly killing him.

'Oh, this is ridiculous,' I say suddenly, because it is. 'You can't go anywhere, not yet. Give yourself time. Look, this is all my fault, and I'm sorry. Tell me where you need to be and I'll help. Please. Let me put this right . . .' I can feel the eyes of the pictures staring at me. I'd really like to be out of the cave right now.

He looks at me, and then back at the pictures on the wall.

'Let me go instead,' I say. 'I can get help . . . send someone back.' Once I get down from here, I certainly won't be coming back.

'OK . . .' he says finally, 'but on one condition.' He looks straight at me, the gold flecks in his green eyes sparkling in the firelight. My breathing becomes shallow and fast. He grabs hold of my wrist and my breathing quickens again, like a musical score stepping up to double time.

'Sure. Anything.' I'm tingling all over, my nerve endings standing to attention.

'You mustn't tell anyone where I am. No one must know about this place. Please. I'm begging you.' He suddenly looks like the old George, softer, kinder, before whatever happened to him . . . happened.

'But that's ridiculous. You need help. You need to get down from here.'

'Please, agree to do this one thing for me and then . . . then I will tell you everything.'

We both look around at the pictures at the back of the cave, my heart beating so fast it feels like it may never find its natural rhythm again. When I turn away from them, he's still looking at me. The smell of the wild dittany fills the air between us.

'What is this place? Why are there these pictures here?' I push. 'Tell me what the hell is going on and I'll do whatever it is you need me to do for you.'

He lets out a long sigh and then says evenly, 'It's a shrine, to lives lost.'

'But why is there a picture of you there too?'

He looks straight at me. 'And for lives spared,' he says slowly. 'I was in the car with Stelios when it crashed.'

My heart leaps into my mouth. I can't speak.

'Look, I will tell you everything if you just do me this favour. It's really important. There are people relying on me.'

'Who?' I frown.

'I am the gods' messenger,' he says. 'I'm the one who delivers the dittany to those that need it.'

'You?' I pause to take this in. 'But why? Why not just let people get their own? I thought you were the one *stopping* them from getting to the dittany?'

A flash of frustration crosses his face. 'The mountain is in danger. At the moment, it has protected status. As long as we can prove that the dittany is growing here, it will stay protected.'

I shake my head, not understanding.

'That's who you saw me meeting that day. The man in the car park, he's from the office of protected sites. I bring him samples to show him we still have fresh, growing dittany. It's nothing like it used to be when it covered the mountain and the bees thrived, but it is here.'

I think of the honey farm and my heart sinks. What are we going to do?

'By keeping people off the mountain, I have been trying to make this place safe and keep the dittany growing. I harvest a bit and dry it in the other cave, then I store it up here, where no one will find it, and deliver it to the people that need it. But if anyone knew where it was coming from, this place would be stripped by poachers in no time. I need to keep it safe until it finishes flowering in a few weeks' time.'

I'm starting to understand. 'And you need to deliver the dittany this evening, or at least . . . the messenger does?'

He nods, wincing in pain.

'And if I go and deliver it for you, you'll tell me about Stelios. Why he never came to find me. You'll tell me about . . . the accident.' I swallow hard.

He nods again, gripping his leg, and somehow I know he means it. He's relying on me to do this for him.

'OK.' I must be mad, I think. I hear a voice in my head:

Think it through. But instead of listening to it, I say, 'Tell me what you want me to do . . .'

Once Georgios has explained what I need to do, I take three bunches of dried dittany from the pile at the back of the cave, then step outside and walk to the edge of the ledge.

'Nell!' he calls me back. 'Take this.' He reaches up, and I bend forward so that he can put his hat on my head. 'Hide that red hair away. Makes you stand out a mile.' He almost smiles, but then winces in pain. 'This too.' He hands me his jacket and I shrug it on, comforted by its scent of pine and cave smoke.

'You have it all?'

I nod and hold up the three bunches, tied with crocheted ribbon.

'So one for Christina's husband, on the main street, next to the tablecloth shop, for his gout. One to the restaurant, for Stelios's father's arthritis. And one—'

'Yes, yes, I know.' I cut him off, the nerves getting the better of me. I have to get the third one to Mitera, without being seen. Easier said than done. He's right. If anyone realises where this dittany is coming from, the secret will be out and it will disappear for good. It will mean the end of the mountain as we know it, and the honey farm. No one must recognise me.

I walk out of the cave, take a deep breath and sit down on the edge of the ledge. I mustn't freeze with fear like I did coming up, because this time there is nobody to help me. I put the dittany in the top pocket of Georgios's jacket, then look back at the mouth of the cave. I can't let any of them down.

Chapter Thirty-nine

I can hear Maria in the concrete milk store, metal churns clanking. I have to do it now, I think. My heart is pounding so loudly it must sound like the Salvation Army coming into town. I mustn't be seen. I crouch down behind the wall at the front of the house. The moped is parked just beyond the drive, outside my bedroom. To my huge relief, the key is in the ignition. The getaway vehicle: I allow myself a little smile. Once I've dropped the dittany off, I'll have to leave as quickly as possible.

Running in a crouched position, I reach the moped and flip it off its stand, then wheel it down the drive to the main road and park it up behind the wall, next to the gates, ready to go. Hands shaking, I return to my hiding place and pull out the dittany.

Just then there's a loud bark right behind me, and I nearly jump out of my skin. I look down to see Georgios's little dog.

'Oh ssh, please,' I whisper, putting my finger to my lips. I pull the hat down further over my face. 'Go home,' I hiss. The dog doesn't move. Just sits next to me, his tongue hanging out. He's as stubborn as me. I look at him. 'Well come on then. We have work to do. But no barking.' He pants in reply.

Dropping down as low as I can, I scuttle towards the front door. I place the dittany on the step, then pull myself up slowly to knock on the wood before running into the shadows of the vine growing outside my room. I feel like I'm playing knock-down ginger, like the kids who live on my street back home. Once again I get the strange feeling that home is a whole lifetime away.

The door opens and I see Kostas's head poke out nervously. He looks around and then down at his feet. 'Maria! Maria!' He picks up the dittany and holds it up like the Olympic torch. 'Maria!' She comes running from the milk store, wiping her hands on the apron tied round her middle, and the two of them bustle excitedly into the house, no doubt straight to the kitchen to make Mitera's tea. I smile and look down at Georgios's dog, who is sitting at my feet, still panting. I realise I've been holding my breath. I suddenly feel exhausted, but I can't stop now.

'Come on,' I say quietly to the dog. 'Two more deliveries to go.'

I can hear Kostas and Maria exclaiming happily to each other in the kitchen as I creep down to the moped. Luckily it starts first time, and I send up a word of thanks to whoever might be looking down on me. I'm about to set off when the dog hops on to the running plate between my feet. I smile.

'Come on then. You'll only bark and give the game away if I don't let you.'

As I head off down the road, Georgios's dog warm between my feet, I know that Maria is lighting a candle in thanks to the messenger, and I feel very good indeed, like part of the hole in my heart has been filled. In fact, better than that, I feel fantastic. With the wind in my hair, I bend and weave my way into town feeling like I've finally got somewhere I have to be.

Heading back up the mountain with a huge smile on my face after I've made my deliveries, I start to climb the rocky path towards the first cave.

'You stay here,' I tell the little dog firmly before I start the main ascent. 'Your master will be back soon, I promise.'

I make my way up the path, pulling myself up on the rocks, feeling the weight of my bag slung across my body. I've got some figs I picked from a tree on the roadside, and a bunch of wild rocket from the mountain, as well as a loaf of bread that was cooling in the kitchen window when I dropped the dittany off at the restaurant, and a piece of feta from there too. It's not much of a meal, but it should help Georgios get his strength back to make his way down the mountain.

'Woof! Woof!'

I turn, and the little dog is right behind me. He stops and cocks his head to one side, then barks again.

'Go home,' I say, firmly but kindly.

But he just barks again, more insistently. I turn back and continue my climb. He won't come much further, I think. He'll go back and wait for Georgios at the house. But when I get to the first cave, I see that he's still behind me, hopping from rock to rock on his three legs, slow but determined. I tut and shake my head. He's starting to struggle, taking longer, more sideways routes, fighting to keep up, but when I try and send him home again, he just barks. I can't help but admire his determination. I turn and look at him. Oh . . . for goodness' sake, I can't believe I'm going to do this. I pick my way back down to where he's standing and scoop him up with my free arm. He stops barking. I look down at his little face, wiry beard and moustache, dark brown eyes. He sticks out his pink tongue and licks my face, making me laugh.

'Come on then, little one,' I say, and start to head towards the first cave again. It's not going to be easy with the added complication of the little dog, but I need to get back to the secret valley. I can't just leave Georgios there, and I have to know about Stelios.

As I reach the vantage point of the first cave, I turn and see a candle flickering in Maria's kitchen window, giving thanks. I smile, satisfied that I've done some good here today.

Chapter Forty

'You did it? You delivered all the dittany?' Georgios looks like he's been sleeping, but pulls himself upright when he hears me arriving back at the cave.

I nod, out of breath but beaming widely. I can't help myself. I delivered the dittany and made it back up through the secret gorge to the cave, and I feel amazing.

'I was so nervous at getting caught, but I didn't, and God, it was really exciting.' I find myself telling him how I hid behind the vine, and about Maria and Kostas's ecstatic shouts when they realised their guardian angel hadn't let them down. When I tell him how I managed to get the bread and cheese as well, he gives me a stern look.

'I'll pay them back,' I say quickly. I knew it was wrong, but I also knew that Georgios needed food, and I couldn't stop by the farm to pick something up without being seen.

The little dog wriggles out from where he's tucked inside Georgios's jacket, under my arm. He's delighted to see his owner, and he can't wait to be set down to greet him.

'He wouldn't leave me alone. Came with me on the deliveries and then followed me all the way up here,' I tell Georgios. The dog runs and hops to his master, his little body wriggling this way and that, despite his three legs. He licks Georgios's face ecstatically until Georgios is laughing, and I find myself looking at the two of them and smiling too.

'What's his name?' I ask.

'Filos. It means friend,' Georgios says, rubbing the little dog's head. 'We all need good friends, someone who needs us and we need them.' He doesn't look up at me as he says it.

'How did he lose his leg?'

'Poachers. People wanting to pick the dittany and sell it for their own gain. Like I said, it's big business and something I'm trying to stop happening here.' He gives me a pointed look, and I blush. 'They want to keep the wildlife away from the dittany, particularly the wild goats.'

'The kri-kri goats?'

He nods. 'The kri-kri will seek the dittany out when they're injured. But in recent times, the mountains have been overgrazed, another reason for the herb disappearing. So someone set a trap for the goats, and this little one got caught in it.'

'How terrible!' I'm appalled at the barbaric act.

'Some people will do anything to get their hands on the wild dittany. It is a valuable product. But very soon there will be none left for anyone.'

I hold out the bread to him, and he takes it gratefully. I empty out the fat purple figs and the square of cheese, and then go outside and rinse the wild rocket in the tumbling waterfall.

'Thank you,' he says on my return. 'For this,' he nods at the food in his lap, 'and for bringing my dog to me.' He strokes Filos's head, then, for the first time, looks up and smiles at me.

'No problem,' I say, with no idea why I suddenly feel like I've been blindfolded and spun round three times, leaving me feeling a little disorientated. It must be the altitude so high up the mountain, I tell myself.

'And the bees? How were they? Did you get stung?' he says suddenly, with a concern I haven't heard before. I shake my head.

'I kept calm and sang to myself.' I must have looked ridiculous, I realise. The only song I could think of as I sidled past them was 'Rudolph the Red-Nosed Reindeer'. God, if Angelica and Grace could see me now, they'd never believe it.

'That's good. If you respect them, they'll leave you alone, I'm sure.'

We fall into silence for a moment. I stoke the fire, feeding on more sticks from a pile in the corner, and stand back as the smoke puffs ups and then curls out of the cave. With a nod of satisfaction, I add a bigger log.

Georgios is watching me. 'You seem different,' he says suddenly, stopping my daft smile.

'So do you,' I reply quietly, blushing. But actually, he's right. I *feel* different. Not the holidaymaker helping out, a WWOOFer, but like I'm working with the mountain, in the heart of it, and at the thought, and a flash of his eyes, my heart starts up its drumbeat again.

'Hello again, George,' I say quietly.

'Hello again, Elinor.'

We smile at each other as if the last few weeks haven't happened, and I find my head falling to one side to touch his. It feels like a new start.

I tear the bread I've lifted from the restaurant into chunks, then crumble in some cheese and figs with the peppery wild rocket and hand a piece to Georgios. Then I pass him my water bottle. He sips, smiles and nods.

'I feel like Zeus being cared for by Melissa.'

'Zeus?'

'He was hiding out in a cave. Melissa, a wood nymph, looked after him and brought him milk and honey. The name Melissa means honey bee. She cared for him just like the Cretan people looked after the partisan soldiers in World War Two. We are a small island, but a proud one. And we will fight for what is ours.' His face darkens. 'For what we love.'

'Georgios,' I say, 'tell me about Stelios.'

Filos turns a circle and snuggles into his master's side. Georgios takes comfort in stroking him, and then draws a big breath, as if this isn't something that has been spoken of for a very long time.

Chapter Forty-one

Outside the sun is setting in the west, casting a long, low orange glow over the mountain tops. Georgios's voice is low and gravelly, and he takes a sip of water to cover the cracks that appear as soon as he starts to speak.

'Stelios was my best friend. I loved him like a brother.'

I nod, listening.

'We did everything together.' He manages a smile. I settle back and listen, feeling closer to Stelios as he talks about the times they shared together. And then finally, I ask the question that has haunted me all these years.

'After I left . . . did he talk about me? Did he say he loved me?' My mouth was dry.

'He loved you very much,' Georgios says. They are the words I've been desperate to hear, and I feel myself take a big gulp of air as I stare out over the valley, like I've been holding my breath until this moment, unable to carry on with life. I feel like my rusting joints have been oiled, like the tin man in *The Wizard of Oz*, and that I've been catapulted forward on to a new path after years of staying in the same place.

'There was never anyone else for him.' Georgios looks into the fire, lost in his memories, while my mind is full of what might have been, for me and for Demi. A tear tips over the edge of my eye and down my cheek. I brush it away, but more follow. Georgios swallows, and his Adam's apple bobs up and down in the orange firelight. 'He found what we're all looking for,' he says. 'He had a whole new life to look forward to. A family.'

'So you knew I was pregnant when I left?'

'I only knew what Stelios told me. He said that you argued on the day you left. You told him you were pregnant, but he was confused and didn't know how to tell his family. But as soon as you'd gone, once you'd left for the airport, he realised that it was you he wanted. You and the baby. He came and found me, and we went after you. He told me he loved you, and about the baby, just before . . . just before the car left the road.'

'Huh?' I take a sharp intake of breath. 'The car accident? He was coming after me?' Hot tears start to build and I let them fall, like a tap that has been stuck shut for years suddenly being turned on. 'He was coming after me,' I repeat quietly, as if imprinting it on my memory. 'You were in the car? Is that . . . Your face . . . your leg?'

He pauses. 'At first, after the accident, I couldn't remember any of it. It was months before I could put all the pieces into place. Stelios was driving as fast as he could to stop you getting on that plane. He wanted to ask you to stay and marry him. It all came back to me eventually. You had told him he had to think things through and to come and find you when he was ready. You always were the stubborn one, making your plans and going through with them.'

'And then what happened?'

'There was a hire car, tourists, driving up the mountain.

They were coming too quick. They didn't know the road. There were no markings and the car just cut straight across in front of us. Stelios swerved, and we left the road and rolled down the mountain . . .' He tails off.

'Where the shrine is?'

He nods. He looks back at the pictures of him and Stelios.

'For lives lost and lives spared,' he practically whispers, and I nod, slowly understanding.

'But you did remember, eventually, about me and the baby. Why didn't you come and find me? Tell me what had happened?'

He shakes his head. 'I didn't know where you lived. I had no idea.'

'And you never told his family, about me being pregnant . . .' I trail off. He shakes his head, holding a hand to his temple.

'I thought it was for the best. And maybe I was angry too.' He looks up at me with regret in his eyes. 'But now I can see that was wrong.'

This time it's my turn to shake my head, trying to take it all in.

'I thought you coming back here would cause them more upset. I thought it would be better for them not to know.' He has a penknife in his hand, and he picks up a small stick from the fireside and begins whittling at one end, sharpening it, as if it's helping him to concentrate, focus and remember.

'And now?' I push. 'Do you still think it's right to say nothing? For his family not to know about the baby? Is that for the best?' I don't have the answers myself. Should I tell them? I could just leave here in a few weeks' time and let them get on with their lives as before.

He carries on sharpening the end of the stick. 'I think you should consider it. Maybe . . .' he says slowly and thoughtfully.

I don't wait to hear his response, the memories of those days, weeks and months that followed my return to the UK flooding back. 'I was so angry when Stelios didn't come after me. I couldn't believe that he'd abandoned us. Everything he'd said about loving me, how his parents would come round to the idea of us being together. It was a shock finding out I was pregnant. That's why we rowed. So I returned home as planned and waited. When he didn't come, I was determined to look after our baby on my own. I told everyone that her father was just a holiday romance.' I feel so ashamed. 'He was so much more than a holiday romance. He was my . . . well, my one and only.' I swallow. 'He hurt me and I tried to cut him out of our lives. Except every time I looked at her, at his daughter, I could see him.'

Georgios is slumped now, the pain at the memories I'm asking him to revisit etched on his face. His head tilts towards mine and mine towards his, just touching, drawing comfort from the past and a shared love. Outside, dusk is turning to darkness, wrapping itself around us like a velvet cloak. Lost in our thoughts, and safe in the knowledge that Stelios loved me, we both drift into an exhausted sleep.

Chapter Forty-two

I wake with the dawn and look out from the cave, and it's like I'm in heaven . . . literally. White mist is rolling around the wild beauty of the gorge, and the sun is a huge orange ball in the sky, telling us that it's going to be a hot one later. But in the thick early-morning mist here in the cave, there is still a damp, chill air. I start to build up the fire again, putting small sticks on orange embers.

'Maria and Kostas will be worried about you. We'd better go.' I turn to see Georgios sitting up, with not so much bed hair as cave hair sticking up at the back, making him look kind of sweet. But he's clearly still in a lot of pain.

'Do you think you can make it down now? How's your head? And your leg?' I ask, but he doesn't reply. He doesn't move. He just looks at me with those green and gold eyes, and the staircase from my heart to my head shifts and rocks.

'Isn't there someone else we should be talking about first?' he says.

'My daughter, you mean?'

Outside the cave I hear a cry and turn away briefly, grateful for the distraction, to see a huge eagle gliding through the valley outside. The mist is dispersing, and in its place the hot August sunshine begins to reach in, bringing with it the smell I will always associate with this place: wild thyme, marjoram and dittany.

'I just thought . . .' He pushes his hand through his hair and I suddenly find myself snapping, taking out my grief and anger on him. The injustice of it, the life I was cheated out of by the hire car on the wrong side of the road, driving too fast.

'What *did* you think, Georgios? Did you think about me waiting for him? Day after day, week after week? Never giving up hope that he would come for me and his daughter and tell us he loved us. Then believing that his family here meant more to him. Believing he had chosen them over us. They told him not to fall for me; they wanted him to find a nice Cretan girl. They didn't want to lose him, he told me that. And that's what I assumed had happened. They had got to him, and he had done what they wanted and moved on with his life.'

'I thought at the time . . . that not saying anything to anyone was . . . for the best.' He stumbles over the words and I actually let out a laugh even as the tears roll freely down my face.

'For the best . . . for who?'

For a moment he says nothing.

'I realise it was wrong now. Seeing . . . seeing your daughter's face on the computer.'

I bite my lip. The day I discovered Stelios was dead, when I was talking to Demi on Skype.

'So you did see her then?'

He nods, the guard down from in front of his eyes, leaving

243

him looking vulnerable, like he's the one trapped in the poacher's trap, waiting to be released from his pain.

'It was just like looking at Stelios. A living image of him,' he says.

My heart fills up as I think about Demi, and a smile pulls at the corner of my mouth despite the waterfall cascading down each cheek. 'She has that dimple he had,' I hiccup, 'just here.' I point to my own cheek. 'Whenever she smiles.'

'Just like him,' he agrees, and the sparkles in his eyes are like tiny diamonds catching the light.

My anger is seeping away. 'We were all doing what we thought was best at the time,' I tell him. 'Me included.'

He nods.

The eagle is joined by a second one, and a smaller one in the middle of them. A family by the looks of it, looking out for their young one, trying to keep it safe and doing the best they can. Keeping it from harm. We both watch them glide down the valley. Filos walks to the cave entrance and sniffs the air.

'For what it's worth,' Georgios says, 'I think you should tell them – Stelios's family. I think you're scared, and that's why you've said nothing.'

I go to argue, but he puts up a finger and stops me.

'You're scared of being rejected . . . You feel Stelios rejected you and you think his family will do it all over again.'

I can't say anything else. Georgios is right. What if they don't want to know me or Demi? I don't think I could bear to feel pushed away again.

'Will you . . . will you come with me? To see his family?'

I breathe in the herb-scented air, taking strength from it. 'Will you come with me to tell them about Demi?'

'Demi?'

I nod and swallow.

'It's a lovely name,' he says, surprising me with his warmth and kindness.

'Short for Demetria.'

Georgios raises an eyebrow; not the one with the cut over it.

'Stelios's grandmother?'

I nod again. 'He loved her very much. I thought it would be a nice surprise if he ever did . . . if we ever met up. So he'd know I was thinking of him.'

Georgios nods this time. 'It's a beautiful name. Demetria, sister of Zeus, mother to Persephone, who was taken to the Underworld; only when she returned would spring return to the island.'

We look at each other, the meaning running deep between us.

'So will you come with me?' I finally say.

'Of course, but first I think I'm going to need some help getting down off this mountain.'

Georgios is clearly still battered and bruised from the fall, and I help him to his feet. All questions about the dittany and the bird scarer have been forgotten for the time being – it is Stelios's family and Demi who feel important now.

This is something I should have done years ago, and I'm terrified. Terrified of how Stelios's family will react. Suddenly descending the rock face and coming down the mountain doesn't seem half as scary any more.

Chapter Forty-three

I stand by the restaurant entrance and look in through the gates. I can hear Yannis calling to his father from the upper level. He's holding a tray, putting candles on the tables. Despite the heat of the day and the lack of customers, they don't stop trying. I haven't been here since they found out who I was. I didn't wait for Yannis to sack me. It was clear I wouldn't be welcomed back.

'Ready?' Georgios is standing right beside me, shoulder to shoulder. Well, my shoulder to his elbow, practically. It has taken us a long time to get down off the mountain, me guiding Georgios, and him moving slowly and carefully, one hand on my shoulder. And now, finally, we're here.

I nod. I can't speak. My head is pounding and my stomach is twisting and tangling itself up. 'Ready,' I finally manage to say with more confidence than I'm feeling. I straighten my tie-dyed T-shirt and dust myself down, pushing my shoulders back just like my nan taught me to do when I came home with Demi, when I knew people were talking and whispering about me behind my back. Eighteen and a new mum on her own. I held my head high then, and I'm going to do it now. But God, I wish Nan was here with me. Then I feel Georgios's little finger reach out and brush the side of my hand, letting me know he's there, and it feels like the fairy lights have been untangled and switched on inside my stomach. Now I'm ready. I push open the gate.

'Yannis?' I say as he appears down the stone steps, still carrying the tray of candles. He stops suddenly and stares at me, and his face darkens.

'I thought you'd gone,' he says. 'Please don't tell me you've come to ask for your job back. I thought it was clear the other night. There is no job for you here any more. Not now I know who you really are.'

'No . . . nothing like that.' I lift my head higher. 'I have something I want to tell you, you and your family.'

'I'm not sure there is anything they would like to hear.' He carries on down the steps and continues putting candles on the tables, lifting the mood in the dark recesses of the enclosed courtyard.

'I think you should listen to what she has to say.'

'George,' Yannis says, as if only just realising he's there. 'We don't see you here much these days.'

'Gather the family, Yannis,' Georgios instructs, and Yannis slowly puts down the tray and with a look of speculation goes to the kitchen.

His mother is the first to come out, wiping her hands on her apron, followed by Stelios's sister, who is waving her arms and protesting that she has things to do. She's followed by Stelios's father and then finally Demetria, wearing an apron and slippers, her hands red from hard work and hot water. They all stare at me and then, on Georgios's instruction, sit down at a long table. Oh God! I'm not sure I can do this after all. It's been eighteen years. Isn't it just going to cause them more pain? Won't they hate me for all the time they've missed and can't get back?

I go to open my mouth, but then drop my head and shake it gently. Where do I start?

'I don't think I can do this,' I hear myself barely whisper. My chest is tight and I just want to turn and run, if only my feet weren't rooted to the spot. I suddenly have an image of my mother leaving for Australia, of Stelios the last time I saw him, and then of Demi looking out at me from the bus window. Everyone I have ever loved leaving me. I couldn't bear it if these people did the same to Demi. Then I hear Georgios beside me clearing his throat.

'Nell has come here today because,' he takes a deep breath, 'she has something she wants to tell you.'

I lift my head and look at him, straight into those eyes. He holds my gaze and it feels like we're back up the mountain, and he's promising me he won't let me fall. He turns slowly back to the table.

'Someone she wants to tell you about . . .'

Finally, with Georgios's help, my courage returns. I look around the table at their faces, familiar and yet strangers. Then I lift my chin just a little bit more and begin.

'My daughter . . . she's eighteen.' I think about Demi. Brave, independent Demi. I should be thrilled she's gone off, flown the nest, grabbed life by the scruff of the neck. And I am, I think, deep down. I'm proud of what she's done.

'I'm afraid we don't have any seasonal work. You can see what it's like. We don't have enough customers to keep us going, let alone to take on British students,' Yannis says matter-of-factly, and then stands up and picks up his tray of tea lights again. 'Now if you'll excuse me . . .' he adds, and the rest of the family start getting up, presumably to go back to their jobs: Stelios's dad to wait outside at the end of the lane in case any passing tourists can be tempted in; his mother to the office, to pore over the accounts; Demetria to the kitchen to prepare the vegetables that will be eaten by the family if no one comes to the restaurant.

'Yannis,' Georgios says sharply. The rest of the family stop in their tracks.

'I'm sorry, George, we can't help. Especially not after . . . what has happened.' He looks at me with coldness in his eyes. I knew I shouldn't have come. They won't want to know! I want to turn and run and run . . . but maybe that's what I did when I found out I was pregnant. I like to think I was giving Stelios time to think. But maybe I really was running away.

'Just listen,' Georgios says, like an older brother telling off a younger sibling, and amazingly, Yannis stops and does as he's told. The rest of the family too turn back and look at Georgios and then, almost as one, sit back down.

I don't know how or where to start.

'Show them a picture,' Georgios says quietly, his hot breath on my ear and my neck making a shiver run up and down me. Yannis tuts and exaggeratedly swings one leg over the other, showing his tedium.

I reach for my phone with shaking hands and pull up a picture: Demi's last birthday, when we had cake and cava at the house with Gracie and Angelica. I show it to Georgios. He nods and gives the tiniest of smiles, and I step forward and hold up the screen.

The whole family stares at the picture. There is silence, followed by a collective sharp intake of breath. Then slowly they look up at me. Stelios's father is the first to speak.

Chapter Forty-four

'What is her name?' he asks.

I take a moment, lift my chin again and say, 'Demi.'

'After the American actress Demi Moore, is it?' Yannis says, still snippy.

'After Demetria,' I say quietly, and Stelios's grandmother looks at me and her eyes fill with unshed tears.

'Is this true?' She finally speaks.

'How do we know it isn't some kind of sick joke?' Yannis is angry now, standing and pointing at my phone. The air is full of emotion being held back but about to burst the flood defences.

'You only have to look at the picture to know it.' Georgios steps forward.

They all look again at the phone in my still-shaking hand. I feel so hot, I'm almost cold. My top lip is damp, as is the back of my neck.

'She is Stelios's daughter,' I say finally. 'I was pregnant when I left here. I told him about it. He needed time to think, how to tell you. I told him I was going back to the UK; that he should come and find me if he wanted me and the baby. I wanted to give him time to tell you. We rowed and I left anyway, hoping he would follow.' I swallow, and the next words barely come out. 'But he never did . . .'

'She is beautiful,' Stelios's mother finally says, and she reaches out and takes the phone from me, running a hand across the screen, staring at it as if she is holding a baby in her arms for the first time.

'Did she sleep as a child? Stelios never slept!' his father suddenly says, and they all, unexpectedly, laugh; tearful, watery laughs. Even Georgios smiles. 'And talk . . . once he learned, he never stopped!'

Now I join in the laughter. 'That's Demi!' I tell them.

And now the floodgates burst open, letting the tide of emotion flow freely. Only Yannis is quiet. But he pulls up a chair and sits close to his parents.

'Do you remember the time Stelios said his first word, just like that? We were up the mountain,' his father carries on.

'*Melissa!*' his mother grins. 'Bee,' she tells me. 'Buzzz,' she adds, just in case I don't understand. 'The mountain was full of them, buzzing happily. The mountain was a different place then. He dreamed of having a hotel there.'

'I know, he took me there,' I tell them, and we all smile as we share Stelios's dream for the place he loved.

They pull up a chair for me to join them and ask me about Demi: her job in London. Can she speak any Greek? And I shake my head and tell them, 'Only to order a kebab,' and we all laugh, and I feel like a huge weight has lifted off my shoulders and I'm breathing freely again. Laughing too, like I haven't laughed in a long time. I turn round to thank Georgios, but he has slipped away.

Stelios's sister disappears into the kitchen and reappears

with a big pot of coffee and a plate of little cakes – the ones like spun golden thread, soaked in syrup; filo pastry parcels; cherries and quinces made into fruit preserves and served in spoons – then we talk all over again, about the sweet treats Stelios adored as a child and the food he loved to cook at the restaurant, food from the mountain that he was so proud of.

Finally it's time for me to leave. The family stand up and hug me one by one.

'We want to hear more,' Stelios's mother tells me, wiping the tears that keep falling from her eyes despite her smile.

'You are part of the family now,' Stelios's father says, holding me by the tops of my arms. 'Please, you will come back and work here? I know there are no customers, but we look after our own. Besides, we want to spend more time with you. Won't you stay and eat with us?'

'Thank you, but I have to go now,' I say. It's been lovely, but I want to speak to Georgios.

'Just out of interest, who is the young woman in the photograph with Demi, the one who looks like Britney Spears?' asks Yannis casually, pointing at Angelica. We all laugh.

When I finally manage to leave, amongst hugs and tears and more laughter, I have a warm glow inside me. I have to find Georgios and thank him. And then of course there's Demi. She doesn't know about any of this . . . where on earth am I going to start?

Chapter Forty-five

Georgios looks surprised to see me when he opens the door of his little stone house.

'At least you knocked this time,' he says with half a smile, but he opens the door wide for me to come in. I smart at the memory of snooping round the day I found the bird scarer.

'Thank you for doing that, back there,' I begin. I look around the living room, my eyes drawn to the amazing view from the floor-to-ceiling window at the far end, leading out on to the balcony.

'It was the right thing to do,' he nods. 'Coffee, or something stronger? I have wine or raki.'

'Wine would be lovely.' I'm surprised to find myself accepting his offer; wine might actually be just what I need. He takes two glasses from the wooden shelves in the corner where the kitchen runs under the open staircase.

'The woodwork, it's the same as Stelios's shrine on the roadside.' I find that now I've started talking about him, I can't stop. I watch Georgios as he pours wine from an unmarked green bottle into two tumblers.

'I made it, from my own trees.' He nods to the window. 'Come, let's sit outside.'

He leads the way to the small terrace looking out over the

mountains. Bending down, he picks up a newspaper, scrunches a few pages into balls and takes some kindling from a pile neatly stacked on the decking, then pulls out a lighter and lights the laid-up fire in the fire pit. The wind makes the flames flick and flack.

I take a sip of wine as I watch him feeding the flames. The sun is setting in between two mountain peaks, and I'm mesmerised. It's not cold, but the wind is whipping round us and the fire is comforting.

'This is good.' I nod to my glass as Georgios sits in the chair next to me.

'My own wine. From my vines.' He indicates the vines that are growing in straight rows on a tiny triangle of land on a ledge down the mountainside, and another patch below that. Order amongst chaos.

Putting a log on the fire, he sits back, holding his leg out straight in front of him. Filos jumps up on to his lap.

'Hello, little friend.' I rub his head and he pants happily, his pink tongue poking out from his wiry whiskers.

'How are you feeling?' I ask Georgios.

He looks straight at me and then says evenly, 'Like I've been hit on the head with a rock!' and breaks into a wide smile, wrinkles appearing at the corners of his eyes.

Any nerves that might still be hanging around disappear as I can't help but let out a little laugh. Then we both turn, smiles on our lips, and look out towards the setting sun, like a big orange and red ball sliding out of the sky. The smoke billows and curls and around us like a cat, winding itself in between us and all around as we sit for a moment in contented contemplative silence.

Suddenly Filos barks, interrupting our thoughts. I turn, and there behind me is the little fawn-coloured pup from the litter back at the honey farm. It stops in its tracks when it realises it's been spotted. I must have left the front door open. It's ventured a long way from the barn. I look back at Filos, who is no doubt going to send it home, his headstrong, independent child straying too far from its mother. But Filos barks again; not in his usual snappy way, telling the pup off, but more encouraging, and this time the pup bundles forwards towards me, nearly tumbling head over heads in its excitement, and I put out my hands to scoop it up, holding it to my face, losing myself in its soft fur and puppy smell. Georgios is smiling and nodding gently, looking out over the mountains as I fuss and cuddle the little dog.

'Thank you,' I say to Filos, and put out my hand and pat him. Looks like we've finally learned to trust each other. He holds up his head and pants, showing his pink tongue, as though he's smiling too.

'Looks like you'll have to stay around for a while now. You have a Filos too.'

'Oh, I couldn't keep her.' I look at the puppy's big brown eyes, and the white patch around her dark nose. 'But . . . well, maybe if I could look after her, just while I'm here. I've never had a dog.'

'Looks like she's chosen you. And Filos seems to approve.' Georgios has pulled out his penknife, and with one foot up on the wooden terrace wall is idly whittling a piece of wood from the neatly stacked pile there.

'I think I'll call her Angelica, after my best friend back

home.' I settle her in my lap, where she turns three circles and then curls up contentedly and shuts her eyes. 'Maybe Angel for short,' I add. I pull out my phone and take a picture of her, and then send it to Angelica. Then I put away the phone and sit back and smile at the pup in my lap.

With peace and harmony in the air all round, and buoyed up by my success as messenger yesterday, I feel the time is right to ask him more about the dittany. I take a sip of wine, then stroke the puppy, which has a hugely soothing effect on me.

'So, the man I saw you with in the car park that day, when I put two and two together—'

'And came up with seventy-two?' Georgios finishes for me with an arched eyebrow, and my toes curl in embarrass-ment.

'Yes.' I manage to smile. 'You said he was from the office of protected sites?'

Georgios stands and goes inside, returning with the wine bottle, and tops us both up.

'That's right. The dittany is on the red list of threatened species. The mountain is a protected site.'

'And when will it be safe again? When do you think the bees will want to start to move down the mountain?'

He puts the bottle beside his chair and sits, resting his foot on the terrace wall again, making himself comfortable. He shrugs. 'It's at its most vulnerable right now, whilst it's flowering. In a couple of weeks, the poachers won't be interested. But right now, I have to keep what we have safe. If I can't show the inspector evidence of freshly picked dittany, the mountain will lose its protected status. If that happens, the developers will move in, put up buildings and construct solar panels all over the slopes.'

'But surely that's a good thing? What's the problem? Stelios always wanted to build a B and B on the mountainside. He said he wanted everyone to come and see how beautiful his home was.' I'm sitting up straight now, and Angelica, the puppy, has woken at the sound of raised voices.

'This would be very different. Building an all-inclusive resort would choke the town, suffocate it. They will have everything they need up there – restaurants, bars, cafés; even a medical centre. No one will go into the town at all. It will die. Every single business, including Stelios's family's restaurant.'

'An all-inclusive resort?' I think of Zeus's Vista, the resort where we worked down by the coast; no one venturing out of it, every need catered for from drinks to food to souvenirs.

He nods. 'There's been some company sniffing around apparently, Henderson's Holidays? They want to bring tourists, yes, but they want to build a resort, here on the mountain. The guy has an investor lined up, and a lawyer from the city. It will be totally self-contained, even bringing in their own solar energy from the panels that will cover the mountain.'

A slow, sickening feeling is starting to spread over me. 'Did you say Henderson's Holidays? How do you know about this?' I say, with a very dry mouth and a sudden thumping headache.

'The inspector told me. An offer has been made on the land, a serious one. If they think there is no threat on the mountain, no drugs gangs with guns keeping people at bay, they will start to invade it and seek out the dittany until it's all gone. Whatever happens, no one must know what's happening up here.' He nods his head to the mountain peak. 'No one must know about the secret valley. If they find it, and the dittany is stripped from it, any chance of saving the mountain and Vounoplagia will be gone.'

He stares at me, looking straight into my soul, and my blood runs cold as I realise what I've done.

Chapter Forty-six

My head is swimming and I focus on breathing. In, out, in, out, I tell myself firmly, watching my chest rising and falling. I've told Harry Henderson exactly how to get his hands on the mountain and carry out his plans. Plans that will ruin the town, including Stelios's family business, Maria and Kostas's too. The bees will all die. The honey farm will never happen. How could I have done this?

'So,' I say very slowly over the sound of the whooshing in my ears. I struggle to get the words out. 'If the holiday firm and its developers get to know about the dittany . . .' My mouth goes dry.

'This town will die,' he finishes for me, all hint of his earlier good humour gone.

I look out over the streaks of red, orange and yellow where the sun has left its mark in the sky. Tears prick my eyes. I want to tell Stelios I'm sorry. Georgios too. I have to think of a way to put right the damage I've caused.

'I could help!' I say suddenly, making Angel jump. 'Sorry,' I soothe her.

'What?' Georgios frowns.

I start to gabble. He has to agree. I have to put this right before he finds out what I've done. 'You said yourself I did a good job yesterday, delivering the dittany.' I'm gripping the arm of the chair tightly with one hand, my wine glass in the other held out in front of me.

'Well, yes, but . . . it's a lot more than—'

'I could help you,' I insist again. I'm on a roll. I can't let him turn me down. 'You could concentrate on guarding the secret valley and looking after the dittany, making sure no one comes near it, helping it thrive. I could take over the messenger duties. I go to the crocheting circle and hear about everyone's ailments, so I'd know exactly who needs it and when.'

Georgios looks at me suspiciously, and then his dark eyebrows lower over his green eyes as his face becomes more thoughtful.

'You could spend more time up there,' I point towards the secret valley, 'and if you see anyone coming up the mountain you could call out to me and I could create a distraction or diversion to stop them. We could work as a team! Just until the flowering is over.'

I'm actually convinced this is the answer. I have to do it. After all, I have spent the last few weeks trying to scupper everything he's done. I have to make sure that Harry Henderson and his developers stay away from here. I can't believe I was so gullible. Harry doesn't want to share the wealth the tourists will bring; he wants it all for himself. How could I have been so stupid? A bit of flattery and a glass of wine and I thought he was Richard Gere to my Julia Roberts. There I go again, thinking life is some kind of romantic film with a happy-ever-after . . . well it's not! I've made a huge mistake, and I need to put it right.

'Please, Georgios, let me help . . .'

The silence between us is excruciating. The dogs don't move a muscle.

'I'll think about it . . .' he says finally, and falls silent again, reaching out and stroking Filos.

'Please . . . for Stelios. Let me help save the mountain.' I don't know what I'm going to do if he says no. How can I leave knowing the damage I may have caused? I'm going to have to tell him, and then any bridges we have built will be well and truly burned. I take a deep breath, trying to work out how to broach the subject.

'Georgios . . . I've done something awful . . .'

'You made a mistake. You let your head rule your heart.' My own heart lurches. He knows! 'You thought you were doing the best thing for Stelios and the baby.'

I realise we're not talking about the same thing. He doesn't know, and my shoulders drop in relief. But I *did* listen to my head instead of my heart. When I met up with Harry, my head was telling me this was a great opportunity, a way to put a stop to Georgios, when my heart should have told me that Georgios would never do anything to hurt the mountain he loved.

'We have to keep the secret of the mountain safe!' he says earnestly, and I stop thinking about what I'm about to tell him. He looks like nothing has ever mattered more to him. He's doing this for Stelios and his family, and I want to do it for them too.

'You promise to work with me? You'll do what you're told, no more climbing up rock faces and getting stuck?'

I nod vigorously. 'I mean no! No more getting stuck!'

'And you must deliver the dittany to those who need it without getting caught. No one must find out it's me . . . us. That way they won't follow us or ask questions and the location will stay secret.'

I nod again. 'I'll do whatever it takes,' I say, and mean it. I'm doing this for Stelios, for his family – and, I realise, my daughter's family too. A whole family I have shut out for all these years. A whole life she could have had. I need to start putting my mistakes right.

'How do I know I can trust you?' he asks.

I feel sick to my stomach. 'You don't. But if what the inspector has told you is true, and there are people who want to get rid of the dittany in order to build, you're going to need help with keeping them off the mountain and keeping the valley hidden and secret. You can't be everywhere. You can't do this on your own, Georgios, and you don't need to. I'm here.'

He sucks air through his teeth and looks as if he is agreeing to possibly the biggest mistake of his life. Eventually he speaks.

'OK, get your things. I'll move up to the cave in the secret valley; that way I'll have a good view over the mountain, and the road to Vounoplagia too. I'll be able to see if anyone is getting close. You can stay in my house, look after my sheep, and you'll have to check the bees as well.'

'The bees?'

'Yes, you'll have to make friends with them so they know you're not threatening them.' His face softens as he talks about the bees. 'Soon we must collect the honey, if there is enough for us to take. But we must leave enough for them for the winter.'

'OK,' I agree. 'I'll check the bees. If you tell me what to do . . .'

'You must open the lids and take out the frames where they make their hexagonal wax cells, the honeycomb where they keep their larvae and honey stores. As you lift them from the hive, you'll see the bees doing the waggle dance, moving in circles, telling the other bees where the flowers are in relation to the sun. They don't need words to communicate.' He looks at me, and I feel like a whole swarm of bees is flying round and round my stomach, doing the waggle dance as they go.

'Check and see if they are making honey, if there are capped stores in the hive. They are collecting from the dittany here. That honey will be very good. If the bees are thriving and they have enough dittany, they will want to start moving out of their overcrowded homes and look for new ones. Hopefully they will find Kostas's farm. I'll show you what to do. Introduce you.' He smiles, and the bees waggle in my stomach again.

'And what about Maria and Kostas; what do I tell them about you not being here and me looking after your place?'

'Tell them I've been called away. Family business back in Athens,' he says. 'No more than that.'

Oh God, he's actually going to let me do it.

'I'll let you know if I see anyone on the mountain, and you try and head them off before they start up the path. You'll need to do whatever you can think of.'

I nod earnestly.

'And if they still come, well, then I'll let off the bird scarer and hope that they think it's gunfire. It's worked well enough in the past.' He gives me a hard, dark stare. 'Until someone decided to go snooping in my house.'

'Sorry . . .' I say, and swallow.

He leans towards me, staring at me all the time, green eyes flashing in the orange sunset, making my insides jolt again. Then he reaches up, takes off his hat and places it on my head.

'Looks like you'll need this, to keep that red hair covered,' and he breaks into a smile, the corners of his mouth lifting, making the dark skin around his cheeks crinkle, and the corners of his eyes too.

I feel more excited than I have in years, and at the same time absolutely terrified.

Chapter Forty-seven

'Georgios? Gone to Athens?' Maria says the next morning as she prepares a tray of coffee for us to take outside after we've finished our morning chores. 'We don't see much of him but he's always there if we need him. He's a good neighbour.'

There's nothing more I can do in the honey factory until the bees come, so instead I've been feeding the cows and helping Maria with the goats. Kostas has made bread and sweet rusks and raisin cake, and he has also decided to carry on with Mitera's crocheting while she's in bed. The dittany I delivered seemed to have lifted her spirits a little, but she still refuses to get up. It's as if all the fight in her has gone.

'Georgios never goes anywhere,' Maria says, deep in thought, preparing another, smaller tray of coffee and cake to take to Mitera, who probably won't touch it.

I'm worried Maria doesn't believe me. I'd like to say I'm not good at lying, but I have realised to my shame that I'm better than I think. I have been lying to Demi all these years, and it's something I have to put right. I'm just not sure how. I've barely heard from her this week, but I remind myself that she's getting on with her life and I have to let her. Just like I know she'll want me to get on with mine.

'He hasn't left the mountain in . . .' Maria is still puzzling over Georgios. She looks at Kostas.

'Years!' he finishes for her.

'Since Stelios . . .' She looks at me as if stepping on eggshells, not wanting to upset me again. Kostas looks at me softly too. These are such lovely, kind people, I think as we follow Maria outside to the table in the shade, looking down the valley to the sea in the distance.

'Since Stelios died,' Maria finishes. It's as if no one has actually been able to say the words until now. But now that they know who I am, they seem to be talking about him more. It's as if the floodgates have opened for everyone in the town.

'Now we will have no one on the mountainside looking out for us,' Maria tuts. 'It must be very serious family business for him to leave.'

I hate myself for lying to her. But it's for the best. I've learned my lesson. It's my loose tongue that has made this problem a hundred times worse.

'I've said I'll stay in his house, look out for his sheep and his dog while he's away. But I'll still be able to help you out with anything that needs doing on the farm.'

'Are you sure you don't mind? Up there, alone?'

I smile. 'I won't be alone; I'm taking this one with me,' and I look down at Angel, sitting in my lap as I accept the steaming cup of coffee and one of Kostas's rusks. 'As long as you don't mind, that is,' I add quickly. 'Me being up there and not here.'

Maria shrugs. 'Until we have bees, there's little for you to do in the honey factory. I'm glad you're helping Georgios out.' She smiles as she hands me a plate for my cake, then wipes her hands over her apron and sits as Kostas pours her steaming coffee from the battered pot. They are such a team. Even now, with the roles reversed after Kostas's terrible encounter with the bees, they just fit in with what the other needs. I wish Stelios and I could have been like that, being there for each other, getting old together. But heck . . . I have Angel for now, and she is lovely company.

'But if you aren't happy, or you're scared, or you see something that worries you, just come home,' Maria adds, like an older sister stepping in when there's no mum around. I want to hug her.

'I promise.'

'I feel so useless!' Kostas wails, throwing up his hands. 'What good is a honey farm without bees?'

'Don't worry, they will come soon,' I say, not feeling as confident as I sound.

Maria smiles fondly and then, with a teasing look, she imitates Mitera, saying, 'Only when love returns to the mountain.' She takes hold of Kostas's hand and we all laugh gently. Then we tuck into yoghurt with figs and cakes, and as she always does now, Maria apologises for there being no honey.

I take a spoonful of yoghurt and follow it quickly with a bite of cake to chase away the sharpness. 'Maria? Why does Mitera keep talking about love returning to the mountain?'

'Well . . .' Maria looks at Kostas, who nods as if giving permission. 'Mitera had a love, the love of her life; they were at school together. But they were both young and foolish and one day she heard . . . well, that he had been seen with another girl. Mitera was stubborn and strong-willed. She finished with him and started to see another boy who had been asking her out. A much more sensible boy. Eventually they got married.'

'Kostas's father?' I look at Kostas, and he nods.

'He was a fine man, honest and hard-working, and they had a good life together,' he says. 'But he died when he was still young, rebuilding the villages that were destroyed after the war.' I can see how proud Kostas is of his father as he looks towards his photograph, one of many hung skew-whiff around the fireplace. Here, it's the people in the pictures that matter, not how straight they are on the uneven wall.

Maria tops up our coffee. 'Much later, just a few years ago, Mitera came across her old love by chance on the ancient mountain path that was once filled with wild thyme, oregano and marjoram. She knew him straight away by his big smile and the gap in his front teeth. His family had moved to a village on the other side of the mountain and he had brought up a family of his own there. But he was now a widower, and they began to meet up on the mountain and walk and talk.' Maria's fond smile drops. 'But now . . . now the path is closed off to everyone, and she hasn't seen him for a very long time.' She shrugs. 'She may never see him again.'

'Mitera is sick.' Kostas looks at me. 'Lovesick.'

When love returns to the mountain; when the dittany flourishes again, I think to myself. I know I'm doing exactly the right thing.

Once we've finished eating, we clear away the plates and cups and Kostas insists on washing up, shooing me away to put my feet up after a hard morning's work. I thank him and go to my room, where I pull my case from under the bed and start to look around at my belongings to pack and take up to Georgios's cottage. I hear the Skype ringtone on my laptop. It's Demi! Calling me!

'Demi? Everything all right?' I'm immediately panicking that she's in trouble. I go hot and cold, heart thundering, like I've had a caffeine overdose.

'I'm fine, Mum. Just thought I'd call and say hi,' I hear her say, but I can't see her face. The picture's faint, then it disappears and comes back quite blurry. But I don't care; it's Demi, just wanting to say hi!

'Oh bugger!' I stare at the computer screen, wondering if I've done something wrong or if it's just that the computer is old and slow.

'What's wrong?' she asks, and I can hear the concern in her voice.

'Nothing, love, just this computer.' I pick it up and look at the underside, as if that's going to help.

'Mum?'

I set the computer back down and wave my hands about madly in front of the screen. 'Don't worry, I can hear you and that's the main thing. Now, how are things?'

There's a slight awkwardness in the air, and I hate it. I fan my face and blow upwards. A horrid cocktail of heat and nerves. Since when did I find it awkward to chat to my own daughter?

'Fine,' she says.

'What have you been up to?' we both say at the same time, and then laugh.

'You first, Mum,' she says, and I'm wondering how to tell

her that her birth father is dead and that I should have told her the truth about him years ago, but that his family are wonderful and want to meet her. How on earth do I put all that into a Skype call?

'I've finished the honey factory,' I finally say. 'It's all ready to go. Now all we need is bees.'

'I don't believe it! A honey farm with no bees!' Demi shrieks with laughter, making the mic crackle, and I'm terrified I'm going to lose the sound as well. 'How did that happen?'

'It's complicated. But . . . well, there are bees living up the mountain, but they're not doing very well. Their habitat is dying out so they're very agitated. Kostas keeps trying to tempt them to new hives he's built, attempting to catch them in a cardboard box and rehome them, but so far it's just resulted in him getting badly stung.'

'Oh no!'

'And I'm riding a moped,' I tell her.

'Mum! You always said those things were death traps,' she scolds. 'You never let me have one. And what if anything happened to you? It's not like I've got a big family to turn to.'

I bite my tongue. Should I tell her now?

'Oh, and I'm learning to crochet.' Damn! Missed my moment.

'Much safer. You'll be picking up your pension before you know it,' she teases. I want to tell her it's so much more than an old people's hobby. There's real skill involved in it, and the crocheting circle is a fantastic place where I meet with wonderful, strong, funny women and where everyone keeps in touch and looks out for each other. But I don't. I just laugh with her.

'Oh, and I've got a new friend.' I pick up Angel and hold her to the screen.

'A dog! You never let me have a dog! I'd have loved one!' she practically wails, but she can't help but add, 'Ahhhh, she's gorgeous!' as Angel tries to nip my nose.

'So how are things with you?' I say, settling the little dog in my lap. 'How's the job? How's the family?'

'Fine,' she says brightly, but I can't help but think something's up.

'Demi?'

'It's fine, Mum,' she says crossly now, and I'm cross with myself for pushing it. 'I just wanted to chat, that's all.'

'Yes, of course.' I try and smooth things over, but it's like a game of croquet with the Queen of Hearts in *Alice in Wonderland*, wondering when she's going to yell, 'Off with her head!'

'I'm just tired.'

'Make sure you get an early night,' and I bite my lip as soon as I've said it.

'So, you doing anything tonight?' she asks.

'I have to help out Maria and Kostas's neighbour Georgios with something on his farm. Looks like I'm going to have to look after his sheep!'

Demi bursts into laughter again.

Good, I think. Job done. Steered out of the choppy waters and back into bluer, calmer ones.

'You seem really different, Mum. Have you met someone? Are you and this Georgios having a thing?'

'Good God, no!' I shake my head emphatically and wave my hands again. 'He's . . . no . . . just no. He can't stand me!'

She laughs. 'Well, whatever it is, you've certainly got a sparkle in your eye!'

'Demi, you're the only one I need to love me. You and me, that's how it's always been, hasn't it?' I want to reassure her. 'I'm here if ever you want me.'

'Mum, I'm fine. Stop fussing. I can ring you for a chat without you fussing, can't I?'

'Of course!' I make a mental note not to fuss. I mustn't imagine there's a problem every time she rings. I don't want to put her off calling.

'So, no big love affair then?' She returns to light-hearted good humour and I breathe a sigh of relief, glad she hasn't got all cross with me and ended the call. I look up at the mountain from my bedroom window and over towards Georgios's house, suddenly finding myself wondering if he's waiting for me, wondering where I've got to.

'Definitely not.' I turn back to the screen, nodding and shaking my head at the same time so that it becomes a circle like a nodding dog in the back of a car. I take a swig of water from my bottle.

'Good, I'm not sure how I'd feel if I suddenly discovered you'd met someone and I had a whole load of new uncles, aunts and cousins to contend with,' Demi laughs, and I practically choke, water spilling out of the sides of my mouth and down my chin.

'Um . . . about that . . .' I try and say through the coughing fit. 'The thing is . . .' I take big gulps of air and then more water, and try and breathe again.

'Really, Mum, I'm joking!' she says brightly. 'I know you wouldn't do that to me!' She laughs again and it tinkles around my head as I cringe inwardly.

'Look, Mum, I'd better go.' I can hear a woman calling her name sharply in the background, and again I want to ask if everything's all right. But she's saying goodbye, quickly.

'Oh, OK. Be happy!' I blow kisses. 'I love you.'

'Bye, Mum. Thank you. You're the best.' And she's gone, the dull ache, the yearning to see her, returning.

I wish I was the best, but I'm feeling far from it. How can I drop this bombshell now? Will she stop calling me, missing me if I do? I couldn't stand it. I can't.

Chapter Forty-eight

Standing on the stone step in front of Georgios's door, I knock. When he doesn't answer, I knock again, just to make sure, then push the door open tentatively.

'Hello?' I call. It all looks the same as last time. The little kitchen under the stairs, the fire in the corner with its blackened surround against the whitewashed wall. Just as before, my eyes are drawn to that big picture window looking out over the valley beyond. It's a view you could never get tired of, but I must get on and work out where I'm going to sleep. Angel is sitting at my feet beside me. I bend and stroke her.

'Looks like it's just you and me,' I say, thinking about Demi with her family in London, hoping they're looking after her too.

Reluctantly dragging myself away from the view, I turn around slowly and catch my breath as Georgios dips his head through the low front door and steps in carrying an armful of chopped wood.

'Oh, sorry, I thought you'd gone!' I feel like I'm intruding again. 'I did knock.'

'It's fine.' He heads towards the wood basket by the fire and dumps the armful of logs in there with a clatter that makes Angel leap backwards. I scoop her up until she

275

wriggles to be put down again to chase and bravely tease Filos, although he remains stoic and uninterested.

'Just wanted to be sure you had enough wood for the burner. Are you ready to come and introduce yourself to the bees?'

I gulp.

'We'll go up there together and I'll show you what to do.' He raises one of his dark eyebrows questioningly. 'Then I'll go on up to the cave and you can come back here. OK? You may even have some honey for your breakfast if you talk nicely to them!' he smiles.

I nod.

'Sure?' he checks, and I nod again.

He picks up his rucksack and swings it on to his shoulder before turning to the door, his limp definitely more evident than usual. 'Let's go and meet the bees. Oh, you'll need one of these.' He takes a white suit with a hat and mesh face covering from one of the hooks behind the door and hands it to me. 'Always advisable.'

The wind is there as it always is up the mountain, and as we climb, the dogs weave in and out of our feet. A merry band of four. Just before the plateau, Georgios tells me to stop and put on the bee suit. As he reaches round to zip me in around the neck, my heart is racing, and I'm not sure if it's the prospect of meeting the bees up close and personal or the fact that Georgios has got his arms around me and I'm face to face with his chest and can smell his pine-scented shower gel mixed with the fragrance of the chopped wood he was carrying earlier.

As we approach the hives, I can hear the gentle buzz of the bees on the wind and spot a few of them flying in and out of the boxes.

'The thing is not to get in their flight path,' Georgios tells me. He is clearly quite an expert at this. 'Always stand behind the hive so they can get in and out. Bees are amazing creatures.'

He puts his rucksack on the ground, along with the stick he's picked up to help him walk, and approaches the hives. As I watch, he opens up a box full of equipment and pulls out a billy can with a lid. He lights some sort of dried debris in it, then closes the lid, and it starts pumping out plumes of smoke from an opening at the top. Inside the white suit, a trickle of sweat rolls down the back of my knees, and I try and stand in the shade of the olive tree.

'We use this to move the bees aside. They don't like smoke because they know it means fire. By wafting a little, we can get to see how healthy their hives are looking.'

'Is this the right side?' I double-check I'm not in the flight path. He smiles and nods. 'You see, they are flying in and out on the other side, heading in the direction of the secret valley for the dittany. They are very clever. They know where to find the nectar to make honey from. They know what time of day the flowers will be opening too. Here . . .'

He lifts the lid from one of the hives and puts it on the ground. I can hear the buzzing now, but it's not high-pitched and agitated like it was the other day when they chased me. It seems quite a gentle sort of buzz. He raises the smoke can and waves it a little.

'Come . . .' He encourages me over to look in. Feeling

like a Teletubby, my suit all bunched at the ankles, I shuffle over and peer in. There are wooden slats inside the hive and bees crawling all around them. I remind myself to keep breathing.

'Lift one of the frames out,' he instructs, standing right behind me, and I'm feeling that waggle dance in my tummy again. 'Here . . .' He puts his arms either side of me and guides my hands to lift the slat and slowly draw it up from the hive. The buzzing gets a little louder, possibly a little more excitable, but I don't find myself running for cover.

'You see? The bees have collected the nectar and turned it to honey.' He points to the wooden frame. 'They have been working hard all summer, while the herbs are in flower, and it looks like their efforts are finally coming to fruition. It's all about teamwork. After the worker bees bring the nectar back to the hive, the younger hive bees store it in these hexagonal capsules, then they cover each capsule with a wax cap, like here.' He indicates. 'It's early September now, so they'll want to have made enough to get the colony through the winter before they shut down.'

'My factory at home shut down,' I say, thinking of everything I've left behind.

'It's much the same. The worker bees will go quiet for the winter.' He drops his voice and speaks quietly into my left ear. 'But first they throw out or kill all the men!' I nearly laugh out loud, but stop myself. 'It's true. The males do not make honey. They are only there to impregnate the queen. They do not want extra mouths to feed.'

'And is it really true that they don't like the colour black?'

I smile, thinking of the bees' reaction to me that day I ran from them up the mountain.

'Quite true,' he nods. 'And here,' he lifts another frame, his arms still around me, 'you can see they are moving in the same pattern, telling each other where to go for the nectar: the waggle dance.'

'The code to the secret valley?' I smile and look up at him, and he smiles back, and the waggle dance in my tummy becomes a full-on rave.

'Now, we must look at the rest of the hives. Others may not be doing as well.'

We check each of the hives with varying degrees of satisfaction. 'You see here?' He points to a cell. 'Here they are laying. That's a good sign. They are breeding. If they continue to breed, eventually the hive will become too full and they will need to find new hives. The queen will be thrown out and will take half the adult bees, her children, with her. They will swarm and look for a new home. Another queen will take over the existing hive. And the old queen, we must hope, will find Kostas and the honey farm.'

'Do you think they will?'

'If they are making honey, they are happy. So let's hope.'

I stand by while he checks the next hive. 'How come you know so much about beekeeping?' I ask, trying to keep my voice low and calm despite feeling nervous about being this close to so many buzzing bees.

'After the accident, I spent a lot of time up here. It made me feel close to Stelios somehow. One day I found a swarm, wild bees, building a nest in the hollowed-out trunk of that old olive tree over there. I made a hive, and then very gently moved them into it. I found that spending time here with the bees, it helped; the nightmares weren't as bad. I felt calmer and so, I think, did they. I began to build more hives, and they bred and moved into them. They've helped me through some very dark times.' He looks up at me. 'Now it's my turn to help them.' I nod, understanding.

Finally we check the last hive, and Georgios smiles widely. 'This hive has a good coating of capped honey. It is ready to take for extraction. I'm sure they won't mind sharing a little. You must scrape off the wax cap and then put this in the extractor and spin it.' I nod. 'You know the extractor?'

'Yes, at Kostas and Maria's. I've taken it apart and cleaned every bit of it, so I know how it works.'

He brushes the bees from the frame and hands it to me. 'I tell you what, since you've worked so hard to get it ready, how about we christen that extractor together?'

I beam. 'Really?'

He nods. 'But we must make sure we're not seen. After all, Maria and Kostas think I'm in Athens. But if we are very careful . . .' He looks at me, and I feel a whoosh of excitement right around my tummy.

'Are you sure the bees will be OK with this?' I ask. 'Us taking their honey?'

'Call it a welcome gift.' He smiles again, and we close up all the hives, clipping the lids shut. I find myself feeling surprisingly disappointed that my date with the bees is over. Georgios reminds me that I will need to check them regularly. Without these bees, other plants won't get pollinated and all the mountain plants will die. I nod, taking in the seriousness of what he's saying.

* * *

We make our way back down the mountain, past Georgios's little stone house, where we drop off the bee suits, and then through the cows' field towards Maria and Kostas's farm. Georgios waits there, in the shadows of a big pine, for my signal to say that it's all clear, there's no one around.

I go on, past the honey factory and the goats, and pop my head into the farmhouse. Kostas is sitting in the big rocking chair by the fireplace in the cool front room, crocheting. Maria has gone to the cheesemaking factory, he tells me, and then to visit her family in the city, and Mitera is still in bed. Hopefully some of the mountain honey will help her back to her feet, I think.

I run back to the honey factory, next to the empty beehives, and wave to Georgios, and he joins me at the entrance. We pull back the doors, and I can't help a sudden rush of nervous laughter.

'What's the matter?' Georgios asks.

'Nothing. It's just . . .'

I pause, and he tilts his head and looks at me.

'I feel like the elves and the shoemaker, that's all.'

'The who?'

'The elves and the shoemaker. It's a fairy tale. There was this shoemaker, and when he went to bed at night, the elves made shoes for his shop.'

'So we are elves, making honey?' He shakes his head, smiling. The time with the bees has obviously lifted his spirits. 'We'd better get on with it then, before the shoemaker comes. We can't be found here. Maria and Kostas must not learn the truth about the secret valley.'

I nod, fully in agreement, feeling full of excitement and nerves too.

He pulls the door to behind us, shutting out the hot dust that is rolling around the dry path and field. Then he puts the frames full of honey from the hives on to the shiny clean work surface.

'You've certainly done an amazing job in here,' he says, looking around the cool interior of the barn. 'Now, first we scrape off the wax . . .' He shows me how to do it, revealing the hexagonal honey stores. I copy with another frame, and when they are clear of wax he says, eyes alive with excitement, 'And now, to the honey spinner.' He goes to the big extractor that I have spent all these weeks cleaning, takes off the lid and places the frames inside it, like spokes on a wheel.

'How did you learn all this?'

'Like the bees, you have to build your knowledge, find your way.' He brushes any residual pieces of wax from his hands and puts the lid on the cylindrical drum. His green eyes dance in excitement. 'And now, we spin the honey.'

'Don't we add anything to it?' I ask.

He shakes his head. 'This honey is pure and natural. The flavours and all the medicinal qualities come from the nectar of the wild herbs up in the secret valley. Now, you go first.'

I take hold of the handle on top of the drum and begin to turn it. Finally, the honey factory is coming back to life. The drum moves slowly at first, and I can feel the muscles at the top of my arms working hard. As it spins faster and my arms ache more, my smile grows wider. Georgios reaches forward and puts his hand over mine, spinning the big wooden handle even faster, and I can't help but go with it, the two of us beaming at each other, our eyes locked.

Eventually he starts to slow it down. 'And now, the other way,' he says, and I feel like I'm on the waltzer at the fairground, not knowing which way I'm facing but loving the ride anyway.

Only when we have spun the honey the other way, and then back the first way, and then the other way again, am I finally allowed to take my hands from the handle. Georgios pulls back the lid.

'See?' He points for me to look in. There, slowly sliding down the sides of the big steel drum, are strands of golden honey. 'Try it,' he tells me, beaming. Then, seeing me hesitate, he dips his little finger in and sucks the honey from it, closing his eyes as he does, as if it is indeed pure nectar.

Carefully I run my finger along the rim of the drum and scoop up some of the sticky amber honey. It smells of the wild herbs I have come to love up on the mountain, the wild thyme and that little hint of something extra . . . the dittany. I touch the end of my finger to the tip of my tongue. My eyes on his and his on mine. His eyes have flecks of golden honey running right through them, and they sparkle as I take my first taste, letting the sweet, aromatic honey sit on my tongue, the flavours reaching all around my mouth, taking me back to the mountain, to where I walked with Stelios, and to the verdant gorge that now needs all our help.

'So, how is it?' he asks, still beaming.

'Just gorgeous . . .' I say, remembering the mountain as it used to be and feeling tears prickle at the back of my eyes at the bittersweet memory.

'That's because it's made with love – with *erontas*,' he says, and I feel a shiver of pleasure run through my body. Now I know why everyone wants Vounoplagia honey.

'Now we just have to bottle it,' Georgios says quietly. He shows me how to first filter the honey, in case of any stray bits of wax, and then bottle it in the clean jars that are ready and waiting on their shelf.

We tighten the lids on the jars and hold them up to the light streaming in through the clean window, admiring the deep, rich golden colour. And then Georgios produces crocheted ribbons, like the ones around the dried dittany, from his top pocket, and ties them round the rim of each jar.

'There, now take this to Mitera.' He smiles, handing me a jar. 'Say the messenger left it. A sign of things to come, hopefully.'

How could I have thought that this kind man was up to no good! As I reach to take the jar, our fingers meet and electricity sears through my body once more. I quickly snatch my hand away. Clearly the excitement of reawakening the honey factory has set my nerve endings alight.

'Now we just have to make sure we can do this over and over again.' He holds me in his gaze, his eyes full of excitement and what seems to be a glimmer of hope for the future.

We clean down the extractor and filter in companionable silence, so that, just like in the story of the elves and the shoemaker, nobody knows we were here. Dusk is falling as we walk quietly back through the cows' field towards Georgios's house and the path leading up the mountain.

I notice that Georgios is still holding the stick he used to go up to the beehives. 'Will you be OK getting back up to the cave?' I ask. I feel strangely reluctant to leave him.

He smiles. 'I'll be fine, really. I have lived with this,' he looks down at his leg, 'since the car accident. The fall in the gorge just aggravated it. I broke it badly in the accident, and it never really healed properly, but I was lucky. The medics saved my leg and I'm still here.' He slaps his hands to his sides. 'We have to be thankful for second chances.'

I don't know what to say, so I say nothing.

'You go back to the house.' He nods towards the little stone building. 'And remember to deliver the dittany. I've left it in the kitchen.'

I nod and think of the pile of little dried sprigs tied with crocheted ribbon. 'I'll remember,' I confirm. 'And if you see anyone coming up on to the mountain, give me a signal and I'll do my best to head them off before they go any further.'

'A goat bell.' He pulls one out of the side of his rucksack and shakes it. It's just like the one I hear on the farm as the lead goat moves around the field. It's a sound that I hear all day and night.

'How will I know it's you and not the goats . . . or the sheep, for that matter? Couldn't you just text me?'

He shakes his head. 'No signal; remember when we were in the cave?'

I do, of course.

'So, I will ring the bell and then whistle, like this.' He lets out a long, loud whistle that makes me and the dogs stop in our tracks. 'OK?' He drops his fingers from his mouth.

'Fine,' I agree.

'You must listen for the call and then stop people going any further, whatever it takes. Tourists, poachers, it could be anyone. They mustn't find the valley!'

I know how important this is. Maybe I should admit to what I've done and tell him about Harry Henderson. I wish I knew how to, but our new-found friendship will be blown out of the water if I do, and right now, I don't think I could bear losing that too.

'Look, are you sure you're up for this?' he asks, seeing my worried look.

'Yes, of course. Now go! I can look after things here.'

'I'm worried about who will keep an eye on you!' he jokes as I shoo him away, laughing.

'Go!'

'OK, OK, I'm going.'

I stand and watch him take the worn path up the mountain, leaning heavily on his stick, Filos by his side. I'm about to make my way to the little stone house when he turns back and looks at me. My heart leaps and I feel like I'm riding the moped again for the first time, but this time with no brakes. He raises his hand to wave goodbye, and I wave back, even though I know that reckless behaviour like this can only end in a painful fall.

That evening, at Georgios's house – my new home for now – I replay the thrill of spinning the honey and then tasting it, the most amazing aromatic flavour; I remember with a wide smile Maria and Kostas's cries of excitement when they found a pot left on their doorstep. I am about to settle down for the night when I get a text from Angelica.

Factory is nearly finished. Reopening in two weeks. We can go back to work! You can come home! ☺

I take a moment to think. It's nearly time for me to leave Crete and I'm not sure how I'm feeling. I'll have to go if I want my job back, and I can't stay here forever. I have just two weeks to help Georgios keep the mountain and the secret valley safe until the dittany finishes flowering, or our hard work will have been for nothing.

I walk up the stairs holding on to the smooth olive-wood handrail and enter the open-plan loft room. A large, low bed faces the picture window. I undress and slip under the covers, with Angel curled up beside me, looking out over the valley and the skirt of the mountain that I know is towering above me; where Georgios is. I gaze at the dark sky, the huge white moon casting its silver light, and as I shut my eyes, I finally feel like I'm living again.

Chapter Forty-nine

The next day I'm up early with the morning mist, which is rising like steam off the dewy ground and round the glistening trees. I've fed Maria and Kostas's cows, the dogs and the geese, and not forgetting the duck. I've been up to check the bees too and am just finishing when I hear it.

At first I think it's the eagles circling in the late-summer sky. I look up and around, my hair flick-flacking around my face. Then I hear it again, and this time I know exactly what it is: the ring of a goat bell followed by a long whistle. It's Georgios's signal. My heart starts thundering. It's time.

Putting down the water bucket in the sheep enclosure hastily so that the water slops over the sides, I make a dash for the mountain path at the back of Georgios's house, Angel following hot on my heels. I have no idea what I'm going to do. All I know is I need to see who it is and work out how to keep them from going any higher up the mountain.

I reach the plateau on the way to the first cave and head straight to the outreach of rock beyond the bees. I can hear voices, so I drop to all fours and crawl forward, the sharp stones sticking into my knees. I lie on my stomach and wriggle to the rim of the ledge, my fingers gripping the edge. I can see the road clearly from here, right over the cows' field.

There's a family car parked at the viewing point, and I glance up to see if I can spy Georgios further up the mountain. But the cave, like the valley, is well hidden.

The car doors open and a group of holidaymakers climb out. There is a large lady in a floral dress, sunglasses and a big straw sunhat, which she's clinging on to in the whipping wind. A man gets out behind her, just as large, in long shorts and a T-shirt stretched over his big belly. He's holding an iPad, which obviously has a map on it, and is complaining about the car's sat nav taking them the long route round. There is only one route here, I think with a smile: up the mountain road. He's turning the iPad this way and that, trying to work out where they are.

There's a young boy, about twelve, wearing big head-phones, an expensive make by the looks of it, ones I could never afford for Demi. He's holding a smaller tablet with both hands as if he's driving, very fast, through downtown streets, being chased by cop cars. He focuses on the job in hand and not on his mother's squawking as her hat takes off and she and her husband have to chase it. A tall, long-haired, long-legged teenage girl gets out of the car reluctantly and is handed the iPad and directed to take photographs whilst her father chases the hat down the road.

I have to stop them coming up here. They mustn't find the secret valley. The woman's hat is still leading them a merry dance back down the hill, and the whole family is now trying to round it up. I take my moment. Running quickly and confidently down the mountain path, past the wild greens, I pause among the pine trees to check that the family are still huffing and puffing their way back up the hill towards their car, and run over to the cows' field. The animals look up at me and I shove my hand in my pocket and find dried carob pods, their smell like dark treacle, malty. I wave one at the cows as I'm trying to untie the string on the fence, but drop it as I work away at the tight knot I've been so particular in securing. Finally I get my nails right into it and loosen it, then quickly pull back the panel and step through. By this time the calf has spotted the carob pod on the uneven dry ground and is heading towards it, his mother following close behind.

The tourists, German by the sounds of it, have started to walk towards the steps of the mountain path carrying fold-up chairs, a huge picnic hamper and a sunshade.

'That's it, this way,' I whisper, chucking another dried husk in the cows' direction, and suddenly they're all moving towards me in a straight line, one after the other, like I'm the Pied Piper. 'Yes! Come on.' I break up the husks and keep throwing them behind me as I step through the gap in the fence.

Once they're out of the field, the cows begin to spread out, over the wide path and up on to the lower slopes of the mountain, through the pine trees, investigating and seeking out fresh grassy tufts. I stand behind a tree and wait.

'Arghhhh!' The shriek finally comes and I can't help but giggle, like a child playing a prank on April Fool's Day. I pinch my nose to try and stop myself, and find myself making a funny snorting noise, which makes me laugh even more. I clasp my hand over my mouth.

The family are retreating back down the slope, surrounded by the cows, who seem to want to investigate their pockets for carob pods. The woman has her hands in the air and is shrieking. Her hat has now blown off the mountain edge, and is floating away in the breeze like a parachute. The man is shouting, 'Shoo!' and waving his hands. Their son has stopped playing his computer game and is checking behind him as the calf chases after him towards the car, where his parents are now arguing over who has the keys, and the daughter is doubled over with laughter.

Finally they get the car open, sling the picnic hamper, chairs and sunshade into the boot and jump in, slamming the doors shut. By now the vehicle is surrounded by cows, and both the man and the woman are leaning out of the windows and waving their arms. Finally they manage to turn the car around and spin off down the winding road, way faster than they came up it, and a quiet falls over the mountainside again, apart from the sound of munching and mooing cows.

Smiling and dusting off my hands in satisfaction, I glance up at the mountain, hoping that Georgios was watching as I chased away the intruders – and with not a bird scarer in sight.

That night, with the cows back securely in their field, and after an afternoon helping at the restaurant, I return to the mountain with a small pot of lamb stew that I've smuggled out of Maria's kitchen. I know that if I asked, she would let me have it, but I don't want her to know that I'm taking it to Georgios. It's better this way. Negotiating the narrow ledge and the climb up to the second cave with the pot under my arm is precarious, but worth it, as the stew warms over the fire, the smell of the slow-cooked lamb and soft, fluffy potatoes, tangy lemon juice and herby wild thyme filling the gently cooling air and wrapping itself around the inside of the cave.

I think back to Georgios telling me how families in these parts fought German parachuters who dropped into the mountains, and used these caves to hide the British allies, some injured, who worked closely with the island's resistance movement during the Second World War. 'Protecting what cannot look after itself,' as he put it. A little like now, I think, as we sit watching the sun set, eating from tin cups with metal spoons produced from my pocket. Afterwards we sip raki, and Georgios works on the trunk of the fallen olive tree, turning it into a new shrine for Stelios, which he plans to put in the main square of the town, next to the church, so we can remember him every time we pass it.

But as we relive the triumph of the day, I know the reality is that although we may have been able to keep one family off the mountain, the next intruders may arrive at any time. Is Georgios really going to be able to keep this valley secret forever?

Chapter Fifty

For the next few days there is no signal from Georgios telling me that there are tourists on the mountain. But each evening I climb up to the cave with food and the news that the bees seem happy and are continuing to make honey. We may have more to spin soon! The days are still hot, but up here in the mountain, in the early-evening breeze, it's much cooler.

Georgios smiles, accepting the Greek salad I bring him one evening, full of olives, tomatoes, cucumber and onion, along with fresh tangy yoghurt with home-grown figs.

'And honey!' I say, producing one of the jars we spun.

'How does it taste now? Did Mitera like it?'

I nod. 'Wonderful! They all loved it. Maria says that Mitera will be well and back on her feet in no time now they have wild mountain herb honey. It's like . . . well, like nectar!' We both laugh.

'Well, it is made with love,' he says, smiling.

He insists on sharing the salad, and pours us raki, and we sit on the logs by the mouth of the cave, his woodwork to the side of him. In contented silence we spoon feta and black olives and chunks of the knobbly, crunchy cucumber into our mouths.

'Did you know,' he finally says, 'that the word for boyfriend or girlfriend in Greek translates as "the one I'm eating with"?' He smiles, and my cheeks burn and I look down into my salad.

When we've finished, we dish out the yoghurt and plump purple figs into the metal cups, which I've washed in the cold clear water of the waterfall outside the cave. Then Georgios hands me the honey. I undo the jar and breathe in its aroma again, then I tip it, and the golden liquid pours into my cup, catching the sunlight as it cascades slowly down. I hand the jar to Georgios, who does the same, and we spoon the yoghurt and soft figs into our mouths. As the sweet, aromatic, herb-infused honey melts across my tongue, I think I'm in heaven.

'So, you never fell in love again, after Stelios?' Georgios finally says, and I open my eyes and look at him, his face so much softer than when we first met.

I spoon up more honey and yoghurt and shake my head. 'No, there was no one else.' I glance back in the direction of the picture with the little tea lights in front of it. 'At first I was waiting for Stelios, of course, and I wasn't interested in meeting anyone. But once Demi went to school and started to have her own friends, well, I thought it would be nice . . . for her and me. But I didn't want to get it wrong. That's why Mike, my ex, made so much sense at the time. He was happy with our arrangement. I'd see him once in the week and then at weekends.'

'But you never married him?'

I shake my head. 'I didn't marry him, or even live with him. He had a bag under the stairs that he brought with him when he arrived and took again when he left. I didn't want to get it wrong, for Demi's sake. I wanted stability. I didn't want anyone to ruin what I'd built for the two of us, Demi and me.'

'Too scared,' he nods.

I sigh. 'I suppose. Let's be honest, at that point I felt that everyone I'd ever cared about had left me. And I'd made a mess of things so far. The likelihood was I would probably get it wrong again. And . . . well, I didn't want it to be like when I was growing up.'

'In what way?' He takes a sip of raki, and so do I.

'Let's just say my mum kissed a lot of frogs before she met her prince. I had more uncles than I had pairs of shoes!'

We both laugh gently.

'And now?'

'For someone who keeps themselves to themselves, you ask a lot of questions!' I tell him. But I don't really mind. It feels good to talk, like we're in a bubble where what's said in the secret gorge stays in the secret gorge. 'Well, my mum finally met her Prince Charming, on holiday in Majorca, and out of the blue they decided to emigrate to Australia. She offered me the chance to go with them, but frankly I felt like a spare part, so I decided to stay with my nan. And that's how it was: me, Nan and Demi. I loved my life. I wish I could have it all back, our little family. But Nan died, and then it was just me and Demi, and I didn't want to get it wrong, although in the end I think I did.' I lean my chin on my hand and look into my raki. 'Otherwise I wouldn't be back here trying to find who I used to be, would I?'

'Sounds to me like you've tried your hardest to be the best mum you can be.'

I put down my mug, and roll my lips together to get the final sweetness from the honey off them, watching the sun set down the valley.

'Doesn't mean I got it right,' I say. 'So what about you? Did anyone finally manage to tame Gorgeous George?' We both smile, and he blushes at the memory of his younger, flirtatious days. Then his face drops.

'Ssh!' He puts his finger to his lips.

'All right, I didn't mean—'

'No, ssh!' he says again, and I realise he's not talking about our conversation. I fall silent and listen. At first all I can hear is the gentle sound of the goat bells down at the farm, but then I hear it. Cars. And doors closing, and then voices.

Chapter Fifty-one

It's not the German tourists back. It's Harry Henderson. Still as good-looking as before, only this time I don't feel half as excited to see him. In fact, I'm appalled that I ever found him remotely attractive. He's in a group with three other people, who look like holiday reps. Young, tanned and eager. Just like when I worked at the resort. They're wearing a uniform of orange T-shirts and matching shorts with a holiday logo. One is in trainers, one in Greek sandals and one is wearing flip-flops.

I've made it down from the cave, out of the valley and down to the ledge at breakneck speed, and am still trying to get my breath back and eavesdrop on their conversation at the same time. I hold my hand over my eyes to protect them from the low evening sun.

'So, what we know is, this plant, dittany, grows here.' Harry is showing the three reps a picture on his iPad. 'This dittany is disappearing off the mountain. If it goes altogether, the mountain will lose its protected status and we'll get the planning permission we need. So—'

'But isn't that like . . . illegal. I mean, if it's got protected status?' The girl in flip-flops has got a very Home Counties voice.

'We're just giving nature a helping hand. The herb is dying out anyway. And your jobs on this new project up here depend on it.' The girl in trainers suddenly looks like she's well up for it, bending into a sprinting position like she's about to take on her colleagues at the hundred-metre dash.

Harry, looking cool in cream cut-off chinos, deck shoes and a polo shirt with the collar turned up, reflective shades on, looks around at the group and lowers his voice. I shuffle forward to hear what he's about to say, and as I do, a shower of stones tumbles down the rocks below me, making the group glance up. I dart back, lying as flat as I can, my heart thundering. Brilliant! I berate myself. Mission two and I've nearly blown it!

When I don't hear them comment on the stone shower, I wriggle back to the edge and peer cautiously over. The girl in trainers is still looking from side to side, poised, obviously keen to bag herself a new job on the new hotel complex that Harry is planning.

'Now then, there have been rumours of gangs up on the mountains.'

'What kind of gangs?' The young woman stands up, hands on hips, rethinking things.

'But,' Harry holds up a hand, 'I have it on good authority that those rumours are false. Put about as a way of keeping people away.'

I feel sick. It was me who told him that. Thinking I was doing the right thing and completely stuffing it up, once again.

'I need you to get on to that mountain, and if you see this plant, rip it out . . . by the root. Take it home with you. Do whatever it takes. Like I say, your jobs on this project depend on this. Get help if needs be. I've spoken to the office of protected sites. If we can convince the inspector there is no evidence of fresh dittany here on his next couple of visits, this project will get the green light for sure. They'll be a beach barbecue in it for you all if we pull this off.'

I have absolutely no idea what I saw in this man. Why am I such a bad judge of character – first Mike and now Harry Henderson, one-man planet assassin!

'No probs,' says the Home Counties girl.

'It's done!' says the one in trainers, resuming her sprinting position.

'On it!' says the third rep, a tall, dark lad in sandals, and they all high-five each other, making my hackles rise. I can practically hear a growl in the back of my throat. This is my fault. But I can't believe they would stoop that low, ripping out the dittany to get control of the mountain – to wipe out the town!

Just then I hear a scrabbling among the rocks and turn, catching my breath. To my relief, it's only Filos. He gives a little bark of greeting to Angel, who is beside me and who wags her tail and wiggles her body in reply. There is a call from up high, and this time it's the eagles, three of them, circling in the light wind against the clear blue sky and the cotton-wool clouds.

I have to get these people to stay off the mountain. I scoop up Angel under my arm and head towards the pathway, where it looks like they're starting to climb.

'Please don't hate me for this . . . I have my reasons,' I say to the two dogs.

I reach out and sit Angel on a little stone ledge, then call to Filos to follow me down the path. As the three reps get closer, I back away behind a nearby pine tree. Filos stands in the middle of the path, barking steadily and incessantly, like a metronome, while Angel watches with interest from her vantage point. I can see the climbing party now, looking like invading troops marching up the mountain. But when they see Filos, they stop in their tracks, trying to weigh up the barking and growling dog.

'It's just a dog,' says the Home Counties girl.

'An angry one,' says the sprinter.

'Give it a wide berth,' says the lad in sandals, putting out his hand protectively. Trainer girl knocks it away with annoyance. I start to climb up the rocks ahead of them, hoping that Filos and Angel will keep them at bay.

'Ah look, a puppy,' the sprinter says, and I hear Filos growl, slow and low.

'Leave it,' commands the Home Counties girl.

'Oh look, it's jumped down,' says the lad. 'But I don't think he wants us to pet it.'

Filos is still barking. I'm out of breath and hot. The path narrows here, making it a perfect place to cause a blockage. I scamper up to the ledge above, take a deep breath and kick at some of the smaller stones lying around. A few scatter down the hill but stop. I can hear the invaders climbing once again, scanning the plants around them. Angel suddenly bounds on to the ledge next to me, and I hold her close to me gratefully, then pull my leg back and thrust it forward again, harder this time. Dust flies up, and many more stones shift and start to tumble. I hear the three reps shouting to each other – 'Watch yourselves!' 'Mind out!' 'Shit!' – and watch from my vantage point as they run back down the path. Breathless, hot but smiling, I think I may have done it.

But when the stones slow up and finally stop falling, the trio start climbing again, undeterred.

'Boy! They must really want those jobs,' I say to Angel, but I'm beginning to panic. What now? I'm out of ideas. I duck down, hiding behind a big rock just off the path. I've got to move further up or they'll spot me.

And then I hear it . . . and tense up. The buzzing is getting louder and angrier. The landslide has upset the bees. I clutch Angel right into my tummy and hold my other hand over my head, listening as the buzzing gets closer and then, to my huge relief, passes me by. I poke my head up above the rock and take big gulps of air. The three orange-T-shirted reps are shouting and shrieking as they run from the bees. There is the sound of car doors slamming shut, then a reversing car spinning off on the stony ground.

'We did it, Angel!' I say as I rub her ears.

There's a scrambling noise behind me, tiny rocks rattling down. I turn to see Georgios sliding down next to me, his leg outstretched. He sits beside me, shoulder to shoulder, leaning against the rock, then turns to me and smiles, and my insides suddenly feel like they've been melted by the hot Cretan sun.

'We did it!' I grin, my head tilted back in exhaustion.

'*You* did it!' he corrects, holding up his hand and smiling some more. I high-five him, and then Filos comes and joins us, sitting by his master, smiling and panting, his long pink tongue lolling out of the corner of his mouth.

I rest my head against the rock and close my eyes. We did it, but I'm not sure what I'll be able to do if it happens again.

'Look,' Georgios says. 'A kri-kri goat.' I open my eyes to see him pointing up to a rocky outcrop, but the goat dips and turns and is gone before I have a chance to get a proper look at it.

We clamber to our feet and say our goodnights, Georgios smiling widely at me, taking hold of my hand. Slowly I let it slide from his as I turn and head back towards the cottage, using the torch on my phone to guide me.

Back at the little stone house, I shower, get into bed, and watch from the window as the moon rises, whispering goodnight to Demi, and then to Georgios, up in his cave. Then, with a trace of wild mountain herb honey still on my lips, I drift off into the deepest sleep I have had in a long time.

Chapter Fifty-two

It's early morning when I hear the signal from Georgios again, the goat's bell followed by the whistle. My eyes ping open and my heart immediately starts racing, like I've drunk three strong coffees, one after the other. I lie there for a minute, then I hear it again. I'm not dreaming it. It's the signal.

'Oh God!' As I roll out of bed, everything aches from putting off Harry's holiday reps last night. I turn to the huge window and quickly drink in the valley and the mist curling through it. Then I pull on a checked shirt over my T-shirt to keep off the early chill, which will burn off by mid-morning. Despite September rolling in, there's no let-up in the heat – if anything, it's getting hotter. The kind of heat that burns the inside of your nostrils when you breathe it in.

Downstairs, I grab a thin scarf from the coat hooks by the door and hold it to my nose. It smells of . . . I pause just for a moment . . . woodsmoke and a hint of wild thyme. The smell of Georgios. He seems to be creeping into my dreams more and more. Where once all I dreamed about was the fire and Demi, now Georgios is popping up everywhere I look. I quickly wind the scarf round my neck, and then, with Angel at my feet, wriggling her body in excitement and giving my ankles a succession of little licks, I pull open the door and head up the mountain path to my vantage point.

I hear them before I see them; the clanking of the bell and the bleating. Goats! Kostas's goats! Climbing this way and that, grazing their way up the mountain, spreading out wider and wider, like a river that's burst its banks and is continuing its journey every which way. There's no way Maria would have let them out on to the mountainside. Surely she wouldn't have left their gate open after milking.

Then I spot him. Harry Henderson, back again. This time he's getting into his car, parked at the vantage point at the end of the lane, and disappearing in a cloud of dust back down the hill. Looks like he wasn't going to let himself be chased away from the mountain even if his reps were. He's going for the natural approach this time, letting the goats out to seek out the dittany and eat it. This is all my fault. I should never have told him about the dittany, never!

I head up the mountainside as quickly as I can, stepping from rock to rock, waving my arms manically at the goats. But the more I wave and shout, the faster they run away from me.

Then I see him, Georgios, leaning heavily on a stick again. He's obviously whittled it from a branch from the olive tree up by the cave. He's moving slowly across the rocks, goat bell in his other hand. One by one the goats seem to hear it, and change direction to follow him, until they are all moving together as a herd. Georgios goes one way and I go the other, corralling the goats on to a wide flat ledge, with Filos doing his best to help round them up, jumping from rock to rock, barking for all he's worth. Angel joins in too, yapping, tail wagging, like this is the best fun she's had ever.

'Thank you!' I say, out of breath and sweating as I finally reach him. I peel off my shirt and tie it around my waist over my denim cut-offs.

He nods. 'It's me who should be thanking you. Here,' and he hands me a bundle of dried dittany, tied into tiny bunches. 'Are you sure you're OK to deliver them today? You're not too tired?'

'No, I'm not actually.' I smile. 'I'll drop in at the crocheting circle later this afternoon and find out who needs them most.' I put the dittany into my top pocket. 'Agatha has arthritis in her hands again. And Nadim, who lives near the school, has stomach pains, but the ladies from the circle says he's been finishing up last year's vintage from his wine cellar to make room for the new one coming in. Oh, and Samir at the supermarket, I saw him drop a slab of cans on his foot when I was in there yesterday getting rice for Maria.'

'Are you sure you don't have too much on, what with your jobs at the farm and the restaurant as well as my place?'

'I'm fine,' I tell him, and I really am. I'm so busy I've hardly had time to sit and brood over missing Demi. Maybe it's because she's ringing me more. She must be settled. And as long as she stays in touch, I think I'm finally starting to come to terms with it. 'I'm actually . . .' like a wave slowly washing over me, I realise, 'I'm actually really enjoying myself. I think I needed to feel needed again.'

'How are Maria and Kostas?' he asks. 'Any more bee stings?'

I shake my head. 'No more bee stings. And Kostas is loving crocheting again. Says it keeps him occupied while he waits for the bees to come.' For a moment we both laugh, leaving behind the worries of the past and of the future, enjoying the thought of Kostas sitting crocheting by the fire in one of Maria's aprons. 'He's started experimenting with a new stitch.'

'And Mitera?'

I shake my head. 'No better.' I make a mental note to drop off some more dittany to her too. 'I ought to get these goats back to their pen. I have to collect mountain greens before going to the restaurant. Stelios's mother is going to see her sister, and I said I'd help out for a couple of hours at lunchtime.'

He nods. 'You did good work again this morning, Nell. Thank you,' he says while my back is turned, as if it is somehow easier to say what he wants to say when he's not looking me in the eye. 'Stelios would be very proud of you,' he finishes, and I hear the catch in his voice. I lift my face to the breeze and let the compliment feed my soul, but this time there are no tears.

I turn and start to guide the goats down the mountain path, arms wide open. Stelios may be part of my past, but this place is about who I am now, and right now, I'm not going to let some developer and a flock of stray goats take the future from the people I have come to care about. I wonder, just for a moment, if Georgios is becoming one of those people too but tell myself to stop being silly. Gorgeous George is never going to be interested in someone like me; besides, the last thing I want or need is another holiday romance. I'm not settling for second best any more. Not a holiday romance or a relationship built on convenience, like the one with Mike. If I ever get together with someone again it will be because I love them, like I loved Stelios, and because I want to be with them for the rest of my life.

As I walk down the mountain slope, my phone rings. It's Demi, calling for a chat. It's a welcome distraction from thinking about Georgios.

'Hello, sweetheart, how lovely to hear from you. How's things with you? . . . Nothing much going on here . . . No, not much longer until I'm home . . .'

But the buzzing bees in my belly flutter about madly anyway.

Chapter Fifty-three

Another week has nearly passed. The weather is sweltering, and there's been no sign of rain since the day I got caught up the mountain with Georgios. The ground is dusty and hard. Maria and I are watering the herbs in the meadow. Kostas is making bread in the kitchen and singing. We can hear him, the sound rising up through the window to the low slopes of the mountain.

'He would have made a wonderful father,' Maria says suddenly and wistfully. Then she looks at me and smiles. 'How is Demi?' she asks, as if she has known her all her life. And I suddenly get a pang, wondering how it's going to feel when I have to leave this place and actually go home in a week's time.

'Fine,' I say. 'In fact, she keeps texting me funny photos of herself, and then ringing, just to chat . . .' I tail off, still surprised by this turn of events, and anxious, although I have no idea why. 'I'm still worried, although I know I shouldn't be.'

'But that's a great thing. She wants someone to talk to about her adventures and it's you she wants to tell.'

I nod. She's right that it's me Demi rings when she wants to chat. And I'm delighted that she knows I'm there if she needs me. I feel a new sense of peace. It may not be the same as it used to be, but at least I'm still a part of her life.

'It was never meant to be for us, sadly,' says Maria. She is bending over the herbs, her big bosoms rising to meet under her chin, her apron tied between the two rolls of her waist. 'There haven't been children in the town for such a long time. It would have been wonderful. It would be lovely to have a school again, to hear the sound of children playing outside in the school yard. We need more young people to move here to bring up their children. Soon there will be no one left, no one to pass our way of life on to.'

'Not until love comes back to the mountain,' and we both turn to see Mitera walking slowly towards us, supporting herself with a stick.

'Mitera!' we both say, and straighten up and walk towards her, catching her by the elbows. 'I thought you were in bed,' Maria says, concerned but pleased to see her up and about. Mitera is wearing a headscarf and slippers, but she's lost a lot of weight and her teeth shift and slide around in her mouth.

'I thought I would walk the mountain path myself, show them we won't be scared off it. Just like during the war, we won't give up without a fight!' she says, and then dips as her knees give way. 'I want to see for myself who is keeping people off the mountain.' She looks from Maria to me.

'Let's get you back inside, Mitera,' Maria says, putting down her hosepipe.

'I just want to see them!' Mitera shouts at the mountain, and shakes her fist.

It's then that I hear it. The bell and the whistle, and then the whistle again and the bell ringing like billy-o. Maria looks up and frowns.

'I have to check on Georgios's sheep. Sounds like there's a ruckus going on,' I say by way of explanation.

'Yes, of course, go, go!' Maria waves her hands at me, the tea towel tucked into her apron swishing to and fro. 'But stay away from any signs of trouble,' she calls, 'and come and get me if you need help.'

'And me!' adds Mitera, shaking her walking stick and clinging on to Maria with the other hand. She has aged so much in the short time I've been here.

I run towards the path, grabbing the handrail and leaping on to the first stone step, worn in the middle from hundreds of years of local people taking this same route. Then out on to the dusty road, past Georgios's house and towards the back route up the mountain.

By the time I reach Georgios, I am panting and out of breath. He's standing on top of the grassy roof of the cave.

'Look!' He points without bothering with greetings. I follow his finger down the mountain to a lay-by. There are two cars there. 'I spotted them coming up the mountain road. See? One is a hire car, the one with the dents in the passenger door. The other, the truck, is from out of town.' He takes a pair of binoculars from his eyes and passes them to me. As our fingers brush, my body gives a surprising jolt, as if I've touched an electric cable. Must be static, I tell myself firmly.

'More tourists?' I ask, recognising Harry's car straight away and wondering if the cows will be enough to put him off.

Georgios reaches out and takes back the binoculars. I look down at his dark arm, covered in black hairs, the same colour as the stubble around his chin, apart from where the scar cuts through it.

'Not tourists,' he says. 'Looks like they mean business . . .' and the muscles in his arm tense and ripple.

'What? What is it?' I reach up for the binoculars.

'It's worse, much worse. See for yourself.'

'What? How can it be worse?' I frown. 'How do you know?'

'Look at the men in the truck.'

I watch as four men climb out of the blue truck covered in beige dust. They are wearing an assortment of joggers, checked shirts, worn open with the sleeves cut out, baggy T-shirts and baseball caps. Two have dark moustaches running along their top lips and down the sides of their mouths. They're looking around, pulling up the backs of their sagging joggers and turning this way and that, talking intently amongst themselves.

'Do you know them?' I frown, and he shakes his head. They lift the boot of the car and start unloading pieces of equipment.

'What's that? What are they doing? Georgios, who are they?' My heart starts pounding.

'Poachers, professional poachers,' and by the look on Georgios's face, things have just got a whole lot more serious.

Chapter Fifty-four

'What's all that equipment?'

'Traps,' he says coldly.

'Traps?' I repeat in disbelief. 'What do they need traps for?'

He shrugs. 'Times are hard on the island. They're trying to make a living, look after their families. They'll strip the mountain of dittany and take it to the shops in the bigger towns and cities to sell to tourists.'

'And the traps?'

'They won't want animals getting to the herbs before them. Every plant is money to them.' He looks down at Filos, who lies down and whimpers.

'We have to stop them, Georgios!'

'These guys aren't messing around. You must be careful. They won't let anything or anyone stand in their way. This is big business.' He looks at me and my mouth goes dry. 'These are the men this town has been terrified of, believing them to be already here. And now they have come. They could be armed,' he says, taking hold of both my hands.

'What are we going to do? More landslides?'

He tips his head to and fro whilst thinking.

'What about the bees?' I ask desperately. 'What will happen to them?'

He shrugs. 'If these men get what they've come here for, it's over for all of us.'

'Maybe the bees will guard their hives, like they did last time,' I say hopefully.

'I reckon they will have been tipped off about the bees after the last time he was here.' He nods towards Harry, who has got out of his car, dark glasses on, and is walking over to the group of men. 'I don't think bees will stop them.'

'Filos? He could do his protective-dad routine again.'

Georgios shakes his head, almost as if he's beaten. 'These guys are not going to be scared off by a three-legged dog.'

We fall into silence, both racking our brains.

'They might not find the valley,' I try hopefully.

'With any luck not. But still, if they do find it, there will be nothing more we can do.' He looks at me, and I can see he feels he has let everyone down.

'Georgios, we have to keep going, for Stelios! We have to fight for what we believe in.'

He is silent again for a moment, his eyes staring straight into mine, as if we are sealing a pact. 'You're right. Men stood their ground and fought to defend these mountains during the war. I can't walk away now. I have to stand and fight too. It's the right thing to do, but we don't have a chance of winning, you and me against them.' He manages a smile that sets my insides alight. 'Though actually, I do have one other idea. It's risky, but if we're careful and manage it properly, it might just do the job. Scare them off and convince them there's nothing worth coming back for. We'll need to collect lots of wood . . .'

Chapter Fifty-five

When Georgios has finished explaining his plan, I look at him incredulously. Have I heard him right?

'You want to start a fire?' I say.

'Not *a* fire. A number of little ones, dotted along the mountain edge. That way, when the wind picks up and creates lots of smoke, they'll think the mountainside is ablaze.'

I feel my hands starting to shake. I remember the sound of the fire as it took hold of the factory. You couldn't hear it at first, as Noddy Holder was blaring out and the girls from packing were singing along – well, more like shrieking. And the smell . . .

'Nell? Look, if you don't want to do it, I could just use the bird scarer. Fire off rounds. Hope they'll be put off.'

'No, it needs more than that.' I swallow. 'They look like they're ready to take on an army. Let's do it!'

He breaks into a smile and I find myself doing the same. Adrenalin scoots through my body like a roller-coaster ride, dipping and turning, zooming so fast it feels like my senses have been left behind, and I think they probably have! Then, breathing heavily, he takes my face in his hands and gazes at me. 'You are one amazing woman,' he says, his jewelled eyes intense, and the adrenalin surges and what I really want to do is reach up and kiss him, like my life depends on it.

But instead I pull away, my heart racing. I look down and see Harry counting notes into the chief poacher's hands. 'Let's do it!'

As I put the match to the first little fire, making sure that there is no other shrubbery around it, my hands are shaking, but the dry grass immediately starts to smoke and glow and take hold. Further up from my vantage point I can see Georgios's fire sending up smoke too.

We worked quickly, collecting kindling and moss and building small fires on each of the plateaus and vantage points on the route up the mountain path, with the final one just by the cave into the secret valley. Beside each of the little piles, surrounded by a circle of stones, we left a billy can of water from the stream in the valley, ready to put the fires out as soon as we can.

Now I can hear the men working their way up the mountain, their rough, deep voices giving out instructions to each other. I quickly move on and light the next fire. By the time I'm on to the third, the smoke catches in my throat from the damp moss and olive leaves. It's smoking well. I look up and see that Georgios has at least three fires going too. One or two more should do it. I wipe my mouth and my forehead.

Then I hear the signal and I know that the men have noticed the smoke and it's time to create some panic!

'Fire! *Fotia!*' I call over the edge of one of the rocky plateaus, lying on my tummy so as not to be seen. They're looking around but don't seem to be slowing down. I have to stop them.

'Fire! Fire!' This time I stand up and shout. The wind is picking up and swirling the smoke around. I see them pointing at me, but still they aren't retreating. I jump from stone to stone down the familiar mountain path, waving my arms like windmills.

Suddenly I come face to face with the four rough-arsed poachers. I have no idea what I'm going to do next if they still won't leave.

For a moment they stare at me in surprise.

'Fire! *Fotia!*' I shout again, and suddenly the wind whips the smoke up and through the trees around us, catching in our throats, making us all cough, as if the gods are helping to waft it on its way.

'*Fotia!*' they all agree, and they turn as one and start hurrying back down the mountain, thick legs moving as fast as their baggy-bottomed joggers will allow them.

I follow on as far as the steps, making sure they don't turn back. Too late I realise that Harry is still there, watching the poachers get back in their truck. 'We don't want to take the blame,' I hear them tell him. Harry is dumbfounded and throws his glasses to the dusty ground in frustration. As he spins away from the departing truck, he spots me.

'Nell? What are you doing here?' he frowns. 'There's a fire. You'd better get away. You don't want to be here when the authorities turn up.'

'No, you're right. Anyone found trying to damage the mountain could be in terrible trouble. Maybe a jail sentence, I heard your friends saying,' I lie.

'Um, can I give you a lift?' He looks up nervously at the smoke, one leg in the footwell of his car.

I wave a hand. 'I'm fine, really, I know where I'm going.'

He takes one more look up at the billowing smoke, then slams the car door and spins off back down the mountain road, following the poachers in their truck.

I can't help but smile triumphantly. They've gone. But then I hear a voice that I hadn't bargained for. It all happened so quickly, I hadn't worked out what I was going to say to anyone else about the fires.

'Nell? Nell? What's happening?' Maria is waving her tea towel at me and pointing to the smoke.

'It's fine. No need to panic . . . Holidaymakers having a barbecue. Henderson's Holidays,' I stutter.

'They started a fire?'

'It's fine. Honestly, Maria, it's all under control, I promise you.' I'm edging away from her as I speak. I need to go back up the mountain to put the fires out before they do get out of hand. The smoke is starting to build.

'Tell them no more barbecues!' She shakes her head at me as I turn and sprint away.

Using the cans of water from the stream, I watch as each fire is extinguished with a hiss and a fizz until they are all out. Then I climb up the familiar route to the cave in the secret gorge, where, hot, out of breath and with a dark smudge across his forehead, Georgios is standing beaming, and this time I can't stop myself. I throw myself towards him, riding on the crest of the wave of adrenalin that is still coursing through my body.

'We did it! They've gone!' I say gleefully, and like two magnets finally drawn together, I fall forward into his arms and my lips find his, and I kiss him, on and on.

Chapter Fifty-six

I wake the next morning with the rising sun warming my face. I open my eyes and remember where I am. On a sheepskin rug, by a fire, high up in the Cretan mountains, lying next to . . . Zeus. I smile, looking at Georgios's soft sleeping face – relaxed and as if all his worries have finally been lifted from his shoulders – then lean in and run my finger down the line of the scar on his cheek, still smiling at him and at the memory of last night.

Slowly I turn around and look at the shrine. The candles have gone out. I slide from Georgios's arms and from under the red Aztec-print blanket covering us, pull on my crumpled clothing and creep over to the shelf where the matches are lying. Suddenly the warm, happy feeling that was wrapping itself around me disappears, replaced by the frosty feeling of guilt.

I turn round to glance at Georgios and see that he's sitting up, arms wrapped around his knees, looking at me. At first he says nothing and I don't know what to say either. At last he speaks.

'He would be pleased for us. That we have found each other.'

'Is that all it was? Comfort?' Because if it was, it was the most amazing comfort I've ever had, I think, blushing at my own brazenness and unable to look at Stelios's picture.

'No,' he smiles. 'This is not about comfort. This is about so much more. Come, come back,' he says softly, patting the place I've just left.

I leave the matches and walk back towards him, sitting down on the sheepskin rug. He wraps the blanket around my shoulders, then puts his arm around me and pulls me in close. We stare out of the cave mouth, smelling the fresh morning air, watching the mist curl around the gorge as the sun slowly pushes its way through the morning chill.

'I have to go and water the herbs down at the honey farm, and then check the bees on the mountainside,' I say, resting my head on his shoulder, though really I don't want to go anywhere.

'Stay, drink something first,' he says. He stands and pulls on his trousers, his belt hanging undone, his chest bare, making my insides shift and shift again as he puts more sticks on the fire and then fills the billy can of water to make mountain tea; a taste I'm beginning to get accustomed to. Will I miss it when I'm home? I wonder. Will I miss all of this?

As I stare out of the cave, I spot a goat standing on a nearby ledge. 'Oh no, looks like we've got a straggler, a stray from the herd,' I say. 'I'll take her down.' I sigh and begin to stand.

'No, wait. Ssh.' Georgios stops me by putting a hand on my shoulder. I look down at it: tanned, with a smattering of dark hairs across the back. A hand that is now so familiar I want to bend to kiss it gently. He raises a finger to his lips.

'It's the kri-kri. The wild goat. He's back.'

We both watch the goat as it tries to move forward. It seems to be struggling.

'It's come for the dittany. It's injured. Look . . .' He points as the goat tries to reach to a high plant.

'What shall we do?'

'It will only take what it needs . . . not like poachers!' he growls. 'And if I'm not mistaken . . .' He moves carefully further out of the mouth of the cave. 'Bastards!' he hisses.

'What is it?' I jump up, pulling on my jacket, and stand next to him, shoulder to shoulder.

'We may have sent the poachers packing, but it looks like they left their traps behind.'

'Oh God.' The goat is dragging its back leg, a metal trap clasped around its bloodied foot. 'We have to help it!' I say, grabbing hold of Georgios's forearm.

'Wait . . . let's see how bad it is first,' he says, and I suddenly feel a rush of something that feels a lot like love towards Georgios. Maybe he's right. Maybe I shouldn't feel guilty about what happened between us. Maybe Stelios would be happy for us. My heart begins to soar, like the eagles above us.

We creep out on to the ledge outside the cave and watch the goat as it tries to reach the clump of dittany.

'We have to help it,' I repeat, and he turns to me and nods once in agreement.

'Looks like the gods were right to send you to help me,' he says quietly, and leans in, kissing me gently. Then he picks up some of the tools from where he has been working on the fallen olive trunk, which now has a large eagle carved along the side of it.

'That's beautiful,' I tell him quietly.

'The new monument for Stelios,' he says. 'I thought it was fitting. A bird, free to fly, made from the olive tree, for peace.' He nods and turns away. I can't speak for the lump in my throat. Then he starts to climb out on the rocks towards the goat and I set off after him.

'Be careful. Follow me exactly,' he says and I nod and do as I'm told.

The goat doesn't flinch and lets us do what we have to do. I hold its head, stroke its nose and soothe it whilst Georgios works at releasing it from the trap. Once it is free, it dips its head and reaches straight for the dittany, a trickle of blood still coming from its ankle. Georgios kicks the trap off the edge of the rocky ledge, down into the deep green gorge below.

'Can't we help clean up the wound?' I whisper.

'The dittany will give it all it needs,' he says. The euphoria of saving the goat and seeing off the poachers seems to have completely disappeared, and he is frowning, his face like a black cloud.

'Georgios, what's up?' I ask. 'Is it me? Is it Stelios? Because if it is, I've been thinking about what you said, and I agree, he would be happy for us.'

'It's not that,' he says. 'The thing is, if anyone has seen the goat and knows it's injured, they'll also know that it will be looking for dittany. They will follow it and it will lead them here, to the secret valley. Right to the heart of the mountain.'

I look down to see Harry Henderson's car has returned whilst we've been asleep. He's in it now, on his phone.

My heart sinks like a stone in water.

Chapter Fifty-seven

'We'll light the fires again,' I say quickly.

'You need to check the bees first. Bees hate fire. Check they're OK, that they're still there. Try to reassure them. Act normal. We don't want to raise any suspicions.' He looks worn out, practically beaten. I feel the same. This may be it; we may have lost the valley. But we can't give up yet.

'Keep a lookout,' I say. 'If you see them, make the signal as soon as you can.'

'OK. I'll lay up the fires this side.' He rouses himself into action. 'Stay safe,' he says and kisses me again, giving me wings to hurry down the mountain.

'I was just asking Kostas if he'd seen you this morning,' Maria says as I let myself into the farmhouse kitchen. 'I was getting worried, what with the fire up there and you staying on your own at Georgios's.'

'Early-morning walk, just checking the fire hadn't damaged any of the wild *horta*,' I say quickly. 'It's all fine.' I even manage to pass over a handful I collected on the way down from the mountain, just in case I needed the excuse.

'Oh thank goodness. You must be exhausted with all this work you're doing, for us and for Georgios. I can't think why he has been away so long. I mean, I know he has a lot of family business to deal with, but . . .'

I wonder what business that might be, but the imminent arrival of the poachers pushes the thought out of my mind, and then my phone rings. It's Demi.

'Hello?'

'Hi, Mum, just wondered if you had time to chat. It's my day off. I tried a few times this morning but couldn't get it to connect. You free now?'

I think of the lack of signal up in the mountain cave where I've just come from, my cheeks pinking up at the thought.

'Of course!' I lie, turning away from Maria, who starts trimming the *horta*, looking out of the window over the kitchen sink. I move out of earshot.

'What are you planning on doing today?' I ask.

'Oh, nothing really, just hanging out. I might head to a coffee shop. But coffee is so expensive here,' she says.

'Well, if it's a treat, I'm sure you deserve one. Are you meeting friends?'

'Um, no, there's no one free today.'

'What about the family? Are they doing anything?'

'Nah . . . think I'll just have a day to myself.'

Demi's never been one for having time on her own. She hates her own company.

'What about you, Mum? What are you doing?'

'Well . . .' I won't tell her I'm about to fight with a group of don't-mess-with-me poachers and set light to a number of fires high up on the mountaintop. Or that I spent last night having the most glorious sex I have ever had up on that same mountaintop, on a sheepskin rug, looking out over a blanket of diamond-like stars, and that it was the closest I am ever going to get to heaven. 'I've got the herb meadow to weed and water and then Georgios's bees to check on,' I tell her, my heart leaping at the mention of his name.

Demi laughs, and it feels really good to hear. But I have to get a move on, before the poachers come back. I look anxiously out of the window towards the mountain.

'Actually, sweetheart, I have to go. The bees need me.' I hate cutting her short.

'OK, Mum, go and look after your bees.' She laughs again.

'You have fun,' I tell her, proud she's getting on so well.

'Bye, Mum. I love you,' she says, and it takes me by surprise.

'I love you too.' My voice cracks, tears gather, and we both hang up. I quickly wipe my eyes with the back of my hand and walk back into the kitchen to Maria, who hands me a tea towel.

'You must take some time off, time for yourself, I insist,' she says, scooping up the *horta* and rinsing it under the tap. 'You're exhausted.'

'Actually, Maria, strange as it may sound, I don't know when I've felt more alive,' I say, handing back the tea towel, heading off to Georgios's bees up the mountain.

'OK, ladies, no messing this morning. I have to get back up there.' I look up to the higher rocks. 'So, no fussing and definitely no stinging,' I say, zipping up the neck on my big white suit and carrying my smoke can towards them. But the bees aren't happy, not happy at all. Their buzzing is high-pitched, urgent and agitated. I can feel one of the insects on my neck, like a screwdriver trying to drive its sting into me. I wave it away. I need to get back to Georgios and tell him.

The sun is high and warm in the sky and I'm heading back down to Georgios's cottage to put the bee suit away when I hear the call. I look up and can clearly see the kri-kri goat standing high above the secret valley. If I can see it, so will others, including Harry Henderson and his poachers. I just have to get up there before they do.

I'm on my way back up the mountain when my phone rings. It's Demi again. Oh lord, I really can't stop and chat now. I'll ring her back as soon as this is done. She probably wants to tell me about the sights she's seeing in London, or some restaurant the family are taking her to. I'm delighted she wants to share things with me and so happy that she's happy, but just this once, I decline the call, sending it to voicemail, then shove the phone back in my pocket. A little higher and I wouldn't have had any signal anyway, I tell myself, puffing slightly as I try and make it up the mountain as quickly as I can. My phone buzzes, letting me know that Demi has left a message, and I put a hand on it, feeling reassured that I have a long chat to look forward to when I've finished what needs doing here.

Chapter Fifty-eight

With the fires lit and the smoke curling, Georgios pulls me to him and kisses me hard, as if his life depends on it. Then he breaks away and looks at me.

'You're sure you're OK to do this?' he asks.

'Absolutely,' I nod. I'm out of breath and I'm not sure if it's from running round lighting the fires or that deep kiss that seemed to say so much more than either of us can put into words right now. The heat has been rising for days and it's so hot. An Indian summer, they'd call it back home. 'What about the bees?'

'It's a risk we're going to have to take. If the poachers find the valley, this land will be stripped and there'll be nothing left for them anyway. I'll stay here just in case they make it up to the valley's entrance.'

'Stay safe. I don't want to lose you now that I've . . .' I give a little cough. 'Now that I've found you.'

He looks down the mountainside towards the on-coming trouble and then back at me. Like we thought, the poachers are back, their truck pulling up on the road beside Harry Henderson's. They get out, pulling up their sagging jogging bottoms like they mean business. 'I don't want to lose you either,' he says, but I can't help but think about the impending end on the horizon, when I have to return home.

'And after this, if we get rid of the poachers, you'll come back down to the house? The dittany will have practically finished flowering and will be safe until next year, won't it?' I look into his set face and he nods in agreement. 'Let's do this then. One last push to keep the dittany and the mountain safe.'

I take a deep breath, glance at the injured kri-kri goat grazing near the dittany and then turn back to the now-familiar route down to the lower cave and the mountain path.

'Fire! The fires have started again!' I wave my arms as I stumble, slide and skid down the path just like last time. 'The authorities are on their way!'

It doesn't take long for the poachers to turn tail and leave, clearly keen not to be in the frame if someone is going to get blamed for the fires. I watch from high up on the mountain as they give Harry his cash back and roar off in a cloud of dust to match the dust that's clinging to my clothes and body. As Harry makes his way angrily up the mountain path to see what's going on, he's met by a swarm of agitated bees, and he quickly follows his workforce down the road for what I hope will be the last time.

I stand on a large rock sticking out from the mountainside, hands on hips, watching him go. Then I take a huge breath and let it out slowly, revelling in the glorious view over the pine trees and the farm below. We did it! I think. The dittany will have finished flowering in a few days, just when I'm due to leave. It's worthless to poachers if it's not in flower. We've kept the mountain's secret safe for another year. Let's just hope it's finally enough for the bees to come back to the honey farm.

Chapter Fifty-nine

Early the next morning, as I make my way down the mountain, I hear jubilant shouts of joy from Kostas at the farm.

'Bees! There are bees in the hives!'

The queen must have taken some of her children and moved there for safety when we lit the fires on the mountainside. Probably the same swarm that saw off Harry Henderson.

'We have bees!' Kostas is still shouting. 'Maria! Mitera! They've come!'

Vounoplagia is starting to wake as I slip quietly through the narrow back streets delivering the dittany that's needed. I've tucked the bundles of herbs into the pocket of one of Georgios's shirts, which I'm wearing open over my vest top. The cafés and shops are alive with talk of the fires being started on the mountain.

'Is it something to do with the drug dealers?' I hear, as I leave a bunch of dittany on the back doorstep of the florist's, for Gabriela's bad hip. I'm able to pick out more and more Greek now.

'The heat?' someone else is saying as I slip another one through the kitchen window of an arthritis sufferer. 'It has been a very hot September. I can't remember when the heat rose like this before the autumn.' It's hotter and closer than it has been since I arrived.

The only other talk is of Georgios. Is he still visiting family in Athens? Is everything OK? Why has he been gone so long?

I smile, knowing that he is safe and well in the cave and will soon be back in his little house, having seen off the poachers and kept the mountain safe. I get a thrill of excitement at the thought that he might join me in his bed tonight, and a feeling of warm satisfaction, the same sensation as when I've just eaten *loukoumades*, the delicious little doughnuts drizzled in honey and sprinkled with cinnamon. With any luck it won't be long before the whole town is eating *loukoumades* with honey from Kostas and Maria's farm.

I am in the alleyway, on the corner next to the *kafenio*. I can hear the two old men sitting out front talking loudly across the road to Agatha from the tablecloth shop.

'What of Georgios?' Agatha is asking as she winds out the awning over the shop window with a squeak.

'Apparently he's gone to visit family in Athens,' one of the old boys shouts. They're talking about my Georgios, I think with a buzzing in my tummy. Who isn't? I smile to myself, feeling proud of his efforts to save this town that he loves and cares about. I want to shout about what he's done and why he's done it. But I know I can't. Not yet.

I'm about to make my last delivery, to the crochet circle in the taverna next door, an extra big bunch for them all to share, by way of celebration. I go round the back entrance, leaving the dittany on a pile of menus by the till before sliding back towards the alleyway, which will bring me out on the mountain road above, where I've tucked the moped out of sight behind a big conifer.

'He's been gone a long time,' Agatha is saying.

But he'll be home tonight, I think to myself with a smile. Home from his hiding place in the mountain.

'Maybe he's finally gone to visit his wife,' I hear the other man say as I go to turn towards the moped. I'm rooted to the spot, rerunning his words in my head. I put out my hand and steady myself against the cold stone wall in the dark passage. 'She's been trying to get in touch but he won't answer, so the family say.'

What are they talking about? His *wife*? Have I actually heard them correctly? Is this the 'family business' Maria mentioned? He's married?

Just like that, I feel the ground crumbling beneath my feet.

Chapter Sixty

I swerve and swing the moped up the mountain road back to Maria and Kostas's farm and head straight to the beehives, listening to the sound of gentle buzzing coming from them, sniffing and wiping my running nose with the sleeve of Georgios's checked shirt. I put my hand on the hive and quietly thank the bees for coming. Angel, who I left behind while I went into town, is circling round and round my feet, giving my ankles quick little licks as if trying to cheer me up, and I'm happy for her to distract me from what I think I've just heard.

'We are so excited that we have bees,' Maria is chirping as she busies around the kitchen making breakfast. Kostas is singing and he pulls her to him, insisting she dance. They laugh and hug and she turns back to me. Her jubilant smile drops.

'Are you OK?' she says, seeing my face.

'Just a cold coming,' I tell her, and rub my swollen red eyes, hoping against hope that what I heard in the town wasn't true.

'I told you, you are working too hard. Eat this then go to bed. You need sleep,' she instructs. Maybe if I'd done more sleeping and less going to bed earlier I wouldn't be feeling such a fool right now. She hands me a bowl of *fasolada*, bean soup, and a plate with a square of *spanakopita*, shiny flaky pastry filled with feta cheese and wild mountain *horta* that she has no doubt made for lunch later. 'And here, I will make you mountain tea with some dittany,' she tells me, and I feel another pang of guilt, knowing it will be made from their limited supplies that I've delivered.

I take myself to my bedroom, unable to face going to Georgios's cottage, and replay what I've heard over and over again. I sit on the small bench under the window, looking out on the herb meadow and the bees in their new home in the valley below, and try to sip the soup, but I can't. The wind is picking up outside There's a change on the way. The sky is dark, leaden and grumbling. I put the bowl down next to the untouched pie and think about what I've done. How could I have been so stupid as to think I could find love in the same place twice? Why couldn't I have learned to be happy with who I am, rather than giving away my heart to have it broken all over again?

I pick up the mug of tea from the bench beside me, breathing in its herby scent. Angel is curled up in my lap. Suddenly my phone pings a text. It's from Demi. It just says: *Mum? Did u get my message?*

Oh God! I practically drop the tea. I completely forgot to listen to her voicemail yesterday. I hold the phone to my ear, hoping that hearing her voice and her laugh will cheer me up. But as I listen to the message, I know straight away that something is wrong. The blood drains from my face. I knew there was something up. She wasn't phoning just to chat. She wasn't OK. She needed me. And I wasn't there.

Leaving my mug of tea next to the untouched food, I run to Georgios's cottage and head straight up the wooden staircase, where I scoop up my clothes and start to throw them into my case. I have to leave, as soon as I can. Demi needs me. She wants to come home and I'm not there! I'm sure Maria will understand. I was due to go home in six days' time anyway. The bees are here. I said I would stay until the bees came, and I have. They can get another WWOOFer. They don't need me any more. And Georgios certainly doesn't need me. I have to go home to be with my daughter. Back home where everything is real, not some Greek fantasy filled with sunrises over the mountains, secret valleys full of wild medicinal herbs and long nights of fabulous lovemaking in a cave on a sheepskin rug!

It's time to go home.

Chapter Sixty-one

I pick up the case and run down the stairs. Georgios is standing in the doorway of the cottage.

'You didn't come back. I was worried,' he says.

'What about the mountain? Shouldn't you be up there?' I march out to the terrace, where I yank washing off the wooden railing and roll it up into a tight ball.

'The mountain can wait.' He follows me outside and stands behind me, frowning. My emotions are all over the place. I'm angry, so angry and hurt and bewildered, yet what I want to do more than anything is to lean back into his chest and feel his strong body against mine and draw strength from it. I want to breathe him in and let him love me all over again. But I can't, and that makes me even more frustrated.

'Nell, what's wrong? I'm worried about you.'

I finally turn and glare at him, squeezing the bundle of washing tightly, like I'm wringing the life out of it. A bit like my insides feel right now. I have to find out the truth. I have to ask him. I can't leave here with unfinished business again. Before I can stop myself, the words tumble out. 'Or are you worried about your wife finding out about me!'

He stares at me dumbfounded, his mouth open but no words coming out.

'So it's true! You're married!' I drop the washing into my open case, managing not to hurl it straight into his face.

'I . . .' He pauses for what seems like forever, and then finally speaks. 'It's true. I do have a wife. I can't lie. But let me explain . . .'

'Oh save your breath!' How could I have been so stupid? I didn't see it with Mike, having an affair with Gena, and now it's happened all over again, only this time I'm the other woman! 'I assumed you were free to be with me!'

'Please, let me—'

'No!' I chuck in my wash things from the bathroom. 'You . . . you . . .' I let out a loud exasperated sigh.

'You're right,' he says. 'I was wrong to fall in love with you, to take you to my bed. I promise you it won't happen again. I'm sorry. I . . . I couldn't help it. I just . . . I have never felt like this before. I can't help the way I feel. I love you.'

I can't bear to hear this. I hold my hands over my ears and snap back, 'Too right it was wrong.'

'But it doesn't mean you should go yet. Please don't leave early because I have behaved badly. You're needed here.' He puts a hand on my elbow, but I shake it off.

'Go! Go back to the mountain!' I'm worried my treacherous heart will start to believe every word he's saying. 'Just let me leave. If you really want what's best for me, then stay away until I've gone. I have to get back for Demi. I'm needed there. It's best for all of us that I'm going.'

'Doesn't Demi deserve to know about this place? Her family here? Are you going to tell her, bring her here to meet them?'

And break her heart like this place has broken mine? I think to myself. Right now Demi and I need to be back at home together, just her and me. I zip up the case.

'Just go, Georgios. Do this one thing for me and go.'

He drops his head and turns to leave. I pick his hat up off the table, the one I've been wearing to make the dittany deliveries, and hold it out to him. 'Here.'

He turns back, but I avoid any eye contact. He looks down at it but doesn't take it, as if telling me to keep it, but I thrust it towards him. I don't want any souvenirs from here. I'm not a silly schoolgirl any more. I'm not the person I was when I left here eighteen years ago with Stelios's pendant around my neck.

He takes the hat from me, puts it on his head and yanks it down, then pulls the scarf up around his face. Then he stoops through the low front door, and, with only a moment's hesitation, walks away.

My heart wants me to run after him, to tell him I don't care about his wife, that I want to be in his arms again, that it felt like home. But my head is telling me it was someone else's home, and I was just a guest.

Chapter Sixty-two

I've finished packing. I put my case by the front door, my thoughts focused on getting home to Demi, on wondering how I'm going to get to the airport. That's when I smell it. It's like burning toast, but herbier. Woodsmoke with a scent of thyme. Then I hear Kostas shouting out on the lane, followed by Maria.

I throw open the door and look past the cream Cretan cows down to the road and the turning point. Kostas is there waving his arms. Maria is behind him, wiping her earth-stained hands on a tea towel. They are shouting and pointing upwards.

I look up. There is smoke billowing off the mountain. Not just smoke, but orange, yellow and red flames too. A fire! Not like the little ones we've been making; a real fire, on the mountainside, licking up the trunks of trees, setting the bushes alight. The mountain is on fire!

'Oh God! Oh my God!' I say over and over, picking up Angel and running down the road, where Kostas is opening the fence panel and starting to herd the cows away from the thick smoke pouring down the mountainside. He has his hand over his mouth and is coughing. I can see the flames, burning, crackling, spitting and hissing, just like the ones at the factory, only this time the smoke smells different.

I race towards him and skitter and slide to a halt. My limbs, though attached, feel like they're arriving at a standstill at different times, as my body tries to realign itself in an upright, orderly fashion.

'What's going on? I don't understand,' I stutter, aghast.

'Another fire, but this time it looks to have really taken hold. We'll have to get the animals away.' Maria is shaking her head and waving the tea towel in the direction of the cows, who turn and look at me as they pass in a line. Even Mitera is there, looking small and frail.

'Love will never return now. It's all gone.' She sniffs into her hanky.

'But this can't be happening!' I hold my head in my hands. 'I put the fires out. I definitely put the fires out!'

'What?' Maria's face screws up in confusion and then darkens. 'You? You did this?' Her voice is quiet and deep over the crackling and spitting of the fire taking hold above us. Kostas stops in his tracks and turns to stare at me as if looking at a complete stranger. Even Mitera stops blowing her nose and scowls.

'Oh God!' I hold my head again and spin round. 'I mean, not intentionally. I mean, I did the other ones . . .'

'You started the other fires?' Maria says. I feel like I've kicked a puppy; I'm sick to my stomach, hating myself.

'Not like that. I mean, I did start them, but I put them out. I definitely put them out . . .'

I replay going to each of the fires, making sure one was out before moving on to the next, using the billy cans of water I'd left by each one. I was so careful. How could this have happened? Did I get distracted, just wanting to get into bed with Georgios? Oh please say I didn't! Oh God! Did this happen because I was so desperate to get into bed with a married man?

'Why? Why would you do this to us? We took you into our home. Treated you like family . . .'

I've never, ever seen Maria cross. But the look of hurt in her eyes will stay etched in my memory forever, branding itself there and burning painfully. A look of betrayal. The sky is turning orange now to match the flames spreading across the hillside.

'We have to do something!! Call the fire brigade! Get everyone to come and help!' I bunch my fists as the panic bubbles up.

Maria and Kostas are still staring at me.

'The fire brigade will come, but I fear it will be too late by the time they make it up here. We have to get the animals away . . .'

'Too late? What do you mean, too late?'

'There is nothing we can do. It is too much fire for just us.'

Mitera starts coughing. 'All the love will be gone,' she says again. 'The dittany will be destroyed. Men have risked their lives for this herb to show how much they love, and now it will be gone.'

'Oh God!' The panic bubbles up and explodes from me. 'The dittany! Georgios!'

'What?' Kostas, Maria and Mitera all stare at me.

'Georgios! He's up there! Up the mountain!'

'But you said he was in Athens.' Maria looks like I've kicked her again.

I shake my head. 'He's up there!' We all look up. The kri-kri goat is standing out on a rocky ledge, not far from the cave where I know Georgios is. 'On the other side of the fire!'

Chapter Sixty-three

'Kostas, get the villagers!' Maria commands, then she turns to me. 'Moped keys!'

I toss them to her, and she throws them to Kostas, who gets on the moped and starts it up. Mitera climbs on the back.

'What shall I tell them?' he asks.

'Tell them the fire is moving down the mountain. Tell them to hurry,' Maria instructs. 'The last time we had a fire like this, it swept all the way down to the town. We nearly lost our homes. It only just missed the farm. Maybe this time we won't be so lucky.' She wrings her hands in anguish, tears rolling down her cheeks.

'Tell them I'm sorry.' I can't think what else to say. 'But tell them to come. The mountain needs them. Georgios needs them. Tell them to bring buckets.'

'What if they won't come?' He looks at Maria, who shakes her head and shrugs.

'Ask them who they think has been protecting the mountain.' My voice is hoarse. 'If the dittany disappears altogether and the mountain loses its protected status, the holiday company will build an all-inclusive resort.' I look at them, hearing the crackling of fire, the wind whipping up and fanning the flames. 'Georgios has been keeping the developers away, stopping their plans to build. If they do, the town will die. And if we don't hurry up, so will Georgios!'

Kostas opens up the throttle and swings the bike on to the road with Mitera clinging on for dear life, dropping her teeth as he goes. Maria dashes into the road, picks them up and pockets them and then runs back to me.

'What can I do?'

'Pray to the gods, Maria, pray for rain . . .'

Handing Angel to Maria and telling her to look after her, I run to the mountain path and start to climb, but the smoke pushes me back, filling my lungs, stopping me from breathing. I'm hot, sweat gathering over my top lip and running down between my shoulder blades. I hold the back of my hand to my mouth and cough and cough. I look up. There's no sign of him. It's like all my nightmares finally coming true. Just like the nightmares I had when I first got here. The fire, not being able to get to the one I love. Georgios; I love him! I realise, like a great big wave crashing over me. I have to get to him and save him.

'Georgios!' I shout with all my heart.

Chapter Sixty-four

I race back along the path past Georgios's house and up the longer, wider route. The fire doesn't seem to have taken hold there. I start to run up it, like a kri-kri goat myself. Once the road peters out, I'm hopping over stones.

How could this have started? How? I was so careful. I checked for overhanging branches, arranged stones round each of the fires and put each one out with water. I know I did!

I pull my T-shirt over my face and put an arm up to cover my eyes. The fire is coming this way, but there is still a clear path if I'm quick. I push on, climbing, leaping nimbly from rock to rock. I don't look down. I don't look back. I have to keep moving forward. I have to get to him. The smoke is thickening as the wind whips it up.

My heart is banging in my chest. How could I have caused even more hurt to this community? First Stelios and now this! What kind of a fool am I? *One who was doing her best for the people she cares about*, a small voice in the back of my head replies. I was just trying to do my best, because I do care, I realise. For Stelios's family, for Maria and Kostas, for the town. For my daughter's family.

The smoke is choking as I run through the first cave and

reach the valley. Beyond and up high I can see the kri-kri goat.

'Run!' I shout. 'Run! Shoo!' And as if understanding, it dips its head and runs off, over the mountain path, hopefully to safety.

My heart lurches. The route to the secret valley is utterly blocked by thick smoke. I can't see any way to get to it. 'I'll do anything,' I say to whatever god Maria talks to. 'I promise I don't want anything more from him, but just keep him safe.'

'Georgios!' I shout. 'Georgios! But the smoke catches in my throat, making me cough. Then I hear it.

'Nell!' he shouts back, and like the eagles cruising on the thermals, my heart dips and then soars and swoops.

'He's alive,' I shout to absolutely no one. 'Thank you,' I mouth up to the heavens.

The smoke begins to clear and I see him scaling down the side of the mountain, the new monument he's been carving for Stelios gripped under one arm.

'Stay there,' he calls.

'Pass it to me!' I shout back, reaching out for the olive trunk. 'Pass it to me!'

He stretches out, but he's not close enough. The smoke is pouring into the gorge.

'I'm going to throw it!' he yells over the wind and the noise of the fire and, in the distance, the sound of voices shouting. 'Put out your arms.'

I do as he says. He turns, and with one hand scoops it from under his arm and throws it. The smoke is making my eyes smart and sting, no matter how hard I try to blink it away. Blindly I reach out both hands, but no sooner has it landed in my arms and I'm forming the words 'Got it!' like a greased goose it bounces from my grip and out again. I try to grapple for it, knocking it, missing it, dropping it, and it falls from my arms, bouncing, crashing through the smoke-filled valley, way down to the silver snail trail of the river below.

'Oh God!' I make a move to try and go after it. But it's useless. I know that.

'Leave it!' Georgios instructs. 'It's not important! We have to get down from here, now.'

'But it is!' My heart is thundering.

'It's not. What's important is that you came back. It means you don't hate me.' Or at least I think that's what he says. I can't be sure. Because, as if our pleas have been answered by the gods, there is suddenly an almighty lightning bolt across the sky, and with it a crack of thunder, and just like that first time I climbed up this mountain, determined not to be put off, the heavens open. And as the fire starts to hiss, sizzle and spit, we smile, then laugh, and finally hold our faces to the rain.

'I could never hate you, Georgios. I hate the fact that I've found you and we can't ever be together,' I say. And my heart rips open all over again.

Chapter Sixty-five

'I think it would be a good idea if you told us everything that has been going on, Georgios.' We are back at the restaurant with Stelios's family, getting dry, and Stelios's father is the first to speak.

The line of water carriers from the town was disbanded as soon as the heavens opened; using their buckets and tin baths to protect them from the deluge falling from the sky, they trooped back to Vounoplagia, glaring at me as they went and muttering words I haven't yet learned in Greek.

'They're saying I started the fire,' I tell Stelios's father.

'That's impossible,' Georgios says earnestly. 'You were careful. I know you wouldn't have let that happen.'

'But I must have done. How else could it have happened? I started the fires to scare off the poachers. I must have left one of them smouldering. I burned the mountain!' I hold my head in my hands, unable to take in what I've done.

Yannis appears from his small apartment upstairs, rubbing his wet hair with a towel.

'Yannis!' his father says. 'Where were you? We have been putting out a fire on the mountain.'

'Sorry, Baba.' He gives his hair a final rub. 'I had no idea. I was in the shower . . .' He looks around at the group of us there, but doesn't meet my eyes. 'I'll get some coffee for everyone,' he says, turning back to the kitchen.

'I must go,' I say. 'My daughter needs me. I have to go to her. I have to get to the airport to see if they will change my booking for today.'

'You will never get the flight now,' Georgios tells me. 'Leave it until tomorrow. Demi is a young woman. She will understand.' He's right. Of course she'll understand. I'll be home soon enough, and there are things I need to put right here before I leave.

'Stay just for one more night,' he implores me with those green and gold eyes, and I can't help but feel another pang of longing. If only I could. I trusted that he was free to be with me, but he isn't.

'Join us, Nell. We are all family here.'

But someone is missing, I think. Not Stelios . . . Demi. This is Demi's family and I can't keep it from her any more. She has to know.

I pull up a chair at the family table next to Georgios, making sure my leg doesn't touch his, and finally Georgios tells them everything – all about the secret valley, and keeping the dittany safe and delivering it to those in need.

'So you see, it was for the best,' he says when he has finished.

'But you should have told us.' Stelios's mother brings more plates of *mezédhes* from the kitchen, mouthfuls of moreishness: thick chopped country sausage and smoked pork, fried zucchini flowers, meatballs in tomato sauce, soft aubergine baked in olive oil, garlicky hummus sprinkled with paprika, and vine leaf parcels. 'We could all have helped.'

'It was safer this way,' Georgios explains. 'All the time the dittany still thrived in the hidden valley, the mountain maintained its protected status. No one could build on it. The bees managed to survive. The future of the mountain is safe. That's why I've had to keep it secret. That's why I had to deliver the dittany anonymously to those who needed it.'

Maria, Kostas and Mitera arrive at the restaurant gates and Stelios's family wave them in. I can hardly meet Maria and Kostas's eyes. Not after seeing the look on Maria's face – the look that said 'traitor' – when she realised I'd lit the fires. I stand up and offer Mitera my seat as Georgios starts his explanation again for the benefit of the newcomers.

'I'm so sorry,' he says when he has finished. 'I have no idea how the fires restarted. We thought we had been so careful.'

'I believe you.' Stelios's mother stands up and reaches for the empty water bottle.

'No, let me.' I try to smile. 'We are family.' And she smiles back and lets me go to refill it.

As I step through the kitchen doorway, Yannis jumps and shoves something away with his foot. The look on his face reminds me of Demi when she's hiding something, doing something she shouldn't. I frown.

'What's that, Yannis?'

'Nothing,' he says quickly, again just like Demi.

'Let me see.' I push him to one side, and he sighs and moves away from the sink, where he's standing in front of a bottle of what looks to be . . . petrol.

Chapter Sixty-six

'Well, are you going to tell them or am I?'

As I march Yannis into the restaurant, he has a smug, self-satisfied look on his face. He knows that no one is going to believe me.

'You sold out the mountain,' I say, staring at him. 'You gave away the mountain's secret. Tell them, Yannis.'

'Nell!' Maria scolds like the older sister she has become.

'Nell, we're all upset . . .' his father says.

'You knew, didn't you? Tell them, Yannis. You knew about the dittany and where to find it!'

He folds his arms defiantly.

I march back into the kitchen and pick up the petrol bottle, and the rags and matches I found by the sink. I return to the restaurant and hold them up.

'Well?'

'It's for the car . . .' Yannis says, but there is a slight hesitation in his voice. His mother's eyes narrow, and at her stern glare he suddenly crumples.

'I only told the man that was here, that Harry guy from the holiday company, that if he found the kri-kri goat, he would find the dittany,' he says, throwing his hands up as if I'm being ridiculous. 'That's all! He and his workers came in for lunch a few times, when I was here coping on my own!' He scowls. 'He told me they had plans. That they needed to check if there was dittany on the mountain.'

'Pah!' I say out loud. I don't believe for a minute that that's the full story. I'm a mother, after all, I know when I'm having the wool pulled over my eyes.

We all stare at him, mouths open. Mitera's teeth drop down but she catches them and pushes them back in quickly. Yannis is looking very uncomfortable. Suddenly he goes to make a run for the main restaurant door, but in one quick move – not bad for a man with a damaged leg – Georgios jumps up and steps in front of the door, blocking his way. Yannis looks at him and for a moment thinks about challenging him. Georgios lifts his head and his chest swells. He stares at Yannis and then says, quietly and slowly, 'Did you start the fire, Yannis?'

Yannis pulls his glare away from Georgios and stares at the floor, saying nothing.

'Yannis!' Georgios snaps, making me jump. 'Did you start the fire?' He speaks even more slowly this time.

Yannis looks away and throws his hands up in the air again, higher this time, as if addressing a huge amphitheatre.

'You . . .' his mother says slowly. 'You would do this to us? You would kill off the mountain and put us out of business?'

'Just tell us, Yannis, was it you?' I'm desperate for him to admit it.

He drops his arms abruptly to his sides and glares at me.

'I wouldn't have done it if it hadn't been for you. All this is your fault.' He's back to performance mode. 'You come back here, and my family embraces you like some long-lost relative, but really it's all your fault!'

'Yannis!' his mother reprimands, but he's in full flow.

'Yes! Yes, I started that fire. I knew it wouldn't harm anyone.'

'It could have killed Georgios! We don't need any more sorrow. Why did you do it, Yannis?' His father slaps the table and Yannis looks up at him slowly. 'Why?'

'For money. For a new start. To see the world. It's not like I'm ever going to meet anyone here. No one under the age of sixty, anyway.'

'What?' His father is aghast.

'Vounoplagia is dead on its feet. There are no tourists, Baba. I've always said something needs to happen here. When the new resort comes, which it will, this place, along with every other business in the town, will finally die. A whole new world will be born and this restaurant won't be a part of it.'

'But this is our family business . . .'

'When Stelios was here!' he says. 'It was Stelios who loved Vounoplagia. Not me. I never wanted this. I wanted to go to London, remember? Or America, or Australia. Anywhere but here!'

'You love this place.' His father stands shakily.

'Only as my home. I never intended to stay here. I want to travel, like other young people. But they all went a long time ago and I have been left to keep the restaurant limping along on my own. I never wanted to stay. If it hadn't been for *her* . . .' He turns and points at me, the accused, and I move my hand away from where it's resting against Georgios's.

'Yannis! Enough!' His mother stands up.

'You leaving like that! If Stelios hadn't followed you that night . . . All this is your fault! Everything changed for me when Stelios died.'

No one says a word.

'That developer friend of yours wanted to know where the dittany was. I told him to follow the goat. But then he came to me with the idea of a fire. He said there had been a couple of small ones, but he wanted one big one to wipe out the wild herbs, in return for this . . .' He pulls out an envelope from under the till, and opens it to reveal a wad of euros. We all gasp.

'How could I refuse? This place is going to die anyway. It's my fresh start . . . away from here.'

'Enough!' It's Demetria's turn to stand. 'I have heard enough. This is all my fault. I was the one who told Stelios he would be better off with a local girl. We didn't want him to leave, you see. That day you came to speak to him, when you rowed, I told you to go; I said that if he loved you he would follow. This is all down to me.'

'You remember,' I say quietly. I can picture it as if it was yesterday. I remember being here, meeting the family, feeling nervous. And the day Stelios and I rowed. I was so cross and unsure of what to do. It was his grandmother who convinced me to leave.

'I am deeply sorry.' Demetria walks over to me and holds both my hands in her bony ones. 'Please forgive me. I was a fool. I thought I was doing the right thing but I know now that I was very wrong. No one can tell where you're going to find love, and when you do, you must hold on to it tightly and treasure it.'

I can feel the heat of Georgios's body next to mine and it feels so wrong and yet . . . so right.

'Yannis.' Demetria turns to her grandson. 'You have been foolish. But we are all guilty of that in our lives, listening to our heads instead of what's in our hearts. This was not the way to make your brother proud of you.'

Yannis hangs his head in shame.

'You should have said something if you were so unhappy here,' his mother scolds. 'We didn't want you to feel trapped or pressured to live a life you never wanted. We could have run the restaurant, we would have found a way. We thought we were giving you a future.'

'But this was a shameful way to act,' his father adds, voice shaking. 'Shameful! You no longer work here. I will take over whilst you make your plans, whatever they may be . . .' Yannis leans his arms on the table, muscles twitching, head hanging. 'Nell is part of our family too. We will not protect you and let her take the blame. You must own up and tell the town what you did.'

My heart leaps at the thought of being part of this family, but I feel truly sorry for Yannis as I watch him run from the restaurant to his apartment. A door slams and a moment later Britney Spears blares out at full blast.

'Thank you,' I tell his father.

'I'm sorry for what he did,' he replies.

I attempt a smile. 'We were all young and foolish once,' I say. 'We all do things we regret.' My throat is tight and hoarse. Stelios's father takes my hands and holds them tightly.

Demetria looks at me. 'Stelios loved you, but that was

then and this is now. I believe there is more than one love for all of us, and I hope you can find yours.'

And the relief I felt on the mountain when I realised Georgios was alive washes through me all over again.

Chapter Sixty-seven

It's time for Maria, Kostas, Mitera and me to return to the farm. As we leave the restaurant, Georgios walks with us. I'm still hurt and angry but so relieved he survived the fire. At the farm, Maria hugs me, telling me she's forgiven me and I'll be missed.

'Will you walk with me to the house?' Georgios asks. 'To say goodbye.'

I look at Maria, who smiles and nods, and I turn and fall into step beside him, dropping my head as we walk. Tomorrow I will be gone. Back home to be with Demi. In a few weeks' time, Maria and Kostas will be making honey again in the factory.

'Stay with me,' he says quietly, taking hold of my hand when we reach his door.

'I can't.' It comes out as a whisper.

'Just let me explain, that's all I ask; let me explain before you go.'

We sit out on the terrace, watching the sun set between the two triangular mountains, and dusk wraps itself around us. Georgios fills glasses with raki, and it's surprisingly soothing on my rough throat, still sore from the smoke.

He takes a sip of raki, then puts his glass down and looks

out over the terrace. 'After Stelios died and you had gone . . . well, everyone was so unhappy. I was young, just twenty. It took months for me to recover from the accident. After the car left the road, I was thrown from it and hit rocks and trees. My leg was broken in three different places, my cheek deeply cut. I was in and out of consciousness. But Stelios wasn't thrown clear, and the car kept falling, down the mountain. There was nothing that could be done to save him. I couldn't believe I had survived, that the mountain had spared me and not him. He had so much to live for. I felt . . . I felt so guilty, all the time. I wanted to put it right.' He sips again and so do I.

'Carissa – she is my wife – was a nurse in the hospital. That's how we met. I thought that by marrying her . . . well, that I would be bringing love to the mountain, bringing some happiness back.'

'And were you happy?' I asked.

He shook his head. 'We both knew it had been a mistake. We had an apartment in town, but even that was too quiet for her. She was used to the city. We thought that maybe having a baby would help, but the gods had other ideas and never blessed us. I spent more and more time up here on the mountain, with the bees. It helped. I felt so guilty about Stelios dying and me still being here. I had terrible nightmares and hated the noise in the town. Somehow I felt close to Stelios here.'

The dogs curl up around each other and sigh.

'And Carissa? Where is she now? You're still together, right?' I take another fortifying sip. He takes a deep breath and I watch from the corner of my eye as his chest rises and falls.

'No, we're not.'

'But I thought you said . . .' I turn to him.

'I am still married. You were right. It was wrong of me to sleep with you whilst I am not free. Carissa lives in the UK now, in London. She got fed up with waiting for me to come down from the mountain, and so she went to London and told me to follow when the mountain was safe.'

'And will you?' I can't help but ask.

'When I know the mountain is safe,' he says flatly.

'And is that now? Do you think it is time?'

'I don't think there is any more I can do to help the mountain,' he says quietly.

He puts out his hand and I take it. Turning away from the setting sun, he leads me upstairs, where we lie on his bed, on top of the covers, fully clothed, the dogs curled into a ball together, and there we watch as the sky darkens and turns black, both of us wondering what the future holds for us. Our little fingers touch, just like they did that day he came with me to tell the family about Demi, and as the stars scatter themselves across the dark blanket of sky, laying on their best performance yet, and the big white moon gazes down like a dinner plate, silent tears roll down my cheeks for what might have been but can't be.

Demi needs me at home. The town at large still think it was me that started the fire. I can only hope that Yannis will own up and tell them what really happened. And as for Georgios? Well, he isn't free to love me, and that's something I will have to live with. I look out at the sky, our little fingers curled in and around each other, and try and imprint this moment on my memory, so that I can put it in a box in my mind and pull it out whenever I need to remember him.

In the morning, I wake, still fully clothed, to see Georgios staring at me. We spent the night in each other's arms, just holding each other while we still could.

'Walk the mountain with me,' he says. 'Just one last time before you leave.'

I nod and rise from the bed, and hand in hand, with the dogs scampering around our feet, we walk up the mountainside, blackened, burnt and damp in the early-morning light. It's as if the storm has finally opened the door to let the start of autumn in.

'You'll look after Angel for me, won't you, when I'm gone?'

He says nothing but nods, just once, firmly, reassuring me she'll be safe.

At the first cave, we look down into the rocky gorge to where the new memorial that Georgios carved fell when I dropped it during the fire. There's no sign of it. Smashed on the rocks on the way down, no doubt. We leave the dogs in the cave and climb out to the second cave, in the secret valley. Inside it feels cold and damp, nothing like the warm hideaway we've enjoyed for these past two weeks. The candles by Stelios's and Georgios's picture are out. I walk over to relight them.

'Leave them,' Georgios says, and I turn back to him. 'Stelios lives in our hearts. We don't need shrines and memorials; it's what's in here that matters.' He puts a hand over his heart. 'This is where he lives on for all of us. Life must move on too.'

We take in the empty cave, feeling like this is goodbye. Then I walk out to the ledge. There, to my right, higher up the mountain, is the kri-kri goat, and my heart leaps.

'Georgios, come and see!'

He comes out and stands beside me and smiles. The goat has brought his family: a smaller adult and two kids. He dips his head towards us.

'You see?' says Georgios. 'Hope. If the goat is here, the dittany is still here too. They will always seek it out. It hasn't gone completely. All is not lost. If the dittany is here then the bees will find it and make honey again. Love hasn't disappeared altogether.'

If the bees can survive and make a new life for themselves at the honey farm, maybe one day, who knows, there'll be a new life out there for me too.

Chapter Sixty-eight

There is no need for words as we finally turn to make our way back down the mountain. As we descend from the lower cave towards the fallen tree, now burnt, blackened and disintegrating, Filos turns back towards the mountain peak and gives a bark, and Angel joins in. We both gaze back up at the mountaintop, holding our arms up against the bright orange sun that is rising behind it, looking at where the goat was standing with his small herd. But it's not the goat the dogs are barking at. I squint and strain to make out if what I'm seeing is real. A small, wiry man, in a jacket two sizes too big, is walking right over the top of the mountain, down the path that hasn't seen walkers on it for . . . well, since it was closed off, over a year ago. He's wearing a flat hat, despite the clear, bright but much gentler September sunshine. His coat tails are being lifted by the wind that is whipping up the blackened ash and dust. But he doesn't falter, walking determinedly like the kri-kri goat down the hill, holding out his right hand with something held firmly in it.

He reaches the big trunk that has stopped the villagers passing this way and hops through the middle of it.

'*Yassas.*' He nods his head in greeting and we stare back at him in disbelief.

'*Yassas*,' we acknowledge in return.

'Where have you come from?' Georgios asks him in Greek.

He points. 'Pefkódasos,' he says.

'Pine Forest,' Georgios translates for me. 'It is the town on the other side of the mountain. He heard the mountain path was safe to travel again, that the bad men had left after a fire. That the path was clear.'

The old man's face is dark and lined, but his eyes are sparkling with excitement. 'I just hope I'm not too late,' he tells Georgios, and smiles widely, revealing a dark gap where a tooth to the side of his front ones used to be. I look down at his right hand, held in front of him. He is clutching a small bunch of dittany.

Both Georgios and I stare at it.

'Where did you get that?' we ask at the same time, in Greek and English.

'Just up there, right on top of the mountain. A valley where it still grows, by a waterfall and a cave. I saw it as I came over the top of the mountain. I saw the kri-kri goat and her kids. Here . . .' He pulls a tiny bunch from his lapel and hands it to Georgios. 'You look as if you need it. Now . . . *kalimera*.' He nods to us. 'I have a young lady I must pay a visit to. A long-overdue visit. I have waited for this day for a very long time. I just hope she hasn't given up on me altogether.' He points to Maria and Kostas's farmhouse, and then with a tip of his head continues down the mountain path.

We watch him go. Georgios looks at me in surprise, and then together we smile.

'Do you think . . . could that be Mitera's long-lost love?' I say, wide-eyed.

'Looks like love really has returned to the mountain.' Georgios leans in towards me. Our foreheads rest against each other, drawing in the love that is there. When I look up again, the kri-kri goat is walking along the mountain path, silhouetted against the big orange ball rising in the sky behind it. The eagles are circling once more and the smell of wild thyme, heightened after the fire and the rain, is in the air, wrapping itself around the town at its feet. I feel like I'm saying my final goodbyes.

'You could stay,' he says, his forehead still against mine. I shake my head, sniff and run my hand under my nose, which is starting to run, mingling with the gentle tears.

'I can't. Demi needs me. And you? Well, you don't need me.'

'But I love you. It wasn't just a fling,' he tells me. 'I would do anything for us to be together.'

'But you have the mountain to keep safe. And you are married. You have to stay and I have to go.' I quickly pick up Angel from beside my feet and rub my face in her soft coat. Then I hug her and hand her to Georgios.

'Take good care of her,' I say, but it catches in my throat.

It's time to go home, I know. Why then does it feel as if I'm leaving my home behind?

Chapter Sixty-nine

Four weeks later

The Pogues are blaring out of the speaker next to me. Darren on Christmas CDs is singing along tunelessly, like it's the first time he's heard the song all year; despite the compilation having been on constantly since I started back here at the factory three weeks ago.

I don't want to think about Christmas, but it's hard not to now I'm back assembling singing Rudolphs with flashing red noses all day long. I remember giving Demi one of these years ago. I think the nose fell off after about three days, but she still kept it. It's in the box of decorations up in the attic that I pull out every year. Now she's here working with me in the factory, and I wish with all my heart that there was something more for her out there.

When I arrived home, she was waiting at the house, overjoyed to see me. I think the memory of that hug she gave me will last a lifetime. She told me that she'd been so in awe of her new family to start with, what with their big London house and their busy lifestyle. She'd thought she was part of the family too, but she soon realised that they only wanted her to look after the kids and do the housework twenty-four-seven. They were never around, and when they were, she'd be shooed out and ended up wandering the streets because they didn't want her in the way during their scheduled family time. They didn't give her enough free time to meet any other nannies, let alone boyfriends. The kids were rude and never did as they were told. Wouldn't go to bed unless their mother brought presents back from business trips. It made Demi realise what a brilliant family she had: me, Angelica and Gracie. How loved she'd felt and how homesick she was.

That final day she was wandering streets brimming with overpriced coffee houses, watching other families in the park and wanting more than anything to come home. That's when she rang me. And when she couldn't get a reply, she just left and got on a train and came home anyway, and sat with Gracie and told her all about her awful time in London. She'd been worried when I hadn't called her back, but Gracie had reassured her that she was never far from my thoughts. The only thing I ever wanted was to be there for Demi. At least she knew where home was, because home is always where your heart is.

'I realised there isn't any better family than the one I've got here, Mum. You and me. We don't need anyone else.' She snuggled into me on the settee, smiling just like when she was small, and I wanted the moment to last forever, but there was something I had to do and so I took a deep breath. A very deep breath indeed.

When I first told her about Stelios, and the crash, I

thought she was just going to pack up again and run back to London, head first into another disaster. But the more we talked, and the more photos I showed her of the restaurant, the family, the town, the mountain, the hives and the honey farm, the more interested she became, poring over the pictures and asking questions.

Finally she said, 'And you wouldn't mind . . . if I contacted them?'

Tears prickled my eyes. All this time it had been just me and Demi. I'd thought I was doing the best I could for her, protecting her, not wanting her to get hurt. But I'd been listening to my head instead of my heart. 'You can never have too many people to love you.' The words caught in my throat as I said them.

'And would they love me? What if they don't like me?' She looked worried and I had to reassure her.

'Believe me, they will love you.' I grinned. 'Who wouldn't? You have to just let them.' This was our second chance at family and we had to take it. Everyone should grab hold of a second chance of love.

I rubbed her head, just like when she was a little girl, and we fell into a wonderful big hug, and I squeezed her and shut my eyes. It was a hug that told me she knew that wherever she was, I'd always be there for her, forever.

The Pogues are still ringing in my ears. 'Oh for goodness' sake, Darren, can't you change the CD just for once!' I march over to the player and turn it off, much to his horror, then sit back down heavily on my stool and start a new Rudolph. I try to picture myself back in Crete with the bees on the mountain. Even checking the hives didn't have my nerves frayed like this place. I imagine the morning air, thick with low mist and the promise of a hot day ahead. I shut my eyes and allow myself to think about lying in Georgios's bed, looking out through the valley, waking to the sound of the goats bleating gently, the soft chime of the bell on the herd leader's neck. I wish Demi could see it for herself and meet her family there. The last thing I wanted for her was this: working in the decoration factory with me. I wanted her to have more.

My mind flits back to Crete and I can almost hear the sound of the goat bell followed by Georgios's whistle. It's as clear in my head as if I'm there. I can hear sheep nearby like they're in the car park outside the factory, like they've come in off the hills and are gathered there. I can hear the bell really loudly now. I must be going mad. I shake my head. I have to stop this. I have to stop thinking about it, about what could have been. I need to put it away in the box in my mind, shut it firmly and leave it there. But try as I might, the bell and the baaing still ring in my ears. There it is again, the whistle, the call he made when I was needed on the mountain. I ping my eyes open to try and push the memory away. I even stand up and put Darren's CD back on to drown out the sounds. But I can still hear them, pushing my thoughts back to Georgios.

I decide that I need some air. A bit of British drizzle and five minutes in smokers' corner should bring me back down to earth. I head to the fire doors, which are surrounded by dark green fake-fir garlands, covered in plastic pine cones. Unlike the ones on the mountainside in Vounoplagia, they don't smell of pine. Over the doorway in a cross are two big red and white candy canes left over from shop window display kits.

As I yank open the doors, the drizzle hits me in the face and I catch my breath, not knowing whether to scream or laugh. If I'd seen this in a Richard Curtis film, I wouldn't have believed it.

There, framed by the fake garlands and the candy canes, to the sound of Noddy Holder, is Georgios, in his hat, rain dripping from its brim, his scarf around his neck. He is surrounded by a herd of confused sheep. Now I must really be going mad. The sheep mingle and one or two try to come into the factory itself.

My heart is beating so loudly, it's drowning out the music. I hold my hand to my face.

'Georgios? What are you doing here? Why are all these sheep here?' I look around this way and that.

'They followed me from the car park. I rang the bell to see if you would hear it and they came.'

I put the back of my hand over my mouth and try to hold back a laugh.

'But what are you doing here?' I ask again in amazement.

There is a scraping of stools on the factory floor and I turn briefly to see that the whole factory is now standing, craning their necks and watching as Georgios steps forward and looks around in wonder at the colourful plastic fake world. Darren's jaw has dropped and he is positively speechless, as is Gena.

He looks so out of place. This world – my world – couldn't be more different from his. I glance around to see if there is anyone with him; his wife maybe? Wondering if this is some kind of cruel joke.

Little pools of water are gathering at his feet, glistening in the bright light. He looks down at them, oblivious to the cheap decorations festooning the doorway where he's standing.

'I have been to see my wife . . .'

There's a sharp intake of breath from the gathered group behind me.

'I see,' I gulp, my cheeks burning like never before, feeling like this is the ultimate humiliation.

'Was she knocking off a married man?' Gena asks.

'This is Gorgeous George, I'm guessing.' I hear Gracie putting two and two together from the photographs I've shown her since I've been back and the tales of my time on the mountain.

'Gorgeous, but married,' I hear Gena sneer, and I'm tempted to shove her deely boppers right up her nostrils. But right now, I want Georgios to go. Or do I want him to stay? My head is spinning and my heart somersaults.

'Look, I think it would be best—' I begin, feeling like I have a mouthful of sand.

'Demi said I would find you here.' Georgios continues as though I haven't spoken.

'You've met Demi?' I turn around and she waves from her position on packing fake trees. It's an itchy job.

'We met on Skype, when she was talking with Stelios's family.' He nods and smiles. 'She's very beautiful. The family love her. She is the image of Stelios.'

I manage a watery smile.

'But she has something of you too. She told them of her time in London. She is fiery, independent, brave, just like you.'

'Hear, hear!' I hear Gracie shout, and I blush, blinking away the hot tears in my eyes.

'Is he talking about Nell?' Gena says. 'Mike never says things like that to me.'

'Ssh.' I hear Angelica hushing them. Oh, they're all seeing my public disgrace! My toes begin to curl.

'So, you left the mountain. It's safe, then?' I try and make it sound like a conversation with an old friend. But my insides are shifting and spinning, reminding me that he is so much more.

He nods. Droplets of rain fly around like glitter.

'The dittany is back. The developers have gone. The bees have started to make honey again. Kostas's hives are full. More swarms moved in after the fire. He will be opening his honey factory again very soon!' He looks around *our* factory. God knows what he makes of it.

'I'm glad for you, Georgios, but I really have to go. I'm not on an official break. I'll . . .' I look around. 'We'll get into trouble.'

'Mr Evans is on a phone call. You take all the time you need,' Angelica calls, arms folded.

'I have been to see my wife,' he starts again.

'Yes, so you said.' I look down, shamefaced. 'I'm glad you've got everything sorted.' Oh God, this is killing me.

'We have agreed the terms of the divorce and made all the arrangements. She has a new life and there is a new one I'd like too . . .'

'I'm really pleased, but—' I look up. 'Sorry, what did you say?'

'I couldn't ask until I was free to, but I'm asking now.' He looks at me with those familiar green and gold eyes.

There is silence on the factory floor.

'Will you have me, Nell? Will you be with me?' He reaches out a hand towards me. I look down at it slowly.

'Did he just say what I think he said?' Gena asks exactly what I'm thinking.

'Ssh!' Angelica silences her again.

'But . . . but the mountain . . . the town . . .'

'The mountain is safe. It's time for me to move on. If being with you means living here, well then, so be it. My home is with you, wherever you are.'

He looks at me, and with my eyes full of unshed tears, I rush forward and hug him hard, so that his hat tips off backwards, falling into the sheep, who start baaing and milling again. He lifts me off the ground and then slowly lowers me.

And then he kisses me, just like I remember, the kiss I've longed for ever since that night up the mountain. Like a tidal wave, joy flows over me, drenching me.

Finally we part, and I realise the whole factory is cheering.

'Go on, girl!' I hear Gracie call.

Angelica is whistling with two fingers and Demi is whooping and clapping the loudest.

'What on earth is going on out here?' It's Alwyn Evans, looking short and angry. But then he always looks short and angry. He's obviously finished his phone call. 'Nell, what is all this commotion . . . and what are all these sheep doing in my factory?'

I look at the sheep milling around and suddenly can't stifle my giggles any more.

'Get them out or you're fired! You've already nearly burned down my factory!' He's got it into his head that I'm to blame, just because the beam fell in over where I was sitting.

'Hey! You can't fire Nell! She didn't burn down the factory.' We all turn to look at Gracie. 'If you're going to blame anyone, blame me. I did it. I was having a crafty fag in the tinsel packing cupboard. Thought I'd put it out, but . . .' She shrugs, 'Well, all that having to go outside to the smoking area malarkey. I thought no one would notice.'

Now I'm thinking with my heart rather than my head. 'Actually, I did it. I started the fire,' I say.

Gracie looks aghast. 'No you didn't. It was me,' she argues.

Angelica steps forward and lifts her chin. 'No, *I* started the fire!' she declares.

And the three of us turn to each other and smile. Who knows where we're going, but life is certainly about to change for all of us.

'Out, the lot of you!'

I look at Georgios.

'Your job?' Georgios is wide-eyed. 'I thought you wanted things to go back to how they were: your job, your home, your life here.'

'I want to go back to the mountain, if that's all right. I want to wake up to that view, with you, every day for the rest of my life.'

'But you have a job here . . . a life.'

'Not any more. I'm doing what you told me to do. I've stopped thinking with my head and started listening to my heart. My life is in Crete. With you, if you'll have me . . .' I look over at Demi, my head to one side, and raise a questioning eyebrow. Like the bees, we don't need words. Demi beams and gives a single nod back at me. I look at Georgios again. 'If you'll have *us*?'

And at that point he does the one thing I never dreamed could happen to someone like me. As the sheep pour in out of the car park and fill the factory floor, milling and baaing, he scoops me up in his arms and carries me out of the fire exit, just like in *An Officer and a Gentleman*. I grab his hat and put it on my own head, and he stops only to kiss me again before we pass over the threshold of my old life on my way to my new one, back to the mountain where we both belong.

Epilogue

'A double booking!' Demi cries. 'Today of all days. I'll have to cancel them.'

'Don't panic. We can do this.' I smile at her. 'We'll all pull together. There are plenty of villagers you can ask to waitress. There's Agatha from the tablecloth shop now that her arthritis is cleared up, and Gabriela from the crocheting circle – she's got over her cold – and Christina, now her husband's gout has gone. Just ask them. They'll be happy to help.'

'But Mum, we have loads of tourist parties coming. It won't hurt to cancel this one.'

'Yes, we have lots of bookings because they've heard about the mountain and the power of its love. We can't turn people away. Georgios can take them up the mountain on one of his guided tours . . . he'll show them Kostas's honey farm, and point out the valley where everything grows. They should be back at our place, at the herb factory, by about twelve thirty.' I find myself grinning. 'Oh, and Gracie has finished packing the dried mountain tea and the wild thyme, so she's free. We'll all pull together, it'll be fine. Could you man the shop in the factory today, Gracie?'

'Sounds good to me, love.' She slides off her stool at the little bar in the Wild Thyme restaurant, where Demi is managing the day's bookings and we're sharing our regular morning coffee as we plan the day ahead.

'Oh, and I need more wild thyme for the lamb *gamopilafo*!' Demi puts her hand to her forehead. 'And I have to do the wedding rice. Granny Demetria is showing me how to make it.'

'No worries, love. I'll ask Angelica if she can drop the thyme off on her way to the shop.' Gracie knocks back the last of her mountain tea and pulls out her mobile.

'*Kalispera!* Cretan Bridal Gowns, how can I help?' comes the crisp, efficient voice at the other end.

'Angelica, be a love and pop into the herb shop at Nell and Georgios's and grab some wild thyme to drop off to Demi at the restaurant; she's got a couple of coachloads of tourists coming in today.'

'No problem, Gracie. I'm just off to pick up some more crocheted patches to take up to Kostas for the final touches to the dress. You're not going to believe it, *Hiya* magazine heard about Mitera's wedding last autumn, and her dress. They want photos . . . and an actor from *Holby City* is interested in one. This is it! Cretan Bridal Gowns is going to be huge!' I hear her shout.

'Well with you running the show, love, why wouldn't it be? Anyway, got to go. See you at the church later. Come on, you,' Gracie says affectionately to Angel, always at her feet.

'Oh, and there are more WWOOFers coming today to help Maria and Kostas at the honey farm,' I tell them. 'With the twins on the way and Kostas making the wedding dresses, they need all the help they can get.'

Georgios pokes his head in through the restaurant gates.

'You can't come in here! It's bad luck!' Demi shouts good-naturedly and throws a napkin in his direction.

'What are you doing here?' I ask.

'Just checking you're not having second thoughts.' He grins around the wrought-iron bars.

'I'm not. Now go!' I laugh and also throw a napkin in his direction, and it lands in the lemon tree, the one I hid in on my first visit here.

'OK! OK!' He moves away, then turns back. 'And you'll definitely be done by four?' he double-checks.

'Of course! I wouldn't miss it for the world. We'll be ready.'

That evening, in the small flat-roofed church in the square, as the sun begins to set between the mountains, Georgios and I make our vows.

Everyone that matters is here: Demi, Maria and Kostas, Mitera and her new husband, Angelica and Gracie, Stelios's family, and of course Georgios, right beside me, promising to be there forever. As the warm, thyme-scented summer evening wraps itself around the mountain and the town, we leave the church, me clutching my bouquet of wild mountain flowers and herbs, and walk through the streets, where everyone has come out to see us, smiling and clapping and wishing us luck. As we reach the wrought-iron gates to the restaurant, there are butterflies flying around my stomach – or is it bees, doing their waggle dance no doubt? Georgios, holding my hand, stops, turns to me and kisses me. I look up and see the outline of the kri-kri goat high above the mountain cave.

Georgios pushes open the gates and I catch my breath. Demi and Stelios's family have worked wonders. The whole courtyard is filled with white candles, fairy lights and lanterns, and my eyes are drawn upwards to two white doves that take off through the courtyard to the opening above, their wings flapping, like they've finally found each other and are starting a new life together.

'It's beautiful,' I whisper, knowing that I never, ever want to leave this place again.

'Everyone is happy for us. Stelios would be happy too,' Georgios says. 'Happy that we have found each other.'

That evening we sit in the courtyard, in the light of the candles and lanterns, a jug of wild herbs and mountain flowers on each table, along with sugared almonds scattered across the white tablecloths. Demi has organised the waitresses, all the villagers that Georgios delivered dittany to: Agatha, Christina and Gabriela, in rude health and wearing black with white aprons, smiling and darting between the tables. We eat wonderful melt-in-your-mouth morsels made by Stelios's mother and sister, and then lamb slow-roasted with lemons, olives and bay, with the wedding *gamopilafo* – rice coated with butter and lemon made with love by Demi and her namesake, Stelios's grandmother Demetria – and huge bowls of Greek salad, full of fat tomatoes, crunchy cucumber, crescents of onion, and crumbling white feta contrasting beautifully with the firm black olives tumbling across the top. Then the lightest sponge-and-buttercream wedding cake made by Agatha; glistening spoon sweets, made from cherries and quince; and bowls piled high with *loukoumades*, the warm fluffy doughnuts the size and shape of golf balls, sprinkled with sesame seeds and soaked in glorious golden Vounoplagia honey.

We drink chilled wine made from the vines in the town, and firewater raki, and Georgios tells us to raise our glasses because love has returned to the mountain. And then, as two guitarists and a violinist begin to play, we dance in a circle in the sultry evening, men one side, women the other, arms outstretched, eyes locking on to each other. Mitera is there with her new husband. Gracie is beaming at one of his cousins. Angelica is dancing opposite Yannis, who has decided he doesn't want to leave any more. Stelios's parents sit and laugh with Demi, who is organising the kitchen and waiting staff and looks right at home. Because that is exactly where we are.

Maria takes a break from dancing, rubbing her big swollen belly, and I sit beside her, placing my hand on her tummy too.

'Mum?' Demi walks towards me. 'There are some lads outside, say they're WWOOFers?'

'Oh, they're here. Great. Tell them to come in . . .'

Demi blushes and then beams as three Canadian lads, one tall and dark-skinned, one shorter, blond and cute, and the third thinner, with crazy black curls, step into the restaurant and stare around in wonder.

'Wow! Looks like a wild time . . .'

And as the sun disappears and the mountain wraps its shadow around the town like a great big hug, the music plays on, like a steady drumbeat, just like the heart of the mountain. Love has finally returned, and this time it's here to stay.

Bonus Material

Discover some of Jo's favourite Cretan foods

Cheese
Crete has many wonderful cheeses, almost every town or village has its own local variety. Probably the best known is *mizithra*, made from sheep's milk or a mixture of sheep's and goat's milk. I love the way it crumbles over salad. And don't forget to try the Greek pies – flaky pastry with a cheese filling, or even cheese combined with spinach or *horta*, Cretan greens. Just delicious.

Olive oil
Whilst in Crete I went on a cookery course taught by the wonderful Koula Varydakis-Hanialakis and bought her book, *Foods of Crete*. She signed it and wrote in it: 'For Jo, Enjoy cooking the way we cook in Crete, use olive oil!' Olive oil is considered the basis of the diet that helps the people of Greece live long and healthy lives. And it tastes fabulous too!

Honey
Honey is probably the best known Cretan produce alongside olive oil. It is thyme that makes Cretan honey so distinctive, amber in colour with a wonderful floral flavour. Drizzle it over Greek yoghurt or figs. Just gorgeous.

Jo Thomas

Herbs
Apparently Crete has the greatest number of species of wild herbs in Europe. These herbs make simple food special and I came home with a case full of them.

Calamari
Deep-fried squid rings in crispy batter with salt and pepper and a generous squeeze of fresh lemon is a Thomas family favourite . . . served on a plate to be shared and eaten with fingers.

Smoked pork
Cretan smoked pork is marinated for days and then smoked over local herbs such as sage, bay and rosemary. I ate this in the local family-run taverna where we were staying, just outside of Rethymno, washed down with home-made raki. I also had the most wonderful slow-cooked pork up in the mountains at Dounias Traditional Cretan Food eatery in Drakona near Chania. Everything was locally grown and sourced and cooked over open wood fires. It was such a memorable meal. Fantastic setting, fabulous food!

Loukoumades
These are honey-soaked doughnuts sprinkled with cinnamon and they can be found on every street corner, served in cafes and bars, and they are the very best of Cretan traditional home cooking. Like a great big hug on a plate! Need I say more?

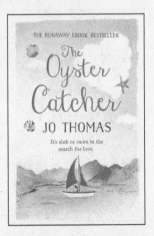

THE RUNAWAY EBOOK BESTSELLER

The
Oyster
Catcher

JO THOMAS

It's sink or swim in the
search for love.

'A world you long to live in with characters you love' Katie Fforde

Dooleybridge, County Galway: the last place Fiona Clutterbuck expects to end up, alone, on her wedding night.

But after the words 'I do' have barely left her mouth, that's exactly where she is – with only her sequinned shoes and a crashed camper van for company.

One thing is certain: Fi can't go back. So when the opportunity arises to work for brooding local oyster farmer, Sean Thornton, she jumps at the chance. Now Fi must navigate suspicious locals, jealous rivals and an unpredictable boss if she's to find a new life, and love, on the Irish coast. And nothing – not even a chronic fear of water – is going to hold her back.

Join Fi as she learns the rules of the ocean – and picks up a few pearls of Irish wisdom along the way . . .

REVIEW

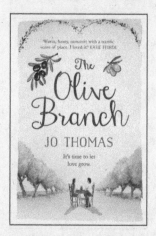

'Sun, good food and romance, what more could you want?' *Heat*

You can buy almost anything online these days. For Ruthie Collins, it was an Italian farmhouse.

Yet as she battles with a territorial goat and torrential rain just to get through the door of her new Italian home, the words of Ed, her ex, are ringing in her ears. She is daft, impetuous and irresponsible.

But Ruthie is determined to turn things around and live the dream.

First, though, she must win over her fiery neighbour, Marco Bellanouvo, and his family . . . Then there's the small matter of running an olive farm. As the seasons change and new roots are put down, olives and romance might just flourish in the warmth of the Mediterranean sun.

Escape to Italy with *The Olive Branch*

REVIEW

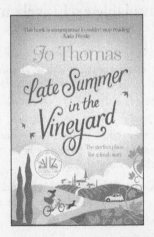

'A fabulous French feast of fun' Milly Johnson

Emmy Bridges has always looked out for others. Now it's time
to put down roots of her own.

Working for a wine-maker in France is the opportunity of a lifetime
for Emmy. Even if she doesn't know a thing about wine – beyond
what's on offer at the local supermarket.

There's plenty to get to grips with in the rustic town of Petit Frère.
Emmy's new work friends need more than a little winning over.
Then there's her infuriatingly brash tutor, Isaac, and the enigmatic
Madame Beaumont, tucked away in her vineyard of secrets.

But Emmy will soon realise that in life – just as in wine-making
– the best things happen when you let go and trust your instincts.
Particulary when there's romance in the air . . .

REVIEW

Why not try one of Jo Thomas's delightful short stories, available exclusively in ebook.

When Ellie Russet leaves home and her restaurant in the wake of disaster to housesit in the Kent countryside, the last thing she wants to do is cook for a living – ever again.

Ellie's new neighbour, Daniel Fender, is struggling to make ends meet as a furniture maker. Could the answer to his problems lie in the chestnut orchard at the bottom of the garden?

Only Ellie can help Daniel unlock the delicious secret that will bring them the fresh starts they need.

When Layla arrives in the Welsh coastal village of Swn-y-Mor with new fiancé Rob in tow, she plans to carry out her dad's final wishes, then return to Cardiff quickly, before too many unwanted memories surface.

But the longer Layla remains, the harder it is to resist the lure of the autumn skies and memories of family holidays gone by. With fishing trips and firesides to enjoy, is Rob *really* Layla's future, and is Swn-y-Mor going to remain in her past for ever?

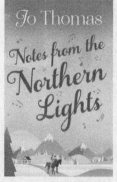

Wardrobe mistress Ruby Knightly has been sent to Iceland on a very special mission that could save her opera company's opening night. And she's determined that her fear of the dark – and the incoming weather – won't stand in her way.

But as Ruby follows her nose across Iceland's wild, volcanic landscape to the warmth of the smokehouses, she will soon discover that there is shelter to be found from even the most turbulent of storms. Particularly if there's romance around the corner . . .

A James Villa holiday inspired Jo's new novel

Starting to write a book is a bit like opening up the fridge and seeing what ingredients you have and what you're going to make for dinner. If you start to find out about the food of an area, it takes you by the hand and introduces you to the people, the culture and the history of the place and the stories within its walls. And Crete was no exception.

Arriving at our villa was like moving day! Excitedly, we explored the house. Within minutes of getting the bags in through the big, ornate metal gate and deciding who was sleeping where, my three young teenagers had opened up the French doors leading onto the covered terrace and were in the pool, with shrieks of delight; surrounded by fruit bushes, and set against a backdrop of a rocky mountain. On our first night there we sat outside and watched the sky darken to the colour of blue-black ink and a big, round, silvery moon came up silhouetting the rugged mountain. I knew that mountain was going to be a main character in my new book.

Every morning of our stay I sat out on the terrace of our villa, surrounded by pomegranate trees and oranges hanging from branches like golden Christmas baubles, whilst my early-bird son swam in the pool and a local cat kept me company. In the distance, my mountain. And there I began to write. Not the story I set out to tell, but the one that I'd discovered when I arrived in Crete, in the heart of the mountains.

James
VILLA HOLIDAYS

At James Villas we take the emphasis off arranging a holiday, giving you the freedom to live one. With the best selection of over 2,800 villas across more than 50 destinations you'll be spoilt for choice.

THE
LITTLE THINGS
THAT
MAKE A **BIG**
HOLIDAY

When one book ends, another begins...

Bookends is a vibrant new reading community to help you ensure you're never without a good book.

You'll find monthly reading recommendations, previews of brilliant new books, and exclusive features on and from your favourite authors. We'll also introduce you to exciting debuts and remind you of past classics.

There'll be a regular blog, reading group guides, competitions and much more!

Visit our website to see which great books we're recommending this month.

welcometobookends.co.uk

/welcometobookends

@teambookends